the infinity chronicles

Works by R.R.S:
Piercing Midnight (book one of the Infinity Chronicles)
Blood Moon (book two of the Infinity Chronicles)

PRAISE FOR PIERCING MIDNIGHT, PART ONE OF THE INFINITY CHRONICLES:

"Sometimes in life you get lucky…I was not sure what to expect, but I certainly didn't expect anything as incredible as what R.R.S produced– a story both **immersive** and **original**."

–Michelle Ray, author of *Falling for Hamlet*, the inspiration for E!'s hit show *"The Royals"*

GOODREADS MEMBERS ACROSS THE GLOBE RAVE:

"The story started gripping me like nothing I've ever read. Just couldn't put it down. Loved everything about it– the realistic and identifiable characters, the description of the sceneries that took your breath [away]. Hopelessly waiting for the sequel"
–★★★★★, India

"Oh my god, just wow. Beautifully done [descriptions] and the characters just simply perfect. I can't wait for the next one."
–★★★★★, Canada

A beautifully written novel…full of suspense, fun, humor, cute and lovable characters, and surprises around every corner. This novel flows perfectly with a fun, new, completely original plot. I can't wait to see what happens in the next novel, but I bet it'll be amazing!!!!
–★★★★★, USA

R.R.S PRESENTS

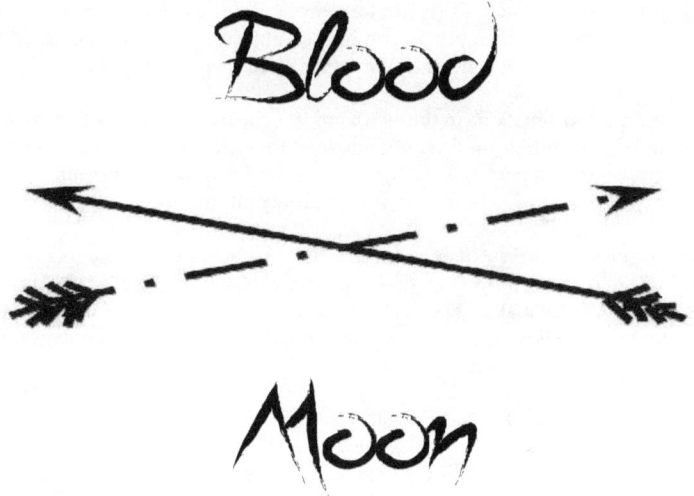

Blood

Moon

∞ PART TWO OF THE INFINITY CHRONICLES ∞

All rights reserved. Published in the United States by Faery Ring Press,
a private publishing platform in Baltimore, Maryland, USA. Printed by CreateSpace, a DBA
of On-Demand Publishing LLC, part of the Amazon group of companies. CreateSpace
headquarters located at:
21 North Pennell Road, Lima, PA 19037
Phone: (610) 566-7828

The characters and situations in this work are (for the most part) wholly fictional and
imaginary, and do not portray and are not intended to portray any actual persons or parties.
Any resemblance to a person living, dead, or undead is (most likely) unintended and
(somewhat) coincidental.

This novel includes an English adaptation by R.R.S. of a popular Chinese folk song titled 花
儿为什么这样红 written by Chinese composer Lei Zhenbang in 1963 for the movie
"Visitors on the Icy Mountain." The author cannot claim ownership of the translated lyrics
or concept, but has taken creative liberty and added original lines that connect it to the
book series.

ISBN-13: 9780692630877 (Custom)
ISBN-10: 692630872
BISAC: Fiction / Dystopian

Summary: Alone in the dangerous forests of Mythland, Raine Ylevol sets out looking for her
companions, striving to make it through all obstacles the woods throw at her to the
mountain on the other side where she can find sanctuary.

1. Fiction, 2. Young Adult, 3. Science Fiction/Dystopian, 4. Romance, 5. Coming-of-Age, 6.
Sexuality, 7. Action/Adventure

Printed in the U.S.A

The main text type was set in Garamond. Additional fonts include A Quiet Sleep, Cedarville
Preferred Cursive, Nothing You Could Do Bold, Arsenale White, good vibes-regular, DJB
Chalk It Up, Permanent Marker, Swanky and Moo Moo, La Belle Aurore, Hill Country,
Alywriting, Gigi, and James Fajardo.

Cover artwork by Ronen Yakubov
Other featured artwork by Mia Kaidanow (graphic novel portion) and Rachel Szpara.
Book design by Rachel Szpara.

For Dahlia

Daisy,

Sandy and George,

Clover,

and Ivy;

*for guaranteeing my safe passage
through the ever-changing wilds of Mythland,
throughout all of these years.*

Hello readers. **Please Note...**

...as happy as I am that you've picked this book up (whether you've read *Piercing Midnight*, walked by this at a bookstore and thought the cover was sexy and wanted to check out the full package...) there are some aspects of this book I need to make quite clear, right away. While *Piercing Midnight* touched upon serious matters of its own, this sequel goes even darker, and into certain subjects that can be **triggering** for some individuals. I also understand that I have a number of young readers, and if you are a parent of one of these readers I would like you to consider reading it first and deciding for yourself if you think it is appropriate for their eyes. When I say appropriate I'm not referring to my use of the f-bomb or the fact that the protagonist has had sex (pretty PG-13 sex, mind you) but that **this sequel not only touches on topics such as severe depression, rape and sexual abuse, and PTSD, but a number of characters experience this first-hand.** I have of course not written the actual occurrences in explicit detail, but these are still serious matters that I'm sure many young readers are not simply unfamiliar with, but could be seriously affected by. I'm also mentioning this in case you are a victim of these terrible things and may not feel ready to go through it again or could be triggered.

Then again, you're your own person, your own reader and this isn't me telling you to put the book down by any means– good lord, I'm the author, after all! Please read! I didn't go through all of this trouble to publish just to tell you it's too hot to handle! I just don't want to potentially trigger anybody or expose them to something they did not want to see. These elements are not in here for shock value and they are most definitely not treated lightly. They serve as vital catalysts in developing the characters' perception of themselves, humanity, and the world around them. I didn't avoid these topics because I believe they are not only important to my story, but to the genre as a whole. These issues exist and affect real people outside of this book. It sucks, but it's the truth and I'm not going to sugar-coat it and write a series about war and corruption and overcoming great obstacles without detailing the realistic bumps in the road– physical and psychological. I'll leave you with that. Thank you for taking the time to read this little note of mine, and I look forward to hearing back about your thoughts on this second installment in the series.

All my love,

Part Two:

BLOOD MOON

The door slammed loud,
and rose up a cloud of dust on us.

Footsteps follow—
down through the hollow sound, torn up.

And you will go to Mykonos,
with a vision of a gentle coast;

and a sun, to maybe dissipate,
shadows of the mess you made.

I remember how they took you down;
as the winter turned the meadow brown.

You go, wherever you go today,
you go, today.

-Fleet Foxes, "Mykonos

chapter one

I was almost out of strength.

Palms pressed to the roof of ice, I pushed up with all my might, bubbles gurgling from my nose. I could feel my lungs pulsing in desperation, and I floated away from the ice momentarily to reach back at my quiver to keep the arrows from floating out.

Believe me, I hadn't intended to go swimming in a stupid frozen lake. But when my bow had skidded across, I'd cautiously gone out to retrieve it and fell through the thinner ice. And because at this point I was sure Mythland was out to get me, the hole I'd fallen through had somehow sealed back over as soon as I'd been dunked, and I was trapped.

I reached back for one of the crappy arrows I'd made. Since the Majesty Council had offered the bow and arrow separately before kicking us out, I went with the bow deciding I could surely fashion some sticks and feathers into something I could shoot. I hadn't done too badly, either, but now with my head bursting from lack of oxygen, I doubted the arrows would hold up if I stabbed at the ice to get free. Despite this, I thrust an arrow forward over and over, watching splinters of ice streak through in webs above me. Then the arrowhead snapped off, and I grabbed another, hacking at the punctures in the ice. My ears rang, my mouth couldn't stay closed any longer and I sucked in freezing water as I furiously hammered at the ice and watched the arrow tip begin to dent and loosen like the last one had. And then with a last jolt of energy, I drove the arrow straight through, jerking it to the side as an overwhelming rush of water swirled around me. Blinded, and with muscles giving out, I shoved chunks of the ice away and launched myself up and out.

I couldn't give myself a moment to rest, the rest of the lake was creaking and threatening to collapse on me again, so I crawled ashore, my entire body numb and quaking. Once back to solid ground, I shoved aside reeds and plopped onto the bank. I rolled onto my back, the muddy moss seeping into the back of my sweater. *Well, it doesn't matter. I'm already soaked,* I thought, fondling the grubby red sleeve with my fingers to try and gain more feeling in them.

Dizzily, my eyes focused in on the sky peeking out from the thick tree cover; dark blue velvet shot through with silver bullets. I spotted the three consecutive stars forming Zhanshi's belt and suddenly felt my stomach heave, but not from the water sloshing inside me. The wooden infinity pendant around my neck suddenly felt heavy and cold. I tucked it under the collar of my shirt and forced myself to sit up. *Keep looking, keep looking.*

With a shudder, I rolled onto my knees, where runs and holes webbed through my sweater tights. I dug around in my shorts pocket and pulled out his hat, now sopping and twirled with lakegrass. I stuck it on over my bun and nocked an arrow on my bowstring to keep alert.

Eyes glinted at me from the dark depths of the woods, the multicoloured glares fading in and out. It would be pointless to shoot at them; they'd be after me in an instant. I'd just have to pass through quietly until I got to my stuff. I climbed over the colossal fallen oak tree, my gloves tearing for the hundredth time on the rough tree bark. I dashed through the swamp, leaping from tree stump to tree stump

2

lithely as the brown, putrid water frothed and heaved around me. It took only a few more minutes to make it back to where I had my stuff stashed; a big tree with a cavern sized hole in between the roots. The trees here made me feel like a bug; tiny and only the size of a leaf while everything else towered hugely around me.

I jogged toward my cave as raindrops heavy as buckets began smashing through the tree-cover. I clutched the beanie to make sure it wouldn't fall off, and squinted to see through the downpour, increasing speed as I neared the cave. Lightning clawed the sky with its long white fingers, and thunder shook the ground, making me stumble and hold onto a tree to regain my balance.

I escaped the coming storm just in time as I ducked inside the tree and fell back onto my pile of stuff, chest heaving as I tried to calm down. My hand was over my heart, feeling my chest rise and fall as I made sure to breathe in through my nose and out through my mouth. Once I felt a little less shaky, I reached for the flint and struck up a fire. Sparks danced onto the damp twigs, trying to catch hold, and slowly I relaxed, taking off my quiver to check my arrows. Only two of the shabbier ones remained since I'd made the newest dozen a week ago. I paused. *Hold on...one week? Five days ago? I really can't seem to remember.*

Keeping track of time was a chore in itself. The days blurred together and sometimes it was so hard for me to know when they started and when they ended because of how constantly dark Mythland was. But I'd been trying my best. On the side of my left boot, in the cleanest spot of black leather, I'd cut in a dash for every day. There were now four groups of five dashes and two dashes standing alone. Twenty-two days. A little over three weeks and I was still alone.

Closing my eyes, I hugged my knees to my chest and listened to the storm. *Destan could be out there right now, escaping lightning and the trees that fall every night. Or he could be in a tree cave like me wondering about me or not wondering about me because maybe he's lost a limb or is bleeding to death.*

The tree creaked ominously, my heart beat at a hyper speed. *Or maybe the moment we were shot into this goddamn place, he hit into a tree and died instantly on impact and I'll never see him ever again, not his crazy hair, or rough fingers, and never hear him call me Bluehead.*

I blinked away the buildup of tears and forced myself to swallow the spongy fungus I'd ruled safe to eat this morning. I know it didn't really matter if I cried; no one would see me. But I didn't want to, anyway. Because these days when I started, I couldn't stop. I needed to focus on living just in case Destan did happen to be out there somewhere, chopping wood and slaying giant bugs and slashing through tangles of vines and dancing through the swamp so that he could make it to my cave and we could hold each other all night and make it out of here together.

Even though my craving for food was beyond intense, I'd been vomiting more often than ever lately probably due to the nasty air and weird raw food, so I set the shrooms aside and rubbed my temples. Took a sip from my gourd. The storm thrummed and thrummed the tree, and from the mouth of the cave the woods were a grey-green ocean; incomprehensible through the thick downpour. Some water dribbled steadily down the wall of the tree-cave, running off an ivy leaf and dripping slowly to the dirt. I missed when things could actually be dry for a full hour. Even the air was full of sticky moisture that made me feel drowned inside.

I looked in my bag to check on the egg Chantastic had given me, and seeing it was still unharmed, I moved it closer to the fire, her words echoing in my head. *Keep it warm. Keep it warm.* And without another thought, I scooted away from the fire and puffed up my rucksack to use as a pillow. Lying back on the dirt, my eyelids suddenly felt like thick curtains being released over my eyes, two windows of blue, and I let them black out everything. Sleep was my favourite part of my schedule these days. Morbid as it was, I couldn't deny how comforting it was knowing the risk that maybe a tree would fall on me while I slept and I wouldn't ever have to wake up from the dreams of Thgindim and Destan and Chantastic and Irene that I'd have every night. Through practice, I learned to control my dreams. I could now run around wherever I wanted on the mountain and see whoever I wanted and these dreams were just so much better than real life in the Mythland.

But I worried about how realistic the mountain in my dreams was to Thgindim. Sometimes I'd go places that I knew didn't exist on the mountain, or Destan had a house and not just a pile of clothes and hammock at an old temple. I'd end up replacing memories of my real home with the dreamworld ones.

I took off his beanie and tucked it close to my cheek, pretending it still smelled like him. Like pine and wood and fresh air, not freezing lake water and swampy sludge. I slid into sleep, the rain only getting louder and more threatening outside the mouth of the tree cave. It fell in wiggly glass ribbons, shattering as it hit the ground, and slowly the wiggly lines became fuzzy lines and then no lines at all as my eyes finally shut.

"Just jump, Bluehead! It's not that far!" Destan yelled, face glowing and golden from across the valley.

A waterfall tumbled clear cerulean water beside him, and I held onto my arms, shaking my head, "I can't, it's too far."

Someone launched off beside me, and I grinned seeing Irene propel herself across. Her legs bent for her landing, and she spun around, black ponytail glinting blue in the sunlight. "C'mon, Raine, if I can do it, you can."

"Yeah! You're gonna miss all the fun over here!" Destan called, putting his hands on his hips. Even though he was shirtless and only in some knee length shorts, he still had his hat on and I couldn't help but laugh at how silly he looked. Irene was wearing a black bathing costume, her spy mask on her face so that only her dark, owlish eyes showed. I considered the jump. If I fell, I'd only land in the water at the bottom, and something inside me told me that I'd made the jump many times before. There was nothing different about this time.

A soft hand touched my arm, and I turned my head to see Chantastic's serene smile and beautiful eyes watching me. "We can go together," she said, in her low, musical voice.

I nodded nervously, preparing myself for the leap. "One," I counted, "Two...Three!"

I grabbed her hand and jumped, the world a sparkly green and blue haze around me, but when I looked to smile at her as we flew over together, I saw that she wasn't holding my hand anymore, she was still on the other side, crying and looking utterly betrayed. In mid-air, I tried to fly in the opposite direction, but suddenly I was hit with a wave of exhaustion. And even when I tried to reach out my hand to her and move my legs, I was too tired and couldn't move.

"Ray!" she wailed from the other side, but her voice was all wrong. I blinked and it was Gwen, her dark eyes streaming as JPs pushed her off the side of the landing. And it wasn't a valley filled with water, but it was the Mythland swamps, and trees were tipping over everywhere and I started falling at full speed into the swamp, Destan and Irene staring coldly down at me and moving away as if they didn't even care. And as soon as I knew I would smack into the swamp and sink down below the toxic brown sludge, I closed my eyes and—

My tree was falling. Scrambling up from the ground with sleep still bleary in my vision and my limbs still unbalanced and shaky, I felt the cave around me rumble dangerously. I scooped up my rucksack and tossed in the fire starter stones, dashing out before it could tumble down. But as soon as I was back in the thick of the storm, panic seized me. My fingers knifed through my mess of hair realizing that his hat wasn't there anymore.

I glanced back desperately, the tree hadn't come down yet, but branches triple my height and weight were crashing down all around. I could see the scarlet hat balled up by the fire, and I hesitated, jumping out of the way of another branch. I could almost hear Destan telling me to just keep running, find another shelter and stay safe because I mattered more to him than a silly old hat. But that was all I had left of him, the only hard evidence of me ever having a life before toxic Mythland storms and scrounging for food every day. The tree thundered with snapping sounds, having only moments left before crashing down, and I forced my eyes to look away and my feet to start running full speed in the other direction. My rucksack and quiver bounced against my back, my bow in my fist.

I skipped through the swamps, the splashes of acidic mud burning my calves as I rushed desperately forward. My eyes combed the woods for somewhere to take cover, finding nothing in the blur of rain and falling branches. Something I'd learned about Mythland: it was alive. When I say this I don't just mean the trees and creatures are alive, I literally mean Mythland is a living, breathing clever being of its own. I have never been one to believe in the spirits or the mystical or anything, I'm not sure if it is some kind of magic or maybe just that the woods are so big that it tricks your mind. Trees disappear

6

and reappear, the holes in frozen lakes seal over the moment they are made, there's no dependable landmarks. Mythland has a way of trapping you, of trying to drive you absolutely mad so that you never truly understand anything. I'm shocked I had been able to stay in that one tree for so long in the first place.

Suddenly, something leapt out from a grove of trees beside me and tackled me to the grass, knocking the breath out of my chest. It drooled yellow saliva onto my face, red eyes gleaming as the beast's lips curled back from its slavered fangs and growled. I couldn't tell if it was a wolf or a bear, or maybe somehow a cross between the two, but without any more contemplation I unsheathed my dagger. The monster caught my hand instantly in its jaws, sending my dagger into a deep swampy puddle where it sank and disappeared. I ripped my hand out before its teeth could snap down on my wrist, and I struggled to roll out from under it as its mouth came down again, jaws wide open to take a bite out of my throat.

Just as the beast slammed its clawed paw onto my back and had me trapped, an arrow soared through the rain. It must've pierced the animal somewhere because it leapt off of me in pain and spun in a circle to shake out the arrow. Another three animals came bounding in, all circling me growling, their noses up and sniffing for whoever it was that had shot the arrow. I felt as if I'd gone into hysterics, rain poured down, knocking me off my feet with the heavy drops, and more arrows shot out from the dark, making the beasts quickly scamper off to safety.

A gorgeous grey wolf revealed herself from the dark, on her back a hooded rider. I struggled to my feet, squinting in the downpour and nearly going deaf from the thunder. The wolf's eyes shimmered in recognition and I felt sobs rise up in my throat as I ran toward her. "Siri! Oh, Siri!" I called, pressing my forehead to her soft muzzle that was slick with rain. She whined, rubbing me affectionately and pawing the dirt as I threw my arms around her in disbelief.

The rider slid off and I felt my lungs seem to die out in wonder. I moved away from Siri, approaching the figure slowly, trying to see through the dark of his hood. But my whole body had come alive with tremors– I already knew who it was. Almost in slow motion, I raised my shaking hands to touch his face, and I lowered his hood, expecting the grey eyes and a beanie-less blond head.

"Destan?" I croaked, and it felt odd to speak aloud seeing as I'd been alone and silent for so long. But it wasn't him. And I stepped back in horror as the shiny black mask of a JP officer glared back at me. His spiked glove grasped my sweater collar and he lifted me with one hand onto Siri's back before I could even think of escaping.

"You're coming with me, sweetheart," he growled, cuffing my hands and tying a soiled cloth around my eyes so that everything went dark. "You're a lucky, lucky girl."

chapter two

"What's your name?"

"Irene Abrasha."

"What's your real name?"

"What, you're saying you don't believe me?" I countered, narrowing my eyes as he and some others paced around me. I was beyond confused at this point. He was the only one dressed like a JP, the others were in colourful leathers and patterned vests and muddy boots. They all had their mouths hidden by bandanas, and their hair was long and wild, their eyes a variety of browns and blues. They seemed completely unrelated to each other in every way, only furthering my confusion. I struggled in my binds, glancing around the violet tent as sunlight peeped through and turned everyone's skin purple. "What I would like to know," I began, voice quivering, "is where you found that wolf. She belongs to me."

They cackled, exchanging amused looks. One apparently blind man answered, "She's yours, is she? We don't see them kinds of beasts around these here woods, so you both must be foreigners." He bent down close to me, brandy tingling in his breath. "So tell me, why are you so far from Fluxaria, girly?"

The hairs on my neck stood straight up. "I'm not a Fluxarian," the words came out cool and clipped, "But I do happen to be on my way there, so I would appreciate it if you could release me and I won't be getting in your way anymore." I thought it sounded like a perfectly reasonable deal. What did they want with me in the first place?

The JP shook his head, crossing his arms in front of his armoured chest. "Mmm, I don't know about that. You see, you might be our ticket back to our home. Thgindim would just love to get a purebred Fluxarian princess."

"I. Am. Not. Fluxarian!" I insisted, saying it slow enough so that I knew they understood every word. "If you want specifics, I'm an Underbrusher; Ex-Laundress. And Thgindim most definitely does *not* want *me*. They banished me not even a whole month ago."

They exchanged wary glances, some shifting from foot to foot or whispering into one another's ear. One man wearing a red bandana came close to me, crouching to stare straight into my eyes. His were a crystal blue, with lashes caked in black makeup.

"Maybe she's tellin' the truth," he murmured, his words muffled by the mouth covering.

"Course she's not telling the truth. You see her hair and eyes, she's pretty much a Fluxarian poster-child. She's just trying to save her own skin," said the man with his arms around my rucksack.

The JP waved a hand to brush aside the comments and plopped down on a pile of pillows, propping his boots up on a tree stump. I implored him with my eyes, begging for him to believe me, to show some kind of mercy.

"Why would Thgindim kick a girl like you off the mountain?" he asked sharply, and even though he seemed to be one of the few actually listening to my argument, I could tell he still clearly wanted me to be handed back over to the Majesty Council. Without another thought I twisted my story into a half-lie.

"My name is Irene Abrasha, and my companion and I were banished from Thgindim a month ago." A hush fell inside the tent and I added, "At first, the Majesty Council wanted me killed, but we were able to be let off with banishment to Mythland."

To my surprise, I saw the red bandana crinkle over the blue-eyed man's mouth as if he had smiled. He stood up and went around to the back of my chair. I heard the sound of a knife being unsheathed, and he started sawing away the rope binding my wrists together. "Hear that Rong? She's one of us."

Rong, or the JP, rubbed his jaw curiously, lifting up his mask to get a better look at me. "I...I suppose you're right. What were you banished for?"

"And be specific!" the blind guy ordered, still seeming immensely suspicious of my story. I started from meeting Irene (changed her name to something random) and ended with getting captured and interrogated, skipping unnecessary bits in between and desperately mentioning bits about Destan's appearance to see if maybe they had spotted him. They didn't twitch at the mention of his blond hair or set of fancy Majesty Council arrows or even ratty crimson gloves. He was still completely missing in the big sea of storms and trees.

"What do you call yourselves?" I asked, tentatively. "Do you... travel together?"

Rong lifted his chin somewhat proudly. "We're the Shuishan. A people born of the exiled and banished from both mountains. The name comes from the trees that dominate the valley."

"Shuishan..." I repeated quietly. And then a head poked inside the tent, a pale man with a cherry red ponytail and single emerald earring dangling an inch from my head. He looked only a few years older than I was.

"Lilah wants to know if you want the elderberries for cider or save them for tonight's moonshine," he said, his voice smooth as honey. His dark blue eyes flickered onto me and his mouth twitched into a brief smile. "Who is this?"

"Banished Thgindimmer. Found her getting chewed up by a tiangou during the storm last night," Rong explained, laying a hand on my shoulder. Meanwhile, the man came closer and closer, sunlight glinting green off of his earring. "She calls herself Irene Abrasha."

"Thgindim? She looks completely Fluxarian," he mused, skeptically looking me up and down. I tried not to roll my eyes again. Just great. The JP and the new guy exchanged conspiratory looks that made my skin crawl.

"Exactly what I think," the blind man grumbled, spitting a seed of some kind into a bowl on the ground. I watched it spin around on the dirt floor and I became even dizzier and unsettled.

"Let's have Lilah check Miss Irene out and see if she can be useful until you decide...otherwise," the JP said, and he kicked my chair. I jumped up in surprise and he cut my foot binds with a short knife. As he bent over me, I read his rusty old Justice Police badge; 15003. 15003? That was ancient, the JP's were now in the 30000s. He noticed my looking and averted his eyes, saying, under his breath, "Staring's not polite."

"I'm sorry. I just wanted to see if maybe I knew you..." I said quietly, "I haven't seen a JP officer since being back home."

"I'm not in the force anymore. Banished for freeing some rebels from Peak. I never was the most civil officer," he sighed, winking, then glancing away. "Follow Tieran out. He'll show you to your quarters and a bit around the camp."

I gulped, trying to keep from stammering, "W-well, I really can't stay here, I have to k-keep looking for my companion—"

"You'll die out there searching, and for all you know, he might wind up here," Tieran said dryly, beckoning me out of the tent. I reluctantly ducked under his arm and squinted in the sunlight that came through the webbed canopy of gigantic Mythland trees.

There were tents all around like the one I was just in, but they looked like patchwork with random bits of pelt and fabric sewn together. Mismatched men and boys wandered in between tents, transferring weapons to each other or trading baskets of food. It didn't take long for me to realize there didn't seem to be any women in sight. Slowly, all heads swirled to look my way. There was one large cage where tiangou, wolves, and large cats were crowded in to fit together,

Siri butting heads with two much larger beasts. She turned to look at me as I passed by, and whined and whimpered, clawing at the strong iron bars. She looked emaciated, new scars streaking her body, a small piece missing from her ear and still bloody. I hesitated, drifting toward the cage and away from Tieran, who continued walking with long strides. *Siri how did you end up here?* I thought, pain clogging my throat as I tried to recall the last time I'd seen her. She'd disappeared with Irene the night Destan and I were taken to the hot springs. I didn't want to think about how long she and the Fluxarian spy had been separated, and thinking of how beat up Siri looked, I was scared to imagine what might have happened to Irene.

There was a sharp tap on my shoulder, breaking me from my daze. "Is there a problem?" Tieran asked, suddenly at my side again.

"It's just…" I began, finding it was still hard to keep my voice from shaking. "That's my wolf. I recognized her the moment Rong found me last night. He was riding her."

"Interesting. Seeing as she's been in our possession longer than you've claimed to be in Mythland," he rose an eyebrow.

I flushed. "If you need proof she's mine, I can show you. I can call her name and I'm confident she'll come."

"We'll discuss this later in my tent. Now keep up, I have more important things to take care of today." He turned on his heel, lazily waving me to follow. I looked longingly back at Siri, making her a silent promise to come back, and forced myself to keep walking.

"When's the last time you ate something real?" he cut in, elbowing me in the ribs and gripping my arm hard as he led me through the crowd.

"What qualifies as real?" I whispered, my eyes scrunching as his fist enclosed even tighter on my arm.

He smirked. "Cooked. Not berries or bark? You're a skeleton."

Shooting him a look of hatred, I wrenched my arm free from his grip, rubbing where he'd held me. He didn't even blink, only sped up his walking and knocked on the door of a sleek fur tent. The door was a huge slab of tree bark attached to the tent's fabric with some thick looking thread.

"Busy," a voice from inside called out. Tieran licked his lips.

"It's me. And a new girl."

"Oh?"

A head peeked out. It was a young girl; Gwen's age, maybe, with waist-length blonde hair and giant grey eyes. The hair and eyes combination made my heart clench as I thought of Destan. But hers were a darker grey, almost black, and her body was thin and willowy, no muscle anywhere. Suddenly she looked nothing like Destan. "Where'd you get her?"

"Rong found her in the last storm."

"Bring her in," the girl said monotonously, still refusing to look me in the eye. It was like Tieran was delivering a doll rather than a girl; she wouldn't speak *to* me, just *about* me. A bit ticked off, I stepped inside the tent and was overwhelmed by the fragrances emanating all around me. There were bottles upon bottles of tonics and perfumes, pots and pans bubbling and fizzing with soap and flowers and berries and meats. The girl glided from station to station, adding dashes of this and that, and relighting fires beneath each pot. It reminded me of my Mom bustling about in her kitchen while she brewed, but the girl was so graceful and quick that it seemed like a dance. She continued speaking to Tieran as she brewed.

"Are you going to keep her?" she asked, and I opened my mouth to protest, but Tieran raised a pale hand.

"I would like to. Do you need her?"

"Do I look like I need any help around here?" she fluttered her eyelashes coyly and the edges of Tieran's mouth curled into a smile.

"I'm not sure why I even asked such a question," he said.

"My poor, innocent Tieran. I don't need her, so have fun with her. Did Rong say anything about moonshine vs cider by the way?"

"Just keep on brewing the moonshine, we need him drunk tonight," Tieran said, winking.

"I agree. Does she need anything?" she jerked her thumb towards me and I made sure to meet her eyes. I was not a doll. I was here and I needed to say something.

"Could I have some water, actually?" I interjected, before Tieran could open his dumb mouth again. The girl's face went red in shock.

"I...I didn't think you could speak," she said, giving Tieran some odd look and picking up a bucket of water. She dribbled some into a big leaf and held it out for me to take, not meeting my eyes.

Ignoring her bizarre comment, I drank deeply from the water pooling on the leaf and asked, "So...what do you do for the Shuishan? Cook?"

Lilah's lip curled, her eyes shooting daggers. "Do I look like a cook, new bitch?"

"Lilah, play nice," Tieran warned, draping an arm across her tiny shoulders and squeezing them affectionately. His eyes flashed to mine, a wooden smile on his lips. "Lilah's our witch, our distiller, our apothecary, everything to me. Aren't you Lilah?"

She smirked, slinking out from under his arm and moving back to her pot. "And don't you or your girls forget it."

"Sorry for misunderstanding," I muttered, averting my eyes to the floor. I could see the imprints of her little bare feet in the dirt, tracing her patterns of movement.

Tieran's voice appeared beside my ear again, his arm suddenly snaking around my waist. I felt a hot blush creep from my neck up into my cheeks. "She accepts your apology. Well, I have to get Irene to where she needs to be so she can be all ready for tonight, so I suppose I'll see you at the feast, Lilah."

"Tonight?"

I blurted it out before I could stop myself. They looked at me strangely, scrutinizing, as if staring at me through a fogged window. And then Lilah suddenly smiled like the bright little girl she was supposed to be, her voice high and sweet, "Don't worry about it. Tieran will take very good care of you, won't you Tieran?"

"Of course I will. See you later, Lilah," he said, taking my arm again in his stony grip, tugging me out of the tent with him.

I stifled a yelp, "Would you stop holding onto me so tightly? I'm not going to dart away."

"Oh, yes you will. Let's have a chat. You want something from me."

"I don't even know you."

"Keep your mouth shut for now and walk with me. And stop looking so damn pathetic," he chuckled, digging his nails into my arm and making me gasp, tears budding in the corners of my eyes. He shot me a terrifying, handsome smile and we continued traipsing through the camp. His tent was strung in one of the trees, and right by a huge set-up of tables and benches. People were lighting candles and carrying out goblets and trays for whatever celebration was going on tonight. It was then that I noticed something strange about all of the servants.

They were all girls, my age or younger, with hair that glinted a jewel tone in the sunlight. They were Fluxarian, they had the tanned skin and dark eyes of Irene and all of their lips were pale white, as if they were painted over. A number was scrawled on their foreheads, along with an adorned letter 'T'. I met the trembling eyes of one girl carrying a bundle of unlit torches and she shook her head at me. I drew my brows together questioning her, but she hurried away as Tieran touched her shoulder.

16

"Just ignore them for now. You'll be properly introduced soon enough," he said quietly, motioning for me to start climbing the ladder up to his tent, first. I nodded and started picking my way up carefully.

"What's wrong with their lips? They're so pale," I asked.

"They're mute. But like I said, just ignore them for now," he said quickly, obviously wanting to change the subject. "How old are you, by the way?"

I paused in my climbing, wondering if I could pull off another lie right now. He nudged my foot so that I kept climbing. "I just turned seventeen about a month ago."

"Really? You're so small and short, but you did seem a bit sharp for a child so I took you to be about that age." He laughed, pleased with himself.

"How about you?" I asked, reaching a landing at the top and waiting for him to catch up.

"Twenty-one. Not that it matters all that much," he sighed, pulling aside some golden drapes for me to go inside his tent.

I didn't even have to crouch to slip inside, and once I had made it in, all of the air in my lungs faded out. The colours and patterns of the silks draped about were beautiful and mesmerizing; they could only be Fluxarian, maybe Emergent. Tieran's bed was a great heap of pillows and wolfskin blankets, and around it was a canopy of gold chains. He had a small stump table beside it with a knife, some handcuffs, scraps of cloth, and two tall bottles: one of whitish liquid, another of gold. The golden bottle was shut with a bolt and padlock, the key nowhere in sight. I knelt on a cushion by a table in the middle of the room, candles and bowls of fruits and steaming breads laid out before me.

"Help yourself to any of that," he said, tossing me a greenish looking fruit the shape of a pretzel. I turned it in my hands for a few moments and set it down in my lap, staring at the ceiling. A chandelier made of some kind of bone swung above me.

"You're pretty."

I gasped, hearing his voice behind me, and hesitated; taking a small bite of the green-pretzel-fruit. It tasted like a pomegranate, but had the consistency of an orange. I wiped my mouth on my sleeve, bowing my head slightly in appreciation. "Thank you. That's nice of you to say, but I'm engaged, actually, so please refrain from saying such things."

He chuckled, "If you're referring to the companion you're searching for, I promise you that he is most definitely dead by now."

"You seem to be doing just fine out here, I don't see why my fiancé wouldn't."

"Not everyone is as resilient as I."

"Or maybe you're just lucky," I said, unable to keep from smiling. He narrowed his eyes in amusement, his gaze extremely unnerving as it travelled over my body. I pointedly looked away, setting down the fruit and trying a piece of bread instead. Then I recalled his earlier comment. "What do I want from you? You told me that earlier. What could I possibly want?" I asked, sounding braver than I felt. My hands shook uncontrollably under the table as he came closer and touched my chin with his smooth, pale fingers. I winced, but as I leaned away, his touch followed.

"You want to leave, don't you? Find that fiancé of yours? Make a deal with me, Irene," Tieran said.

"I don't like deals," I breathed, heart pounding against my ribs.

"How about you give me a shot? Just hear me out?"

I sighed. "Fine."

"All I ask of you is a performance at the feast tonight," he said, absently playing with a piece of my hair, "and that I can keep you for one week. Then you can leave."

"A week?" I gasped. "Are you crazy? What kind of 'performance'?"

He crossed his arms. "Dancing. Nothing fancy. And come on, Irene– a week in a real bed? With real food and actual people instead of storms and beasts? Doesn't sound all that crazy to me."

"I have important things to take care of, things you couldn't understand," I said, steadily. "I appreciate your offer but I have to politely decline. I really have to get going–"

He suddenly knocked the bread out of my hand, roughly grabbing my chin between his thumb and index finger. "Leaving wasn't an option," he hissed.

I wrenched out of his grip, slapping his smooth, cleanly-shaven cheek. His head whipped to the side as my palm made impact. I leapt to my feet, brushing off my shorts and stuffing some of the bread down my sweater before making for the ladder. But before I could reach for the first rung, Tieran's fist had secured on the neckline of my sweater and yanked me backwards, throwing me down. I crashed to the floor of his tent, the wind knocked out of me and lights popping in front of my eyes. Then I saw his face, the red handprint on his cheek.

"You're leaving me no choice, Irene," he growled, a hand gripping around my neck and squeezing, the other digging under my shorts' waistband. I yearned against his grip, trying to peel his fingers off my throat, but he squeezed only tighter and soon black patched across my vision. The hand he'd put down my pants wrenched out my hidden dagger, and then hastily tossed the knife aside. Tieran pulled me up and slammed me against the wall, knitting his fingers in my hair, yanking my head back as he whispered into my ear, "You belong to me now."

"Why...why do you want me?" I rasped, my head flaming in pain, lungs trying to catch some oxygen.

Tieran didn't answer. Only stared, his eyes cold sapphires. And then he smiled, bringing his mouth to my forehead and leaving a burning kiss. "You're a shiny new addition to my collection," he said, one hand still holding me, the other reaching behind him to grab that white bottle on his bedside table. He tipped his head back, drinking carefully, licking his lips. And before I knew what was happening, he had my face in his hands and he was kissing me, taking no break to breathe, the shock of his mouth on mine making my stomach turn. But as soon as his mouth touched mine, I knew this wasn't just a kiss. It was punishment. My lips felt like they'd been embraced by a live flame, a burst of lava, a solar flare. The pain was so intense I felt my bones jellify, my blood boil. As his tongue pushed through, the fire invaded every reach of my mouth, and then my throat. He tasted medical and like chemicals and as quickly as it had started, it ended. It had been so horrible that it wasn't until it was over that I realized he'd only kissed me for less than a minute, barely thirty seconds.

He released me and I crumpled to the floor, my whole body racked with tremors, my mouth a hot, numb, hole in my head. I laid there, my forehead pressed to the cold floor of his tent, gagging and eyes streaming until I felt his hand gently rub my back, his voice no louder than a whisper. "Shh, shh, it's all done, Irene," Tieran said, kneeling by me. I raised my streaming eyes, looking at him, horrified. He smoothed my sweaty bangs off of my forehead.

"W-what did you do to me?" I rasped, choking as I tried to swallow, grabbing at my throat. He took my hands and lowered them, wrapping an arm around my waist as he helped me to my feet.

"Just fixing the problem all beautiful women seem to have," he said, going over to his set of drawers and rummaging through. "You talk too much. Ask too many questions."

"I don't understand–"

"Get dressed in this," Tieran said, tossing me a handful of silky garments. "Your clothes are filthy, and when skin is as exquisite as yours, it would be a crime to hide it from admiring men, don't you think?"

I opened my mouth to speak, and then stopped myself, eyeballing the outfit. The servant girls below had all been wearing something similar; a short, black robe that wrapped around and tied in the front; a pair of red silk shorts; a lacy brassiere.

"And let your hair down. I've never seen a Fluxarian girl with hair as vivid as yours. Were you kicked off the mountain for being so pretty?"

Heat flooded my face. "Were you kicked off for being such a bastard?" I retorted, my voice coming out broken and jagged.

A shadow passed over Tieran's face, icy dread seeping through my veins. I didn't have a moment to regret my words before he struck me on the side of the face and thrust his knee into my stomach. He placed his foot squarely on my back, making my bones creak. "Get dressed and take out your hair. Come down and Lilah will be there to show you to where I need you to be," he said, through gritted teeth. I nodded, trying to keep breathing as he leaned his weight onto me, then lifted his foot off and walked away. "That's my girl," he said, his voice now distant as I heard the rope ladder creak under his feet. I lay there for a while, listening to the quieting sounds of his climbing, shaking so violently my teeth chattered.

"Destan, Destan, Destan, where are you?" I said, my lips not wanting to move any longer, stiffening on the last word. Fat tears bubbled from my eyes and rolled down my cheeks, the world seeming to tumble and roll like thunder, everything falling away like the tree had been chopped down with me still inside it. I couldn't just lie here. If I let myself start crying again, I knew I wouldn't be able stop this time. I would cry until Tieran came back and beat me until it killed me because I hadn't listened to him again.

It took everything I had to stand up and start undressing. Once I was bare, I slipped on the shorts first and found that the brassiere actually fit better than the worn out thing I'd been wearing before. My chest felt sore and tender. Then I undid the tie on the black dress and shimmied into it. It fell just to my skinny thighs and hung loosely everywhere else. I couldn't look in the mirror. I tried to sigh, but my lips remained sealed together. Confused, I touched my mouth and felt that the skin had hardened and turned white, just like the servant girls below.

"What's wrong with their lips? They're so pale."

"They're mute. Just ignore them for now."

No, I attempted to say, but now my cheeks only filled with air. I pulled aside my lips with my fingers, I could still open them this way, but when I touched them I couldn't feel my fingertips on their flesh. All burning sensations were gone, but now left a dry, empty numbness. I tried to scream, make the loudest noise I possibly could, but my throat felt like it had been coated in cement.

My voice was gone. And Tieran had it.

chapter three

At the foot of Tieran's tree, I looked around me in a panicked haze, my thoughts spiralling out of control. *That Lilah girl. She must brew some sort of poison for him that does this. This is how he controls all of his servants. They can't talk back and have no choice but to stay, because without a voice it's almost impossible to survive, isn't it?* All around me were men and trees; Shuishan and shuishan. My gaze caught onto the smirking girl leaning casually against a nearby tent, her long blonde hair over her shoulder.

As she combed through it with her dainty fingers, Lilah smiled evilly. "Cat got your tongue, new girl?" she asked me.

I narrowed my eyes and strode toward her, feeling terribly exposed as the cold wind breezed between my bare legs due to the stupid new clothes I had to wear. *You are an evil snake with no soul and I hope the nastiest tiangou eats you alive,* I thought viciously, yearning my mouth to move, but just making my jaw throb from the useless effort.

"Nothing to say? You're still having a great time?" she asked, widening her eyes innocently and grinning with yellowed teeth. "I'm so very glad. Come with me to meet your new sisters."

I had no choice but to follow her. We walked behind Tieran's tree to where a lopsided looking tent was strung. It looked to me like one big gust of wind could knock the tent flat. Lilah let the tent's door smack my face on our way in, and my nose was greeted with clouds of perfume and powder. A rusty lantern swung from the ceiling, and girls as mute as I painted makeup on each other's faces; dressing up in jewellery and silks, some even dancing among the cluster of straw sleeping mats. Four cracked mirrors leaned against the back wall, nothing more than haphazard slabs of reflective glass. One girl knelt in front of one and brushed her long, dark hair. The lantern light made it appear violet every time it ran through the brush bristles.

"Listen up: this is Tieran's new doll. He wants her dancing by tonight, so don't mess around and show her the steps so that she doesn't get egged her first time," Lilah drawled. "You don't want your master disappointed or else he'll pull more than one of you into his tent tonight." Her eyes flashed and every girl stood and bowed, touching their index fingers to their foreheads where a number and Tieran's initial was painted on. A sign of servitude?

"I'm told she's a weeker, but let's make her good enough to keep her, don't you think?" she added coyly, and the servant girls made the same finger-to-forehead motion again. Lilah smiled, patted my shoulder and disappeared from the tent. I shifted from foot to foot and would have smiled or said hello, but all I could do was frown at them and have them frown back.

I toyed with the tie of my robe, waving and averting my eyes. Two girls with a 'T4' and 'T11' painted on their foreheads looked at each other, moving their eyebrows and blinking rapidly, obviously communicating something. T4 strode toward me and lifted away my long blue bangs, rubbing the hair in between her fingers. Her caramel eyes met mine and she motioned for me to sit down on a stool by the mirror. All at once, the girls came down by me and began braiding my hair, brushing off my dress, offering me drink and bread and one of them even held my hand. I was overwhelmed at their kindness and couldn't even say thank you or smile, so I just bowed my head at each of them and let them do what they wanted with me.

T8, a short girl with curls, stood up and made a brief dancing motion, wrinkling her brow. *"Should we teach her the dance?"* I imagined her asking, in a warm voice that looked like it could suit her.

T11 shook her head and waved her hands frantically, *"No, no time,"* She pointed at my face and then the powders and paints on a small table, *"We have to do her makeup."*

T7 tapped her wrist, like a Peak worker running late to some important meeting, *"Do we have enough time?"*

T11 gave a thumbs up, *"It'll work out."* She tugged on my shoulders to stand up. T11 circled me for a moment, glancing at my scrawny body; at the ripples of muscles, the bruises and blemishes, and the pale skin stretched tightly over my bones. She lifted up my dress and nodded her head as she saw my flat stomach, *"She's in okay shape."*

Next, T2 came up and touched my arm. I turned to her and raised an eyebrow in questioning. She jabbed her thumb at me and then spun in a circle. It took her a few different moves for me to guess what she was trying to ask me, *"Can you dance?"*

I shrugged, looking dismally at my feet. Dancing. Not good. Is this really why Tieran had these girls here? To *dance* for him? He should've examined me better and realized that I had never danced a day in my life, save for some playful jumping and spinning me and my friends did after a successful thieving. Only girls high up on Thgindim could pay for lessons, and it wasn't as if Underbrush was a celebratory town that called for such things. I had a brief recollection of stepping on Skye Zanying's toes constantly during his 19th birthday cotillion. My stomach heaved and I corrected my shrug to a shake of the head. The girls eyed each other anxiously, and then T11 grabbed my hand and pulled me out of their tent. Two others came skipping out behind us into the woods.

The forest was darkening, and the tables were now fully set with all kinds of food. The Shuishan were crowding onto the benches, hauling in barrels of moonshine, and grinning grossly as they took notice of me and the servants who'd come out. T11 snapped her fingers in front of my eyes to regain my attention. She pointed at herself, and then back at me, giving a questioning thumbs up, *"Watch me, then repeat what I do. Okay?"*

I returned the gesture, *Okay.*

T11 strung a series of bells along my hips that matched hers and she swivelled them back and forth, making the air sweet with the tinny sound. Self-conscious, I timidly echoed her movement. I had never used my hips like this before, it felt sensual and unfamiliar and I stopped after a few swirls. Her shoulders sagged and she widened her eyes, making the movement more rapid. I closed my eyes and forced myself to do it, then she raised her arms above her head and began twirling her hands gracefully in circles, like she was stretching out each finger and fluttering them like butterfly wings. I did the same, and once she saw that I had this much down, she combined these two movements with turning in a circle, slow, and then faster, making me have to stop and watch for a moment as she became a blur. She was so beautiful, and she closed her eyes as if she could be enjoying herself, but Tieran had stolen her smile, and so the dance was without joy.

T6 tiptoed over and rubbed her hands together, staring at me intently. She then did the hand movement T11 was showing me and I translated this as, *"Always move your hands. Don't stop."*

T13 added onto what I should do by demonstrating a series of kicks and a quick leap. I let the movements repeat and change and then I realized what she was trying to tell me. *"Do whatever else you want. A leap, a kick, just keep your hands moving. Make it up,"* she shimmied her hips, *"and use your hips,"* she tapped the 'T' on her forehead and winked, *"Tieran likes that."*

I nodded bitterly. I didn't want to do what Tieran liked. But I had to. The blind man from the tent where I'd first awoken limped over, shooing us with his hands, "Come on girls, get in costume! We're almost ready to feast!" The servants touched their foreheads and I copied the gesture, adding a bow and rushing inside our tent. There was no more time for questions or dance lessons, T11 forced me into a chair and started applying my makeup in thick wet smears and powder clouds. The first addition to my face: T17 on my forehead.

Breathe, breathe, don't panic. I was so anxious, the breaths whistling through my limp lips. They'd put me at the back of the procession of girls, but now we were walking out through the curtain that the Shuishan men had hung and we were about to go on stage and begin the performance. *Move your hands and your hips, close your eyes, spin in circles, give a kick or a jump, don't fall or run into anyone. Oh shit, Raine, don't run into anyone.* I thought in a daze, getting nudged in the back to begin prancing out.

We were all barefoot, but the girls had me slip some glittery gold rings on my toes and bangles around my ankles. They jangled as I walked and I ran instantly to the very back part of the stage as the men began to clap. I raised up my arms in the starting position, glancing warily around. It felt unreal, like a dream. The torches made the stage so bright that the audience appeared as nothing but a black mass. Every girl had her eyes closed and faced turned upward in preparation. At the foot of the stage was a jumble of drummers and other musicians, and all seated around them were the Shuishan. Tieran was draped across a throne-like chair front and center, Lilah kneeling at the foot of it, bringing her mouth to and from his ear, whispering. Her eyes flashed to me, winking. Tieran's lips curled into a smirk, and he stared and stared so hard at me I had to scrunch my eyes tightly closed. *He's going to be watching me the whole time, isn't he?* I thought.

The drummer beat hard on his rabbit skin drum, one, two, three. One, two, three. It was like a waltz, and every time he hit it, one of us would start the dance; first hips, then add arms, then hands, then spin, then let it go. I was waiting for the twelfth beating of the drum to begin my dance, which gave me some time to calm down. There were twelve of us, but I assumed a couple girls in between had died or run away because I was T17. Five of his dolls had disappeared over the time he started collecting them. I peeked out from under my eyelids. Tieran was guzzling a dark, blood-red wine from a goblet and licking his lips at me. I shut my eyes completely again and tried to keep track of the beats.

Ten, eleven, twelve, I had to keep focus. *Focus, focus.* But the men were calling out now, screaming compliments at the servant girls as they danced and whirled like colourful hurricanes, the bells and bangles  adding a metallic stirring to the heavy beat. I tried to drown it out and think. I was last so I wouldn't really have to count, just look out for who was dancing near to me. So I squeezed my eyes closed and held my breath and let myself melt away.

I sent my mind to Thgindim. I was at the Base for that archery tournament, everyone dancing and celebrating my victory, and fire is blazing everywhere and Destan's arm is linked with mine as we gallop around a circle. His eyes are silver moons, his laughter is the drumbeat; low and fast. The sound of the servants' bells is the music the archers are beginning to play on their flutes and chimes.

I love you Destan, I'm dancing for you.

"And you're not stepping on my feet, either! That's an improvement, Bluehead," he'd laugh back, his voice so clear in my mind that it was if he were actually here. I could recall it easier than reciting the alphabet or naming Thgindim's levels. He was the only thing about my old life that wasn't foggy or dusty or tainted. He was here, I could still remember his feel and voice and everything. Maybe this meant I would find him again.

The floor shook beside me and my eyes popped open. T14 began dancing and so I swallowed my last breath and swivelled my hips in a circular motion. As soon as I began, Tieran leaned his chin on his fist, zeroing in. I wouldn't let him shake me. I tore my gaze from his as I raised my arms and turned in a circle, my dress fanning out and gold bells tinkling madly.

"Look at the new girl!"

"She's a natural."

"Give us a twirl, new girl!"

I stumbled and nearly ran into another girl as I realized that the men were shouting at me.

He wants her dancing by tonight, so don't mess around and show her the steps so that she doesn't get egged her first time, I recalled Lilah saying earlier. Egged. As I spun, I caught a glimpse of what they were eating. There were trays and trays of meat and fruit, and then I saw a few gallons of eggs. Some men were rolling the white things between their fingers, their eyes hungry and fingers tapping impatiently. They were looking for a target...a weak dancer?

And in that moment, I decided that it wouldn't be me.

I cut in front of the girls and stood closer to the front, forcing myself to give a kick and twirl that made me feel completely stupid. *I'm not here, I'm with Destan, I'm not here.* But the screaming was so loud, I could distinguish Tieran's voice from the rest calling out to me and I slid down to the floor, moving my arms rapidly, fluttering them down like ribbons. The audience howled in pleasure and roared for more. A rush of adrenaline coursed through me, thrilling and hot.

Men started climbing onto the stage to dance with us. They each seemed to have favourites, but among the twelve of us they had to share. T2 was being yanked back and forth, the pain clear in her eyes. Poor T11 got caught between twins three times her age who touched her breasts and pulled her hair. It wasn't long until a hand slipped around my waist, swirling my hips for me. I gasped and turned around, my hands landing on his shoulders. Tieran smiled, looking at me under his lashes. I shut my eyes, face flaming, my body fighting against his hands as he moved me.

"You sure are special, aren't you?" he chuckled, lifting my hands off his shoulders and pressing them to his buttocks. Shocked, I removed them immediately, backing up only to be caught around the waist and spun around, everything blurring by as the Shuishan exploded with laughter. Tieran stopped me again, pulling me close, touching his forehead to mine. "Let's dance, my blue girl," he whispered, his breath reeking of strong, raw moonshine. He drew back, suddenly scooping me into his arms, and tossing me in the air.

All air whooshed from my lungs as I flew up, and when I thought I'd crash into Tieran's arms, I ended up bouncing on what felt like a big trampoline, soaring up again and being caught in the tangle of fabric. A Shuishan shoved me off and tossed on the next batch of girls to be launched in the parachute, and I staggered down the stage, every limb quaking, tears stinging in my eyes. They wouldn't let me get away so easily. Someone snatched at the tie of my robe, yanking it so hard that the knot came undone and part of the garment tore down the middle, exposing me in the brassiere.

The crowd erupted into a chorus of *oohs* and *ahhs*, a circle of men closing in around me. Their mouths were open and drooling or laughing so hideously I could see their nasty yellow teeth, and I found myself unable to distinguish these monsters from the tiangou that had attacked me the night before. I looked around in a panicked haze for a way out, wanting to beg for mercy or help from the other girls but unable to choke out even a word. They were reaching and lunging for me, trying to pull off the rest of my robe, and I dropped to the ground, wrapping my arms around my head, curling in on myself. Hot tears rushed from my eyes without my permission, and I hid my face, trembling, praying they couldn't see me cry, that it would all turn out to be a nightmare triggered by the assorted fungus I'd been eating the past few days. And then– a hush fell over the stage. My whole body went cold, shaking uncontrollably as the familiar footsteps came slowly my way.

"There, there," he soothed, kneeling by me and putting an arm across my shoulders. His hot breath grazed my neck, sending chills down my spine. "Why are you crying, pet? Are you hurt?"

There was a myriad of mumbling and whispering around me. I shook my head, still tucked in my safe little ball. Shivering. *Go away, go away, go away.*

"Not hurt? Then why don't you come dance, join the party like my other dolls?" Tieran asked, this time coming around and gripping my shoulders, pulling me to stand as I tried to stay put with all my might. The men around were chuckling, calling out again as I was forced to stand before their leader. Tieran tipped my chin up to look at him, my vision quivering behind tears. His smile was playful, but his eyes were hard and dark as stone.

"Give us a turn with her, sir!" someone called out, causing Tieran's eyes to glance away from mine for a moment.

"Not tonight, men," he said. Then before I knew what was happening, he had my wrists pinned to my back, my shoulder blades aching in protest. "This doll's having a drink with the king."

I wasn't done fighting him, I didn't care how humiliated or exhausted I was. I kicked my legs and struggled in his grip the whole way from the stage to his throne. It only seemed to amuse him, though and I ended up sprawled helplessly in his lap anyway. Tieran snapped his fingers and three girls came dutifully over, bearing bottles of drink and bowls of fruit and what looked like salted meat. "Thank you, ladies," he bowed his head, taking T8's hand and bringing her closer so he could peer inside the bowl. He withdrew two bright green apples, handing one to me. "See, Irene? I can be polite."

My eyes narrowed. *Then how would you like it if I return the favour and politely strangle you?*

Tieran nodded at me, motioning at the apple. "Aren't you going to eat? You must be starving after all of that dancing."

I looked at the fruit in my hands, bringing it slowly to my mouth. Even as it brushed my lips, I couldn't feel it. I wouldn't embarrass myself and even attempt to take a bite with this useless mouth. And yet, in the presence of all of these fragrant wines and the warm scent of bread and meat wafting around me, my stomach growled and moaned in desperation for food. I passed the apple back to T8, avoiding Tieran's eyes and he burst into laughter.

"Picky, picky. Who doesn't like apples?" he asked, rubbing my back. I cringed at his touch, shaking my head. Tieran waved his hand for another girl, T2. The smallest servant girl here, with short, glossy hair that looked green in the torchlight. Her dark eyes lowered obediently, presenting him with two corked bottles. Tieran chose one and grabbed one of the large leaves on the table, dribbling a pool of the clear, brownish liquid into the concave center of it. "How about a drink?" I shook my head but he grabbed my chin and forced my head back. "I'll help you, then."

His fingers pushed my lips apart, and my throat was drenched in the horrible sting of vinegar. I lurched forward, gagging, my eyes streaming as I struggled to cough and not choke on my hopeless tongue. Everyone was laughing at me, at my sputtering, at my exposed chest in the stupid brassiere, at the makeup my tears had ruined and smeared.

I couldn't take the shame any longer. I raised my hand to slap him, but time seemed to slow down as my palm neared his cheek, and I caught the deadly glint in his eyes that said if I hit him, I was going to be in a world of even worse pain than what he'd already put me through. I slowed my hand and touched his face rather, a soft caress, and Tieran smiled.

I hate you, I thought repeatedly. I lowered my hand, glancing away and staring at my lap. But no sooner had I done this, I felt Tieran brush the hair off of my neck, chills going down my spine as I felt his breath tingle below my ear.

"That was a wise move, Irene Abrasha," he hissed, a finger trailing down my cheek. "Even a pretty girl like you won't last the night if you keep fighting your master like this."

31

You are not my master.

"What do you say about another dance?" he whispered, pulling me to my feet. But instead of walking us back toward the stage, he turned around and motioned for me to go up the ladder to his tent. He was right behind me, moving fast so I had to climb and climb as quickly as I could.

We made it to his tent. He closed the ladder hatch. I stood across from him, my whole body trembling as he stared and stared with a cold sort of fire in his eyes. "Take off your robe," he said, calmly. I didn't move. "T17," he warned, taking only one step forward, "take...it...off."

Please, I begged, shaking my head, looking away at the window. At the unstripped branches of dark, shuishan leaves. *Don't make me do this, Tieran. Anything but this.*

He came three more steps forward, his face hardening into shadow and bone in the lamplight. And yet, he was still smiling. Even as he strolled behind me, placing his hands on the tops of my shoulders. "It's not a matter of take it off or leave it on, Irene," he whispered, "It's a matter of do *you* want to take it off? Or would you rather I do it for you?" He flicked down the shoulder of the robe and rested his chin on my skin, inhaling deeply. Shivers sizzled through me, and I felt one of his hands touch my stomach, sliding down, down, a heat manifesting between my legs. Ashamed, I tried to wrench myself free from his trap. But his arms were stone and my bones had turned to jelly and I found myself weak and immobilized, my eyes filling with tears and heart hammering in a panicked daze as he reached and rubbed at my core, the layers of silk too thin to keep the feel of his fingers from affecting me.

"You're mine now, Irene Abrasha," he growled, combing through my hair from scalp to tip. "You're mine and no one else's. You're not even your own. And if you cross me; if you keep fighting and fighting like you have been, I'll shoot you before you even think about stepping outside of this camp." He was slowly moving us toward his bed, the music down below fading as we got farther and farther from the window. "Do you understand me?"

Destan, forgive me.

In one quick movement, my robe was on the floor and I was face-down on his bed. His body loomed heavily over me like a storm. And then came crashing down.

chapter four

The world had turned red and hazy.

I'd left a wet, dark spot on his silver wolf pelt blanket. So as punishment, he wouldn't let me cover myself. I was shivering, the pain inside of me searing and hot while my skin and bones felt coated in ice. Meanwhile, he watched me; sick satisfaction on his face. He had just turned out the light, guzzling what remained in the tall, wooden goblet and relaxing into his pillows. Tieran tilted his head to one side, half of his face in shadow.

"Hmm...what to do, what to do..." he murmured, leaning forward and scrutinizing me. I didn't move, just squeezed my eyes shut and tried to appear asleep as I heard him come staggering over. He couldn't do anything more with me if I was asleep. Fresh fear tore through me...or would he? His toe nudged at my cheek, first gently, then harder, causing me to flinch. He chuckled, "Wakey, wakey. Your master needs you."

I didn't want it to get any worse, so I obeyed. I could hardly lift myself into a sitting position, my knees slipping in the shallow smear of blood that had pooled beneath me. I made it to my knees, and forced my eyes to meet his.

"I think that'll be all for tonight, T17," he said, surprising me with the sudden change of address. "We've broken the seal and now you may return to your tent. Unless you would rather pleasure me longer?" Tieran slurred drunkenly, revealing a new robe for me and swinging it in the air.

I shook my head, regretting it instantly as the moderate blood loss sent me into a nauseating dizzy spell. Using the bedside table for support to lift myself up, I reached for the robe. He moved it away, one finger tipping my chin up to look at him.

"Forgetting something, doll?" he whispered, scarlet hair falling into his eyes.

I bowed, touching my index finger to my forehead and looking at him with every ounce of hatred burning in my gaze. He handed me the robe and strode away, back to his bed.

"Very good."

My descent from his treehouse was unsteady and disorienting, the sounds of the woods making loud chatter flood into my ears, the night rain just beginning to pour. Different pairs of glowing eyes stared and stared, my bare feet slipped and stuck to the splintering rungs of the ladder, and after being startled by a particularly piercing howl from beyond the camp, I tripped– falling to the ground a good five feet before I should have.

My back smacked hard against the bulbous tree roots, pain shooting through me, the wind knocked from my lungs. Everything swam before my eyes, icy raindrops splashing my skin. *How did I get here?* I thought, trying only half-heartedly to get out of the mud and roots, my body so tired and aching. *I'm never going to make it out. Tieran will have killed me before I find Destan again.*

I'm not sure how many minutes passed, but it wasn't too long until I heard feet quickly darting through puddles, someone nearby panting. I only feared it was Shuishan for a moment until I realized no one was speaking. Soft hands touched my cheeks, eyes appearing above me.

Another pair of hands slid under my back and helped me into a sitting position, a small lantern hovering between me and a girl with T1 painted on her forehead. She had her hands in front of her, raising them up and nodding at me. *"Can you stand up?"*

I nodded, but once I stood, my knees buckled. With assistance from the servant girls behind me, I was lifted completely to my feet. The small group of them guided me past the stage area and tables, into the tent we'd gotten prepared in earlier for the performance. T6 and T8 had been waiting inside there, moving the tent flap aside as we stepped in. There were two more lanterns sitting on the makeup counter at the front of the tent, and all of the chairs had been stacked in the corner; straw sleeping mats and an assortment of tattered blankets spread out.

They helped me settle onto a mat, T11 wrapping a knitted covering around my shoulders, T1 communicating something to the others that I couldn't translate. Whatever it had been, they nodded and disappeared through the opposite end of the tent, through some hidden opening. Even with T11's warm arm behind my shoulders and T8's fingers combing through my hair, I couldn't stop trembling. I looked at them both, touching my hands to my heart, hoping they understood.

Thank you.

T11 took my hand in hers, shaking her head. Suddenly, her eyes glanced downward, widening as she saw the dried blood on the inside of my thighs. She motioned aggressively to two girls standing by, T4 and T12, and within a minute they were bathing my legs with a washcloth. T9 passed me a cold sponge to press in between my legs and while at first it made the pain worse, soon it subsided to a dull aching, the coolness taming the fire. T11 touched my cheek. With just one look, she communicated what went beyond words. She'd been in my place before, many times. And without warning, without being able to stop myself, I dissolved completely into tears, collapsing against her as she held me tightly.

I was so busy crying that I didn't notice them moving me toward the back of the tent, where the others had disappeared earlier. I found myself in what looked and felt like a cave, but I knew that to be impossible seeing as we were miles and miles away from either mountain. And yet, I was surrounded on all sides by smooth stone, the only opening a small circle to gaze through at the sky above. The servant girls sat along the circumference of the hideaway, a small fire in the center and a crate of bottles and what appeared to be reeds in a mason jar. T1 was at the head of them, by the flattest, cleanest slab of rock. T2 was kneeling at her side, a damp cloth in her hands.

T1 looked at me, waving her hand in front of her eyes and motioning at the wall, *"Can you see the wall clearly?"*

Wiping my nose and nodding, I came to her side. She withdrew a singed stick from the fire and turned to the wall, raising it and beginning to write. The words were thick and black on the light grey stone.

I AM JAY, OF FLUXARIA. DAUGHTER OF THE PAST LEADER OF THE SHUISHAN TRAVELLERS. I WAS THE ONLY FEMALE IN THE CAMP WHEN TIERAN ARRIVED. AFTER EARNING HIS WAY INTO OUR COMMUNITY, HE TURNED MANY OF THE MEN AGAINST MY FATHER AND KILLED HIM AND FORCED ME TO BE HIS FIRST WHORE. BUT AS TIME WENT ON HE WOULD HAPPEN UPON OTHER GIRLS IN THE FOREST AND COULDN'T KEEP HIMSELF FROM ADDING THEM TO HIS HAREM. THE ONLY GIRL HE DIDN'T POSSESS IS LILAH, WHO WAS FOUND AS AN INFANT, ABANDONED OUTSIDE OF THGINDIM. HE'S GROOMED HER TO WORSHIP HIM AND FOLLOW HIS EVERY COMMAND. THEREFORE, YOU CANNOT TRUST HER. SHE IS NOT LIKE US. SHE IS YOUNG BUT SHE HAS BLOOD ON HER HANDS.

She wrote so quickly and fluidly it was incredible, making me wonder how many times she'd had to tell the same story. The stick snapping on the very last word and T2 immediately retrieved a new one, slipping it through Jay's fingers as she continued to write to me.

DO NOT BE AFRAID.
WE ARE YOUR SISTERS NOW.

In spite of myself, I shook my head vigorously, finding a stick of my own and finding a free place to write. It had been so long since I'd held a pencil, my handwriting was messy and all over the place as my trembling fingers guided it.

Thank you for all you have done for me. But I cannot stay here.

T6 lunged forward, stealing my stick:

Do not dare leave camp! You will surely PERISH

Before I could write back, T11 appeared by my side and touched my wrist gently, taking her time to write:

Forgive me, T17, but T6 speaks the truth. Tieran has eyes everywhere. And we have lost so many to the beasts and wilds of the forest.

With her washcloth, T2 wiped away all of the writing that had filled up the wall. Then she dipped her fingers into a pile of ashes and rather than writing, began to sketch something with only her hands. It was breathtaking, how her fingers moved and traced so delicately across the stone, creating images of beasts and silhouettes of girls and a tall, dark figure overpowering it all. Tieran.

The first girl she drew was marked with the number seven. She was by Tieran's side, six other undistinguished girls behind her. T2 dotted her thumb along a path to another man, one with what looked like a helmet for a head. *Could it be that ex-JP Zhaorong?* I wondered, watching as her two hands joined to imprint a heart along the line; connecting the T7 girl to Rong. T2 sat back on her knees, imploring me with her eyes to see if I so far understood.

I squinted uncertainly, pointing from the two figures and hesitantly forming a heart with my hands, in question. T2 as well as the others nodded in confirmation, and I motioned to her that she could continue drawing. She nodded and turned back to the wall; a fresh coating of black ash on her fingertips.

She drew a circle around Tieran, followed by an arrow pointed to the assumed lovers, and an *X*. A new girl joined the drawing, but she was distinctly smaller, thinner, and on Tieran's right hand. Lilah. There was a bottle in her hand, marked with a skull. Dread settled in my stomach like a stone. I knew where this was going. An arrow connected the bottle to T7, and after only leaving the drawing up for a number of seconds, T2 took up the washcloth and viciously scrubbed away at T7, leaving a smeary, black hole in the story.

Somehow, the silence in the hideaway seemed to deepen after T2's story was over. She solemnly cleaned away the rest of the drawing, T1 beginning to write again before she was finished.

THAT'S NOT EVEN THE BEGINNING, T17.

She touched T2's shoulder, communicating with her sad, dark eyes. And after taking a moment to stretch her fingers, T2 went again at the wall. This time, the story was shorter. Simpler. All she had to sketch were three girls. T10, T15, T16. None of them among us. The girls were enclosed in a big orb, and after more detailing of teeth, ears, claws, it sunk in. The servant girls were in a tiangou's stomach. T2 bowed her head at me, looking at T1 to continue. Her words were scrawled beneath the tiangou's paws.

WE DON'T WANT YOU TO END UP LIKE THEM

I understood her caution, and I did not want to insult the girls who led me from the foot of Tieran's tree to safety, but I could not leave them with the impression that I would be settling into the Shuishan's twisted way of life. By now I knew how dangerous Mythland was, how full to the brim it was with new terrors and tricks. But my head was filling with the memories from earlier tonight of the dancing and humiliation and fear. And then came the memories from later tonight. The memories of my wrists pinned down to his floor, his breath reeking, and his body crushing mine into dust beneath his as he forced his way in and smiled the whole while.

Nausea overcame me and I lurched forward, snatching up the stick again and writing with fervour, trying to keep from vomiting:

Please understand. I accept the risk and I must leave. Someone I love is out there and I must find him.

I paused, taking in their disappointment, then added to the wall:

You can't continue to be treated like this. Leave with me, I'll find a way

T6 shoved me out of her way and jabbed the stick pointedly at the wall.

__There. Is. No. Way.__ What makes you so capable? You are no better than the girls who've left and died before you. You're his whore now. Start getting used to it.

T6's addition caused so many divisions among the servants that I feel I can only continue to document the event through their writing, which volleyed back and forth, T2 wiping it all clean in between. T11 was first to respond.

Enough! How dare you let him convince you of such a thing? We are women. Not whores. Not dolls.

Call us what you want. We're damaged goods.
<u>We strip at his command</u>

We do what we need to survive

*We **whore** to survive, just admit it, bitch!*

THIS STOPS HERE. BOTH OF YOU STEP DOWN. YOU'VE MADE YOUR POINTS QUITE CLEAR.

T2 wiped the board clean, and a new girl stepped up. She was very beautiful, with a peachy face and eyes like dark drops of ink on parchment. Her hair was the colour of creamy coffee and cut to her chin. On her forehead was T8.

T17, where do you come from?

I come from Thgindim, Underbrush.
My name is Raine.

Hello, Raine. I'm Xiaowen. I'm from Thgindim, too. Starshade.

Why were you banished?

My father raised me with another man he loved the way men should love women. I adored them and they adored me. We were so happy. They were executed for immoral behaviour one day while I was at school. When I got home, their heads were gone from their shoulders. I was shot into Mythland before nightfall.

I'm so sorry, Xiaowen.

I just hope they can't see me from the spirit heaven. They'd be so ashamed of me.

Would you try to leave with me?

My fathers having to watch me die is worse than having to watch me whore. I hate the Shuishan, but I cannot leave and die. I have no experience surviving alone, and not in a forest this dangerous.

I'll help you. Don't worry. We could steal weapons, we cou

T17, I'M SORRY BUT THE DISCUSSION OF LEAVING ENDS HERE. YOU WILL NOT ENDANGER THE OTHER GIRLS FOR THE SAKE OF YOUR OWN PLOT.

T1 did not look pleased with me. But still, she gave me one more chance.

IS THERE ANYTHING ELSE YOU WISH TO SAY OR ASK BEFORE WE RETURN TO THE TENT?

Chills rolled down my neck and I clutched my arms. There was. I slowly took the stick, writing the words carefully, large enough for all of the girls in the hideout to see.

What has Tieran done with our voices?

T2 returned to the board with her bowl of ashes. It would be story time once more.

The Legend of TIERAN HUANG

The story begins six years after Tieran Huang had been made an orphan, left to his own devices in Mythland. He was twelve, nearly thirteen years-old at the time.

He had mastered means of survival in the forest, learning how to cloak his scent, find shelter in the storms and hunt even the fiercest beasts.

And yet, one fateful day, his intuition failed him, and he happened into a seemingly endless, toxic swamp

He walked for days, starving, growing weak…

RUSTLE

SLUMP

COLLAPSE

…until he could go no further

TRICKLE TRICKLE

GASP

And then, he saw her.

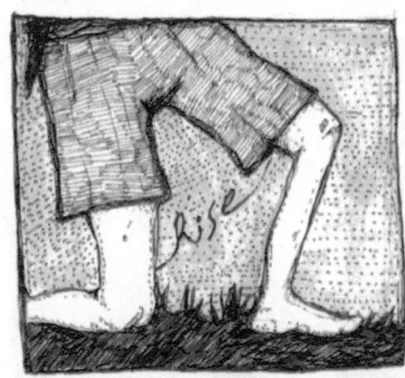

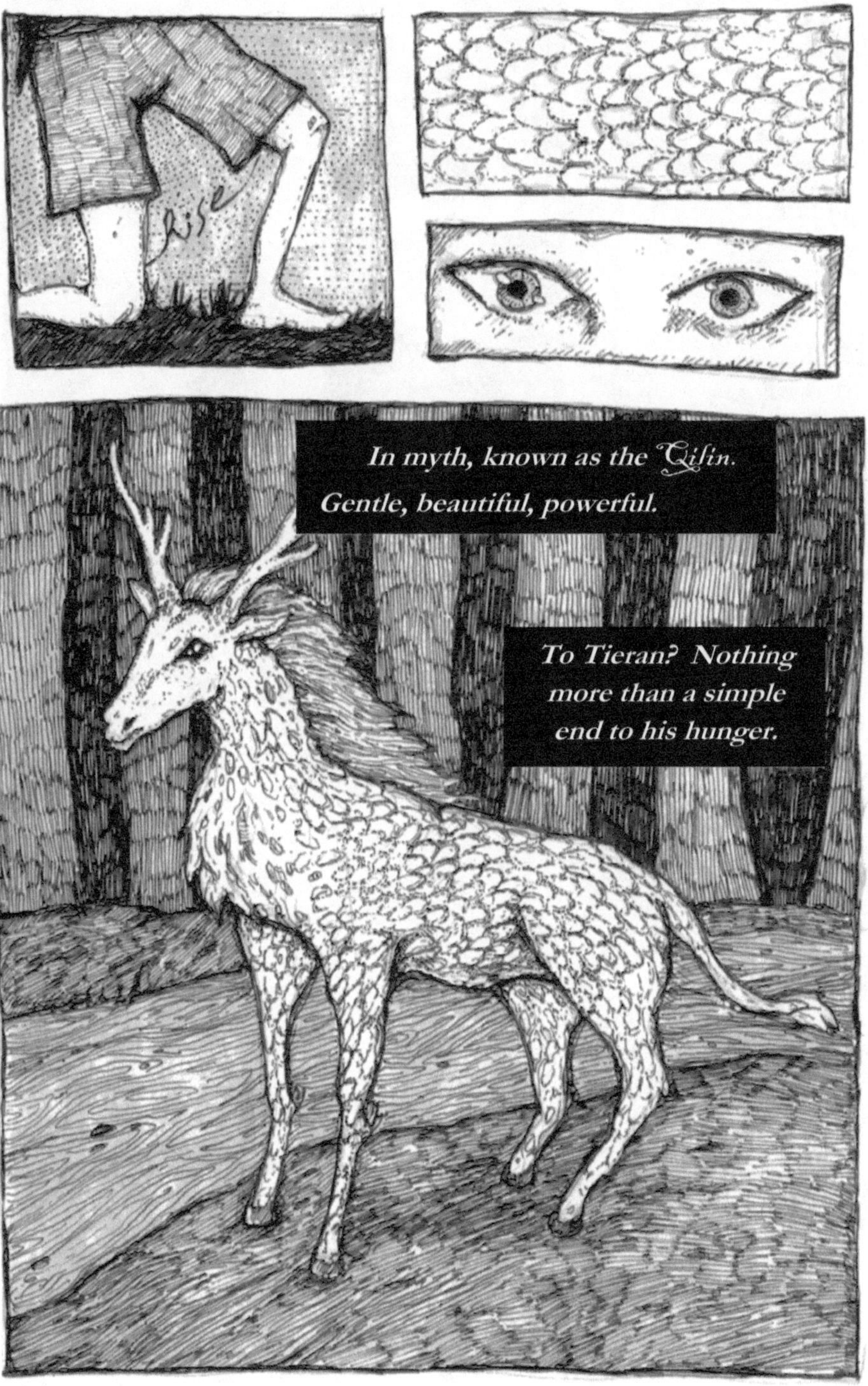

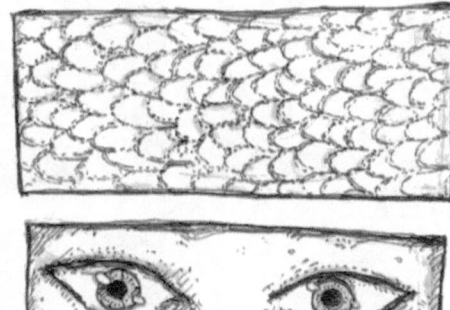

In myth, known as the Qilin.
Gentle, beautiful, powerful.

To Tieran? Nothing
more than a simple
end to his hunger.

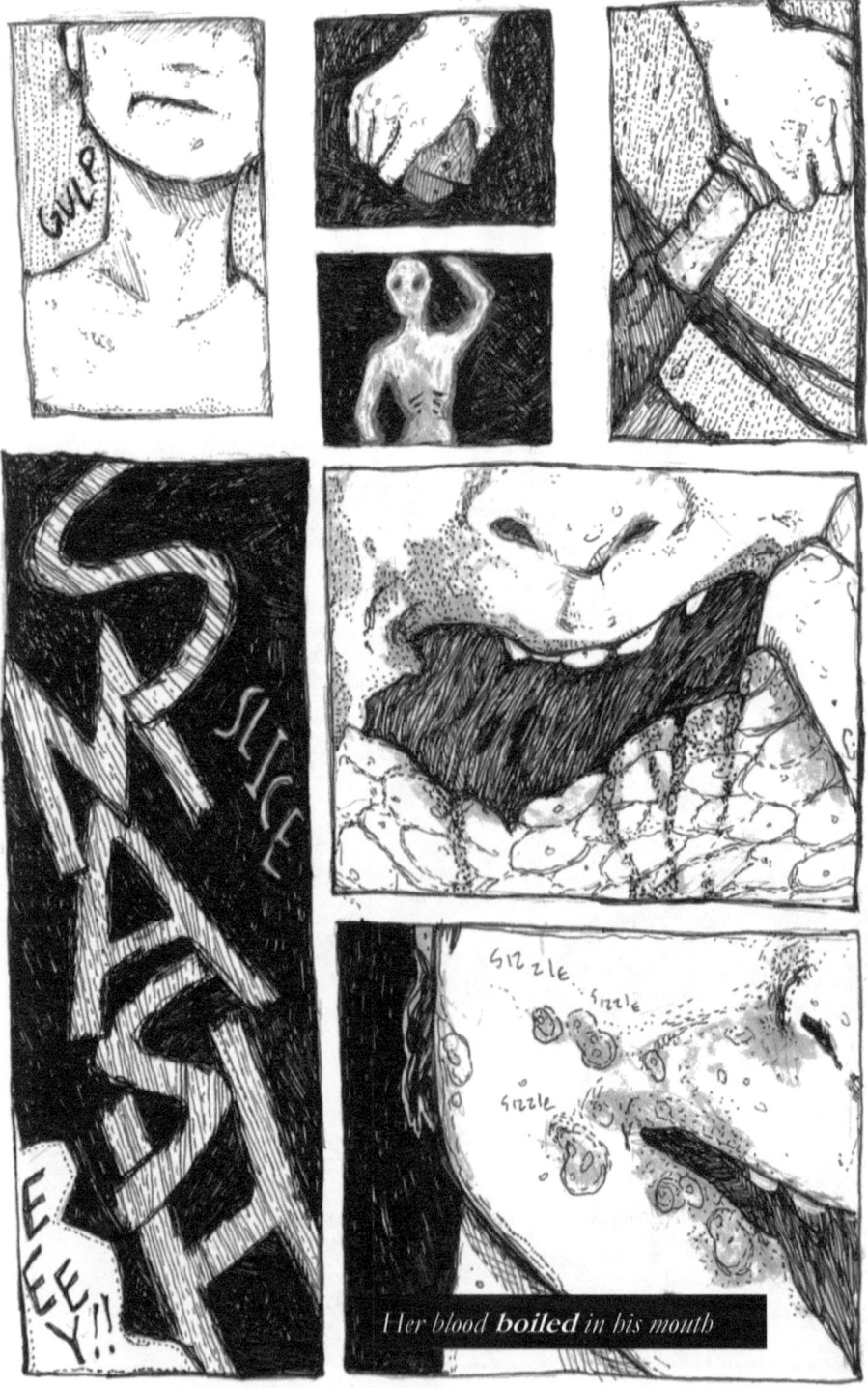

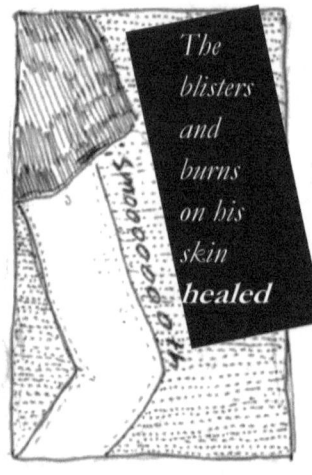

The
blisters
and
burns
on his
skin
healed

And enlightenment struck Tieran Huang

This creature could be nothing more than a gift to him from the spirits.

With blood that could immobilize…

…and tears that could heal any battle wound he could suffer…

…she was too precious for him to simply leave for another to find

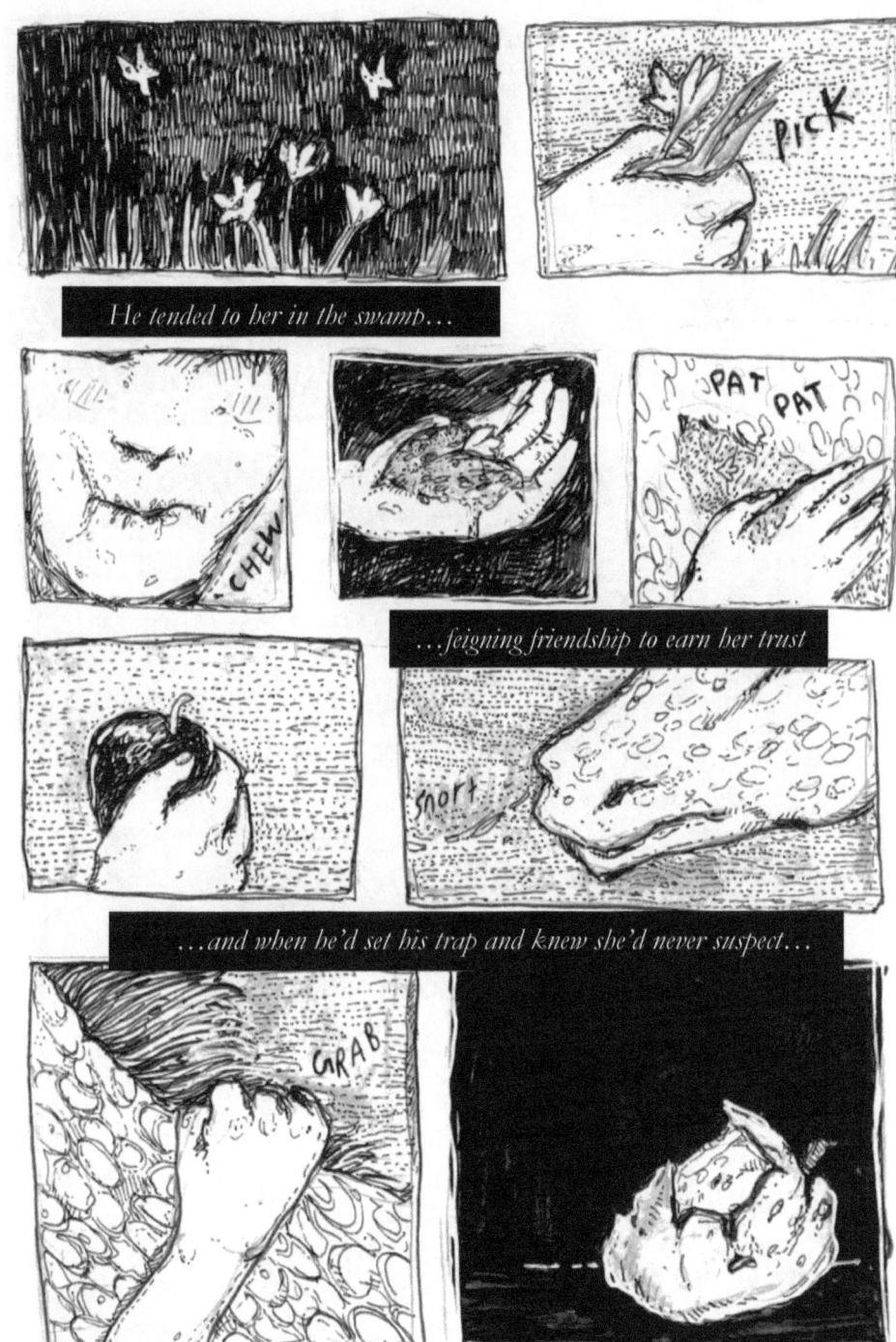

He tended to her in the swamp…

…feigning friendship to earn her trust

…and when he'd set his trap and knew she'd never suspect…

 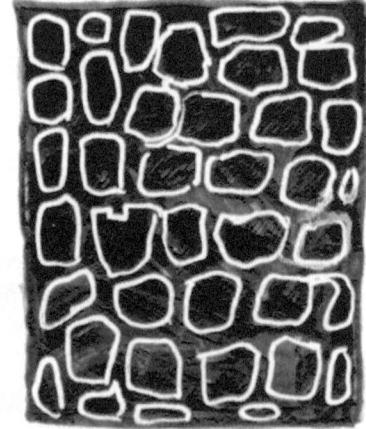

He made her a slave to his every command,

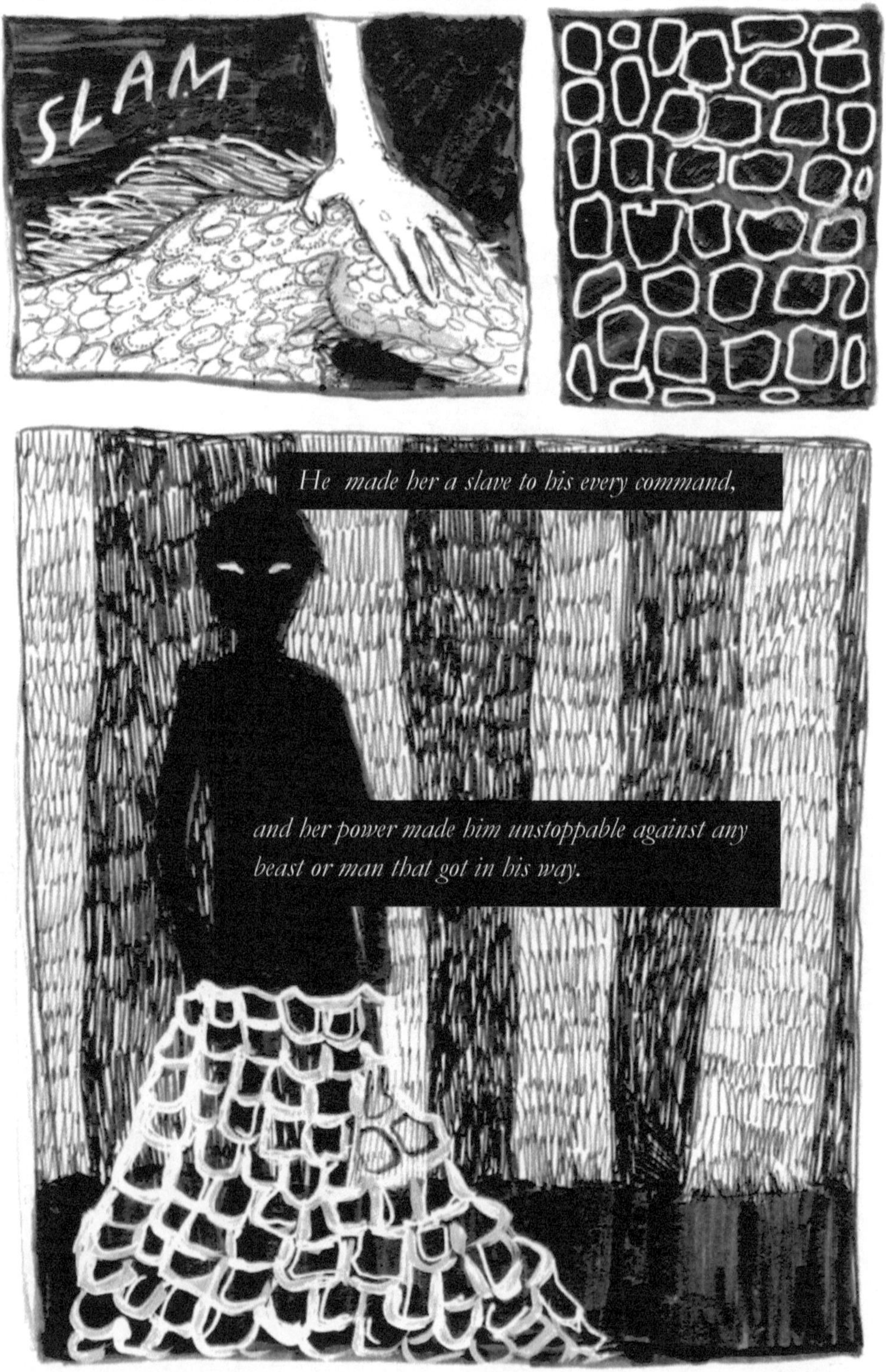

and her power made him unstoppable against any beast or man that got in his way.

THE QILIN IS NOW KEPT LOCKED
AWAY IN A SECRET GROTTO BELOW
THE CAMP.

TIERAN RETURNS TO IT WHEN
HE SEES FIT, TORTURING HER TO
COLLECT AND BOTTLE MORE
BLOOD AND TEARS

Over time he has built a tolerance against the effects of the blood, and has mastered the technique of drinking just enough of it to kiss a girl and leave her mouth in agony. As it coats her throat, her vocal chords are paralysed, and for good measure, Tieran drinks a serving of the qilin's tears to protect himself.

This is his _POWER,_ Raine.

This is how he hunts us.

But without the qilin, he is as _POWERLESS_ as a man can be

chapter five

Powerless, powerless, powerless, the word raced and raced through my head all night and day. Powerless the first morning, waking up in the tent and realizing it hadn't all been a dream. Powerless, as Tieran greeted me with a pair of handcuffs and had me follow obediently behind him all day like a dog on a leash while he managed the camp. Powerless, as I was coated in makeup and dazzling fabric and made to dance. And above all moments, above all humiliations, I was powerless to Tieran the minute he gained that vicious gleam in his eyes and I was taken back to his horrible tent for another night. And another night. And another.

It was the fourth night now, and I sat by the mouth of his tent; watching as the last of the Shuishan's torches went out in a flash. The nightly storm had finally finished just minutes ago, leaving the woods in a dewy, electrified state of silence. The harsh wind had subsided, leaving the hum of crickets to fill the silence. And I'd looked and looked, but there were no fireflies in Mythland. The trees stayed black and cold.

A horrible feeling welled up and stuck in my throat, and I hugged my knees to my chest, trying to hold myself together. Every time Tieran did so little as breathe a little bit louder my entire body seized up in panic. And even once the anxiety subsided, the throbbing was still there, anywhere and everywhere he'd touched me; a bruise or cut that hurt all on its own. I don't know how to explain it and after this I really can't say any more about what he did and kept doing because it makes me want to squeeze myself so tightly that I disappear. I had been touched by something bad, something awful, and no matter how potent the perfumes the other girls gave me to bathe in, no matter how red and raw my skin got from my scrubbing and scrubbing to erase him, I never felt clean. It had been three nights now, and no matter whether I danced badly or beautifully, Tieran stained me with more ugliness. And when he was done, he'd get to dream while all of me seared with the memory of his body invading mine over and over. *Powerless, powerless, powerless.* I was shaking again. Damn that word.

And damn whining, too, I thought. *That's not going to save you. That won't get your voice back.* Pulling a blanket around my shoulders, I concentrated my energy into scheming a way out of here. I technically had three more days left before Tieran said I could leave, but at this point my trust in him had completely dissolved. And it wasn't as if he trusted me either, so I couldn't depend on that original promise. He'd even send Lilah with me when I had to go to the bathroom (which was becoming more and more frequent due to the weird diet), and have me follow him around in that stupid pair of handcuffs otherwise.

Yesterday I was able to slip free from his gaze for a good amount of time. He and a handful of men had left camp to hunt, and he'd put Rong in charge of camp duties. One of his duties, supervising me. So far, ex-JP Zhaorong was the only man at camp I didn't have any major issues with. Even though I still had to follow obediently, carrying various things for him and obeying orders, he'd relinquished the handcuffs. Said they weren't his style. And halfway through the day when lunch came around, he set me free to roam within the camp for a little over an hour. There were Shuishan milling around everywhere and my hair made me stick out like a blue thumb, so making a break for it wasn't an option. Not to mention I would've felt guilty to cross Rong after he'd treated me like an actual human.

For an hour I wandered about the camp, hiding my hair in a bandana to keep attention away, and poking around for where they'd hidden my bow and knapsack. I also was desperate to check on Chantastic's egg and see if it was safe and sound. A part of me was terrified that if my bag had been searched, the Shuishan would add the precious little thing to the carton of eggs used to chuck at the girls who messed up during the dance.

I found the weapons tent within a matter of minutes, and I scoured through it all, but found only the Shuishan's own tools and arrows. At this point, I didn't even care if it was my own Majesty Council-issued bow or what was left of my crummy handmade arrows. When I saw the steel and silver glinting and gleaming, so ready for the taking, I was tempted to just forget Rong, grab something, shoot a few of them in the feet and run; retrieving Siri from that horrible cage on the way out of here.

But of course I couldn't. My voice. I needed it. So I either needed to get my hands on the bottled tears he had somewhere or try and find a qilin and make it cry. If it even existed. The existence of magical creatures was not something I'd even fathomed, even for a disorienting place like Mythland. I guess maybe it wasn't *too* otherworldly to have poison blood, but tears with healing properties? Maybe T2 had gone crazy and made it all up. I wouldn't blame her. Even I felt like I'd gone a bit delusional. But if I didn't believe her story, if I didn't even try to find this creature, I was powerless. Powerless, powerless, powerless. And Tieran was nearly all-powerful.

Nearly.

An idea hit me so hard I gasped. *Who has power over Tieran? Lilah. He adores her, but why? What connects them?* He'd called her his witch, and I'd seen how naturally she danced from pot to pot, brewing whatever she was brewing. She could be his real qilin, couldn't she? Make poisons and cures? So even if there wasn't a fantastical creature hidden somewhere, Lilah, the potion-making-witch-bitch, was my best bet for getting a cure to free my mouth of Tieran's bindings, and she was out in the open. Suddenly my heart was racing, I was beginning to feel hopeful. And then...it passed.

Even if I could identify what's a cure and what might just be wine or another poison, I couldn't just leave the other girls to suffer while I took my voice and ran. Not to mention they had made it pretty clear to me that they feared the beasts outside of camp just as much as the beasts inside, and some had no intention at all to leave. Despite all of the twisted crap going on, we were sheltered from tiangou and storms, we received two meals a day, and had more than just trees and mushrooms to keep us company. At its heart, the Shuishan camp wasn't the problem. Its leader was.

Tieran had tried to bargain with me, so in turn I'd have to make a bargain with him. A bargain to free the girls from their servitude to him and let them continue to live within the shelter of the camp. *The only way I could secure this deal and have him agree would be if I had a knife at his throat while I demanded it,* I thought. *And if he still wouldn't listen...going through with killing him would solve the problem, too. And keep them safe.*

My stomach suddenly heaved, chills running through my arms and down my neck. I glanced tentatively back at Tieran, who was so peacefully sleeping. I'd never killed a human before, or at least not intentionally. When Destan and I had stolen the tablet from Peak, we'd injured many and I even took off a JP's hand, but I hadn't aimed for fatal shots, and if any died from injury, I never found out. I'd shot a few small animals, but never succeeded in hitting them in just the right place for them to have a quick death. As soon as I suffered through my first Mythland night with an empty stomach, I tried my best at hunting a rabbit and ended up only hitting its little leg. I held its wheezing, shivering body for about ten minutes until it bled out and died in my arms and I didn't have the nerve to even cut it open and eat it. It was a rabbit and I was hungry and it was meat, but I just couldn't. I'd shoved some berries down my throat instead and buried the rabbit in a little pile of leaves and wildflowers. Destan would've laughed at me and told me I'd been so stupid and then he'd show me how to do it right. But Destan wasn't here to get rid of Tieran for me. And I couldn't help but feel I had returned to being the fragile Raine Ylevol I was before Destan had pushed me to be stronger. If I didn't even have the guts to kill a horrible guy like Tieran, then there's no way I was ever as brave as Destan had convinced me I was. I was truly powerless.

Could I kill him? Physically, it would be easy. All I'd have to do is wait until he fell asleep, grasp that dagger, drag it across his throat until red slipped out in a crimson curtain and washed down his neck to the floor. But emotionally? Mentally? Tieran was the worst person I'd ever met since Sebastian Lao, but he was still a person, and the thought of killing someone choked me with fear and guilt.

Tieran liked to smoke and tell stories when he was drunk. Tonight after he'd had his way with me, he told me about how he'd come to be in Mythland and with the Shuishan. He didn't mention the qilin, furthering my suspicion. Tieran's mother was of Fluxarian descent, whose family had originally stowed away to Thgindim after it split from the other. There had been so much mixing of blood that at this point she was not even connected to her Fluxarian heritage. But of course, the Majesty Council found out. And without warning, she, her husband, and six-year old Tieran were gassed out of their Canopian apartment and banished by morning. His mother died instantly on impact from hitting a tree during their release into the forest. A tiangou mauled his father that first night and Tieran said he wandered on his own, falling in love with the forest and learning its secrets until he found the Shuishan seven years later. He was welcomed into their arms and taught them all sorts of things he'd discovered about Mythland through his journeys. He was elected leader at fifteen. The dates matched T2's story, but I only wished I could have asked questions. Seen if I could probe any information about what really made them decide he was worth keeping. But without another mention of his past, Tieran took a last draw on the joint he'd been smoking and ground it out in the tray near his bed. Then he touched my lips lightly with his own. "I like you better without a voice," he'd chuckled, pushing back some of my hair and kissing my neck. I'd shoved him away slightly, begging with my eyes.

Please, Tieran, I'd silently asked him, *let me go. Please just let me go.*

Tieran's eyes were all out of focus, but eventually they found my face and he whispered, "Just finish the week. I'll make you want to stay longer. I'll make you stay..." Then he fell asleep and I had crawled over here to think.

Tieran was a man. A bad man, but still a man. Twenty-one-year-old Tieran Huang: part Fluxarian, part Thgindimish; who had slept with all of his servants even though they didn't want him to; who beat them, and stole their voices, and played mind games, and should be *so easy* to kill. But my head was racing and all I kept thinking was that once he was a baby who giggled and had to learn to walk and talk; that once he was an okay part of the ecosystem and an okay part of society and just went rotten.

I could poison him, maybe. Bad berries weren't hard to find. I'd have to watch as he'd take a drink and have his face smash into his unfinished plate of food, eyes wide and mouth frothing from the poison. I would end him. I'd be the one to make sure he never kissed or hurt another girl, but also never got to apologise or even realize how bad he had become. Could I kill him? Snatch away a life that was made out of love and just turned out to be bad?

And if I kept thinking like this, of course I couldn't kill him. If I tried to reason with this utterly unreasonable and untameable beast of a person, I'd end up worse off than I was now.

So stop thinking, Raine. I told myself, tearing my eyes away from Tieran's oblivious, sleeping face. I decided quickly I would take advantage of this time to go to Lilah. I began down the ladder into the freezing night air, and jumped quietly to the ground, wincing as my bare feet touched the rough, cold gravel. Some men had been so drunk after tonight's show that they'd crashed and slept on the tables, mugs of moonshine still in hand. I crept in between the tables, forcing myself not to look at the desolate stage behind me, and then I squinted in the terrible darkness for the tent I needed.

Lilah slept in her brewery. All fires were put out and ointments and potions corked, but there she was: pretty and innocent looking as a little girl should, curled up cosily on a silk cushion under a wolf pelt blanket. She couldn't be any older than thirteen, but even that felt like a stretch because she was so tiny. Her eyes told a different story. I remembered the ashen shadows circling her eyes, as if she'd been running in the world for decades without rest. I felt a tug of pity for her, which quickly faded. She was still dangerous.

Holding my breath, I tiptoed around her and took the knife resting on the chopping-board. It shook in my hand. I knelt slowly, putting the knife to her throat. She stirred ever so slightly. And without hesitation I slapped her cheek, not too hard, to wake her. Her grey eyes popped open in surprise, flickering down to the knife and then back to me, and her lips spread apart for a scream. I immediately slammed my hand over her mouth.

I narrowed my eyes. *Quiet.*

Lilah wrenched off my hand, hissing, "What do you *want* bitch?"

I leaned my head to the side and pointed to my lips. Could she have seriously forgotten I couldn't answer?

"*Well?* What's with the knife?" she demanded, tapping the blade with her pinky and tensing up as I pressed it tighter to her skin. With a more serious expression on my face, and my eyes shooting daggers, I touched my mouth repeatedly, knowing that she must know why I'm here and if she didn't, then she was of no use to me.

"I can't give you your voice back," she said coolly, closing her eyes and letting out a delicate yawn. Furious, I forced the blade down harder and heard her squeal in shock. If I went any harder, I might actually spill some blood and I wasn't planning on killing Lilah. She was still a child. "I mean it, I can't!" she pleaded, her lips trembling and eyes quivering behind a window of tears. I gritted my teeth and tried to stay furious, but she suddenly reminded me so much of Gwen in the midst of a tantrum that I couldn't stand to look at her any longer.

I threw down the knife in anguish and lifted her off of the ground by the collar of her nightgown. I jabbed a finger at her forehead, *Think harder, Lilah. I know you know. I know you made Tieran this potion.* I motioned me drinking from that white bottle and then I grabbed my throat, pointed to my mouth and pointed at Lilah.

Eyes nothing but slits, she shook her head. "You really don't know anything. I didn't make what's in that potion of his, honest. I wish I could take credit."

My stomach flipped. I lowered her to the ground. *What?*

"You heard me. I didn't make it. Do I bottle it? Yeah. Know what's in it? No," Lilah said. "And, no offense, it isn't my place to tell you, whore," she sneered. I shoved her hard against the counter, knocking down some bowls of ingredients she'd left sitting out. They spilled across the ground and Lilah cried out, snot dribbling from her nose. "Okay, okay, I get it, but if you really want to know, then you're going to have to put me down." She struggled earnestly in my hold, and reluctantly I set her down and took a tiny step back, my eyes still glued on her.

Lilah scoffed, rubbing her neck, "Gods, you are even more annoying when you can't speak. I truly have no idea what Tieran sees in you."

I crossed my arms. *The feeling is mutual.* Then I raised an eyebrow, motioning around the tent. *Well? Where is the cure?* I tested a locked cabinet and saw her flinch, obviously pissed I was touching her stuff.

"Okay, stop I'll show you," she grumbled, massaging her temples in distress. She shoved me aside, opening a secret compartment of a larger cabinet. I went on my tiptoes and saw that inside were what looked like a life supply of Tieran's evil white potion. But no cure.

"They're behind the poison, idiot," Lilah said, behind me. I glared, peering again into the depths of the cabinet, leaning forward and feeling behind the bottles. My fingers reached a new texture of glass and my heart quickened with excitement. Craning my neck to see, I saw three spherical vials labelled: *Only to be handled by Tieran Huang.* But my excitement died when I realized the vials were empty. And I shook one gently, thinking maybe the liquid was actually clear, not golden like T2 had said. But there was nothing inside. Not even a cork plugging it up.

"Something wrong?" Lilah asked. Icy dread melted through me, from the top of my neck and down to my toes. I slowly turned around, staring at her. Her eyes had taken on the same deadly glint as Tieran's, a corner of her mouth curling into a half-smile. The tent went dead quiet. Even the bugs outside seemed to be holding their breath in anticipation.

"I'll show you to the cure, blue-hair," she whispered, "but it's going to take a lot more than waking me up in the middle of the night with a knife. Do you trust me?"

I stepped down from the counter, shaking my head. *No, I don't.*

Her face brightened. "Good." She took one step closer to me, and without hesitation Lilah threw her forehead at mine and kicked in my stomach, hard. Colours flashed across my vision at the impact and I staggered away, crashing into the counter as I choked on a scream. "Have fun getting your voice back," she sneered, clearing her throat before yelling, "Help! Tieran! Zhaorong, Dr. Wan, anyone! The new servant girl's attacking me!" She picked up the chopping knife and without hesitation made two incisions on her cheek; wincing only a little as blood came trickling down her jaw.

I struggled to my feet, looking wildly for a way out, only to be slugged hard with a bottle of moonshine, Lilah's face glowing in victory as I crumpled to the ground in pain. Within seconds Rong and the blind man rushed inside her tent, their voices loud and unintelligible. Lilah was crying and touching her bleeding face, looking just like any normal, sad little girl for a moment.

Rong touched her arm caringly, his voice muddy in my ringing ears, "Lilah dear, did she hurt you?"

She pulled her shaky hand away from her face and whimpered, "I-I don't know w-why she wanted to hurt me, I b-barely even know her..."

The flap of the tent fluttered limply as another man entered, and I heard Lilah run into his arms, crying. He heaved a disappointed sigh. And then I felt his hand tip my chin up to look at him. I opened my eyes. Tieran's face was strangely calm.

"Well, well, T17. Now why would you hurt my Lilah?" he whispered.

I stared back coldly into his dark blue eyes.

"You don't know? You don't have a reason?" he probed.

I glanced away, and he roughly yanked my chin back to stare at him.

"Aren't you going to explain yourself? Why don't you say something, sweetheart?" Tieran mocked, "Something wrong with your voice?"

The men in the tent snickered, and I caught Rong roll his eyes. I grit teeth and looked away, focusing all of my strength on not crying in front of them.

Tieran stood up and sighed, "This girl's been nothing but naughty since she's arrived. Rong, Dr. Wan– take her to the grotto. Maybe she just needs some time alone to think about what she wants...oh, correct me," Tieran smiled, "what she needs."

The grotto. Isn't that where...

The men nodded, bowing to him and hoisting me to my feet. As they dragged me from the tent, Lilah brushed past and her lips appeared by my ear, whispering silkily, "I keep my promises. Even to bitches like you."

chapter six

The leather whip snapped against my back, stinging to the bone. I couldn't yell out or howl or scream and it was unbearable to not even be able to release my pain. Zhaorong whipped me about seven more times and then he stopped, breathing heavily, "That's twenty-five lashes. Jeez, new girl, Lilah is one thing, but what did you do to Tieran?" He went on one knee and peered at me writhing on the floor, shirtless and bleeding. His eyes were very sad, even guilty. Cursing quietly, he tossed me a thin, oversized sweater ridden with holes, and I tucked it around my front. The involuntary sounds I made were disgusting. Like a gagging frog.

"I...I'll just leave you to yourself, then. Try not to lie on your back. Keeps it from getting infected and, um...it'll hurt less that way," he mumbled, pausing to give me a thoughtful look through the visor of his beaten-up JP suit.

My eyes begged and begged, bloodshot and streaming. *Please Rong. Please let me go. Let me go.*

Rong shook his head, clearing his throat and turning his back on me. He left the grotto, and shut and locked the door behind him. I couldn't move even an inch without feeling what felt like a thousand lashes at once surging across my flesh, but I had to slip on the sweater to keep from freezing to death. My toes were white and numb with cold, and I flexed my fingers over and over to keep them from stiffening.

The 'grotto' as Tieran had called it, was nothing but a murky hole in the ground filled in with some stones for a floor and with two handcuff-chains stuck into the clay wall. The handcuffs would be put on me at night, but during the day Tieran had confidence that I could not escape while the sun was up. Even so, I couldn't tell what time of day it was because it was so dark down here.

I hugged the sweater around me and flinched as my raw skin brushed the rough fibres of the knitting. My bloody back and the sweater were sticking together. Fire was crueller than ice, so I lifted the sticky knit threads of the sweater away from my skin and let the cold nibble at the bleeding edges rather than feel the whip one more time. Lilah. That absolute demon of a human being. I couldn't believe how stupid I'd been! Why hadn't I just gone through her cabinets while she was sleeping? Or caused a ruse to get her out of there and gain some time? I would've been able to figure out where the cure actually was.

I rested my forehead on my knees. No, I couldn't have. I wouldn't have even been able to find that secret cabinet she had the poison in. I was so angry at myself for screwing up, I found myself wishing Rong would come back and whip me until there was nothing left because being alone with myself and my guilt was unbearable. I was literally now in an even deeper hole than where I'd been just an hour prior.

Lilah's words vibrated in my ears like bees. *"I keep my promises."* I perked up. What did that mean? Was my getting locked up supposed to show me to the cure? As more blood seeped from the wounds, my head was becoming lighter and lighter, like it was filling up with air. I struggled to stay awake, to think through how I could possibly fix this, but the air filling my head now seemed to be weighing me down, down. Pulling me without mercy into an all-encompassing sleep.

Everything was dark, but I could still feel my burning back. Everything was real and cold and harsh. Was I even asleep? Suddenly, something cool touched my skin and I jumped, but then the cold hand pressed down harder, making me lay down flatter on the hard ground. The ground seemed to grow softer at the touch and the darkness get more bearable and less suffocating. The hand smoothed calm circles on my back, and I could almost feel the welts and whip marks fading away into nothing.

"Relax, just close your eyes," she whispered, and so I did.

"I am so lost, Chantastic," I breathed, "I don't know if I can do this anymore."

"Do what anymore?" Her voice in the dark was a halo of bells stirring the silence around me.

"Live. Keep going like this. Without anyone to help me."

She gently laid her cheek on my back, sighing. I felt her fingers dancing delicate waltzes down my spine, her words coming in between, "Oh, Raine...you're stronger than anyone I know. You don't need any help."

Even though I knew it would hurt, even though I didn't want her calming touch to stop, I made myself roll over and sit up. Her eyes were shining beacons ahead of me. I knelt before her, cupping her face in my hands. "But Chan, I do need help. I can't do this alone," I said, "I know I'm supposed to keep going, and I've tried staying strong, but I can't stand the thought of going on any longer."

She smiled. "Well, of course you can 'go on,' silly. Grab your bow and boots and go. What's stopping you?"

On instinct I wrapped my arms around her and held her close to me, smelling her lily-scented hair.

"Well, I'm sort of in a giant hole. And I can't speak, my lips are numb—" I cut off, and for a moment she looked at me really funny because of course I was speaking this instant, and I waved my hands to clarify, "Oh! No, you see, I mean in real life I can't speak—"

"This isn't real?" She cocked a thick eyebrow and glanced warily around the muddy cell.

"No, no it's just..." my voice faded and I said, "I can't just leave, there's stuff I need to do—"

"Then do it."

A hand rested on my shoulder and I didn't even have to turn around to know who it was. The gruff voice and ratty gloves were enough. Chantastic looked down at

her hands and her image started melting away as Destan walked into view.
"Bluehead, you climbed a mile-high building."

"Not the whole way up..."

"Hey, don't cut me off," he joked, nudging my shoulder. "Being in Mythland
has made you impolite or something? Damn. Well look, you are still good enough to
climb out of a stinking hole. Chan patched up your back, and I have your weapons
right here." Destan sat my bow down by the handcuffs. It already had an arrow
nocked on the cord. "And you know how to get your voice back. Think about where
you are."

"The...grotto?"

"The grotto."

I waited a moment and rolled my bow around in my hands, the wood smooth to
the touch and so achingly familiar. I tore my eyes from it and looked around me in
the darkness. On the same wall as the handcuffs, there seemed to be a small, glowing
square of light. I crawled toward it, peering into the radiance and hesitantly touching
it with my fingers. It felt warm and smooth, like glass heated in the sun. Destan's
breath grazed my neck.

"You know what to do. You have everything you need to save yourself, Raine,"
he whispered, touching my cheek and turning me to face him. His forehead gently
rested on mine as he continued, instructing. "Lilah is the next step. After you
knock her out, it's time to bring down the king." He drew back and looked me in
the eyes, very serious. "Don't you dare die. And don't stay down here. It smells.
And I know how much you hate the dark."

I propelled up from the ground and ran into the wall, catching myself
and breathing heavily, the air whistling through my motionless lips.

Destan? Chantastic? I thought fervently, my eyes traveling over every
inch of the grotto and finding not a trace of them. But of course it had
all been a dream, a terrible, wonderful dream, and I felt as if I had been
asleep for a thousand years and completely revived. My back still seared
and I longed to feel Chantastic's soft and snowy-cold hands healing
me. And then, abruptly and without reason, I was overcome with a
burning determination to get moving. I wobbled to my feet and
glanced around the grotto. Destan had laid my bow by the handcuffs in
my dream, and for a moment I panicked seeing that suddenly they were
gone. But then reality struck that they'd never been here at all and I
sank, defeated, to the ground again.

I stared at the handcuffs, waiting for a weapon to appear. After a good minute of waiting for a miracle, I tore my eyes away and glanced over the cell. A chamber pot for my overactive bladder and an empty wooden bowl from which one of the Shuishan had force-fed me earlier. A rusty spoon glinted ever so feebly in the crack of light coming from the cellar door. I lunged for the spoon and followed the chain on the cuffs to where they connected to the wall. Gripping it hard, I shoved the metal spoon's scooped end into the clay and began digging around the bar that held the handcuffs into the wall. Whatever thought brought me to doing this I have no idea. It was all impulse and nothing else mattered but getting out of here and somehow this was the way.

The clay was crumbling, but it was hard and thick and it took a lot of scraping to even chip away a little. But as I scraped away the tougher bits, I found that the wall's clay became softer as I got deeper. Three inches in, I set down the spoon and began to use my fingers, poking through the clay and hearing the clatter of stones falling onto the other side. *Another room?* I wondered, unearthing half of the first pike and fitting my entire hand through the hole I'd made. My fingers reached something warm and smooth. Like glass heated in the sun.

I froze, chills running down my arms. It was just like in the dream. Slowly, I peered into the hole, seeing the outline of what looked like layers of glass in the dark. I reached back in and touched it again, stroking it. Suddenly, the thing moved. It must've raised itself off of the ground because the hard smoothness turned into matted, stringy fur; sprouting from a warm, but very gaunt belly of some kind of animal.

This is unreal. I knew what I was touching, but I just couldn't believe it. I withdrew my hand in fear and tried to gather my courage, worried that if I became too hopeful this was the magical creature T2 said Tieran kept hidden away, I would be ultimately disappointed. In the meantime, I tested the chain of the handcuffs, seeing the other pike strain in its connection to the wall. I worked another round of minutes scooping and scraping with the spoon and shoving big pieces away with my battered, bleeding hands, and soon the gap in the wall was big enough I could quite clearly see the beast in the other cell of the grotto.

The qilin had backed away from me, sitting with her legs crossed in front of her by the opposite wall. She had what looked like a heavy iron brace around her neck, keeping her secured to a ball and chain on the floor. She did indeed have the deer-like body T2 had illustrated, not to mention the scales, the horn, and flowing mane. But unlike in the story, this creature was nearly a corpse. Scales were missing in more than a few places, leaving gaping wounds in some areas and bare patches of skin in others. Her neck was a graveyard of scar upon scar, her eyes hidden under a frightening black mask made of what looked like dried tar. She was missing one of her cloven feet, as well as half of her tail. Her bones looked too big to fit inside her small body, protruding out and pulling the skin taut. I couldn't help but imagine him coming here and beating her, cutting her open until he'd bottled more blood and tears. And I thought Tieran had been cruel to his dolls.

Okay, Raine. Stay calm. Don't scare it, I thought, edging closer and sticking my entire arm inside of the hole. I couldn't call to it, and I had no food to offer so that she might come to me, and yet I reached, my palm outstretched in beckoning. Her tail lashed the ground twice, scattering dust as she considered me. Then, with a stroke of luck, she struggled to her feet, wobbling on her rickety bones as she made it over to me.

I felt like my heart was beating so fast it had up and run away, burst out of my chest, as I felt the soft nose of the qilin nudge my fingertips, sniffing cautiously. I wondered if she could smell the blood left on my hands from all of that digging in the wall. She raised her head, and despite her eyes being covered, I could feel their intense gaze examining me. *Please, qilin,* I prayed, my arm beginning to ache the longer I held it through the wall to her. *I promise I will not hurt you for your tears and especially not for your blood. Please help me, spare just one more weeping for me and I swear I won't leave this grotto without you. You deserve to be free again. We both do.*

I waited, patient, but struggling to keep faith. There were flies buzzing around me, landing on my back and neck. I fought the urge to swat them away, focusing on the face of the creature just on the other side of a crumbling clay wall. She moved gradually closer and I stroked her muzzle, running my fingers gingerly over the twirling branch of her horn, and then scratching under her chin. She leaned her face into my hand trustingly, releasing a soft grunt and her tongue flicking out to lick my palm just once. I could no longer feel the strain of my arm, I was so

72

overcome with emotion at the love still inside this victim after years of trauma and Tieran's abuse. I moved my fingers away from her cheek and reached toward her eyes, gently prying off the mask. It didn't come off easily, but it came off nonetheless. And then I withdrew my hand to see if her eyes were really as magnificent as T2 had illustrated.

They went beyond beauty. There was a chilling sense of royalty in them, of queenliness and wisdom. They appeared at first just as the eyes of any other deer, but when she turned her head ever so slightly, constellations spanned the heavens inside of them; flecks of gold and silver coming out of hiding. I stuck my hand back in, palm up, and let it rest below her chin where tears might fall. And like golden rain, they fell and fell in shining splashes into my hand. She had bowed her head, her long lashes fanning her eyes as they looked at my hand, and cried, no sound escaping her lips. I didn't know how much I'd need. I tried to envision Tieran taking a long draw from his stash of the cure, guessing how much that might be. And when I was worried the precious elixir might spill over, I withdrew my arm again, slowly bringing my palm up to my mouth.

No more powerless. No more waiting. No more silence. It was a command. I bent down and touched my lips to the golden surface, letting them soak. I couldn't feel it yet; my lips were still numb. I waited and waited and then I realized I was opening my mouth wider. I was opening my mouth! I dribbled the tears into my mouth, over my tongue, down my throat, and tried not to splutter at the salty, warm taste. Taste, I could taste for the first time in so long, and they tasted like human tears, nothing magically delicious. Once my tongue cooperated I licked my palm clean, checking the floor of the grotto to make sure none had spilled.

A rough laugh spilled from my throat, and I sounded like I'd aged eighty years in the time since I'd last made a sound. I lowered my head to peer into the hole at the qilin, and I grinned, my face muscles working hard to keep my lips from slipping into that horrible frown again.

"You did it!" I rasped, reaching through the hole and stroking the qilin's neck, avoiding the fresher wounds as she purred appreciatively from the other side. "You're the cure..." I whispered, my voice cracking and a sob threatening to take over, "you saved me. Now I'll save the other girls, and I'll save you, too–"

The metal door of the grotto jiggled as someone struggled to open it. Shocked into action, I stowed the spoon under the waistband of my underwear for safekeeping, and quickly shoved some rocks back into the hole. I scooted as far away from that wall as I could. As the person entered, I laid on my side, shutting my eyes tightly and hoping I could keep my lips from doing something they shouldn't be able to.

My heart beat loudly and my entire body tensed as footsteps came towards me. I tried to steady my breathing and seem asleep, but found it extremely difficult and just decided to hold my breath. The footsteps stopped and I heard a fairly recognizable yawn. After a moment, he patted my shoulder and I pretended to stir ever so slightly, blinking and releasing a sleepy breath.

"Hi there. Did I interrupt a dream?" Tieran asked.

I pulled my knees to my chest and glared, trying to appear less terrified and more hostile. *Go away and let me get back to digging myself out of this craphole.*

Tieran touched my cheek with the back of his hand and I cringed away, scooting into the corner of the cell. I nearly scowled and had to focus on keeping my mouth dead still. His eyes narrowed. "No need to be rude. I'm just checking up on you. You can come back out whenever you want, if you promise to behave."

I feigned struggle, and spat a nice wad of phlegm onto his rawhide boots. *No.*

Tieran raised his hand to strike, but then, in a moment of resistance, grit his teeth and shoved his hands in his pockets. His long, dark cherry hair looked damp and sweaty in its loose ponytail, the long bangs clinging to his forehead. When he began pacing, the light from the candle in his hand made his deep blue eyes sparkle like sapphires. If I didn't know how twisted he was, from afar I might have found him attractive. He was exotic; half Fluxarian, half Thgindimish. But as he settled beside me, my bravery collapsed. My arms were prickled with goosebumps, my breathing rapid and shallow. My skin would always remember him.

We sat in silence for a few extremely awkward and tense minutes, and then out of nowhere he whispered, "I know you're not from Fluxaria."

I caught my breath, turning to look at him. A half smile was rising on his lips, and meeting my eyes, he winked. "Well, at least not all the way. I've met enough Fluxarians to know eyes like that don't come from that half of the great mountain. You're a mutt. Like me. I thought I was the only one."

I'm nothing like you.

"That's what makes you so captivating, so beautiful, Irene. You are the most beautiful girl I've ever seen."

I closed my eyes and felt my back throb suddenly, as if his words had knocked into my wounds. Tieran's hand found mine and I pulled it away, giving him a stern look. For once, he didn't try again. Just kept speaking, softly.

"When you dance, Irene...I stop breathing. I stop everything except for watching you, wanting you," his voice was rough and low, like a rumble of thunder. I could feel his eyes on me again. "I don't know how you do it. It's like you have some kind of spell over me, but you won't even let me touch you, have you...when you're just what I've always wanted," he said, brushing aside a few oily pieces of my hair and touching his mouth to my exposed neck. I could feel his teeth on my skin as he smiled. "You *torture* and *torture* me, teasing and fighting me. You don't have to fight me, Irene. Just stay with me, with the Shuishan. I'll let you speak. I'll let you have a tent of your own for whatever it is you like to do. We belong to each other, there's no doubt. We're meant for each other..."

He moved to kiss me and I turned my cheek, tears burning in my eyes. With one hand forcing my face towards his, he had me pinned against the wall, my back screaming in anguish. His other hand pried my legs apart, wrapping them around his hips as he began to grind his heavy body into mine and kiss me without stopping to let me breathe. I wrenched out my face and pushed him away, my fingers over his mouth. His lips were hard and dry, cracked beneath my fingertips. I knew it had to be from all of the poison he applied to them over the years. Sighing, he grabbed my wrist and wrenched it down, his mouth coming furiously at mine and for the first time since he silenced me, I could feel him. Not completely, but there was a faint tugging sensation that hadn't been there before, and soon I could even taste the sour fumes of his breath and tongue in my mouth. I focused on keeping my mouth perfectly still as he bombarded me with kiss after kiss, and let my thoughts drift away to a better place.

It was over more quickly than I'd thought. I guessed maybe he was tired from the feast earlier, or maybe he'd already been with another girl before coming to see me, but for once all he did was kiss me and touch me. I couldn't have been more relieved. The spoon I'd stowed behind my waistband was nearly ready to come clattering out by the time he had had enough and climbed off of me. Once he'd finished, he put me down and gathered himself, shivering as he put his clothes back on. "Chilly down here," he chuckled, shrugging into his coat and looking at me. I tried not to let my eyes wander to the rather noticeable hole in the wall behind him. "I'll be back in about an hour to check on if you've changed your mind...and if not, I'll send Lilah to...persuade you." He winked and without noticing a thing, left the grotto.

Thank the spirits! I thought giddily, relaxing my face and crawling over to the wall. I pulled out the rocks filling in the hole and reached my hand through, beckoning for the qilin. I whistled softly, waiting until I felt the soft muzzle under my fingertips. I grinned, whispering into the gap, "There you are...thank you, qilin. I owe you my life. I'm gonna get us out of here, okay?"

chapter seven

In the time between Tieran's departure and Lilah's arrival, I was able to free the handcuff and chain from the wall. At this point, my hands were bleeding and stinging worse than my back. So after I'd gotten the cuff and tested its weight, I hid it behind me and took a break. I was only able to doze off for a few minutes before a rude awakening; compliments of Lilah.

At the slam of the cellar door, I jumped awake, gasping on instinct and instantly covering my mouth. Lilah appeared looking the cheeriest I'd seen her, and she grinned at the sight of me curled up and dirty on the floor. "This has made my day. Soon you won't be very pretty at all, will you, 'blue-hair?'"

I ground my teeth. *Ugh. If you're going to call me by the colour of my hair, at least get the nickname right and say 'Bluehead,' you jerk.* I paused in my thought process. *Never mind. That name is reserved for Destan. So just shut up about me altogether.* Outwardly, I just shrugged and tightened my grip on the rusty chain hidden behind my back.

Lilah began pacing about on her tiptoes, looking sinisterly happy. She moved by the hole I'd haphazardly filled in with loose stones, and being so short she noticed something was amiss immediately. She gave me a sly smile. "I see you found what you were looking for," she said, kicking the rocks out with her foot. I heard the qilin scamper away on the other side. "Need help making it cry? Tieran's taught me some tricks."

"That won't be necessary," I said, watching Lilah's blonde brows shoot up her forehead in surprise. I smirked, leaning on the wall for support and standing up. Lilah's shock faded to amusement, and she clapped her hands slowly, emphasizing each clap.

"Well, well, the bitch is smarter than I thought," she laughed, long hair swaying as she danced over to me. "What'd you do? Cut her? Ram her head in with one of those rocks?"

"No, psychopath," I said, horrified, but not surprised she'd assume the worst. "I didn't need to. Why did you help me anyway? I thought the knife to your throat was ineffective."

"I'm glad you're acknowledging the whole whipping and shoving you into a dirty hole of salvation thing as me helping you, because that is what it was. At least that's the best kind of help you could expect from me. I really wanted to see you taken down a peg or two."

"Lilah, really," I said, walking closer to her, "why did you lead me to the qilin? I know you don't like me and want me gone, but isn't this sort of betraying Tieran?"

She crossed her arms over her chest. "We pick our battles, blue-hair. I would never *truly* betray Tieran. But I do know it's about time his little silencing game is stopped."

"So, you think what he's doing to girls is wrong?"

Lilah shook her head. "No, it's not like that. I'm just sick of my brother wasting his time with these girls instead of taking care of what actually matters at camp. And when a hell-raiser like you showed up, I decided you could be useful to me in getting things back to normal."

"What do you mean?" I whispered, narrowing my eyes. Lilah had begun scooping out the rest of the rocks, withdrawing a small spade from her apron pocket and digging away to widen the hole. Soon she would be able to slip through to the other side.

"You're going to help me kill the beast, of course," she said easily, as if she and I were somehow on the same page. "Help me with this. I'm just a little girl."

I backtracked, kneeling and subtly reaching behind me to touch the handcuff and chain. "We are *not* killing it. Are you insane? I still need to get tears for the other girls."

Lilah chuckled, wiping her brow and showing me one of the empty bottles I'd seen in her secret cabinet. "Oh, don't worry blue-hair. There'll be plenty of tears to bottle when we're done with it."

I clenched my hands into tight fists, storming up to her, the cuff dragging behind me on the ground. "That's not the issue, Lilah. You're not killing the qilin. I won't let you." She had begun to climb through the gaping hole she'd made bigger, and I grabbed her arm, yanking her back. Her head whipped around, her grey eyes dark and vicious.

"Won't 'let' me? Won't *let* me?" she shoved me away from her, and as I went stumbling back, she pointed the spade at my throat. "You have *no* say over what I can and cannot do, slut! I showed you to the qilin, I pretty much spared you from getting your throat slit in my tent last night by telling Tieran to take you to the grotto. You owe me your life. And if you refuse to help, I'll kill it myself and cover your entire face in its blood so that you can never use your stupid face again."

She watched me as if waiting for me to snap. To cave in or end up in tears begging for my life. I only sighed, trying to keep from smiling. "Lilah..." I began, striding up to her, lifting the heavy handcuffs off of the ground so that they wouldn't clang on the floor anymore. I met her eyes, resting one hand on her shoulder. "I'm sorry."

She batted her eyelashes, saying coyly, "I don't believe in forgiveness, blue-hair."

I shrugged, "Doesn't really matter to me." And grabbing the chain with both hands, I swung it up with all my might and knocked Lilah on the side of the head with the heavy iron cuff. There was a terrifying cracking sound and a handful of little yellow teeth scattered on the ground as she crumpled to her knees; her mouth a big, red hole. Her face seemed frozen in shock, and as she looked up at me, I kicked her hard in the stomach like she had done to me just last night. She didn't move again. My heart was beating so fast and my breathing was so ragged and that my head was beginning to feel like a balloon. "And don't call me blue-hair..." I muttered, limping toward the door for my escape and adding, "...bitch."

I felt along the wall for a door handle, and using the key I snatched from Lilah's apron, I unlocked and pushed it open. I was in a pitch black tunnel that smelled of rich earth. *The qilin was on the right side of the wall,* I thought, moving down the tunnel a couple steps and reaching forward for another door. I found it. I shoved in the key. And bursting into the next cell, I came face to face with the creature that had saved my life. The qilin was cowering, shaking against the back wall, her body somehow more emaciated and fragile-looking since I'd last peered through at her. Holding my breath, I ran to her and wrapped my arms around her. I tried not to breathe through my nose, instantly struck with the odour of infected flesh and festering. She collapsed into me, and I worked on jiggling the key in the lock of her own neck cuff. The creature cried out in pain as I saw that the inside of her cuff was spiked and barbed, cutting into her neck. And I handled it more gently, taking it off carefully once I had it unlatched. Once she was free, I slipped on the handcuff I'd knocked Lilah out with to keep it with me, and scooped the qilin in my arms.

Even though she was malnourished, she was still an animal the size of a female deer, and I was huffing and puffing the whole way up the pitch-black stairway as I carried her. There was a small window of light at the end, and I began to run sideways, knocking it open with my shoulder and coming into the chilly afternoon air. The grotto was situated in the bushes behind Tieran's tree, the Shuishan camp's torches distant stars ahead of me. I set down the qilin, my aching arms very, very relieved.

I knelt by her, stroking her face as she looked around her in wonder. She struggled to stand and I walked her behind taller bushes, knowing the worst thing would be for such a precious, yet potentially lethal creature to be spotted by one of the men. I brought my face close to hers, petting her smooth, scaly back; careful to avoid the bleeding chinks in her armour. "You're free now," I breathed. "You're free now, okay? I want you to run so far away you can't hear the drumbeat once it starts, and keep running."

She looked up at me with her starry eyes, imploringly. I felt my lip tremble, my eyes threatening to fill with tears. I wiped my nose with the sleeve of the sweater Rong had given me, and then remembered the other tears I needed. I dug around in the bushes hastily, looking for one of the beer bottles Tieran would carelessly throw out the window when he was ready for another. I found the broken remnants of one, holding up the jagged bottom half and watching in wonder as the qilin's eyes leaked gold. How did she know? My throat grew a painful lump and now my own tears were falling and mingling with hers, my sobs muffled in the crook of my elbow.

Once it was full to the brim, I gave her one last hug and kiss, and then I smacked her flank to ignite urgency. She glanced back, still uncertain, still wondering why I wasn't following her or leading her away. I mouthed, *Go. Go, qilin, go. You're free. Run as fast as you can.* I motioned myself running and pointed at the dark thicket of trees waiting so readily behind her. And bowing her head to me in a final gesture of graciousness, she took off, all wobbliness gone from her limbs as she vanished into a better life.

I felt like a raindrop flying fast through the sharp wind. A storm waited to crack the sky open, I could feel it on the rise, vibrating through my bones, rousing my every nerve and telling me that soon lightning would be dancing among the trees and I would finally be free.

I ran to the outskirts of the camp, behind the tents they had abandoned for the nightly feast. I could see Shuishan milling about with trays of food and drink, hear the chants and music thrumming like melodious thunder. The volume nearly made the ground shake beneath my bare feet. My first stop was the tent where I'd first awoken. I scoured the silky tent for where they could've hidden my old clothes, but resorted to whacking the heavy handcuff at a locked chest and stealing some of their clothing when I remembered how short time was. I stripped off the gross sweater and undergarments, doing away with brassieres altogether and pulling on long underwear and a thick wool sweater. I hit the jackpot when I found some long, fur-lined, leather pants. They were meant for a man and were baggy on my chicken legs, but the sudden warmth and lack of exposure was so incredible I did a little spin. I quickly yanked on a couple layers of socks and marvelled at the miracle of finding my old boots, and then snooped into other drawers and goodies the room had to offer.

I found my bow and quiver buried at the bottom of a weapons cabinet, and replaced my crappy handmade arrows with a sturdier dozen arrows that appeared to be crafted with hollow bone. I slung the full quiver over my shoulder and nocked one on my bowstring just in case I had a run in with a Shuishan. I was on my way out when I finally discovered what had become of my knapsack. It hung high on a hook on the wall and bulged with various types of fruits. Dragging a table to use as a stepping stool, I retrieved it and dumped out the bulk of the fruit. Chantastic's egg seemed to have grown since it had last been in my position. Now it was the size of a large apple and strained against the tiny zipper compartment I'd stowed it in. The shell felt a bit softer in some places, but other than that it had not been cracked. I locked it up safe and sound in a little tin that used to hold Shuishan cigars and stowed it deep in my rucksack, taking up my bow and slinging the bag over my shoulder.

I flew from the tent and launched into Lilah's, immediately covering my mouth and nose as fumes and odours drifted from her unattended pots and drifted in hazy clouds around me. Brews boiled and foamed over, some even changing colours. I chucked some water on the fires beneath them and stormed the counter, ripping open Tieran's secret cabinet. Then I shattered every bottle of the qilin's blood against the side of the counter and watched in satisfaction as the pearly poison dribbled down the wood and then died into the soft moss. Before leaving to find the servant girls, I stole some of Lilah's canned soups and preserves and tucked them into my bag for later when I was back in the woods. I transferred the qilin tears from the broken beer bottle into a properly corked vial. Without another glance, I ran out before someone noticed that Lilah was missing and her tent had been ransacked.

The dolls hadn't taken the stage yet, but Tieran had made it to his throne. He lounged across it like the king he thought he was, and yet I could tell by the focused look on his face that he wondered where his princess was. Why hadn't Lilah returned from the grotto? I smiled in spite of myself, glancing away and dashing along the perimeter of the camp, through the prickle bushes and brambles, nothing but a shadow. I made it to the girls' tent during the final stages of their show preparation.

As soon as I breezed inside, now dressed like myself and my mouth spread into a smile, the girls looked at one another in panic and shock. T11 rushed up to me, half of her face caked in shimmery makeup and the other half only primed. Her brow wrinkled with concern and she grasped my hands, *"What's going on?"*

"I have the cure," I said, and a few servants stumbled, another spilled a pot of lip paint. T11's eyes lit up in absolute shock. I grinned, digging around in my bag and whipping out the corked bottle of tears. I thought there would be skepticism, but clearly all of them had paid attention to T2's story because at the sight of the golden liquid, the girls swarmed around me like moths to a lantern. They passed around the bottle and each took a sip, just letting it coat their lips and then handing it to the next girl. There was hardly enough to go around, but each of them were able to take a turn and within a couple of minutes the tent was filled with voices.

"My voice, my voice!" T1 bawled, smiling with trembling lips and saying her name over and over in a hushed tone, "Jay. Jay, Jay, Jay–it's been years, I'd forgotten completely what I sounded like!" A few girls giggled in agreement and started making expressions in the mirror, wiggling their tongues around and reciting poems and their own names. T11's name was Nora, T6 was Sara, and T8 was Xiaowen (which I remembered from my first night).

"I understand how crazy this is, but I have to get out of here as fast as possible. I'm going to take Tieran down," I explained hurriedly. The Shuishan would want to start the celebration any moment.

"But what do we do now?" T2, or Yue asked helplessly, her voice raspy from disuse.

"I'm killing Tieran!" T4, or Audi scoffed, punching the mirror and taking up a jagged shard of glass. It made a loud sound and I cursed quietly, grabbing her now bleeding wrist and squeezing until she was forced to drop the mirror piece.

"No, you're not," I hissed, "and please be quiet! You really have only two choices. Stay or leave."

"T17, as we explained to you before, we cannot just leave safely now that we can speak," Jay was saying, coming between me and Audi. "Our voices are just voices, not weapons."

"That's not true," I urged, looking around at all of them, "Why do you think he took them from us? He's scared of what we could say, he fears we'll tell the truth of how he's tortured us to the camp. I know there must be some good men in this camp. It's time we find them and tell them Tieran's reign needs to come to an end."

They were silent. Nora, or T11 spoke up next. Her voice was warm and beautiful. I could bet that she was a good singer, or used to be, before Tieran. "I think you're right, Raine. And what choice do we have anyway? We can't hide our voices and expressions forever, and I know Rong has been suspicious of Tieran for ages."

"We're running out of time," Yue, or T2 said. She peeked through the tent curtain, turning back to look at us in worry. "They're getting impatient; we have to decide what to do *now*."

"Dress me as quickly as you can. I need to be in full makeup and costume overtop of these clothes," I said, my heart racing as an idea finally sparked.

"You're still going to dance tonight?" Jay asked, incredulous.

I shook my head. Xiaowen and Yue sat me down and started painting my face in shimmering powder. "Not exactly."

Nora paused in applying my lip colour. "So, you have a plan?"

"Yes...I...I think I do." I looked up at all eleven of them. Even Audi and Sara who had once been so against leaving wore expressions of desperate yearning. I swallowed, whispering, "What is a song that you all know?"

After I'd been made up like the rest of them, one of the Shuishan peeked inside and asked what was the holdup. We all bowed, touching our fingers to the marking on our heads and hurrying out in single file; each of us hiding smiles. It was nearly impossible not to grin. This would be our very last performance for Tieran.

The men at the tables nearly toppled over as harsh winds pushed through Mythland. The storm wasn't far off now; we had to finish things before running away became impossible. I discreetly tossed my knapsack and bow into a leaf pile and stepped slightly into the spotlight, finishing the knot to secure my bun. Nora had helped me find a new red ribbon. The drumming changed rhythm to match the usual song, but as each of us fell into place on the stage, we faced straight ahead rather than looking down. Tieran didn't notice any difference yet, he was busy pouring himself another glass of something like clear blood. Even as his eyes scanned the mass of servants, they didn't find me because they weren't expecting to.

As the strumming of string instruments and clanging of gongs and whistles began, we remained completely still rather than dancing on each beat like we normally did. The Shuishan were silent, waiting, beginning to look confused. Jay was supposed to step up and start the song first since she was T1, but she shot me a desperate look and shook her head. She was just too scared. Murmurs of suspicion trilled through the audience, and instead of alerting the next girl in line to begin, I instead came completely into the spotlight. There was a collective gasp the moment I opened my mouth.

"Why are the flowers so red; as red as the flaming fire between the moon and the sun," I sang, my voice timid and hardly beautiful. Goblets crashed and spilled onto tables, drink sprayed from the mouths of a few Shuishan, arguments flared. I had to raise my voice to be heard over the commotion. Tieran's smirk had slid into a cold glower, his eyes murderously bright. I looked away from him and kept singing, "Why are the flowers so fresh; so fresh we tear them from the earth, young blood dripping from their roots?"

It was a song I never expected the Fluxarian girls to know; I never even imagined Xiaowen would know it, but in the minute we had to prepare, this is what we all somehow knew the words and melody to and I was completely dumbfounded. I'd learned it from Canton Ajram, Carmen's father, who during his brief service at Peak Tower, would bring back dozens of ancient videotapes and cassettes the Majesty Council had been tossing out. The majority of them bored Carmen, the twins and me, the quality hardly watchable on the viewing box Mr. Ajram had procured and the melodramatic love stories and war stories went straight over our heads. But there was one we had just about given up on, when this song began to play. It was on a cassette tape titled "Ballads of the Youth," and even though Carmen was just as ready to fast forward and move on to a video or something more interesting, I'd stopped her, captivated from the first lull of the string instruments. I must have listened to it fifty times before the ribbon in the tape came undone. I guess since girls from the other mountain knew it too, the song had to be older than I'd thought. Perhaps from when we were still one mountain.

Nora came beside me, and in her honey sweet voice sang, "Why are the flowers so withered? Watered by young blood, there is infinite distance between the earth and the sky; broken roads from sister to brother. Can we still revive dawn after dawn?" After Nora had bravely come by my side, the others weren't so afraid and chimed in. Even Jay slid her hand over mine and quietly repeated the final line, the volume of the song swelling. None of the Shuishan protested or interrupted, even the dissension died out into stone cold silence. Because of the glare of the spotlight I couldn't see most of their faces very well. But I knew they were listening and that was all we needed from them.

That was, until a gun went off.

chapter eight

"Enough!"

A shot rang out and our song ended with a choke of breath. Panicked, we glanced around at each other to see who had been hit. We all were rattled, but otherwise unharmed. I shielded my eyes from the spotlight and swept to the front of the stage. Tieran stood with one foot on the armrest of his throne, the gun in his hand smoking toward the sky.

"What is this?" he demanded, motioning at us with his pistol. "Some kind of trick?"

"No trick," Sara called from down the line, her eyes beginning to stream with tears. "You don't control us anymore."

Tieran flicked his wrist and the gun's nose pointed straight at her, "The hell I don't control you–"

"Don't you *dare* pull the trigger!" I screamed, moving in front of Sara and spreading out my arms. I averted my eyes from Tieran's own flaming blues and sent my gaze out to the rest. "Don't you see us?

Don't you hear us? We have voices, we're human, we aren't just dolls for you to play with whenever you want."

"But you *are* my dolls, and you do belong to me," Tieran snarled. Zhaorong slid up his visor and gazed at Tieran; his expression of disbelief slowly melted into what looked to me like disgust. Tieran hopped down from his throne and stepped up onto a table, kicking over bowls of fruit and bread as he strode toward us. "You are all mine, rightfully mine, and I can do whatever the fuck I want with what belongs to me–"

"Tieran!" Rong boomed, sliding off the bench and towering over Tieran even when he was on the table. He placed a hand on Tieran's shoulder and spoke quietly, "Enough is enough. You know I respect you, but you are out of line with this sort of talk."

"Even you, Rong?" Tieran scoffed. "How can you take her side?"

"I'm just advising you not to act rashly because of what they are saying," Rong replied, his voice measured. "You've had a lot to drink tonight, so let's just discuss the girls tomorrow. Right now we all need some rest and time to think."

My heartbeat struck against my chest faster than the beat of a dragonfly's wing. Any minute now I felt that my heart would fly free and I would fall from the stage, I knew it. At the terrible clash of thunder and menacing dribble of rain, I interjected, "We have to 'discuss' now. Let them live within this camp like the rest of you, like human beings. And if your king disagrees, then who in his right mind could still admire such a leader? Tieran has to stop treating them like this anymore–"

"Treating them 'rashly' you mean? I'm the bad guy, right?" Tieran called, grinning broadly at me. His gaze sent ice through my veins, and I struggled to keep my composure.

"You don't have to be," I said. "Tieran you can always decide to do what's right, to stop this and start over."

"That's cute and all, but cut the bullshit. You don't really believe that, do you?" he whispered, taking a few steps closer. "How about we take it to my tent and then when you're screaming for death to save you, you can decide if salvation exists?"

"I'm not scared of you," I said. My voice shook, my hands shook, my bones shook. Every cell in my body knew it wasn't true. "And I'm not scared of taking you down if it comes to that."

There was dissent among the men, some moving cautiously to Tieran's side, others rising from the benches and looking for a way out. The stare-down between their king and me continued, finally broken when Tieran blinked his long, dark lashes and turned away.

"You know what, Irene? Maybe I am the bad guy," He glanced at me over his shoulder, a hesitant tremble in his lips before they slid back into that horrible smile. "And maybe...I just don't care."

It all happened so fast. Before I could stop him, he clicked back the hammer of his pistol and fired. A bullet wedged deep into Yue's skull and she tumbled, eyes wide open, off of the stage. An uproar exploded from the audience, the Shuishan launching to their feet, hollering at Tieran, waving their fists, stampeding his throne as he continued to laugh. Rong gaped at Yue's corpse, his gloved hand over his mouth as he became violently sick.

"You monster!" Jay screeched, tripping off of the stage and landing face-down in the grass. She crawled over to Yue and buried her face against her stomach, weeping, "Yue, no...no, no, no..."

"I think you've forgotten who your leader is," Tieran shouted above the roar of the crowd. He pointed his gun straight at me, his arm shaking, "Now do you remember? I hold the gun. I call the shots. And you will not speak or sing your fucking flower songs at me unless *I want you to*." His thumb flicked back the hammer of his pistol again, but then as I felt the shock of the impact, I somehow saw him fall as well from his position on the table. Everything seemed to move in slow motion as the bullet hit my chest. It felt like a bomb had gone off inside me. I thought I must to have flown a few feet because of the shocking force of the bullet, but I only collapsed against the stage floor with my chest suddenly hot and screaming. I couldn't writhe or move, the shock was so indescribably great that as I gasped for the breath that was too scared to come, as I felt the wounds on my back touch the wet wood of the stage, all I could do was lie still and stare up at the sky suddenly splitting with lightning and rain.

I closed my eyes and let the drops land on me for a moment and then moved my hand to see where it had hit. Tieran was a dumb shooter all right, he'd fired nearer to my shoulder than my heart due to his drunken state. I didn't dare touch it, but felt two of the servant girls' hands hoist me up by the arms to stand. Every movement was worse than the whip lashes. I felt like someone was stomping on my bones till they broke again and again. I blinked, lights popping in front of my eyes and I spotted Tieran lying, howling wildly at the foot of the table. There were gun wounds in both of his legs, and Rong was sliding his gun into his pocket. No way.

"Raine? Raine, you can hear me, right?" Nora's voice was clear as day, so I nodded. "We'll get you some help, okay? Tieran's down, we're going to be okay," her voice cracked and she half-smiled, but then her eyes fell onto Yue and the girls weeping around her body and her smile vanished without a trace. She gazed down at me again, cradling my cheek in her hand, her face a swirling blur. And before I could stop it, she and the bright-as-gold stage vanished.

Needles, tiny needles like pesky bugs biting me.

My eyelids fluttered, feeling heavy as brocade instead of thin veiny skin. I was on some sort of bed. A scratchy cotton mattress stuffed with–I prodded the cushion and tugged out a thin green stalk–pine needles. Needles. More needles.

I glanced down near my shoulder and chest where the bullet had hit and found it had been dug out. Roughly by the looks of my frayed, raw and red skin. I sat up and while my back still ached like hellfire, the bullet wound didn't hurt a pinch. I looked dizzily around me. A counter to my left coated in spilled white liquid and broken bottles. Ransacked cabinets. To my right was a tray of needles, syringes filled with different coloured liquids.

"Shh...go ahead and lie back down, honey," her voice soothed behind me. Her small, pale hand pressed my back onto the bed abruptly, and I gasped as the wounds on my back scraped the pine needles piercing through the fibres of my sweater and performance dress. "How are you feeling?" She glided halfway into the lantern light and plucked up a syringe, testing the serum by squirting out a little bit of the gravy thick substance. Before I could answer, she covered my mouth and plunged the needle into my neck as I gargled on a scream.

Lilah moved closer, and I saw a handcuff -shaped bruise staining her once rather angelic face. "I come back from the grotto, completely in shock that a nice girl like you would hit a little girl across the face with a metal cuff...and then Rong says that Tieran is shot, and the servant girls speak, and I need to heal the leader of them." She did a little twirl and playfully drummed her fingers over the other needles. "Hmm..." she mumbled, a smile playing on her lips, "Which one, which one? Oh– I know." She covered my eyes and I heard a rattling of metal on metal before she whispered silkily into my ear, "Guess which one."

"The stupid one," I rasped.

"Err! Nope. The blue one," she chuckled to herself and withdrew her hand. Lilah waved the blue-filled syringe over my face and then stuck it deep into my bullet hole, "Suits you, it's only fair. Zhaorong said to heal you, and he's the one in charge, now, so I have to obey. I'm just giving you the treatment you showed to me and Tieran, aren't I, Irene Abrasha?"

I couldn't breathe. Lilah had plunged past the numbed areas of my wound and shot liquid demons an inch away from heart. I choked on a scream as a boiling hot sensation burst from my chest and seared in my veins, horrible visions flashing through my mind. The explosion in the Emergent Hot Springs. Freezing to death with Destan in the cave. Poison blood on Tieran's lips burning into mine. My mother screaming and screaming, *"You're not my daughter!"* and Gwen calling out to me as I was shoved into the street. My father saying goodbye in ten different voices with twenty different faces. The lift up to Peak in suffocating darkness and Chantastic wasn't there to hold me, the rockalanche but Irene's head was split open against the cliffside, Yue's brains leaving her precious skull over and over, Tieran gnawing at my clothes and skin and saying mine, mine, mine, mine, that I was just like him, and I'd stay with him, I'd be pinned to his floor forever, pins, needles. Needles.

"Safe journey home, blue-hair." Her voice was a carnival. She tossed me my bow and arrows, my knapsack. How had she gotten them?

Suddenly I was walking and Lilah had fled like a dream. Where had she gone? Did the Shuishan leave me? Did I leave me?

"Lilah?" I called out, realizing that it was raining all around. The trees were blue, the kind of blue that comes out before the sun begins to set. It was impossible to walk forward without hitting one, as soon as I'd thought that they were out of my way I'd hit straight into one and the woods laughed.

Panicked, I spun around and shouted, "Who is there?" Someone poked my shoulder, I whipped around again, the blue trees suddenly bursting into reds, *"Who's there?!"* I reached for my quiver but as I grabbed an arrow, the tip bit my finger and I watched my blood burst from my finger like a little scarlet firework. The blood creeped up my hand, my arm; I was getting drenched. I shook it off and ran, waving my arm around like some limp attachment, not my own. I tried to wash it in the rain but each drop just made the blood spread farther, farther, it was coming up to my neck, it was swirling into my bullet wound. I clutched my chest and fell to my knees, closing my eyes where violet lights danced.

"Raine? Raine?"

I lifted my head from my hands, trembling uncontrollably, my voice muffled by some invisible hand over my mouth, "Chantastic?"

"RAINE!"

"CHAN! Chan, I'm coming! Where are you?" I shrieked out into the trees, but they began to spin around me, blocking my every move, their branches twisting, wisting, this way, that way, all spindly black vines. The rain coming down wasn't water, it was a bunch of little flames and as they touched my skin they grew teeth and bit as hard as they could. I howled and ran straight into one tree after the other, my head throbbing, something wet dribbling into my eyes. Backing away from the ongoing carousel of trees whirling all around me, I touched my forehead and felt a smooth metal bullet lodged in between my eyes. And then Yue fell with a thud, eyes open, off the stage on top of me with green foam rushing from her mouth like a sea. I shoved her off and she screeched like a banshee, "You made him kill me! Murderer! Murderer!"

"I'm sorry," I sobbed, I begged, I reached for her but she bit off a few of my fingers and slithered away leaving a trail of seashells, "Yue, I'm sorry–"

"Don't move," he snarled behind me, and I felt a blade press to my windpipe. He dragged it across slowly and I held my breath as butterflies flew from my slit throat. "There," Sebastian Lao said, gliding in front of me with his bald head all blue and grey and his eyes some terrible shade blacker than black, bulging from their sockets. "That's better, isn't it, Miss Ylevol?"

"Sebastian, kill me already!" I screamed at him, but he began to giggle and he pressed a hand over his mouth, eyes squinting and watering with laughter. He was standing on a pile of bones and faces with white lips and he pointed to the fire raining from the sky, the trees still somehow churning around in great circles, whispering, laughing, Chantastic was still yelling out for me and Yue was being shot over and over. He tipped my chin up and I saw Destan swinging from the tree; his neck snapped in a noose, his chest a pincushion for arrows still coming at him.

"Exit through the gift shop, to your right. I hope your visit to Peak Tower was the cat's pajamas," Sebastian grinned, lips sliding from ear to ear, eyes widening as if tugged outward from each corner by some black thread that sewed his wrinkles together. I ran, slammed through the swirl of trees and let the blood pour and flames feast and I saw that at the end of Councilman Lao's wiggling finger was a black oasis. A smooth obsidian surface untouched and waiting for me to take the plunge.

Someone poked my shoulder. I kept running, the oasis farther and farther away. Someone grabbed my shoulder. I shoved his or her hand away yelling, "Leave me alone!" Someone went away and I threw down my quiver and bow and went headfirst into the oasis.

Everything hurt, and then it didn't. It was everything at once again, everything that has happened and anything that could happen, and then nothing. I sank through the water, eyes open, sitting with my legs out in front of me and arms floating up at my sides, watching the ripples curl around me in silver embraces. The current hugged me to its dancing body and swayed me back and forth, lulling me deeper and deeper, whispering that we could go to bed together. Really? I said. Really, it said. I'd like that, I said. Just a bit deeper, it said, let me kiss you, fill you up. And then as I tugged my gaze to look back at the surface I had left behind, I saw it.

A hat. More specifically, a red beanie, made of yarn spun and dyed on a place called Thgindim. Thgindim. Where had I heard that name before? Whose hat was that? I saw the hat and thought of calloused hands. Of honey smeared on bread by a river. A deep kiss lost in a meadow lit by torches and fireflies.

Destan.

I blew bubbles from my mouth and kicked my legs, trying to swim up. The current was fighting me and as I got closer, I began to feel the weight of my body. I was full of chains, the chains were full of anchors, I wouldn't make it, I couldn't make it. The silver ripples in the water wrapped themselves around my throat, and I slashed at them with my hands and shot myself up and out.

As I touched the muddy bank, the blue trees flamed again and that invisible Someone poked me nonstop– and the beanie was gone. Where did it go? The trees made a carousel again and came around and around lashing their branches like whips at me, and I saw that one of them wasn't moving. It was stuck and there was something stuck on it. I crawled towards it, my limbs melting down like wax. The trees were thousands of candlelight shards, I lunged toward one the them and clung for dear life onto the thing stuck on it. And as soon as my fingertips touched it, the trees slowed and became brown and green and dark. No more spinning. It was night. And I was screaming my lungs out.

Lightning flexed electric blue against the sky, dimming every star. I let go and crumpled to the base of the tree, freezing, fat raindrops that weren't flames soaked me to the skin. Reaching for a low branch to pull myself up, I instead grasped something cold and metal. I squinted in the blinding rain at what was in my fist. It was jammed tight into the tree and wiggled when I moved it back and forth in the bark. With all my strength, I yanked it out and found a ratty scrap of fabric at the tip of the thing. A piece of glove.

I took it off, ran my fingers up and down it and realized it was an arrow.

A fancy carbon arrow branded with an *MC*. Evidently given to someone banished from Thgindim.

Given to Destan.

chapter nine

I dropped it with a cry. Then, gathering myself, I bent down and picked it up from the pillow of damp moss, holding it in my shaking hands. Pinned to the arrow's tip was a scrap of fabric that I easily recognized as a piece of his glove. I rolled the fabric in between my fingers and closed my eyes, for a moment imagining his hand in mine.

Seeing the arrow had shaken me from the delusional haze Lilah's drug had put me in. The wind wailed like a thousand cries and blew the ribbon from my bun, sending it into a prickly bush that frayed the ribbon's edge. I snatched it and coiled it around my wrist as I ran, my eyes peeled for another arrow. There had to be more. This was a sign, no accident, and if anything, it was proof that Destan Attila Abrasha was still out there somewhere and trying to find me. A smile split my face at that thought, even though the heavy rain bruised my body, even though whatever Lilah had injected in me had me in a hazy state of euphoria. The thought of no longer being alone heated me to my core and made me happier than I could remember being for so long.

He'd been given a full quiver of twenty arrows, and it's easy to lose them if you have to make a quick getaway and don't have time to retrieve them. I was only expecting to maybe find ten more at the most. But throughout the rest of the night's storm, I didn't find any more. When the storm got so bad that I could barely move forward without being knocked backwards into a tree or snake-infested puddle, I decided to stop my searching for now and find cover.

I crouched behind a big pile of rocks that I knew even a Mythland storm couldn't take down and closed my eyes, letting the storm know that I was done fighting it for now; it could go on with its rumbling and the lightning with its clawing against the pristine sapphire sky, and I'd just lay here and let its tantrum unravel until I fell asleep.

Sitting here brought my mind to a place I didn't expect. It rained a lot in Mythland, but for some reason, this rain brought on something I wanted desperately to forget. I was lying in the Underbrush street, kicked out and unwanted by my mother; screaming and praying I would disappear before the JPs took me away. And I thought, what had my mother been up to after I was gone? Did Gwen argue with her? Did she get slapped defending me, or did she shrink away into her room and not make a sound while my mother cried? Did she cry? Was she crying when I couldn't see, after I'd been loaded into the police truck? Was she happier now that she didn't have to deal with me, or is she regretting everything she said? These thoughts were getting me nowhere because they were questions to which I may never know the answers. And so instead, I focused on Destan and Chantastic and Irene and Velle and Carmen and Gwen and tried to drift off to sleep with their faces the only thing to conjure into dreams.

The last time I'd dreamt of them, it had given me the strength to escape. So I thought maybe if I dreamt of them again tonight, I'd envision where to follow the arrow trail Destan might have left for me. I knew it was a silly thought. I'd never been a very superstitious person and now wasn't the time to start just because I was in the world's most dangerous woods and stumbled upon a creature with magic tears.

As I looked around me, there was a fine coating of frost that hadn't been there when I'd left the camp. And my stomach was in so much pain that I felt as though I hadn't eaten for days. Had I been under Lilah's drug for that long? Just wandering aimlessly without stop? My thoughts swirling, I sank into an unsteady sleep.

Chantastic braided my hair intricately down my back. Her fingers combed in a soothing rhythm, somehow making it through the endless tangles without me feeling a single yank. I turned and looked at her, saying skeptically, "I can't do my Laundress duties with my hair all fancy like this."

She smiled. "You're off today. Jun told me."

I gaped, making her laugh. We were sitting in the middle of a never-ending field of mountain poppies, each flower Chantastic's favourite shades of violet and mauve. She was wearing a pale blue dress and her hair was very long and blowing around her face like willow branches. I glanced down at myself and found that I was covered in white roses, the petals showering fragrantly from the pink sky.

"But...but how do you know that? She never gives me off on a perfect day like this," I insisted, worrying about the Canopia load I was scheduled to wash. Chan touched my lips with her finger, eyes gleaming like dark jewels.

"Hush. It's a special day for you. Don't tell me you've forgotten?"

"Special..." I hummed, plucking at some poppies and yearning my brain to remember. But as soon as I tried to recall what was exactly going on, I realized I hadn't been going at work for months now. Right now I was supposed to be in a rainstorm, miles and miles away, looking for Destan— not calmly having my hair braided in the middle of some unknown meadow that looked far, far away from any mountain or woods I'd ever seen. My eyes landed worriedly on Chantastic's and I took her hand and squeezed it. "I can't be here! I have to find him, he...he left me a trail of arrows." A wrinkle formed in between her brows and I added, "Do you know where I should go, where the next arrow or sign could be?"

"I don't know about any arrows." She shook her head and got up, her pale knees dyed green from the grasses. A gentle zephyr rolled in and she pointed down the never-ending meadow. "He's right there, Raine. No trail or arrow."

I clumsily struggled to my feet and squinted in the sunlight, using my hand as a visor above my eyes as a little shadow flickered among the tall grasses and flowers. A strange shape lay among the plants, being tickled by butterflies and little faerie-like creatures, but not stirring. Chan started skipping that way so I walked alongside her, feeling dizzy and warm and for once unsure if she knew what she was telling me.

As we neared the shape in the grass, I became increasingly, intensely scared. I suddenly wanted to turn back and run as fast as I could away before having to face whatever, whoever was lying there. But my bare feet continued to move on the soft ground and I flinched as the shadow took form. It was Destan, and yet I was still afraid. He was lying there asleep, his head turned to the side, his arms splayed out and being crawled on by fuzzy little caterpillars and rainbow-coloured ants. One of his hands held a thin, pale-looking hand attached to some unknown body. Chantastic bent down and brushed aside some long yellowed grasses, and in that moment I knew the hand he held was mine. I was the body beside him. But when I was revealed to be lying there, my eyes were wide open and staring, my mouth slightly agape. Confused I looked from my body to Destan's lying on the ground, and in horror I saw that there was no movement in his stomach. Destan wasn't asleep. He was dead.

And I was dead beside him. Suddenly, the white suit I wore turned red from a single splotch near my heart, and panicking, I watched his white sweater bloom crimson as well. Right over his heart. Then his mouth curled into a smile and so did mine, and my body's eyes closed and Chantastic's mouth kissed behind my ear and whispered, "For good to rise, the good must fall." She moved away from me, laughing softly. I reached out for her, but suddenly she was gone and so was my corpse and Destan's. The shadow flickered back and forth across my vision again and I tried to run towards it, but my steps sank deeper and deeper among the flowers that grew taller and taller. The shadow became no one other thans Irene, and she grinned at me with tears pouring from her dark, round eyes. And with her mouth splitting open, she screeched one word, "FALL!"

I awoke with a start, gasping for breath in the calm evening air. I scrambled to stand and bonked my head hard on the rock I'd forgotten was above me. "Crap! Ow, ow, ow..." I muttered, taken aback by the weird dream, my head throbbing. I stared at the now completely serene and green woods before me and decided that it would be best to keep moving and not let myself sleep until it was absolutely necessary. "Stupid dream..." I whispered to myself, rolling my hair up into a bun and hurriedly tying it tight. "Not real, not real, you were sleeping, it means nothing..." Even though I felt a little silly talking to myself, hearing my voice was still such a treasured relief that I couldn't help but think out loud.

Slinging on my now rather weighted knapsack, I left the crowd of boulders where I'd hidden from the storm and looked around. Confused, I realized that it was going to be nightfall soon. I'd slept through the night and almost the entire next day. No wonder my

100

dream was so long and peculiar! As I began trekking up a slope riddled with streams and thorns, I combed every tree for another arrow or clue that Destan had been here. I crouched by every pile of sticks and saw if they were charred from a campfire of his. I examined exceptionally snapped logs to see if they had been cut by his axe. Still nothing. Grumpily, I reached back at my quiver to make sure I'd even found the carbon arrow in the first place. I touched its smooth silvery tip and sighed, "Yup...guess I just have to keep looking–"

Suddenly, something ran under me, knocking me off my feet and onto my backside. I scrambled up out of the mud, shaking the filth from my hands and glancing around. *What the heck?!* I thought, turning in a full circle and seeing nothing but trees and swamp. And then– a bark. I whipped around, about to nock in an arrow but finding that my quiver was no longer on me. It dangled by the strap in the mouth of a rather small, rather mischievous-looking tiangou pup. It barked again, wagging its tail happily. The young tiangou stood atop a huge tree stump, how it got to me and then over there so quickly, I hadn't the faintest.

"Hey!" I shouted, cautiously coming closer, "Bring that back!" It didn't flinch, just kept staring and wagging and letting some arrows slip out. I flushed. "P-please? Come here?" I beckoned pathetically and I was surprised to see the animal burst into motion. It leapt down from the stump and came trotting over on its little legs, dragging the quiver on the grass. But then the trot turned into a jog, into a sprint, and by the time it reached me it was running full speed and knocked me down again. This time, it dropped the quiver and snatched my rucksack. And rather than bounding back to the stump to drool and wag its tail at me, it kept running and running and I found myself joining the chase behind it.

This is so stupid! I don't have time for this, I thought, my calves burning as I forced my legs to move faster. Fatigue weighed down my whole body, but I was relieved to notice that the gap between us was getting smaller and smaller. As I lunged forward to snatch back my rucksack, the ground suddenly disappeared beneath me, my breath caught in my throat, and I plummeted down.

I was encompassed in darkness, my head hitting back into something hard and my tailbone aching as it slammed into a pile of stones. I rubbed my eyes, squinting in the black, my heart racing as I felt around me with shaking hands. *Stay calm, stay calm,* I thought, probing the ground with the toe of my boot and moving forward, *Jeez, Raine you've been through so much worse and yet you're still afraid of the dark?* I tripped on something and stumbled forward, catching myself on an overhanging root. It was unusually warm down here. My eyes were adjusting and I could almost make out my hand as I held it in front of me, but no sooner did I begin to relax a little bit, that I heard it. A chipper, faraway puppy bark.

The tiangou pup was forty feet away, grinning in a faint pool of sun where the earth opened up again. He wagged his tail, panting, then burying his nose into the gaping belly of my rucksack, sniffing around. I bristled, taking a confident step forward only to land on something soft and snoring. I jumped back, the hair standing up on the back of my neck as I peered at the creature I'd trampled on. I couldn't quite make out what it was, but it was very large, very hairy and very much asleep; making the air in the tunnel hot with its breaths. And what was worse, it was one of many. Suddenly I could see that between me and my rucksack were at least twenty massively full-grown, soundly sleeping tiangou. And then, of course, the puppy. The goddamn puppy.

The goddamn puppy had started pawing through the rucksack, clearly smelling whatever meat Lilah had packed in the cans I'd stolen, and trying to pop the cap with its claw. There was an innocent curiosity in its big, red eyes as it tried and tried again, plucking up my bag in its teeth and swinging it back and forth as my possessions went flying out. My flint sparked as it scraped the ground, miscellaneous cans spewing their contents and conking some sleeping tiangou on the head. The danger of them waking up wasn't even my greatest fear. My blood ran cold as I saw Chantastic's egg fall out, and a crack shot across its shell.

I sucked in my stomach, pushing off from an earthy wall and propelling over the first sleeping beast. I landed clumsily, treading on the tail of another, quickly sidestepping a pair snuggled together, my entire body going into hyper-drive as the puppy bat the egg between its paws on the floor, causing another crack in its shell. I heard a growl, a tentative yawn and I resisted the urge to bang my forehead against the wall as I saw a mass of more tiangou blocking my way, so many that there was near to no wiggle room, so many I couldn't make it over them in a jump. It was then I remembered I still had my weapon.

Hastily, I nocked an arrow on my bow, coming into a narrow, awkward anchor since I had such limited space. I glanced desperately at Chantastic's egg, now abandoned and in danger of being trampled as the puppy became intrigued by something else it had discovered in my rucksack. My elbow trembled as I held the bowstring taut. Sweat beaded on my brow. *I can't shoot that puppy; it doesn't know what it's doing. I couldn't even shoot Tieran when he deserved it.*

Deciding quickly, I aimed a little higher and shot above the puppy's head, expecting it to stab the wall of earth behind and scare him away. I was once again mistaken. My arrow kept going. It soared into the black and when it lost height and fell I heard a sound faint as a pin drop. The puppy glanced behind him, tail raised in curiosity. Gritting my teeth, I angled my anchor higher and shot again, this time at its feet. The little tiangou released a high-pitched yelp, scampering up the wall and out of the hole above him, and I took my time tiptoeing around the rest of the pack.

Finally at my rucksack, I hugged it to my chest for a moment and then picked up Chan's egg, now cracked and battered. It felt smooth and warm on my skin, somehow warmer than I could recall it ever being. And turning it over in my hands, I saw what Chantastic had meant me to see, all along. She'd told me to keep it warm. And now in the stifling heat of a dozen tiangou breathing soundly, something finally revealed itself. She had written in what must've been a crayon or thin piece of clear wax. Once the egg had been exposed to heat, words gleamed on the exterior of the shell as the once invisible wax began to sweat. There were only six words, and one letter that had been sliced in half from a hairline crack:

Will find me on blood moon

C:

What will find you? I thought, reading and rereading the message until my eyes watered. *The bird inside here? How, Chan?*

There was no more time to waste in the tiangou den. The warmth in the tunnel hadn't only awoken her words, but also whatever was inside. The egg began to shake. And shake. And before whatever it was could come bursting out, I tucked it down my shirt and crawled clumsily back to the surface.

I looked around me in a daze of daylight, seeing I'd climbed out into a bamboo grove. Sun dappled the vibrant green of the grove with yellow, warming the chilly afternoon air as I searched for sanctuary. I wove in between the trees, finally finding a small, shaded clearing where remnants of old bamboo lay withered. Kneeling, I carefully removed the egg from under my sweater feeling less awkward now that the warm, vibrating thing wasn't crackling against my chest. I placed it on a cushion of leaves, nudging it out of the shade and into a solitary puddle of sunlight. I waited, watching the now motionless egg with baited breath. It did nothing. And then it was shaking again, a faint peeping sound greeting my ears.

A tiny clawed foot jutted out through the shell, shiny and wet, toes wiggling. Then came an arm, gleaming with opalescent turquoise scales. I peered through the two holes it had made, hoping to see what would come next, but no sooner had I bent down than the egg rolled over and burst completely. I gasped, backing away as the creature sprang into being before my eyes.

chapter ten

Chan, what the hell did you give me? I thought, hand over my heart as the lizard-like thing dragged itself through the dirt. It was squeaking, a sound similar to a baby bird, and its tiny eyes were squeezed shut. I watched it suspiciously as it tossed its head and squealed, wobbling on its four legs and bumping into a stalk of bamboo. The sound it made was piercing and grating, and to keep it from waking the sleeping tiangou not so far from us, I hesitantly scooped the creature into my hands and cradled it against my chest.

"Shh, shh," I whispered, glancing around nervously and moving my fingers away from its snout. I would not lose a pinky to this thing. The creature quieted, warm air rushing through its nostrils, the two long whiskers above its lips curling and twirling around my thumb. I swallowed, my cheeks growing hot as a memory bobbed to the surface in my mind.

I'd seen this creature before.

It had been after school, just a couple of months before my chip went off and I became a Laundress. I was trying to put together a portfolio for the Career interview; when I still thought I had a chance to be a Sketcher. I was at home and digging through old sketches I'd done, kneeling on the floor with mountains upon mountains of paper surrounding me. The biggest stack of artwork had been from when my dad was still home with us. I had been little and thought that naturally everything I created was a masterpiece, so with the positive feedback from my father, I went through two sketchbooks a week, hardly paying any special attention to individual drawings and just mass-producing silly scribbles and ink paintings. Within my six-year-old art rampage, I'd gone through a mini-phase my dad had called the 'wild-blue-sky dynasty,' in which I drew nothing but the various critters I saw roaming around Underbrush gave them the powers of flight.

There were purple squirrels with bushy tails and aeroplane propellers on their heads, meadowlarks with scissor-like beaks that chopped through the air, flying wolves, flying snakes, and soon I'd given wings to everything I laid my eyes on. I have no idea why I had been so fascinated with flying at that point in my life. Doesn't every kid go through a similar phase? And while I took that weird trip down memory lane, I came across some sketches that just didn't seem to fit in with the rest. It was still the wild-blue-sky dynasty, and yet there were these weird lizard-like creatures I'd paid a lot of attention to that didn't have wings or aeroplane propellers to keep them afloat in the clouds.

They were smallish, with five clawed toes and four little legs. Their bodies were scaly and smooth like a snake's, and they had a large snout with two large nostrils. Stubby horns protruded from their foreheads, two delicate ears perking out to the side of their heads, a bumpy spine traveling down their backs, and a pair of long, whiskers that curled out from above their lips. Despite the lack of wings, I'd always drawn or painted them high in the clouds; soaring above ominous sketches of Peak Tower or across big blotchy portraits of the moon. The wild-blue-sky dynasty came to an end once I started to *only* draw these oddball creatures that my mother was convinced were a product of the same internal malfunction that turned my hair blue. She had never supported

106

my father's encouragement of fairy tales and most definitely was not a fan of the wild-blue-sky dynasty.

But now here it was: slightly damp, warm, breathing raggedly in the cradle of my hands. I had a billion questions regarding where Chan might have found it, if it was actually the creature I thought I'd made up as a child, if it could fly, if it would even last the night. And yet the question on the very forefront of my mind was: *why had my best friend sacrificed our last moments together to give me this?* As I continued to watch the thing doze and whimper, anger managed to clog up my throat. I didn't want this from her. I didn't want a puzzle to solve or another thing to take care of. I was angry at myself for being angry at her and this helpless thing I was now responsible for. Most of all, I was angry I didn't understand her intention. She and I had never had to exchange more than a few words or glances to understand each other. Now I was at a loss and wished to find a hint in her eyes or in the curve of her lips, that if she were here maybe I'd be able to deduce what she expected of me and I wouldn't ruin whatever plan she had going.

"Do you know what you want from me?" I whispered to it, leaning down and speaking into its tiny ear. It opened a bleary eye and squeaked. And without another thought, I swaddled it in a scarf and tucked it safely in my rucksack, beginning to walk again. The bamboo grove continued for another mile, but slowly the trees thinned and began looking more and more grisly, contaminated. What was once blindingly green became a sickly mess of hard yellow stalk rattling in the wind. I knew this was an omen that I would soon be knee deep in the acidic mud of the Mythland swamps, so I changed course, trying to find a new way out.

I re-entered the regal shuishan tree territory, having walked through dense forest for maybe an hour when I decided that I was being followed. I'd first noticed the creeping feeling when I increased speed to get past a wasp hive and heard footsteps that continued once I had slowed my pace again. But I'd glanced back and see no one, not even a shadow or a movement in the trees. I'd checked my back to see if maybe it was just the creature messing with the stuff in my bag, but it was just as asleep as it had been when I'd put it in there. Plus, I'd wrapped it so well in the scarf that even if it tried it couldn't break into anything with its five-clawed feet. The second time

I was put on edge, I'd sat down on a rock by a stream and was trying to cut through the lid of a can of Lilah's food that I'd stolen. I heard what sounded like four twigs snapping, continuously, and rather than changing my lunch spot, I stood my ground, eating slowly and with my ears and eyes wide open.

As I wrinkled my nose and downed the soggy pansy petal sludge that Lilah called soup, whatever-it-was made another sound. This time it was a high-pitched bark, and I flew to my feet, dropping the soup and nocking in an arrow immediately as I expected to come face to face with that tiangou pup again. I rose fluidly into form. I'd been prepared, and brought the bowstring to my nose, narrowing my eyes and searching for my target. "I've heard you for hours. Come out and stop playing games with me," I called, voice quivering despite the ferocity I'd hoped would come across to the beast stalking me. There was that bark again...then, a whimper. I gritted my teeth and focused my arrow more carefully at the bushes where I noticed a stirring. "Just tell me who you..." I trailed off.

Siri stepped out from the shade of the trees, her grey fur matted with mud and some wiry looking branches. Her mouth dripped with bloody saliva and one of her eyes stared off in a separate direction. If I hadn't known better, I would have thought she was some sort of demon or an especially nasty tiangou, but unlike a Mythland beast she meekly ducked her head and whined, red weeping from her mouth. I dropped my bow and rushed at her, pressing my forehead to her muzzle and gasping for the breath that had fled my lungs. I ignored the smell of decay and forest juice clumping up her fur and kissed her nose over and over, crying, "Siri, oh Siri, I love you! I love you...I love you, you're safe I'm so sorry I left you at that horrible place." I threw my arms around her neck and hugged her, feeling her tongue lick affectionately at my ear as my fingers worked into the fur of her back where Destan's body once had rested.

As I hugged her, she sniffed and nocked her snout at my shoulder, her nostrils suddenly flaring. I thought she must have smelled the creature in my rucksack, but she circled me and then dug her nose hurriedly into my quiver, her single alert eye lighting up. Suddenly understanding, I withdrew Destan's carbon arrow and held it in front of me, a hopeful smile rising on my lips. Her nose ran along the metal, my heart going crazy in my chest as I realized what this could mean. Siri was a wolf; she could track him by his scent, couldn't she?

She flicked her face away, beginning to breathe in great puffs of warm breath and sitting back on her haunches expectantly. I dashed back and scooped up my bow and then straddled her back, threading my fingers through her thick fur. Siri's body rose off the ground and for a moment I was transported back to Thgindim, my arms around Destan's firm waist as green pines blurred by and we chased the sun. But then I snapped back to reality as she plunged forward I and clung to Siri for dear life.

She was winding through the woods to an uneven beat, stopping randomly to stick her nose to the buggy air and inhale deeply, and every time her claws dug into the soft ground and we jolted to a stop, I'd bite my tongue or lose my grip or feel my heart seem to stop for a moment. The trees were becoming darker and darker, the light fading as she ran, and then she bounded into the only clearing I'd seen for days, pausing and breathing quickly with her tongue wagging out of her red-rimmed mouth. She unexpectedly sat down again, and with my bones rattled from all of the running, I slid unsteadily from her back and looked around where we were.

Why had she stopped? I ran around each tree, searching under fallen leaves and between roots; no arrows. I hacked through bramble bushes with my dagger and crawled between the barbed branches; no arrows, clues. This place was completely absent of Destan, and yet Siri remained adamant, standing tall with her chin up, waiting for me to understand. I turned away from her in frustration, suddenly nauseous, tears springing in my eyes as I felt something hot and burning rising in my throat. Doubled over, I threw up all of Lilah's pansy soup in a fountain of flower petals and rice. I sank to the grass and panted, wiping my mouth and trembling. Siri stared at me. I looked away. I hugged my knees to my chest as the wolf got up and stalked over, silent as a shadow. Siri nudged my shoulder, hard. Then she whined and laid beside me.

My mouth tasted disgusting. I spat, reaching at my hip for the water gourd I'd stolen from the Shuishan and sucking it all down thirstily. "I don't think we're going to find him," I said, after I'd finished, more to myself than the wolf who couldn't even comprehend human speak. Still, Siri growled what felt to me was acknowledgement. "Show me what's here for me to find, what traces back to Destan. Why did we stop here, Siri?" I motioned all around me but the big grey wolf didn't move and I felt the urge to throw up again. I stifled it, reluctantly swallowing and breathing through my nose. No matter how disgusting Lilah's soup was, I was planning on keeping it down.

On a whim, I glanced back at where Siri had sat down before and suddenly noticed something strange lying tangled in the grass. I got up, brushing off my leather leggings and kneeling by the spot, sweeping away some grass to see an old, chunky looking iron key. My heart sank. It wasn't Destan's, it didn't even look like it was from Thgindim. It probably belonged to another banished troublemaker like me or refugees like the Shuishan. But as I touched it, I heard Siri cry out and she bounded over to me, her nose sucking the scent of the key in so hard that it stuck to her nostrils as she inhaled. Her pupils dilated to complete blackness, she yelped and jumped around, so elated I could hardly get a hold on her fur to climb back on. She ducked her head once to allow my riding her, and she shot back into the trees the moment she felt my body connect with hers.

She flew like a grey phantom, and the force of the evening wind hit my eyes so hard that I had to keep them closed and just hope she knew where she was going. The nightly rain began to splatter my face as she ran and ran, and I hugged her body tightly to mine to keep warm. She looked up at the full pearl of the moon and howled like there was something to howl about, and I felt hope rise in my stomach. Hope, or more of Lilah's crappy soup.

Siri gradually slowed her pace to a lithe sort of slink, her ears pricking and twitching as the wild sounds of night began to hum all around us. As I squinted my eyes in the dark, something suddenly stood out to me between the trees. I dismounted and grabbed my bow, nocking in an arrow. I walked forward to where what looked like very smooth stone glinted in the moonlight. I touched it warily, feeling the cool rock under my palm. It was a curved wall, a part of some building, maybe? *What weirdo built a random tower in the middle of Mythland?* I thought, tilting my head up, rain stinging my eyes as I saw that the rock wall continued upward for as tall as the massive shuishan trees. I pushed aside some ferns and wove in between trees, running my hand

110

along the stone that just kept going and going, curving into the tower I had assumed it would become. The creature in my bag was awake now, and crying. It probably didn't like the cold. And Siri trotted obediently behind me, the key in between her fangs as she panted and became soaked in the downpour. *The key, the key!* I thought, overcome with excitement and letting her drop it into my hands. *Keys open doors, Siri found a key, and even if this didn't mean Destan, it means solid protection for us for at least a night.*

I continued going around the building until I felt a change of texture. It still wasn't a door, but it was glass. A window. I peered inside and saw complete darkness, not a speck of light. I knocked timidly, scared I might break the glass. No answer. Harder. Still no response or hint of movement inside. I jogged around more, tripping over roots and patting down the stone for a door, bow slung over my shoulder, searching. Nothing. The first clash of thunder shook the earth, bringing Mythland to its knees before the sky. I struggled back to my feet and went around the tower another three times before accepting there was no door. Just hopelessly smooth, mossy, stone.

I urged the gears in my brain to keep turning, to keep from freezing up like the rest of me. *C'mon Raine, there's no such thing as a building without an entrance, there has to be a way in.* Siri barked at me, her eyes bright green through the blur of rain and wind. I sprinted back to her, flinching at another persistent clap of thunder. Even the sky was frustrated with me.

I stared imploringly at Siri, patting her nose as she continued whining and pawing the ground. She knew something, she'd found the key she must be trying to tell me something now. She wrenched her head out from under my palm and rubbed it hard at the leaf-coated ground. Over and over. Heart racing, I knelt and began shoving away the leaves, my fingers instantly recognizing something hard and grainy, like wood. Lightning illuminated the woods for a brief moment and with the leaves swept aside, I gazed for a clear moment at a round wooden door. In the center was a rusted-over keyhole, and I jabbed the key in hard through the peeling metal cover and twisted it carefully to the right. Even in the deafening downpour of rain, I heard the definite click of the hatch being unlocked.

Not daring to breathe, I lifted up the soggy door with a scrape of wood against stone and eased myself down, hands finding rungs of a ladder. Siri leapt down once I'd landed on the dirt floor of the dug-out tunnel and we huddled together. Scared that I might be closing myself in, I didn't slide the cover back over the hole and instead felt my way in the dark. This had to be connected to the tower right? Like a secret way in? I prayed it wouldn't only lead to another den of tiangou.

I crouched down, shivering inside the pitch black tunnel and digging through my knapsack for my sparking stones. The creature had freed two arms from the scarf and clawed desperately at my wrists, chirping. Siri brought her face to the mouth of my rucksack and barked, shutting up the creature instantly. It disappeared inside the scarf, and I felt a little bad for it. But there wasn't any time to make amends. I found a spark stone and struck it hard against the wall again and again, fire finally dancing off in specks of gold and catching on a torch fastened onto the wall. I heaved the torch off and tiptoed down the hall, the dual sound of Siri's and my breathing the only sound. The floor felt saggy and well-worn beneath my boots, older than anything still standing on Thgindim. But it felt safe nonetheless and soon I found a ladder ahead of me, with rungs that were rusted and fuzzy with thick spiderwebs. I saw a mouse scrabble into its hole as it came into the firelight. I patted Siri's nose before easing myself up the ladder, and waited for her to reach up with her paws on the landing and then leap up.

There weren't any more torches to guide me, but in the dark I could see the faint silhouette of a chandelier hanging from the high ceiling. I took a step forward and ran into a table, Siri knocking over a chair. We fumbled through the dark, feeling a wooden table and three chairs, one of them more of a high chair, as if for a baby. It was so peculiar, this entire place seemed like it had risen out of a dream and yet the cold sogginess of my sweater and tangles in Siri's fur reminded me it all had to be real. The room ended up being smaller than I'd imagined, and I stubbed my toe on the bottom step of a staircase.

Siri whined softly behind me and I stroked her sides to reassure her, tentatively going up the steps and discovering more torches. I lit them each and came to the second floor room. Now that I had some light, I noticed that gemstones were scattered on the floor in places, and faded tapestries were strung high on some walls. The stories embroidered had bene lost with age and damage, but I could still tell they had been woven from expensive silk. I had never been told of a Mythland kingdom throughout all of school, but then again, I was told only lies about Fluxaria, so I guess it wasn't that much of a surprise that there could've been Mythland civilization at some point. But then...how old *was* Thgindim and Fluxaria, really? How long had we been separate mountains if there was an ancient structure in the middle of a valley supposedly created only to separate us so long ago? Dust and cobwebs aside, this place was eerily well-preserved and seemingly untouched.

This floor had two rooms, the first of which was a bathing room, with a big brass basin filled with leaves that had blown in through the shattered window. The water pump attached dripped dark liquid, and a vanity glittered with ancient bottles of soaps and perfumes. Then, all of a sudden, I heard movement in the next room, and I stopped, sharply in my tracks. Siri pawed at the floor, going up the first few stairs to the next level of the tower. She whimpered for me to follow, but the sound had put me on edge and I instead left the bathroom and raised my torch to survey the hallway. An empty bowl, still dirty with remnants of rice, sat in the middle of the hall. I eyed it fearfully, my heart pounding hard against my ribs as I walked slowly toward it. The torchlight revealed there was significantly less dust on this level. And more of what looked like fresh mud stuck to the floors and walls.

From the next room rose a ghostly wailing, melting deafly in my ears until it became more distinct, more familiar— the low hoot of a meadowlark, a clear and beautiful song that I'd heard so many times drifting through the meadow. I dropped my bow and ran. I couldn't breathe as Siri yelped for me to come back and thunder shook the tower. I barged into the room where the flute was playing; the flute that sang like a bird, played by calloused hands that I missed so much and needed to hold again. The sound cut off. A staredown began between me and the shadowed figure sitting on the floor. The flute lowered from his lips, a collective breath whispering against the walls of the room. I strode forward, no longer able to wait, to guess, to be without him, and I held the torch between our faces, finally seeing him.

No. Seeing *her*.

Big, dark, owlish eyes staring back at me in wonder; her black hair in a low ponytail and her tan cheeks bruised and scratched. "Raine?" Irene asked, her usually lively voice low and hoarse. "Am I dreaming?" She touched her face and pinched it, gasping and then touching mine. "Are *you* dreaming? You...you found me?"

I nodded, a hot tear skidding down my cheek as it sank in that I was mistaken once again. I had the urge to hug her, to cry with her about all of the terrible things that happened in Mythland; to strangle and scream at her for leaving us when we needed her most, for stealing Siri; to grab her and shake her back and forth until she made sense of the mess she'd caused for me and for Destan. But all I could do was stand there. And stare.

"Raine?" she probed, nervously touching my arm. Siri barked from the next room, and Irene's eyes lit up. "*Siri?* How did you find her? I

lost her forever ago...damn...say something? Please?"

I swallowed, my lips trembling to form words as my eyes glued themselves to the little wooden flute in her hand. I took it from her fist, examining the smoothly carved body and finely-drilled holes Destan had given what had once been a broken piece of tree. Clearing my throat, but still not looking at her, I managed to speak. "How do you have...Destan...?"

"Is here," she said immediately, her cheeks flushing red as she took a step back from me. As her words registered, as the flute shook in my hands, as lightning illuminated the room a cold white, her expression began to twist itself into something horrible. She let out one broken sob, covering her mouth with her hand and looking up into my eyes as her own shone in a flood of sudden tears. "Raine..." she began to say, her voice garbled behind her hand, "...I just...I can't take you to him—"

"Why?" I whispered, heart pounding as I came closer to her. "Where is he? Where's Destan, Irene?"

She shook her head, turning away from me and slamming a fist at the wall. "You don't *understand*, Raine!" Irene wiped harshly at her tears, speaking through gritted teeth as her forehead pressed against the stone wall. "He can't see you...and I c-can't let you see him. You c-can't see him like this..."

"Like what?" I demanded, voice rising as I reached down for the spy and pulled her up by the shoulders. She wrenched out of my hold, too strong to be kept in place by a scrawny thing like me. She ducked down the hallway and I pursued her, my gaze trained on the swinging of her ponytail. Irene shoved open a door and quickly shut it, just a second before I extended a hand to grab it. Furious, I grabbed the doorknob and pulled, hard as I could, shoving at the door she held in place from the other side. "*IRENE!*" I screamed, "OPEN THE FUCKING DOOR, LET ME SEE HIM, DAMMIT!" I backed away, and pushing off with my feet from the opposite wall, I charged; ramming the wood hard with my shoulder and feeling a hot numbness tingle along the right side of my body as it made contact with the door. There was a yelp on the other side, and in the instant Irene was impacted and released the door handle, I grabbed the knob and turned it, leaning all of my weight against it and pushing against her on the other side as she tried to close it again. The force of her strength was too much. Every limb of mine quaked in surrender, but my mind convinced my hands to not let go until I was inside. I continued pushing back, kicking my heavy boots at the door and screaming.

"No, Raine, stop it, you'll injure yourself, idiot!" she called back, a noticeable strain in her voice. We were both wearing out. "I can't let you in here!"

"Why not? Why can't I see him?" I said. My throat felt raw and shredded from all of the shrieking. At some point, Siri had appeared by me again and was barking her lungs out, scratching at the door with her big paws, claws shooting out and digging into the wood. And with all of our might against hers, Irene leapt away from the door. All of the energy I'd been penting up against her propelled me through the doorway at full speed, Siri bounding in behind me. I slammed face-first onto the soggy floorboards, the wind knocked out of me as I coughed and gasped.

Before even getting to my knees, I was hit with a horrible smell. A dense, cloying scent that coated the back of my throat and burned. Trembling, I rose from the floor, leaning against the wall for support as the scene swam before my eyes and stench teased at my gag reflex. I was in what appeared to be an old study; a shabby brown desk and chairs with ruined upholstery, shelves of books and dusty jars of supplies lining the walls. What smelled so badly I couldn't deduce, until I noticed what was lying on the floor. There was something long and oddly shaped in the center of the room, hidden beneath a tapestry Irene must have yanked off of the wall to cover whatever it was. Irene had shrunk herself to fit in the farthest corner of the room, her knees drawn to her chest.

"You want to see him?" she asked me. Her words danced dizzily into my ears, and I struggled to keep breathing the putrid air as she continued. "Is smelling him enough for you? Do you get it now?"

I shook my head, unable to come any closer. I could see the words forming on her lips. I stole them from her. "Destan's dead."

∞ R.R.S ∞

chapter eleven

I touched the drape Irene had laid over him and then pulled it off in a quick motion, not letting my mind build up barriers to keep me from seeing it. Destan Attila Abrasha was, in fact, dead. No longer in this body. I knew it was true because seeing him made Siri howl at the top of her lungs and collapse at the side of his corpse. I knew it was true because his face had been marred by a long, deep red gash stretching from his right temple in a diagonal line down to his jaw. Because his skin looked like wax and was cold and hard to the touch. Because his face wasn't his own and instead some weird recreation of him; a doll or sculpture, but no, not him. Not Destan. Not the boy from the woods who could shoot and laugh and give the best advice and was so alive that even when he died I expected him to somehow remain and keep smiling and calling me Bluehead from the spirit world; enter my dreams and be there.

But seeing him now, I knew that he wasn't coming back. Had he already been dead when I was in the tree cave and abandoned the red beanie he loved so much? Dead while Tieran forced himself inside of me or when Lilah's drugs catapulted me into those nightmares? Destan was gone, dead, and no longer thinking of me in any form. He wasn't loving me or looking for me, he wasn't going to be able to save me. He wouldn't march into Fluxaria holding my hand as people cheered for us. He wasn't going to do anything anymore except lay here and smell worse and get eaten by bugs. He'd lay here in a dreamless sleep, no longer existent, as if he never existed because the only proof he ever did was the immeasurable pain inside of me and memories I would eventually forget.

"Irene, what happened?" I said, or at least I think I said it. All I knew was suddenly I was on the floor with the Fluxarian beside me, sitting with her muscular legs pulled to her chest, her chin resting on the top of her knees.

Her voice came out in a gentle whisper. "I don't know. I was following a trail I thought he'd left–"

"Of arrows?" I interjected, and Irene licked her lips, then nodded slowly.

"Mmhmm. Arrows. And I wasn't even sure if it was you or him, you both had the same kind...right? Maybe? Well, after finding, like, four, the trail just stopped." She flickered her big black eyes on mine, sadness casting shadows under them. "I found him not too far from here, curled up under some rocks and his face covered in blood."

If my stomach hadn't shrivelled up moments before, now it was disintegrating inside of me and I felt the urge to throw up again. "Blood..." I repeated dumbly, examining her face and then shaking my head, hot anger boiling in my throat. The question spilled out before I could stop myself. "Irene...how could you leave us?"

The spy rolled her eyes, absently picking at her fingernails as she muttered, "Raine, it wasn't like that..."

"Wasn't like what? We were defending you," I whispered, exasperated, and my heart rate increasingly quick. I stood, "Even after you ran away, we defended you and got kicked out."

Irene jumped to her feet as well and jabbed me hard in the chest with her finger. "Look here, Raine. You and your boyfriend would've been banished whether or not you told your Council that taking me under your wing is justified by my winning personality and peaceful

120

nature or whatever. I couldn't have helped. I would've just gotten my brains blown out and you'd be here anyway. So don't, all of a sudden, try to pin Destan being dead on me!"

I pushed her finger down and tears rushed down my cheeks. "But why did you leave without even saying goodbye, without warning us about the bomb after you cracked the code?" my voice broke. I suddenly wished to be mute again. "You just took off with Siri! Destan and I didn't know what to think, we didn't know if you had just scammed us or used us or..."

"Oh shit, you know that's not true, Raine. I had to go because– I don't know if you remember– I was trying to prevent a war."

"*We* were trying to prevent a war," I said, "we were in this together."

She scoffed, "By choice."

"Yes, by choice," I said, pressing my palms to my eyes and then massaging my temples, "and you didn't give us a choice! You just...left. You left us, even after we protected you, even after you promised you'd stick around until we knew what was happening!"

Irene came closer and I shoved her roughly away, stumbling against the wall as the body's odour overcame me completely. I could still see Destan's corpse from the corner of my eye as I keeled over and vomited up an empty stomach onto the tattered floorboards of the tower. I pressed my forehead to the wood's cool, grainy texture, willing myself to disappear.

"Raine?" her voice rose from behind me. "Are you all right? Does...does this puking thing happen a lot?"

"Go away, Irene," I rasped.

A hand latched onto my shoulder and shoved me into a sitting position. I was met with her fierce, dark eyes. "No. I'm not going away, not again, not ever. Even if you want me to." Irene let go of me and got to her feet. Immediately, she bowed and some of her hair slipped free from the elastic tie and fell around her face. Her voice whispered through the curtain of black hair. "I'm sorry, Raine Ylevol. Sincerely sorry, really, really sorry. I messed up. I just...I got so scared and I panicked." Tears dropped to the floor, leaving dark blotches as her voice began to shake and she sank from the sturdy bow onto her knees, crying, "I didn't mean for anyone to die, I should have left the moment you found me. I'm so fucking sorry, Raine, I'm so sorry."

Too exhausted to argue any longer, I gave in and threw my arms around her. She reacted instantly, burrowing in closer and squeezing me so tightly it became hard to breathe and the wounds on my back seared under the pressure of her hands. We remained like that for a long while, until a thoughtless sort of calm fell over me. I couldn't tear my eyes from the body in the middle of the room, and before the horrible truth of his death would set in again and totally shut me down, Irene eased me up to stand and guided me hastily out of the room. The door slammed behind us, sealing in the stench of death and Siri's wails.

Goosebumps peppered my skin as the drafty tower air frothed around me and the spy pulled me up the spiral staircase. "This place *does* exist...right?" I asked, my feet like dead weights as I tried to keep moving.

"Dunno, maybe we've both lost it," she laughed shortly, plucking up the torch I'd lit earlier and handing it to me as she bounded up to the landing. "I'd heard rumours of Mythland people, but never anything concrete or believable. But now, here it is, stone and mortar and dust. Guess both of our mountains missed something." She fiddled with her knife in the lock and then heaved it open, returning to me and helping me get through.

The room we'd entered had a floor covered in rug after rug, and a huge bed of old, moth-bitten pillows and thick blankets. Tiny little lightbulbs bobbed from the ceiling, some shattered, some blinking on, off. The pointed tower roof had a big chunk of it missing, probably blown off in a storm, and the tiled edges waved in the wind like the frayed ends of torn paper. Rain poured in through the hole, leaving puddles all over the wood and carpet despite the makeshift tarp of curtains Irene had presumably tied together and attempted to secure below the gape. She led me over to the bed, by the large circular window with half of its glass knocked out. Rain was blowing in and soaking the mattress, and so the spy drew the blinds and I felt the cold pricks of water ceasefire. Fire. Irene lit a fire in the fireplace. She stood back and waited for the pathetic sparks to hang onto the wood, her fingers drumming increasingly faster on the wall

122

as the fire failed and failed again. I remembered her impatience. Remembered Destan's patience. No more Destan.

I swayed on the spot, and in a flash Irene was there and supporting me. "Okay, time to sleep, missy. That's the best thing for now. I'll join you soon," she sighed, draping me across the bed and blowing on the dusty covers. She tucked me in, shooing out some small rodent from between the sheets and trading my sopping pillow for a dry one from the dry side of bed. The room looked gold and bleary through my half-shut eyes. I tried to mumble a thank you but felt the storm of sobs rolling up my throat and immediately swallowed them down, trapping them in my stomach. "I'm right downstairs and will be back once I'm done dealing with the..." she paused, her jaw clenching as she tried to come up with something less horrible than *stench* or *rotting corpse*, "...dealing with the mess. Just cleaning up a bit to make things more comfortable. Do you need anything right now? Food, drink, some more light...?"

Irene's voice faded into nothing but a slur, the candlelight growing into a sun hoisted high in the room, blinding me. And then I knew I was falling to sleep or some state of unconsciousness because everything became beautiful and I didn't hurt any longer. I reached up at the light and felt it warmly bathe my hands. I slowly pulled my hand down and found that nestled in my palm was a smattering of stars. So warm, so warm and soft. I ran a finger over an edge and then withdrew it, feeling a keen prick. Blood dribbled down my thumb. *Sharp stars, huh?* I thought, sitting up. Cold washed over me like a bucket of river water and in an instant I was no longer in the tower's top floor.

I watched snow fall from the emerald boughs of pine trees. It was nearly morning, the darkness now more silver than black. Two naked teenagers were inside of a cave, their shredded clothing tucked closely over their torsos as they shivered in the cold. The boy was blond and muscular and breathing quietly. The girl was scrawny, with weird blue hair, and a sheen of sweat dewy on her forehead despite the freezing winter night. Even though it was chilly, it had been nearly the warmest night of the year for them. Us, them. Destan and I. After we'd bonded. My soul seemed to flow into my body lying on the cold stone beside him.

"So," he said, in the soft voice that the end of night commanded.

"So," I replied, too nervous to meet his eyes.

Destan rolled over onto his side, a curious expression on his face. We were so close to each other that I noticed emotions in his eyes that I'd never seen before. It wasn't the usual playful gleam, or the intense hardness they took on whenever he was concentrating on his shooting or thinking deeply about something. Lying so close to him, I was now able to see that he had a child's eyes; big and bright with a hidden innocence, taking in everything they saw with wonder and awe. Considering how I felt about him, I was sure he was seeing the same look of enchantment in my own eyes.

After a few moments of silence, he smiled. He began to laugh. Quietly at first, and then more loudly, his shoulders shaking as it took over his whole body.

"What?" I asked, nudging his arm. "What's so hilarious?"

Destan shook his head, rolling onto his back and shielding his eyes as his laughter got louder. He began to splutter, trying to choke out works. "It's just...it's not that...Bluehead, I'm just so *happy*."

That elicited some laughter from me as well, a blush creeping into my cheeks as I tried not to be overcome like Destan was. "Try to be happy a little more quietly! Good grief, Destan," I said, going up on my elbows and putting my hand over his mouth. He couldn't stop, little tears beaded in the corners of his eyes, and he wriggled his head around until my hand was no longer stifling his guffaws. He took my face in his hands and kissed me, rolling over on top of me and trailing his fingertips over my belly. He took a jab at my ribs and I gasped, bursting with my own laughter and struggling beneath him as he tickled me. The cave echoed with a chorus of our hilarity for a good five minutes until we were over the initial funniness of the situation and returned to cuddling in close, out of breath.

"Well...I guess..." I began to say, a grin teasing the corner of my mouth, "that was...nice."

"*Nice?*" he repeated, turning to me in amusement. In a swift roll, Destan loomed over me again, his skin on my skin, his face so close to mine that his lashes brushed my nose. Fire travelled down my body. "Raine...I've never felt so *beautifully* close to anyone in my entire life as I feel close to you."

124

It was too good to believe. My eyes began to sting with tears I wouldn't allow to spill and ruin the happy moment. "Destan Abrasha," I whispered, smiling, "please, never leave me."

"Who said anything about leaving anyone?" He rolled his eyes, kissing my neck and along my collar bones, "And if anything...we're both wanted criminals, so we'll be disposed of together, right?" I knew he was trying to be funny. But the reminder made my skin crawl.

"Mmhmm," I murmured, trying to remain in awe of the softness of him and the moment itself, rather than worrying what we would do once we left this cave. Even as I smiled at him, stroking along his jaw lightly with my fingertips, Destan sensed the tension returning. He gazed down at me sadly, apparently waiting for me to say something. I glanced away, beginning to tremble. He climbed off of me, sitting up.

"Come here," he said, offering his arms and sliding me onto his lap. I nestled myself close to him, my face tucked to his chest and my calves dangling over his crossed legs. I pressed my wet eyes to his skin and twirled my fingers through the wispy layer of chest hairs, trying to calm down. My heart just wouldn't slow down.

"Raine, you're shaking so badly..." he whined, softly, tightening his arms around me and burying his mouth in my hair. It had tumbled out of its usual bun and now was messy and everywhere. Destan had gotten it in his mouth so many times while we were kissing that just moments ago it had been the last straw, and we'd decided to take a much needed break from all of the new closeness we were experiencing. "Why are you shaking? Did I...do something wrong?"

"No, no, not at all. It was...you were perfect," I whispered. "I just hate that this is probably our first and last time. Since we'll soon be...disposed of."

Destan cursed quietly. "Fuck. I shouldn't have said that. Bluehead, we don't have a death sentence yet. Irene's probably going to come in riding on Siri and scream because of our lack of clothing and save us. The only thing to worry about is all the teasing we'll get from her once we're escaping through Mythland, or something."

I looked up into his eyes. "You really think she's going to come?"

"I doubt she wouldn't. We came for her when she was trapped inside the mountain. I'm positive she's on her way now with some hot tea and dumplings."

"Mmm, that'd be so nice," I mused.

"Well..." Destan bit his lip, walking two fingers up my stomach and circling one above my breast. "I'm sure her dumplings aren't as nice as *yours*..."

I smacked his hand away, gasping in fake disgust but unable to keep heat from flooding into my cheeks. "Destan Attila Abrasha! That was very uncalled for!" I covered my chest with my hands and moved to leave his lap, but felt his arms wind tightly around my waist, hugging me close.

"Don't gooo," he moaned, nuzzling my neck and kissing my cheek. "I apologize for the dirty comment about your boobies."

I shook my head. "Really, Destan? 'Boobies?' You really know how to talk to girls."

"I've never called myself suave."

"Good, because you'd be lying."

He tickled me again, brushing my bangs out of my eyes and kissing me deeply. His mouth was honey and sunshine in the winter night, his skin and body melted into mine until I felt we could never separate. I placed my hands on his chest and gently pushed him down, back to the ground with my body following his. As he kissed me, his hands slid down the small of my back, pressing his hipbones to mine as we kissed long and deep and all my anxious shaking quieted.

"I will be with you infinitely, Raine," he whispered, kissing my neck and trailing his lips behind my ear. "I love you. That's something that will never go away." His finger brushed the pendant he'd made me and then stroked down my chest, warming me to my core. And as our bodies melded, I felt it all start to fade– the chill of the air, the encompassing presence of the cave –and I blinked once again in the stoic darkness of my room, my body still vibrating from the memory of his touch.

I sat up, breathing raggedly, disoriented. Beside me, someone stirred, and I tugged the dusty covers off of me and tucked them in around Irene. Her face was so peaceful. She, too, must have been somewhere better in her dreams. I slowly slid off of the bed, making the floor creak ominously. It was quiet now, and much darker. Every candle and torch had been extinguished by the storm, and now only a shower of downy white snow fluttered in through the hole in the roof.

Entranced, I walked timidly forward, extending a hand and catching big, feathery, white flakes in my palm. I watched as they gave my skin a cold kiss of farewell, and then disappeared into a thin pool of water on the floor. I shook out my hand, padding across the floor to use the chamber pot in the corner, and then wrapping myself in blanket after blanket.

I sat on the ledge of the broken window, admiring the snowfall, rubbing my lips thoughtfully. Destan's kiss still lingered and lingered, even long after I'd resurfaced from the memory. A pang struck my heart and I gasped, refusing to cry any more tonight. I got up and wandered the room, trying to take my mind off of the night we bonded. There was a tall oak bookcase stacked with thick leather-bound novels and heaps of ivory rice paper scrolls. A wardrobe whose doors were ornately painted with lotus blossoms and clouds sagged against the wall, one of the doors hanging off its hinges. I made my way over to it, tentatively opening it up so as not to wake the spy still snoozing in the bed. I was shocked to see it was in fact still packed with clothing. Lovely, warm, woollen dresses and skirts and sweaters. Very different from the scratchy knitwork on Underbrush, and yet not quite as flashy and pompous-looking as something produced in Canopia for upper-level Thgindimmers. I sifted through the wardrobe, discovering a handful of more formal items made of shimmering brocade, with tall collars and braided clasps.

Feeling suddenly uncomfortable wearing something from the camp where so many horrible things had occurred, I took off the worn sweater I'd stolen and I tugged down one of the warm-looking dresses. I shook it out, watching sparkles of grit and dust and little dead spiders sprinkle to the floor. I wrung it out once more and threw it up and down to make sure I wouldn't be covered in ancient dust or critters, and then I slipped it on over my leggings. It was a near perfect fit, except strangely tight around my stomach. I blew off some dust from the full length mirror on the inside of the wardrobe and looked myself over, a bit bewildered. I turned to the side and gazed at my profile. Right above my hips, my belly sloped out just ever so slightly. *Either I somehow gained weight while starving at Shuishan camp, or the previous owner of this dress was even tinier than me*, I thought, considering myself in the mirror. Even my chest looked more prominent than usual. *Maybe*

Mythland girls are built small, I decided, shrugging off the thoughts and moving to shut the wardrobe door. I stopped when I heard the squeak, and peered down into the bottom of the structure to see my rucksack joined by Irene's own big, black spy bag. Something inside my rucksack wriggled, and I slapped my forehead in frustration at for leaving Chan's creature inside there to suffocate.

Carefully, I undid the tie on my rucksack and groped inside for the little creature. My finger was snapped at, and I withdrew it, hissing as a crescent shaped incision began to bleed delicately. "I'm getting you out, idiot," I grumbled, opening the bag wider so that I could see where I was reaching. I grabbed the creature around the neck and midsection, holding it stiff so that it couldn't turn around and bite me again. It squeaked and squeaked and twisted itself in my hands, much harder to keep hold of than I'd thought it would be. Its whiskers and tail whipped my wrists in protest, and its pointed snout managed to make contact with my forearm, leading me to dropping it in fear the moment I felt its hot breath whoosh from its nose onto my skin.

But as it dropped, something curious occurred. It had only been a short fall, and yet in the split second before it hit the ground, its body had seemed to change form. The serpentine body flattened to be no thicker than my red hair ribbon, and before it belly-flopped onto the floor, it floated and swayed in the air. Once it touched down, its body shifted from being thin, to being thick once more, and its claws clicked on the floor as it began to try and scamper away from me.

"You can fly, can't you?" I whispered, watching it in disbelief as it stumbled around, apparently trying to get closer to the window for an escape. I wanted to test my theory. But not at the price of it plunging to its death from the window or waking up Irene with more incessant chirping. Thinking fast, I returned to the wardrobe, flipping through the rack of clothes until I could find one ugly or damaged enough to sacrifice. One sweater dress was a disturbing shade of mustard yellow, with half of one sleeve unravelled. I yanked on the yarn until the rest of it came undone. And just as the creature had struggled its way to the window sill and was sniffing air, I bounded over and quickly tied a loop of yarn around its neck. It wasn't tight to the skin, but I had done a triple knot to make sure it would remain secure. I kept the other end of the very long leash in my fist as I nudged the thing towards the window.

It looked back at me in shock, sniffing, as if to say, *"Okay, so now you want me to escape? Make up your mind, woman!"*

"You were in the wild-blue-sky-dynasty, yeah?" I murmured, picking up and cradling the creature in my palms as it stared at me. My heart was beating so fast. What was I doing? Did I really want to just throw my one and only connection to Chantastic out the window to confirm my crazy childhood drawings? To build up just another ephemeral distraction from the fact that I'd found the love of my life dead downstairs, not even a whole day ago?

I suppose so.

I climbed up onto the window ledge by the jagged area of missing glass, and without another thought, launched the creature into the wind. I held tight to the end of the string, watching the pool of yarn on the floor get sucked up and out the window as the creature plummeted. My heart hammered and slammed against my ribs and then skipped a beat as the string pulled taut. Dread coated my blood in ice. I had most likely just broken the neck or even beheaded the thing, tossed it into the snow which was against my one order to keep it warm. But before the guilt could completely consume me, the string loosened, as if receding, and in an instant I'd climbed completely through the window, legs dangling over the edge as I squinted through the falling snow. There was no glimpse of blue scales or flickering whiskers from my height. However, once I lowered my eyes I could see the string being pulled in a circular motion, and then emerging within the white was what appeared to be a shimmering teal ribbon; riding the wind and gradually ascending.

It was just as I had drawn it years and years before. The creature needed no wings; it simply glided and followed the flow of air, occasionally clawing at it to change direction, and then swirling farther away. Don't get me wrong, the newborn creature had not yet figured out how to incorporate grace in its soaring, but just the fact that it had been in a shell not so long ago and now could fly was astounding. It didn't seem to know what to do with its tail, occasionally dropping clumsily and its body shifting back to roundness whenever the tail lagged behind and didn't keep up with the direction of the wind. Its dark eyes were wide with wonder and gazing around at the trees and snow-covered tower, and the point at which I hesitantly tugged on the leash was when I saw it about to dive straight into the stone wall.

The gentle tug was enough of a signal to get the creature gliding back towards the tower. To navigate the opposite flow of air, its body rose over and under the opposing currents, making it to me in no time. I released the string, reaching and grabbing the creature around the middle just as its body seemed to return to its non-flying state, and I cradled it closely to my chest. It chirped and squeaked noisily in protest, long whiskers slapping against my chin and tail curling twice around my wrist.

I was suddenly overcome with emotion. This thing, serpent, dragon, spirit, whatever it was: could fly. It could fly to Chantastic, to home with a letter tucked in its claws. I could know how she was, what was happening with my family, with Thgindim, everything. And I could reassure her I was still alive. She had given me two instructions. *Keep it warm*, and *reach me*. I pulled some of the silk and brocade dresses I knew me nor Irene would have any use for, and made a small bed by the fireplace. Irene's inferno had dwindled to red-hot, smoking logs, and I set the creature into the little nest I'd made for it. It sniffed around the dusty heap of fabric, pressing into it with its claws and smoothing out an area to rest. As it curled up and laid its head on its tail, eyes peacefully shut, I considered what I should call it. "Thing" and "creature" just didn't do the thing-creature justice, and I didn't know if it was a boy or girl. All I knew, was that it had come from Chantastic, someone I loved most in the world. So, with her original name Chan Ai, in mind, I decided to name the creature Ai. Calling it that made me feel like half of her was here with me. Chan was there, Ai was here. And once I figured out when the solstice was and I could strap a note onto Ai's foot and send her off, the second part of Chantastic's instructions to me would be fulfilled.

I smiled, envisioning her seeing Ai come flying to her doorstep, as if by magic. And then my thoughts wandered to imagining myself somehow flying on the back of a much bigger version of Ai, seeing Chan's face glow with happiness, flowers in her hair, and I'm running into her arms and–

I was thinking about her kiss again. Guilt punched me hard in the stomach, and I scrambled up from the ground. *He just* died, *Raine. How dare you even...how could you...you are such an awful person, you should've been the one who died, not him, not Destan.* I covered my ears, unable to block out the nasty thoughts flooding my mind, my throat constricting in pain. *He's dead, he's dead, he's dead.* I dragged myself off of the ground, trying to keep from having another meltdown and walking to the window to get some air. Morning was just dawning on Mythland. From this floor of the tower, I could see that the structure was only half as tall as a shuishan tree. The tower seemed to be situated on a risen area of land, much like an island, in the middle of a murky swamp, surrounded by fungus-covered trees and mossy rocks.

As I curled my fingers around the ledge of the window, I felt my fingertips brush something much like silky paper. Hanging from two large hooks along the window's edge was a gigantic basket of long-dead flowers. The soil they'd been planted in had nearly hardened to rock, the stems wiry and tough. The flowers were deep red. The colour of blood. *I need to do something for him. One last thing.* I thought, tugging off some crispy blossoms and tiptoeing from the room. Irene continued to snore, draped across the width of the queen-sized bed.

My hand shook on the doorknob to the room where his body lay. I didn't so much notice a smell anymore, and the nausea had all gone, but my feet had seemed to take roots in the doorway. Turning the door handle and ripping my socked feet from the floor before they could grow any deeper where I was, I passed quickly into the room. Irene hadn't returned the drape over his body, he lay flat on his back, eyes closed, the wound on his face still open and fresh but no longer caked in blood or pus. Irene had cleaned him up while I'd been upstairs; brushed his hair as smoothly as it could go, washed the dirt from his face, straightened his grey woollen coat and buttoned every last brassy button to the top of the collar. He could have been asleep, and yet even I hadn't ever seen him so free of dirt under his nails or knots in his curls. Siri slept in a silver curl at his feet.

I walked over and knelt beside him, reaching into my skirt where I'd stowed the flowers. I had beheaded every blossom in the window box, leaving a graveyard of weeds and broken stems in their place. My lips pressed tightly together, I silently placed the scarlet flowers in his hair; imagining his red beanie there. I laid petals over the long red gash stretching across his face, and then I took his ice-cold hand in mine and closed my eyes, imagining him alive and warm.

"Destan, I'm trying to believe you," I whispered, eyes shut tightly, scared that if I cried again I wouldn't be able to stop. "That you're still with me. It just feels so horribly like pretending, though." Lightning lit up the entire room with white, and I jumped, my body suddenly overcome with tremors. "I love you infinitely, t-too. I just wish your heart was s-still b-beating. It's so hard to feel you. We've been apart so long, I don't think I c-can believe you're somehow here or in my heart or something because I'm just so empty. Like not even I'm inside of me anymore. There's just all of this pain, all of the time," I gasped, breathless and using all of my might to keep from weeping. It didn't work. I let go of his hand to wipe at my eyes, but then sobs began rising from my throat, and I was crying so hard I couldn't catch my breath. "But because you promised me, I'll believe you. I'll believe you're still with me. This is me believing you," I said, forcing my lips to smile, "if you're really here, you see this, right? A smile. If you're really with me, I'm...I'm going to be fine. I'll keep going and I'll be fine." I opened one eye and peeked at him almost expectantly. His body lay still and vacant on the stone floor. I let go of his hand and paced away, rubbing my eyes and cursing under my breath. I felt insane and more alone than ever.

Standing in the middle of the room, I wrapped my arms around myself, closing my eyes and pretending they were Destan's, not my stick-thin arms, but his strong, lean arms to protect me, hold me. But it wasn't working, and I fell to my knees, covering my face with my palms and shaking violently. There was sudden movement behind me and I felt guilty for waking Irene. She gasped, and then I heard her cough pointedly, probably after seeing how I'd adorned Destan's corpse with the silly dead flowers.

"R-Raine?" her voice was strangled and low.

"Please let me be alone," I whispered, pressing so hard against my eyes that I saw galaxies and stars and an imprint of my own eyeballs. I could hear her coming closer, her steps unbalanced. Had she been crying too?

"How...Raine?"

"Irene, please..." I sobbed softly, lowering my hands as she rested her own on my shoulder. I reached back to push it off, but as I touched it, I felt ratty knit fabric, not her smooth tanned skin. I froze, gasping for air within my flow of tears, as the pad of my thumb smoothed over it. I stayed planted where I was, dropping my hand as strong arms wound around me and raspy weeping sank into my back. I rolled my shoulders and turned around, facing the living corpse of Destan Attila Abrasha.

chapter twelve

I screamed, running from the room and up the stairs so fast that I swore I could hear extra footsteps thundering behind me. Siri's barks were high-pitched and shrieking, and yet she did not follow behind me. I tripped forward and grabbed a step, climbing up with my hands, hyperventilating and wheezing as I ran straight into Irene. "Raine, what happened?" she asked, seizing me by the shoulders and yanking me to my feet. I shook my head back and forth, taking her hand and dragging the spy behind me into the bedroom, my thoughts racing, my throat raw from gasping for breath that wouldn't come.

"I...I saw...Irene I *saw* him," I choked, trying earnestly to open the door, but fumbling with my trembling hands. Irene kicked it in, unjamming it and pushing me inside. Everything was blurry and bright and scary, and there was a horrible screeching noise ringing through my head I didn't realize was coming from my own mouth until Irene clamped a hand over it and the sound cut off immediately. She started talking at me fast and quiet and I was so thankful she wasn't one of those people who screamed at you when you were acting nutty. Things began to slow down and I began to breathe again, breathe again...

"Raine, I know. I know, it's horrible," she said, her brows drawn together in concern. She made slow motions with her hands, showing me the rhythm I should try breathing. She was still ten breaths behind me, and I could not slow down. "But he looked a little better now, right? All cleaned up? Why did you go back down–"

There was a loud crashing sound on the steps, and Irene leapt to her feet, suddenly very alert. I grabbed her arm but she shrugged my hand off, putting a finger to her lips and pointing at the wardrobe. I hesitated, still out of sorts, but then came deep, throaty gasps from the stairwell, and heavy steps fell closer and closer to the door that definitely did not belong to wolf downstairs. Irene urged me toward the wardrobe, opening the door and hissing, "Inside, *now!* Let me deal with this motherfucker, 'kay?"

I nodded, melting into the hanging dresses, careful not to trod on my knapsack. There was a thump on the roof of the wardrobe, and I guessed Irene had jumped on top. She probably wanted a good launching point for nailing the intruder. A voice was calling out unintelligibly, the sound muffled by the thick clothes. I sat, pressing my eyes into my knees, my heart banging in my chest as I tried to erase what I had seen downstairs. The hand on my shoulder, what had felt like his gloves and calloused fingertips. The gaunt and gruesome face with flower petals falling from his hair, so close to mine after I'd turned around, breath like death, hot and blowing on my skin. Had I completely hallucinated? I'd seen things that weren't there after Lilah had drugged me, and this had felt no different, no less horrifying. But then...who was coming up the stairs?

The bedroom door squealed on its hinges as it opened, and big feet fell clumsily on the floor. Now I could hear what he was saying, clear as a bell. *My name.* "R-Raine?" he called, in a scratchy voice, followed by coughing and more gasping. "Bluehead?"

I looked up from my knees, opening the wardrobe door a crack to see through. But as I moved my hand to see if it could really be Destan the ghost, Destan the zombie, any kind of Destan, there was a shrill battle cry and the wardrobe shook under the force of Irene jumping from her perch. Two cries of shock, the smack of a body getting pinned spread-eagle to the floor. I struggled to stand, pushing through the wardrobe with my shoulder and automatically joining the screaming match as I tried to process what was happening.

"WHY ARE YOU SCREAMING?!?!" Destan yelled, his grey eyes bloodshot, pupils dilated and huge as he scooted out from under Irene, looking around wildly.

"AAAAAAAAAAAAAAAAA!!!!!" Irene replied, backtracking into the footboard of the bed, cursing and rubbing her backside in pain. "WHAT ARE YOU DOING ALIVE?! YOU SMELLED! DESTAN, YOU FUCKING SMELLED! YOU WERE DEAD DOWN THERE!"

"What?!" Destan shook his head, grabbing a chunk of his hair and looking in bewilderment at a flower petal. His eyes found me. I was no longer screaming, but stood dead silent in shock. "Bluehead," his voice broke, eyes dissolving into tears as he struggled to his feet and limped over to me. I didn't move as his hands enclosed around the tops of my arms, his mouth quivering as he touched his forehead to mine, his breath still hot and rotten on my face. "You're here...Bluehead, my gods, Bluehead you're alive..."

He wrapped his arms around me and pulled me tightly to him, his fingers raking through my hair and nose burying in my neck, shaking as he tried not to cry. My body wouldn't, couldn't respond. Slowly, my hands drifted to his waist, scared that if I touched him, he'd vanish. That he really was a ghost and there was nothing to hold. But as my hands laid on the small of his back, I felt warmth. He was still too cold, his skin still felt wrong and strange beneath my fingers, but there was the definite presence of blood flowing, pumping from a heart that worked, a heart that meant he was alive, he was alive. He was alive.

My fingers curled, my eyes welling with tears as I threw my arms around him and squeezed as hard as I could. He lifted me off of the ground, holding me even tighter, speaking brokenly, drawing back again and again to gaze at me, touch my face, make sure I was real as well. "Don't ever leave me, not ever again. Raine, I thought I'd lost you for good, I thought..." He trailed off, looking at me for a moment. He wrinkled his nose, setting me down and breathing into his hand. He sniffed the collar of his coat, eyes going wide and then wider as he touched his face and flinched, lost in bewilderment at the sight of blood and more flower petals.

"I told you. You reek," Irene said, sitting on the edge of the bed and shaking her head slowly in disbelief. "You are so *fucking* lucky I couldn't find a decent shovel downstairs. You'd be six feet underground right about now." He glanced from her to me, clearly oblivious to whatever had gone on while he was...not present. Sort of dead.

"Why did you think I was dead? How did you two even find me?" then he crossed his arms, looking even more perplexed. "How did you even find *each other*?"

"It's a long story," I whispered, this being the first thing I'd said to him since we were blasted from the cannon into Mythland. His eyes softened again at the sound of my voice, and I fought the urge to run into his arms, rather than joining Irene on the bed. "You might have to sit down..."

"He is NOT sitting down in here," Irene scoffed. She looked him up and down in disgust, pointing a finger at his chest. "Actually–you aren't going in any room but the bathroom until you get this death-perfume off of you, you hear me, dude?"

He grinned, a smile that took a minute for me to take in and fully realize the beauty of seeing it outside of my dreams. Destan scratched his head, wrinkling his nose as he sniffed at his fingers. "I hear you. And the bathroom is which way...?"

"Your girlfriend can show you," she said, eyes darting to mine for a half-second and then returning to him. She smiled.

I bit my lip, averting my eyes to the floor and wishing I could control the flood of red that would be invading my cheeks at the thought of having to wash him. Swallowing my embarrassment, I looked up, nodding curtly and motioning for Destan to follow. "Okay. Yeah, um...just...come this way."

"Alrighty," he said, sticking his hands in his pockets and following behind me as I went swiftly down the steps. I didn't breathe through my nose, trying to fight the smell still clinging to him, and found the door to the washroom. I hesitated in front of it, feeling his breath on my neck. "Is this the room?" he whispered, making me shiver. I nodded, opening it quickly and rushing inside.

Stop acting so weird, I commanded myself, hardly able to make eye contact as I strode over to the clawfoot bath and wrapped my hands around the water pump. The brass had become dull and tarnished, and as I tried to work the pump, I couldn't seem to get enough power to push it all the way down and get the water flowing.

"Want me to try?" Destan piped up, moving slightly closer and eyeing the pump. I shook my head, gasping as suddenly my shoulder wound seared, Lilah's stitching up of the bullet hole straining against my skin. The white bandage became dotted with crimson, and I backed away from the pump, my bangs falling into my eyes as I grit my teeth against the pain.

"G-go ahead," I stammered, glancing at him and then back to the floor, my hand covering the blood-spotted bandage. Destan pumped so quickly and effortlessly that after some gurgling, water poured from the old spigot in no time. The water ran orange at first, I suppose from the clay that mingled with the mystery well, and then became clear. Not allowing me to do anything more for him, Destan crouched and lit a fire under the tub, sliding the covering over so that only heat and smoke would waft up to heat the water in the basin. Standing back up, Destan turned to me. I felt like his eyes could see straight through me to the door.

"You know...you don't have to help me. Being the stinky lumberjack I am, I've had practice with soaking out stench," he said, a crooked smile tweaking on the edge of his mouth.

I was able to return a shaky grin myself. Pushing my bangs behind my ear, I shrugged, "Maybe...you could worry about your body and I could do your head? Irene already did a lot of cleaning of the scar on your face–"

His eyes widened. "The *what?*" Destan strode over to the sink and mirror, gaping at his reflection. His fingertips traced over the long, deep red gash, and he winced, pulling off another flower petal I'd stuck over it. He breathed a loud breath through his nose, staring into the sink basin, his face unreadable. Tentatively, I touched his shoulder. His hand drifted up and covered mine, stroking over my fingers.

"Do you know how it happened?" I whispered, resting my cheek against his back.

"Maybe," he muttered, "I think so. It's...it's weird. I don't remember feeling any pain. Just a big, fast impact and then nothing." Destan removed his hand from mine, walking towards the tub and testing the water. "Warm enough," he shrugged, unbuttoning his coat and shrugging out of his sweater and undershirt. I looked at my feet, waiting until I heard the splash of him climbing in to raise my eyes.

He lay with his head tipped back against the lip of the tub, dirty blonde curls dangling over the edge. His knees were bent so that his tall body could fit inside, and the water swirled around him a milky, translucent shade of silver. I knelt by his head, passing him a few bottles of soap I'd found underneath the sink, and uncorking one myself for his hair. The pungent, fresh scent of lavender burned in my nose, and I dribbled a generous amount of the thin, soapy substance across his head.

As I worked his hair into a lather, recalling back to when Irene and I had cleaned him up to get him into Peak Tower, Destan spoke again, this time his voice barely a whisper. "Was I really dead?"

"It seemed like it."

"I'm sorry."

"It's not *your* fault, Destan."

He scooted up to sit and turned to look at me. "Raine. If I were to enter a room and see *you* lying there lifeless and scar-faced and smelling the way I do, I don't know how I could make it through the night. So, I'm sorry. I'm sorry you had to go through that. I don't care that it wasn't my fault. I still hurt you, a lot."

There was a lump in my throat, a stinging in my eyes as I glanced away from him, trying to just forget the whole thing had ever happened. Maintaining composure, I dipped the pitcher into the water and poured it over his head, watching him close his eyes as the dirt and blood freed itself from his hair and skin. The stench was already fading, and with his body soaking up the lavender water and his hair clean, Destan chewed on some dried spearmint leaves I'd found tucked behind some medicine and hairbrushes, and he was ready to go.

We went downstairs, where Irene had cleared the cabinets and both of our knapsacks of any food and set it all out on the table, making Destan's jaw drop and stomach grumble loudly. The grumble made Irene jump, and she nearly spilled the cups of tea she'd poured for us as we entered the room. "Oh. That was fast," she said, setting down the kettle and narrowing her eyes at Destan. "So what made you all dead-seeming if you don't mind me asking?"

He sat at the table, and before shoving a spoonful of Lilah's green onion and mushroom preserves into his mouth, took a second to answer. "I was just wondering that myself. I don't know if this has anything to do with it, but I do remember now getting shot in the face."

"What?" I gasped, looking round from him to Irene. Suddenly my heart was beating very fast. Images of Tieran and the Shuishan were filling my head, memories I didn't want of his tent, of the grotto, of Rong's whip falling hard against my back. Irene watched me in concern from across the dining room. Destan, on the other hand, stared up at the ceiling, yearning to remember.

"There was someone chasing me...it was a man. I'm not sure who he was. But only a few days after being here I started feeling like I was being watched. I hid out one night to see if maybe I was more than paranoid, maybe I could corner the stalker, and the guy walked right past me," he explained. "I didn't jump at him, he was too freaky. He had on this mask with a nozzle on his nose and mouth...like a gas mask. He was sort of dressed like a JP, shiny helmet and no skin showing, really gigantic with muscle, huge metal boots, and these eyes that I felt like could see through the rock I hid behind."

"Did you lose him, confront him...?" I prodded, sitting down across from him at the table. Relief washed over me hearing that it wasn't one of the shabby, but lethal travellers I'd encountered not even a week ago.

Destan swallowed another mason jar of fruit preserves and moved onto the next, shaking his head, "No way! I stayed back there until I saw where he was going and then I took off in the opposite direction." His eyes suddenly brightened, as if another light had gone off in his brain. Swallowing, he looked from me to Irene, his face darkening. "There was one more thing about him." He stretched out his arm, flexing the calloused fingers as he said, "He had one normal hand, and one metal hand; with spiked fingers and what looked like little guns in each one."

"It could have been a cyborg?" Irene suggested.

Destan and I turned to her, the same dubious looks on our faces. Irene was so used to us being clueless about nearly everything at this point that we didn't even have to ask what a *cyborg* was. "Half human, half robot, she explained. "Fluxaria was on Thgindim's case about production of them."

"You never told us this before," I said, unable to hide the worry from my voice. Destan squeezed my hand. I squeezed right back.

"Well, we didn't have a firm grasp on how true this rumour was or not," she explained, picking at some dirt under her fingernails. "I would've said something, but the cyborgs weren't really a priority when bombs were definitely on their way. Speaking of which..." Irene reached behind her and unlocked a drawer beneath the kitchen counter. She pulled out a rather scratched, but bonafide Peak Tower tablet. The one I'd taken myself from Councilman Lao's office forever ago. She woke it up, tapping in the crazy long passcode and swiftly navigating the files and documents before pulling up what looked like a diagram of sorts. She flicked a finger upward and the image floated from the screen to becoming a hologram, floating above the glass and rotating slowly.

"I've done some more exploring, as you can see," she winked, looking from me to Destan's awed expressions and tracing a finger along the ghostly diagram. It had to have been drawn by a computer, with perfect angles and circles, notes typed in and multicoloured lines connecting here and there. I leaned forward, tentatively touching it, causing the image to zoom in and focus on a sketch of an odd clock. My eyes narrowed.

"That's not a clock, Irene," I said.

She cocked up an eyebrow. "Didn't say it was. But how did you figure that?"

Destan rested his chin on his fist, eyeing the hologram coldly. "Because it nearly blew us up. The night you ran away, when we were taken up to the hot springs. Just one of these and the whole

spa was made into rubble. And the Majesty Council has one on hand in each of the Peak offices."

"You're not serious," she said. When we both nodded, Irene's eyes bulged, "They're bombs, too?"

"'Too'?" I echoed, heart racing. "What else do they do?"

Irene sighed, gazing at the hologram and swiping it back down to the screen."That's sort of a loaded question. These things got video surveillance, tracking devices, alarm systems, radio signals, a mustard gas component...pretty much anything except telling time. Guess the blowing-up-feature wasn't put in yet when the diagram was made, or I just haven't hacked it hard enough."

We sat in silence, staring at the now turned off and quietly whirring tablet on the table. Irene made the first move and returned it to its place in the kitchen drawer, then crossed her arms against her chest and smiled.

"I'm gonna build one."

"The clock bomb?" Destan asked, skeptical.

"You know how to put all of those features into it and everything?" I added.

Irene nodded. "I already have the framework made from junk I've found throughout this tower and lovely forest. It won't look as pretty since it won't be factory-made, so forget those fancy numbers. And I'm nowhere near done and might not be able to work out a tracking device part because I won't be able to program a microchip myself, but all of the designs and instructions are here. And if I can deliver a prototype of the weapon to Fluxaria, then we're one step closer to defending ourselves against it and whatever else your mountain has planned."

Destan raised his hand for a high five. "Irene, you are one hell of a spy. It is both freaky and awesome to be sitting at the same table as you."

They slapped hands, and settling back into their seats, Irene snapped her fingers at me. "So! About this cyborg. Do either of you have any ideas as to who could be on a murderous rampage for a banished teenage boy?"

"Not really," I murmured, thoughtfully tracing a finger through the dust on the table. I glanced up into Destan's eyes, "What happened after you lost him?"

He scowled. "It's Mythland, so naturally a lot of...frightening things. I mean, I didn't really lose him as much as get a head start."

"You don't have to talk about it now if you don't want to," I said, noticing the change in his voice, the anxiety creasing his forehead.

"Yeah, really. You've been dead, man, you have all the reason in the world to take a break," Irene added. Destan smiled a half-smile, brushing the comments away immediately.

"No, no, just...there was a lot of wandering, a lot of fighting with animals and running away from storms....at one point I found some bodies, still fresh. Girls, teenagers, shredded apart. And I had a bit of a meltdown. I thought that I'd see one of you two next with your hearts around your ankles and your eyes on the grass." His face turned green, and he picked at the splinters fraying the edge of the wooden table. I wouldn't let myself envision Nora or Xiaowen or any of Tieran's dolls as the girls Destan had mentioned, and just focused on breathing, on the warmth of Destan's hand under mine.

"You guys gotta tell me how long I was out, because the last time I was awake, the 'cyborg' had caught up and had seen me plainly, not just my tracks. He chased me for days without getting tired, and he knew my hiding spots before I did. After the fourth day, I was exhausted and starving and I stumbled right into his frame of vision." He pointed at his face, grimacing, "I'm guessing that's where this comes in. He shot at me with this badass crossbow of his, not hitting straight to the brain like I think he'd meant to. When I ducked the arrow just skid across my face and took some of me with it."

After a few moments of silence, Irene let out a breath, "Jeez. That's...brutal."

"How long have I been here, you two?" He sipped from his cup of tea, curling his lips at the bitterness. I was positive the tea leaves had been far from fresh.

"I just got here yesterday," I said, exchanging a nervous glance with Irene, who spoke next.

"I found you when you already looked deader than dead, four days ago. And then I brought you up to this castle and you didn't stir a wink." She said, flinging a berry pit at the wall and propping her feet up on the table.

144

"There must've been something on that arrow, a tranquilizer, a poison or something," I mused. "Since it didn't pierce you completely, it didn't give you the full death sentence. It just knocked you out for a good while."

"You're probably right, Raine," Irene said, "whoever that guy was, for some reason he's keen on finding and ending Destan. And probably you, too. Just taking a wild guess." She shrugged, crossing her arms against her chest. Frowning, Irene shook her head. "Man. I'm sorry for turning you two into criminals. Now Destan's got this ugly scar and we're getting beaten up by a forest."

Destan reached for his face self-consciously, probably thinking I hadn't noticed. When he saw me looking, he forced a smile and said, waggling his eyebrows, "I am all the more ruggedly handsome and battle-scarred now, right, Bluehead?"

I smiled gently, gazing at him and trying to get used to it. What had once been smooth, creamy skin, riddled with small scars and bruises here and there, was now defined by a jagged valley of blood. There was a small piece of flesh missing from the bridge of his nose, taken off by the arrow. No hair grew where the gash separated his left brow, and the wound ended less than a centimetre away from his precious lips. I wouldn't have to worry about hurting him while we kissed. Then I remembered, face growing hot again...we hadn't even kissed yet since he'd awoken.

"I think it would be best for me to stand watch while you two go up and get some...*rest*," Irene yawned, stretching out her limbs dramatically and winking not so subtly at Destan, who flushed. Oh my goodness.

"You sure?" I asked, nerves making my stomach turn. "I'm pretty rested, I could just–"

"You didn't sleep a wink. When I checked on you, you were staring at the ceiling like the voice of the universe was speaking to you. And then you found Destan the Zombie and I'm sure that wore you out in itself. So you two just head to the top room and climb into bed, alright? Tomorrow night can be your turn to stand watch."

No more bad memories, I thought, sneaking a glance at Destan, a million thoughts racing through my head in that split second before he met my eyes. *What better way to get rid of Tieran and the disgusting things he did than replace it all with a beautiful, second time with Destan? To be with him, completely.*

"So you're definitely cool with us...?" Destan said slowly to Irene, raising a finger and pointing at the stairwell.

"Let's save talking for tomorrow?" I piped, lowering his hand and looking at him under my lashes. I bit my lip, thinking, *Please, please, please Destan don't make me look any more foolish than I already do, let's just go upst—*

"'Nuff said!" Destan grinned, suddenly sweeping me off of my feet and into his arms. I looked around in shock, spotting Irene's eyeroll as she trudged toward the tunnel hatch.

"I'll be down here...where I *barely* exist...where I cannot hear or see either of you and or any grossness at all..." Irene called, her voice fading out into the lower level as she climbed down the ladder.

Destan gazed into my eyes, a faint brilliance behind them. A hunger. It made me queasy, but the sensation didn't last long because he bolted for the stairs, bouncing me up and down as he hobbled up as fast as he could, howling, "BLUEHEAD AND BEANIEHEAD TOGETHER AGAIN!! *WOOHOOO!*"

I laughed every last worry away, my arms around his neck, my face pressed to his chest as we ascended, up, up, him kicking open the bedroom door, charging toward the mess of pillows and blankets and dropping me onto the mattress. I bounced up and down once, still giggling, but stricken with pain as the wounds Rong's whip had given me seared on impact. I sat up and covered my face, forcing out some more laughter, trying to hide the pain as Destan climbed in beside me.

"Raine?" he asked, no longer laughing. I suck at lying. He touched my cheek, the other hand drifting down my back, warm fingers appearing under my sweater dress and on my lower back, timidly moving upward. I winced as his fingertips brushed the first mark of the whip, and he gasped, staring at me for an explanation I wasn't yet ready to give. "Who whipped you, Raine?" His exactness startled me. I prayed he'd never experienced such torture himself.

"It's not...I just ran into some trouble, I suppose."

"Can I look?"

Fear gripped me. *No, no, no,* my head screamed, but my body decided otherwise. Holding my breath, I crossed my arms and grabbed

146

the bottom hem of the sweaterdress, pulling it over my head, gnashing my teeth together in pain as some fibres of the fabric clung to the sticky blood and pus that remained on the wounds. I was bare-chested now, only in my leggings and socks, but Destan didn't seem to care. He had moved to sit behind me, his hands around my waist as he peered at the torn canvas of my back.

There was a clean tearing sound, and Destan had ripped a thick strip of sheet from the bed. Gently, he wrapped it around my torso until all of my wounds were covered, and then he tied it off. He heaved a loud, long sigh, sitting back on his haunches. And just as he scooted

147

∞ *Blood Moon* ∞

back in front of me, he wrapped a thick, wool blanket around my bare shoulders and patted my head like I was a little kid. I rolled my eyes, happy to see he was smiling again.

"Thank you," I said, "Now I'll heal a bit better."

"Mmhmm," he hummed, taking my hand and rubbing my fingers. He was being so soft, so caring. I leaned forward, touching my lips to his, waiting. Destan exhaled through his nose, parting his lips ever so slightly to return the kiss. But seeing an entrance, I kissed him deeper, my tongue exploring his, making him moan, the sound causing me to shiver. His hands cupped my face, I could nearly hear his heart beating faster and faster, saying, *Alive, alive, alive.* We weren't breathing, weren't wasting a single second apart for something as trivial as oxygen. I was reminded of the first time we'd kissed, when everything that had been trapped inside us for so long burst and we nearly went mad with trying to feel it all at once. But during that time, there still had been some restraint, something in both of us that kept us from completely devouring each other.

There was none of that now.

The same blanket he'd previously swaddled me in was torn off in seconds. He pulled my body to his, his mouth traveling from my lips to along my jaw and collarbones. My fingers trailed down the smooth skin on his back, my nails digging in ever so slightly when he began kissing my breasts, burying kisses in my stomach, a thousand shivers sizzling through me at the sensation. I kissed his neck, his shoulders, everywhere in sight, and could feel his body trembling against mine in longing.

No more bad memories, no more bad memories, I thought, as he lay down on the bed and my body followed above his. He watched me in wonder, how I carefully undid the leather belt on his pants, gripping the small metal zipper and tugging it down. I moved myself to sit on his hips, feeling suddenly dizzy. My head felt like it could float away, and beneath my skin ants could have been running amuck, spreading goosebumps as they dashed to and fro. *You're ready for this, Raine, you both are. Just move your hand there and—*

I was being crushed.

My face was smashed against the floor and he was grunting, growling, invading, invading, terrible heat flaming through my veins as

148

he sat on my back. I was being gutted. I was raw inside, outside. He was tearing into me where I thought he'd already ripped and torn with his fingers, with his mouth, loving the blood, loving my screaming, loving me so cruelly it felt like punishment. What was I being punished for? How is it that agony never reaches a peak of numbness? How much farther until it kills me and it's finally over?

I fell backward, voice catching in my throat as I tumbled from the bed to the floor, shrieking. Destan leapt from the mattress, hand beneath my head a split second before it hit the floor. My back was already screaming in pain against the cold wooden boards. He swept the hair from my eyes, fingers shaking, evidently panicked. "Raine? Raine, what's wrong? Did I hurt you?"

"No, no," I gasped, blinking fast, looking wildly around the bedroom to confirm I was in fact in the tower with Destan and not Tieran's tent. What the hell was wrong with me? Destan hadn't forced himself on me, I was even the one on top. So why did it suddenly feel like I was suffocating? Something warm was on my fingers. I held out my hands. What appeared to be soft flakes of skin and blood were caked under my nails. I grabbed his arm, horrified, "Did *I* hurt *you*?"

Destan shook his head, immediately covering his waist with a blanket. I wrenched it off and he didn't fight me. Under the blanket I saw three angry red scratches, one a little bloody. Destan cursed under his breath, cradling my face in his hands and looking straight into my eyes. "They're just little scratches, it was an accident so don't freak out. These...these things happen. It's okay," he said, seeing my persistent look of distress. He touched his forehead to mine. "I'm okay. Maybe...to be continued?"

I felt sick. Nodding, I crawled back into bed with him, our bodies fitting together in the sheets. My back, his stomach; my shoulder, his head. His arms surrounding me. I had never felt so ashamed of myself. I lay still as possible, staring at the fireplace where Ai continued to snooze, unbothered. I closed my eyes, tears burning behind my eyelids.

"I think we just jumped in a little too fast," he whispered. I could feel his fingers getting caught in the knots of my wild blue hair. I didn't answer. Just focused on the warmth of his skin. The drowsy music of the crickets singing me into a dreamless sleep.

chapter thirteen

I had imagined my first night in the tower to be a calm one, giving me a break from the chaos of the forest. I would've woken happily in Destan's arms with the sun piercing through the grand window of the tower. Instead I awoke in a cold sweat at 4AM rushing to the chamber pot to pee and puke. At this point I knew that I couldn't last in Mythland much longer. *None* of the food– even Lilah's prepared soups –would last more than a few hours inside of me. After slipping on my leggings and another warm dress, I tiptoed over to the fireplace and pet the smooth, scaled head of the creature now awake in front of it. It chirped, rubbing against my hand and looking up at me with its big, black eyes.

"Want to have a short fly?" I whispered, showing Ai the leash we'd used the day before. She rolled from her back onto her belly, little arms and legs pushing her up to stand as her whiskers floated around her face.

"I'll take that as a yes," I mumbled, scooping her up in my arms and

padding over to the window.

I set her free, watching her fly in between snowflakes as morning began to dawn and Mythland awoke from its tumultuous sleep. White coated the trees and land like thick, pearly frosting. It saddened me to know that it wouldn't last the evening. Rain always came to poke holes in the white, sparkly smoothness; eventually turning it to mush, to slush, to a deadly sheet of ice. I wondered what it would've been like to live in a white wonderland, like Emergent where it was snowy year-round. Underbrush was ever only guaranteed one blizzardish week a year. My level would go into a frenzy of shovelling and sprinkling chunks of salt on doorsteps, and my friends and I would take out Gwen and teach her how to make perfectly round snowballs. We'd build tiny mountains and decorate them with leaves and twigs, and Gwen would bring out her ragdolls and pretend it was all of us living on the mountain. It wouldn't be along until the neighbourhood boys would show up saying our little snow pile was Fluxaria, and they'd pelt the mountain to powder with iceballs. Carmen would chase after them as Chantastic comforted Gwen, Velle would fuss over the mess of snow and babble to herself about how to repair it, and I would work on building a snowy wall around us so that we could play in peace. I missed those days so much.

I stuck out my tongue and caught a raindrop, backing away as the pelt became heavier. That was so long ago. Life here surely would improve with Destan and Irene by my side now, but I knew I couldn't find peace of mind until I'd sent Ai toward Thgindim with the prospect of receiving news from Chan. She would let me know if she and her sister had gotten in any trouble for being friends with me, if Carmen was rotting in a Peak cell cursing my name, if my mother was being violently questioned in a torture chamber with Gwen held hostage until the Majesty Council was sure I was dead and no longer a threat.

Sighing, I glanced back at Destan and thought of how he'd been tracked down. Of course Councilman Sebastian Lao would find a way around our sentence. Banishment, not death. But banishment was nearly equal to a death sentence unless he was scared we'd actually make it to the other side and warn Fluxaria like we intended. In a way, I felt flattered. Sebastian feared us: two fifteen-year-old outcasts with good shooting skills and treasonous agendas. He feared we could make it through the impossible and ruin his and the Majesty Council's master plan of destruction. Even though I now had another danger to worry about, the thought of a hired assassin boosted my confidence that maybe we were worth fearing.

There was a squeak from behind me, and I saw that Ai had already returned. Snowflakes patched in between her scales, and she shivered and wobbled on her feet. I rushed over to her, smiling as she burrowed into my hand for warmth. I stroked her smooth forehead with my pinky, pausing when I heard a *psst*. I hadn't been planning on keeping Ai a secret, but for some reason, someone else seeing her made me panic for a moment. I first checked Destan, but he was still sound asleep. Then, turning around, I faced Irene, who had only half of her face visible.

"Raine? You up?" she hissed from the doorway. I shrugged, and she motioned for me to come to her, her cheeks bright red. Bewildered, I obeyed, first setting Ai down in her bed by the fireplace and then slipping through the cracked door to the hallway.

"Are you okay?" I asked, carefully closing the door behind me and touching her arm. She scratched her head, and that was when I noticed she didn't have her hair in a ponytail. It made me do a doubletake, my eyes not used to the chunks of black hair falling just past her shoulders. As if on cue, she took a rubber band from her wrist and tied it up.

Giving me a conspicuous look, and her cheeks reddening, she said, "I am having...womanly issues."

I looked her swiftly over, confused, "Womanly...?" Then it dawned on me. "Oh! Oh, yeah, do you need a...?"

"It would be appreciated." Her face reddened, and she hastily readjusted the blanket wrapped around her waist to cover the dark spot forming. "Did the Majesty Council really pack you some before giving you the boot?"

"No, I made some myself to prepare for it a couple of weeks ago. Hasn't hit me yet, though," I said, retrieving my knapsack from the wardrobe and digging around inside.

"I'm sorry. This is so stupid and embarrassing."

I shook my head, taking out one of the pads I'd made from moss wrapped in gauze. "Really, Irene, it's fine, it happens..." I paused, lost in thought and counting the weeks since my last. It hadn't happened in a while for me. I handed the whole lot of them to her, staring forward in a numb sort of stillness.

"Thanks a bunch. I'll go back to keeping watch," she said, saluting me and pointing at the steps. I broke from my trance, remembering the snoring I'd heard and shaking my head.

"I...I'm going to stay up, actually. You go get some rest."

"You sure?"

"Yeah."

"Alright," she shrugged, trotting back to the main floor. I looked at the now empty pocket in my rucksack where the stacked pads had just been. I hadn't menstruated this entire time in Mythland. I counted off on my fingers to make sure I wasn't just forgetting something...when was the last time? Three, five...*seven* weeks? I had never been late before, and the last time I could recall my cycle was during the archery competition, and that was forever ago. I felt like I'd been struck hard on the head, and I fell back onto my butt from my knees, the world dizzying and nauseating.

What did this mean? Am I broken? Has it finally happened, I'm barren like so many Thgindim girls? My thoughts raced and raced in circles. That had to be it. Mythland starved me just as much as Underbrush, maybe I was getting so little nourishment my body just couldn't put energy into menstruating anymore. But did that explain the daily bouts of nausea? The emotional ups and downs, the disturbingly vivid dreams? Possibly. Probably.

Except...

I was startled by a sudden chirp. Ai had travelled from her bed by the fire to my pillow, her whiskers dancing close to touching Destan's cheek. I gasped, hurrying over to her and grabbing around her belly to carry her away from him. She resisted only a moment, clearly curious about the other human in the bed. I cradled her close to my chest, trying to ease her excitement and rocking her back and forth. Destan yawned, rolling from his side onto his back. His forehead wrinkled, his fist clenching the sheets as apparent nightmares burned behind his eyelids. My heart suddenly ached. How would he feel if he knew the girl he asked to marry wouldn't be able to have kids? He'd never brought it up before, probably because of how tumultuous the world was now, not to mention how young we still were and not settled

154

anywhere. But, what about one day? Children had been the furthest thing from my mind, I was still getting used to being engaged! But if Fluxaria and Thgindim one day found peace and me and Destan could settle down in a little house in the woods, all politics at ease and no more looming danger, I hadn't seen having children as being totally out of the question. But there wasn't peace yet, and maybe in our lifetime there would never be so that's why the spirits stole my ability altogether.

Or...

I strode toward the fireplace, setting Ai down and trying to light a fire with my shaking hands. I was trying so hard to clear my head, but the intrusive thoughts kept arising, echoing through my skull like a mantra.

It could be the very opposite, the nasty voice in my head hissed, making chills trickle down my spine. I wouldn't give my brain the satisfaction. I gave up on the fire and stormed over to the wardrobe, opening it up wide and staring into the mirror with flushed cheeks. I lifted up my dress, holding my breath and releasing it once I was reassured nothing had changed. I was still a skeleton. A scrawny Underbrusher. Gaunt face and limbs that looked like they could be easily snapped. My bones looked large and sharp, stretched tightly over pale, translucent skin. Except– around my middle. My eyes widened.

I had seen overweight Canopians and Emergents and Councilmen milling about during my laundress runs and that was not how I appeared now. It was more as if I had just scarfed down a huge meal and had a bloated stomach. As I turned to the side to examine my profile in the mirror, a subtle yet definite protrusion made itself clear around my midsection. It didn't look like a fatty stomach roll or even a normal gut, it was just rounder than usual, and it should have been as sunken as the rest of me, but it wasn't.

"No," I rasped, tugging down my dress and feeling the urge to scream. I rushed back to the window and gulped down the chilled air, feeling like my lungs had been shocked into stillness. The white landscape blurred in front of me, and I backed away to keep from tipping forward and falling straight through. *Impossible, impossible, impossible,* I thought, sickened suddenly by how possible it could be. It was almost perfect timing. Destan and I had bonded long enough for things to have started taking form inside me, not to mention all of the signs I'd learned come with a pregnancy...the intense food cravings but unsettled stomach, the out of whack emotions, crazy dreams, the rounded stomach, the missed period, but how did this happen? I thought I'd known how pregnancy worked; it occurred as a result of bonding, but I thought there was something that you had to do specifically to actually conceive. My father and mother had bonded pre-marriage due to the ritual, but I wasn't born until five years into their marriage. They'd planned it, hadn't conceived during the ritual, but how? Was it random, like a lottery? Or was there a step Destan and I had missed? Skye hadn't had anything different prepared except for those dumb clothes, and those weren't supposed to last long anyway so what is it that might have put a living being inside of me?

If Destan had gotten me pregnant while I was betrothed to Skye, keeping it a secret would be even harder. It would be more than just the two sets of eyes I had peering down on me, and word would spread like wildfire through both Underbrush and Starshade. The Council's handful of spiritual leaders didn't really have much to do with anything anymore since our society became so secularized and industrial, however, when things such as this happened, they'd suddenly be all high and mighty and point their gnarled old fingers and say, "The spirits placed a child inside of a mother who is unfit rather than those fit and sacred and ready. This is a terrible accident in need of being fixed."And then since 'the spirits' have messed up, I'd have a forced abortion and the fetus would be sucked out in little fragments that wouldn't even look like a baby.

I laid back down by Destan and laid my hands on my stomach, straining my brain to remember. But all I could think of was how I felt like the world was unravelling and my mind was shrivelling into ribbons with it. If I wasn't just crazy and there *was* something inside of me, it would get bigger. It would grow and so would I. It would force its way out of me and maybe kill me in the process. And then I'd have to make sure it didn't die in Mythland on top of protecting Destan, Irene, myself, and the information we needed to give to Fluxaria. Then again, it wasn't just some creature trying to take over my body and life.

It was a piece of Destan, willingly given to me, that belonged to no one else but us. That could have his eyes or my hair, his smile and my voice, that would look to us like we're the sun and he or she is a flower growing toward us, needing us. We had made the decision to bond, to risk it, even though our intention hadn't been for it to go this way at all. I was surprised to feel that suddenly it didn't matter if I was ready or not, if we were ready or not. My consequence, a precious consequence that came well before I'd ever dreamed, was already growing and growing and depending on me.

Destan reached out in his sleep for me, his arm patting where my body had been before I'd created a few inches of space between us. I snuggled in closer, letting my body form to his under the covers, my heart beating fast. He tucked his mouth into my hair, his warm breath grazing over my forehead, fingers tightening over my waist as he dreamed. I shut my eyes, listening to the rhythm of his breathing. How was I going to tell him?

chapter fourteen

I wrapped another curl of scarlet yarn around the spoke of the round loom, my eyes flickering over to Destan as he began to wake. He stretched his arms above his head, opening his mouth so wide that I thought his jaw might unhinge. His yawn roared out of him like a beast and he shook his head back and forth, the blond curls dancing like springs around his silver eyes.

"Guess that wasn't just a really weird-good dream," he said, coughing and rubbing his eyes. When our eyes met I blushed, and a broad grin glowed across his face. "It's good to wake up to this. To you, Bluehead."

I raised an eyebrow. "But what about that charming assassin you told me about? Surely that was an exciting way to start your day."

"Nah, you know as well as I that too much excitement will get your face scratched off," he chuckled, scowling. The scar on his face was darker, drier since last night. "Have you been up long?" he asked me, scooting up against the headboard so that the blanket fell away and his bare torso shimmered golden in the sun. The three scratches I'd made on his skin remained dark in the morning light.

I tore my eyes away, returning to the loom and beginning another round of stitches. "A while, I suppose..." I murmured. The bed creaked and floorboards groaned as Destan slid out from the sheets and made his way to the wardrobe, whistling. He paused, and I could feel his eyes on my back.

"Whatcha making?" he asked, walking away from the wardrobe only a second after peering inside and seeing it only held girls' clothing. He came over to me with his pants only zippered halfway.

I lost track of the rows I'd been counting, distracted by the sudden proximity of his body to mine. *Breathe, Raine. He doesn't even know about the maybe pregnant thing yet.* Destan sat and wrapped his arms around me as I stammered, remembering he'd asked me something, "A h-hat. Your hat, or I mean...a replacement." He ran his thumb over the soft knitting and I added. "I'm nearly finished."

"Where'd you get the yarn and loom? Our favourite Councilman didn't throw it in your rucksack as a bonus banishment gift, did he?" he asked, brushing away some of my bangs and gently touching his lips to my forehead. I wanted to just tilt my face up ever so slightly and kiss him, but could not bring myself to as I remembered last night and hot shame flamed through me.

"I found it in the wardrobe, buried at the bottom under some fallen clothes," I said.

"Is that where the lizard came from, too?"

My head whipped around in realization that he wasn't behind me anymore. Destan crouched by the fireplace, rubbing in between Ai's two small horns, a charmed smile on his lips. He glanced up at me, motioning at the little nest I'd fashioned for her.

"You did this, right?" he asked.

I nodded, biting my lip, and knelt beside him. Ai chirped appreciatively at seeing me, and rose from her bed like a ribbon swept up in the wind, swimming through the air and circling my head as Destan jumped away in shock. Her flying was becoming more and more graceful.

"It...it flies?" he gasped, a grin overtaking his face as he reached out and Ai settled on his open palm, sniffing his fingers curiously. "I guess Mythland creatures really are full of surprises."

"Actually...she's not from Mythland," I said, meeting his eyes. "I was given her before she hatched. Back on Thgindim."

His brow furrowed. "Really? How did you manage to sneak it past Sebastian?"

"The egg used to be smaller. It grew since I've been here and it finally hatched after being exposed to a lot of heat a few days ago. You see, Chantastic and my other friends visited me after our sentence in Peak Tower. Chan..." I trailed off, my lips remembering the softness of hers, my cheeks feeling suddenly hot. I scratched my forehead, choosing my words carefully, "...when she said goodbye she snuck it into my hair, hiding it in my bun. I named it Ai."

He nodded, watching as Ai hopped down from his hand and trotted toward the window. Her body lengthened and she rose again, nails scraping the rough windowsill edge as she begged to go outside. She still had the yellow yarn tied around her neck like a leash, trailing it behind her as she moved to and fro. I went over and opened it for her, securing the string to the headboard of the bed so that she couldn't get too caught up in soaring away.

"Why did Chantastic give Ai to you?" Destan asked, clearly enchanted by her as she flew circles around a falling leaf.

I coiled my arm through his, saying softly, "I think she can carry messages from here to home. On the egg, Chan wrote a note saying that Ai could find her way from Mythland to Thgindim on the blood moon. Maybe it's like an instinctual thing, like birds flying south, I don't know. But Ai's something, isn't she?"

He nodded, pulling me close, "Like something out of a spirit legend. It's crazy something this unique could come from a dull-as-anything place like Thgindim." We remained calmly watching Ai fly for only a short time, until Destan touched my arm and spun me around to face him, a curious smile on his lips as he announced, "So, what's the plan for today, Bluehead? We're together, we've got a spy and a flying lizard, and I know it's been a while, but I thought it might actually be a good idea to get in some target practice."

I gasped, an uncontrollable smile glowing on my face, "Target practice? Like before?"

"Well, sure," he chuckled, yanking playfully on the ribbon keeping my bun together, "Except I think it would be even better if I taught you to hunt."

"Hunt?" I frowned. "As in killing things?"

"No, as in tickling things. What do you think I mean?" Destan rolled his eyes, striding away and shrugging on his sweater, padding around the room in search of socks.

I pulled Ai in from outside and returned to my knitting, tying off the final stitch and sliding the finished beanie from the loom. Considering his offer, I murmured, "Well...let's talk to Irene, too just to see what she thinks we should accomplish today."

"'Kay," he said, his voice suddenly at my ear. I jumped, blushing as he guided me back to the bed, pulling me down beside him. "And don't worry about what happened last night. Freaky stuff has happened to both of us here, so don't stress the bonding stuff. I'm just happy to be here with you."

Destan came to kiss me, his lips parting just so that the kiss was delicate and sweet on my mouth. I held him there, wishing I could be freed from what happened in Tieran's tent so that he wouldn't have to hold back or worry about me lashing out, wishing that I wouldn't have to tell him I thought something of ours might be growing inside of me. I even half-wished we'd only ever gone this far so that we wouldn't be in this position of potential parenthood when neither we nor the world were ready for a child. But wishing wouldn't change anything that had happened.

Destan's mouth moved from mine only a centimetre, "You okay, Bluehead?"

"Just fine, Fancy-Beaniehead," I said, sticking the new red hat on top of his curls as he laughed, sitting back up and adjusting it to fit. He looked just like his old self, except for the thicker scrub of facial hair and long scar over his face.

He struck a pose, batting his eyelashes. "This *is* a fancy hat! How do I look?"

"Most ruggedly handsome, Destan," I beamed, watching his entire face light up. I poked his scruffy cheek, "But you really should shave if you can, you look like a grizzly man." He stuck out his tongue.

"You really do, though," Irene's voice chimed in, her head poking through the doorway. "And you've got all sorts of goopy shit left over from those soups you guzzled all stuck in that gnarly beard of yours."

"Food. *Breakfast*," Destan whispered, looking from me to her, leaping to his feet and sauntering out of the room, "Last one to the table is a smelly Fluxarian!"

"Hey!" the spy and I hollered in unison. She and I shoved each other on our way down the stairs, racing and laughing, Siri thundering behind us and panting happily. Irene burst from the stairwell first and smacked her hand on the table in victory, shaking the hair out of her eyes as I came in, exhausted and leaning on Siri for support.

"Just joking about the smelly Fluxarian bit. But seriously, let's eat!" Destan said, plopping down onto a stool and drumming his fingers on the wood. Irene walked past him and smacked him on the back of the head.

"Eat what? I can't believe that after your post-death-pig-out last night you could still be hungry," Irene growled, but there was a smile in her voice.

"Sorry..." Destan blushed.

He had indeed wiped us out of all food, and I'd been counting on the dozen cans of Lilah's goop to last at least a week. Irene's rations had also been donated to him last night, and Destan had lost his stash of food while trying to escape the cyborg. So after some moaning and groaning about trekking through snow, we all bundled up and left the castle to go hunting. Destan still had his grey wool coat with the high collar and brass buttons to keep him toasty, and I found a thick knit jacket with a fur hood to wear over the borrowed sweater dress and the fur-lined leather leggings I'd stolen from the camp. Irene pulled on her black spy hat and thermal bodysuit, and then we were good to go.

Mythland was full of animals, but it seemed that as soon as we dug deep in the woods with our bows and arrows, every living thing went into hiding. Like they could sense we suddenly had ulterior motives. Irene went off on her own looking for critters since she already counted herself a hunting expert, but Destan told me to follow him so he could teach me. My last hunting experience had been horrendous, remember? The bunny funeral?

"Step as softly as possible, we can't see what's under this snow and a snapping twig could scare off even the biggest tiangou," Destan whispered, his previously playful self becoming stony and focused. He was in full teacher-mode, just as he was when first showing me how to shoot in the meadow. He swept back some spindly branches and peered into a clearing. I mirrored his movements, ducking under the branches and coming beside him. But suddenly, Destan stuck out a hand, pressing his palm to my chest and then nodding forward. He nocked in an arrow without a sound on a bow he'd fashioned himself, and rose into a flawless stance. I could never be as natural as he was at archery. Never. I fumbled with snapping it just right on the string, and even though I could get into a strong anchor just as quickly, I saw him flinch as I interrupted the quiet of the forest. It was then that I spotted the target. It was a snow white fox, ice blue eyes and long fluffy tail. I wouldn't have noticed it unless it had looked up at my noisiness.

"Let me get this one," Destan breathed, touching my arm. I lowered my stance, nodding and stepping back silently, my boots sinking deep into the snow. The cold wetness seeped through the laces and chilled my ankles. Destan prowled forward, his huge feet somehow soundless and seeming to float above the snow as he neared his target. And before his aim could get too shaky, he let the string roll off of his fingers and the arrow flew forward, piercing the fox on the side of her neck. As it hit, the fox and I yelped.

Destan rushed forward, kneeling by the fox and petting her belly, his eyes pained and touch gentle. "Shh, shh..." he soothed as the fox cried out softly, her small triangular head on a pillow of snowflakes. I came as close as I could will myself to, but it was hard to watch. "Thank you for giving yourself, your sacrifice is the greatest honour and I thank you and the spirits for granting me nourishment," Destan said silkily, bowing his head reverently. He jerked the arrow abruptly to the side, piercing the heart, and the fox immediately lay quiet and still. He'd shot so perfectly that only a small spray of blood had tainted the pure white of the snow. Concentrating, Destan eased out the arrow, and then ran it through a thick layer of snow to clean it. He glanced up at me and grimaced, whispering, "I hate it." He stood and brushed the snow off of his jeans, lifting up the dead fox and slipping her inside my rucksack, "I've never liked it. Griffin taught me how to make it as quick and painless as possible, and how to send off the animal with the proper funeral words. But all I can think of is what if out of nowhere, somebody shot me and screwed up my life? I wouldn't give a shit if it was quick or painless or gave me a great eulogy, I just wouldn't want it to be over, period."

"Hopefully that fox didn't have a life to get back to then, I suppose," I said, taking his hand and letting him lead.

"Every living thing has a life, Bluehead. No matter how small, it's a life. And it's yours until you give it away or have it stolen from you," he muttered, his face in shadow. Noticing my silence, Destan knocked my shoulder affectionately, "Sorry. So...would you like to try?"

"Er..." I said, putting up my hood as a chilly breeze swept over us, "...I guess so. Sure."

"You sure? I can handle it this time if you're not ready."

"I'm ready."

"Alright, well there's been a cluster of bunnies behind that tree for quite some time," he pointed out, his finger directing my eyes to the clump of fluffy white rodents.

I gaped. "How the heck do you see them so quickly? You said *I* had the archer eyes," I mumbled, fingers trembling as I nocked one of Destan's Peak-issued carbon arrows on the bowstring.

"You're just out of practice. Don't stress it, Bluehead," Destan encouraged, stepping behind me and helping me rise into my hold. I shut one eye and let the world focus into just the biggest of the rabbit family. Its twitchy nose wiggled in the air, the dark eyes watery and innocently unaware that I was about to try and plunge a long metal rod through it. I had a clear shot. I'd just have to pretend it was a target, not something with baby bunnies in a burrow nearby or any sort of life. But as I was about to shoot, I instinctively recoiled and lowered the arrow, my head spinning.

"Raine? You all right?" Destan asked from behind me. Determined, I rose up into my hold again, my feet taking roots in the snow as my vision began to swim. *It isn't alive, it isn't alive, it won't hurt, it's just food.* I released the arrow before I could talk myself out of it and watched it fly in slow motion. With a soft sound, the arrow sank through the bunny's eye. The other rabbits flew off, pumping their legs in terror, but the murdered rabbit fell limply to the ground, the snow polka-dotted with crimson as some blood leaked from the eye onto the ground. It didn't sink into the snow. Drops floated on the powder-light snow as if it were a frosted surface.

"That was very good. That rabbit didn't feel a thing, Raine," Destan said, taking my hand and leading me over to its tiny body. My eyes stung with tears and my nose dripped from the cold and swell of emotions. I crouched by the bunny and felt its silky, velvet ear.

"I'm sorry," I whispered, finding it harder than I first believed to remove the arrow. It pulled out slowly, fragments of the rabbit's insides stringy and clinging to the silver metal. Destan rubbed circles on my back as I took it out and laid it on the snow. "Thank you for giving your life for us, even though it wasn't your choice...we...we are so grateful and hope you are someplace better now." Hours later I would laugh at how seriously I was taking this, but at the time it didn't feel silly at all. It felt necessary. I felt less like a human distanced from the hunt, and more like a part of the food chain trying to make its way through the woods like the rest of the living things.

As Destan and I trekked back to the castle, where we were sure Irene was already skinning and gutting something she'd caught, he tried to catch up with me about what had gone on before we found each other. It began okay. Destan cracked up at how many times I told him my boots got stuck in the swamps, me joining in as he mentioned accidentally consuming hallucinogenic mushrooms and thinking he'd grown a watermelon from his bellybutton. But when I reached the part about being taken by the Shuishan, I stopped walking. I tried to quickly think of a way to explain without telling him too much, but even beyond what Tieran did to me, images of the qilin and Yue's story and then her blasted skull swirled in my head like elusive phantoms unable to be released into reality.

"Travellers?" Destan said, "You found other people here?"

"Yeah. Well...they found me," I said, my hand a tight fist in my coat pocket. "They were refugees from both mountains travelling around."

"That's...that's so amazing. They've been *surviving* here, that's really crazy. They must've been pretty badass tree-people. Why'd you leave them, then?"

"They...weren't the nicest, actually," I said, averting my eyes and squinting through the trees to where the tower loomed. Even looking away, I could sense Destan's smile fading.

"Oh. Did...did they hurt you?"

I think he knew the answer. Because when he asked, he brushed where he'd bandaged the whipping scars just last night. And I still wore the shoulder bandage Lilah had put together after Tieran shot me. I nearly nodded, but stopped myself. I didn't want him to be angry at himself for not being there. That's exactly the conclusion he would jump to, and then this would lead to outbursts and I didn't want to explain how Tieran stole my voice and had his own little harem of mute girls and a magical creature in a cellar, because then I'd have to tell how I'd been forced to bond with him, and the guilt, and shame, and disgust still made my whole body quiver.

"Raine?" he asked, his voice more concerned than gentle now.

"They did hurt me," I whispered, unable to meet his eyes, "but I escaped and those are the only scars that came with me, so I am fine now and none of it matters."

Destan cradled my face in his hands, "You sure? If you ever need to talk about it, you know I'll listen, right?"

I nodded, "Of course. But Destan—"

Someone grabbed both of our arms and yanked us back into a tree so hard that the wind was knocked from each of our lungs. Irene's hard black eyes were only inches away from mine, a finger pressed to her lips and her body shielding both of ours behind the wide trunk of the tree.

"Irene what the—?!"

"Someone's in the castle."

"Who?" Destan gasped, trying to peek around the tree, but Irene pushed his head back.

"Don't *look*, stupid! Didn't you just hear me?" she hissed, her face half frustrated and half worried. I touched her hand. It still had some blood on it from the animal she'd hunted earlier this morning.

"Irene, what did the person look like?" I said, urgently.

"Like a cyborg, the one that shot Destan, I'm guessing."

Destan froze. "No way. He found me again?"

I turned to him, whispering, "Destan, I think it's time for a confrontation. If we keep running, we'll never know who he is or why he wants to hurt us. Maybe he could even be a way out of here to Fluxaria. We could take him hostage, or something."

He and Irene contemplated quietly, and then even though I sensed he was reluctant, Destan nodded. His scar was still angry and red, a thick stripe over his features. He had to be terrified to meet the monster that did this to him.

"We should set a trap," Irene said solemnly, looking from my eyes to Destan's. "Set something he'll stumble right into so we can make sure he doesn't sneak up on us."

"Definitely," Destan nodded, "but...who's going in first?"

"I will," Irene and I said. We looked at each other and she rolled her eyes. I adjusted the quiver on my back, heart racing, "I want to do this. I'll go in to scope out the place and shoot an arrow out of the window to signal when you two can come in and what room is safe. We can set a trap from there."

"Sounds decent," Irene said, patting my shoulder. "Scream if there's trouble, got it?"

My stomach lurched. "Okay. See you soon." Then without waiting another moment, I sprinted toward the hatch that would lead me into the tower, and leapt through.

Pressed against the tunnel's curved wall, I didn't dare breathe. I could already hear him; the dull click of metal against the stone, a scrape of what I guessed to be the robotic limbs digging through the abandoned cabinets in the kitchen. His footsteps thunked above me like a mechanical heartbeat. *What if he breaks into the drawer where the tablet is stashed? I have to get him out of there now.* I lowered my bow and instead plucked up a medium-sized, loose stone from the wall, thinking up a plan.

I climbed up the ladder into the dining room, ducking under the table. My knees ached against the frigidly cold floor, the toes of my boots squeaking as I scooted completely under. I could hear movement in the kitchen. Then, pushing back the tablecloth, I threw the rock as hard as I could at the stairwell. It leapt from step to step, sounding like someone was running down them, and hearing a sudden crash in the

167

room beside me, I pressed myself up into the table, my limbs supporting myself in between each leg. I'd done this so many times before when stealing mountainberry cider from the Justice Police canteen on Underbrush, it felt natural to rise up there. But I didn't have to worry about being blown to pieces by a maybe-murderous-cyborg at the canteen, only clumsy JP 21996 who'd I'd tricked time and time again.

While at first the leaden steps of the intruder seemed to be heading for the stairwell, crashing farther and farther away from me, then the thumping stopped. He knew no one was actually upstairs. In my mind's eye I could just see him picking up a rock at the foot of the steps, connecting the dots. The floor went nearly silent. Even in the quiet, I could tell he was only a few feet away from me, keeping vigilant, waiting for confirmation someone was here and trying to fool him. Now that my plan hadn't worked, I didn't know what to do. I couldn't stay up here forever, and Destan and Irene were expecting some sort of signal to come in and tie him up. In between the silence came wheezing breaths, inhaling and exhaling with a mechanical rhythm. Surprisingly soft steps tapped the floor, creeping closer. I had my bow awkwardly pressed in the space in between the table and my back, and with my eyes glued to the ground, I realized with a sickening jolt that I'd tracked in a fine, hardly noticeable grit of snow onto the smooth wooden floorboards.

Oh no.

There was a grind of gears, shadow danced in the sunlight and appeared behind the hanging edge of the table cloth as he crouched down and gloved fingers appeared at the floor. He swabbed the pad of his thumb across the thin layer of frost, rubbing it in between his fingers, then stood back up and paced away from the table.

Please don't look under here, I prayed, *Please, please just turn your back and go upstairs or get out so I can send a signal.*

This time, not even breathing broke the silence. The clicking of gears and rush of air had stopped. But I didn't dare move yet. A cold sweat had condensed on my forehead, and a single drop trickled from my temple to past my eye and sticking to my chin. The only thing keeping me calm was the fact that if I closed my eyes, I felt invisible–

CRASH!

The table split in half with a deafening crack and I felt the thick heel of the man's boot jam into my back, the pain traveling up my entire spine like a flame. My face connected with the floor, and as I struggled to push myself up with my hands, he increased the pressure and my cheek slammed down hard again. He didn't make a single sound aside from the steady, unnatural breathing, and I heard a whoosh and suddenly there was a metal belt of some kind under my chin yanking my neck back slowly and painfully. I couldn't open my mouth to scream because he'd pulled my jaw completely shut. I was stuck and only seconds away from having my neck snapped from my spine. I flapped my arms about wildly, smacking his metal-clad calf to no avail. I couldn't fight him, he was stronger than me and I had moments before I was done for.

I rolled my eyes to the back of my head and let my arms flop, forcing myself not to keep gagging as he increased pressure on my windpipe. After only a few seconds of feigning death, I felt the belt slacken under my chin. My head crashed onto the floor and his heavy metal boot left my back. I could feel his hot breath on my face as he bent down to observe me, and as soon as he got close enough, I grabbed an arrow from my quiver and shoved it deep into the crack between his knee guard and thigh plate where a small window of fabric connected them.

His scream was that of a scraping of gears, a high pitched screech not half-human but completely mechanical, only very quietly was there a deep male voice howling in the background. I rolled onto my back and then leapt up, avoiding his kick and nocking in an arrow. Strangely enough, we raised our bows in the same manner, at the same time. But unlike my standard recurve bow, he had an official, military crossbow equipped with gleaming obsidian arrows. His mask was silver and  hard, with the strange mouthpiece Destan had described. He was a JP who'd been upgraded, made impervious. The only note of humanity was through the bulletproof visor where bright blue eyes stared.

"Who are you?" I said, loudly, receiving nothing, not even a narrowing of eyes. "Did Councilman Sebastian Lao send you? Did Sebastian send you?" I demanded, watching his chest heave up and down as he waited with his weapon raised. Then he made almost a nod of sorts and began to lower his bow, eyes still piercing into mine. As an act of mutual fighting, my bow lowered as well so that we were on equal grounds. Maybe he'd want to talk? Unlikely. We continued staring, my knuckles clenched white on my bow handle. Then at once we both broke form and struck, him kicking over a chair, and me sliding between his legs and sprinting for the stairs.

"Now!" I screamed toward the window, trying not to focus on the heavy footfalls coming closer and closer behind me. The adrenaline kept me up to speed, my lungs and back aching from when he'd tried to break me in half. I ran in zigzags down the hall to avoid his onslaught of arrows and then ducked into the master bedroom, locking the door even though I knew how easy it would be for him to bust through it.

I ran to the fireplace and shoved Ai quickly down my dress, tucking the hem of it into my leggings to keep her from falling out. And thinking fast, I wrapped up a pillow in my coat and tossed it straight out of the window, hoping that maybe it would convince him that I'd jumped or fallen out to escape. From up here it could have easily been my small body lying in the snow.

The instant he crashed into the room, I slid out of the window and plastered myself to the outside wall of the tower, making sure he'd gotten a glimpse of me. It worked. He ran to the window and stuck his metal head out, staring straight down at the heap on the ground. There was a screech of gears and he propelled himself from the windowsill and straight down to my coat, landing on his feet.

Unable to stand any longer on the sliver of a ledge going around the tower wall, I eased myself back toward the windowsill, Ai frightened and nipping at my collarbone from inside my dress. But just as my boots touched down, I felt Irene and Destan's hands yank me in, their faces flushed and frightened.

"Raine! What—?"

"BOARD THE DOORS AND WINDOWS!" I said, running to the stairs and down as the cyborg realized his mistake and released a terrible scream I thought would echo in my ears forever.

chapter fifteen

We'd blocked every entrance, boarded every window with whatever we could find; we'd stacked boxes upon boxes to block the hatch from opening from the outside, and now we sat, in sweaty silence, inside the chilly castle tunnel below the dining room. There wasn't much we could do about the top room's ripped roof and windows, so this was the only spot that felt secure enough to hide in when there was a vengeful cyborg on the loose.

Around where the hatch dropped down into the tunnel, an archway of mossy stone was set in place; dripping with dew and liquified clay. On either side of the archway, the tunnel took off into two separate, endless directions. Thick spiderwebs coated the walls surrounding us, and we made our way down each side for a couple of minutes, feeling for a cutoff or endpoint. And yet, the farther we walked, the more it seemed that the underground caverns could go on for miles.

"You don't think they could run under the entire valley, do you?" I asked, pausing to peer into the endless dark ahead. I waved my torch from side to side, hoping for a gleam of something to catch the light, but in front of me remained flat blackness. My heart began to thrum anxiously in my chest, that horrible suffocating feeling squeezing in my lungs. Just as I thought I might be on the verge of a panic attack, Destan's hand appeared in mine. My breathing slowed, and feeling the warmth of his skin pressed to mine helped to bring my breathing back to normal.

"Let's see..." Destan murmured, releasing my hand and pulling at the various roots spiralling from the tunnel wall. He stuck a small clump of the dead plants and dirt on the tip of an arrow, and moving fluidly into an effective anchor, shot straight into the darkness. Collectively we sucked in a breath and held it, Irene counting softly as the orangey flames dimmed and the arrow kept flying. Ten seconds later and we never heard the arrow strike a wall. We didn't even hear it drop once it had lost its height and energy to fly. "Well..." Destan sighed, slinging his bow over his shoulder and taking my hand in his again, "I wouldn't go any farther after that."

"Wait! Over here, we have to check out this shit," Irene called, after jogging back below the tower entrance and kneeling by the piles of boxes and barrels. She kicked open a rickety wooden cabinet and then sifted carelessly through what sounded like glass bottles. It took only seconds before she hoisted above her head a tall jug of corked victory. She grinned widely, "I knew there had to be something special stashed. Anyone care for a drink while we wait for the murderous cyborg to give up and fight another day?"

She chucked it into my beckoning hands, but once I caught it I was suddenly unsure. Watching the amber liquid slosh inside did not help to ease my nervous stomach. "I don't know, Irene...shouldn't we stay sharp until we know he's gone? What if he breaks into the tunnel?"

"Judging by the fact that the dining room window had been broken, hinting that the cyborg has no idea of the tunnel entry, and we have with us what is most likely the only key to the tunnel door, I think we're actually pretty good, Bluehead," Destan said, shrugging and joining Irene to paw through for more alcohol. He withdrew what looked like a full tank of ale, and Irene sniffed what she had in her hands and confirmed it to be brandy.

"*You* don't have to if you don't want to," Irene said, nodding at me and taking the first long draw from her bottle. She grimaced as the drink touched her lips, and then smiled as the gulp washed down. The spy wiped her mouth, adding, "Not trying to be all peer-pressure-y or anything but it's not as if we're going to have much of a chance any time soon to take a break and just relax like this, sweetie. Do you really not have any sorrows to drown?"

I considered the bottle, tentatively yanking out the cork and wafting the fragrance of the drink to my nose. My head filled with the harshly sweet aroma of whiskey. Very well-aged whiskey. I bit my lip, definitely tempted. And after throwing my quiver on the ground, I drained half of the bottle in a minute.

"And I said to that tiangou beasty, 'Go find another spot to take a shit, will ya'?'" Irene hollered, retelling the same stupid story for the fourth time now and waving her arms frantically as some of the drink escaped from her bottle and dribbled down her arm.

"No, no, don't spill the happy juice!" I cried, stumbling over to her and leaning the bottle safely against the tunnel wall. Irene looked at me and hiccupped, sending me and Destan into a woozy, nauseating fit of laughter. I toppled over onto my back, the torchlights spinning above me as I felt beside me for my drink. Instead I caught Destan's hand, and felt him roll over on his side to share a stale kiss. Irene started gagging and we pulled back from each other to tell her to screw off. I took another shot of brandy, welcoming the warm, silly numbness that came with it.

I had never, ever, ever, been drunk in my entire life until now. I'd drank with Irene and Destan before the Peak Tower thieving, I'd drank at the archery competition, but it wasn't until now that there had been much of a purpose and that purpose was to break the promise me and my friends had made long ago to never sink to the level of a drunkard. So many of them cluttered Underbrush's alleys and streets, crying and embarrassing themselves, until the JPs dragged their pathetic carcases to a holding cell for the night. Carmen's father had been one of them, and after seeing the damage that caused, the Song twins and me saw drinking as just something for the weak and pitiful. It wasn't until now that I realized we had been wrong to judge so harshly. Once you know how cruel life can be, how can you still belittle those who seek a moment of escape from it? When so many strong people succumb, how can you still say it is because they are too weak and not that the world is too merciless?

Anyway, I had never been drunk. And the only marker that let me know I was headed there was the growing stack of empty bottles in the middle of the tunnel. And, of course, the sudden funniness of everything.

"Man, my face is one ass's ass," Destan said, scowling at his reflection in one of the puddles gleaming on the floor, "I used to be so pretty."

"I think you're beautiful," I said, yawning as I rubbed my tummy. I felt so warm, my head was filled with a comfortable level of sleepiness, my eyes fading all harshness to a blearier shade. Siri laid calmly behind me, Ai fighting her own reflection in a puddle a couple feet away. A drowsy, peaceful warmth echoed all around us, coming in waves with every sip we took from a new bottle or mug of old moonshine.

Irene hiccupped again, crawling over to take Destan's and my hand in hers, "You two are my best friends. BFFs." She kissed our foreheads and tossed her mug at an empty crate. It missed by a few feet and conked off the wall, making us all crack up again.

"Don't flatter us knuckleheads, don't you have some spy besties back home?" Destan asked, hands on his hips.

"Nope, nope, nope. No one digs Irene back home. But you two? You dig me. And you get me," Irene said, nodding and smiling. "And the added bonus? You got some good faces for me to look at. You're both sexy as hell. Sexy..." Her voice trailed off and suddenly she screamed, clapping a hand over her mouth and shaking with laughter as she yelled, "SEXY! Get it? Because you make babies together!"

"Hey! No making fun!" Destan retorted, "You're immature, miss 'super-secret spy oh no I'm gonna be blown up blah blah blah.' No babies made."

"Oh, baby's made, all right," I said, patting my stomach and smiling as Destan's eyebrows shot up his forehead. "This baby makes me awfully pukey pukey."

"Liar, you don't have a baby," Irene snorted. "You're not even fat."

"It's a skinny baby," I said, suddenly overwhelmed by how good it felt to say it out loud. Who knew that in my drunken state I could get such a huge worry off of my chest!

"Okay, okay, let's stop joking now. My Bluehead can't have a baby," Destan rolled his eyes and then squeezed them shut, his arms crossed tightly over his chest. He scooted up against Siri and buried his face in the fluff of her silver tail, spitting as some of her fur got in his nose. She growled warningly and then settled her chin back on her paws, her green eyes following me as I crawled forward and brought my lips to Destan's ear.

"Bluehead can," I whispered. An eye blinked opened and peered at me through the thin veil of fur.

"Bluehead can?" he asked.

"Mmhmm."

"Raine…" He shook his head slowly, both eyes fluttering shut again as the sigh morphed into a snore and I knew I had lost him. The bottle in his hand rolled to the floor, spinning twice in a circle before bumping into my knee and stopping. His breathing calmed, and his face relaxed into a slack mouth, loose jaw, and eyelids smoothed by the dreams gliding beneath them. He'd fallen asleep. Or, was faking to change the subject. I frowned and Irene chuckled.

I went to move and my balance was off kilter. I tipped over and landed on the towering pile of bottles, rubbing my backside and looking around me in a daze as Irene helped me clumsily to my feet Maybe drinking hadn't been a good escape. I felt more nauseous than ever, my stomach had completely balled up, and the warmth inside of me was now uncomfortably hot. It was hard to breathe, but I was wary of going outside since I might just topple over and land splat on the snow for the cyborg to find.

Irene burped a loud, froggish burp, looking accusingly at the drink in her hand and glaring. "No more. This gal is done. I am waaaay too drunk."

"I'm not drunk enough," I murmured, my head full of cottonballs and my stomach churning all of the alcohol into a sour ocean. The sorrows inside me had found a life raft and were sailing ashore back to my consciousness, not drowned in the slightest. If anything, they were cheering and celebrating their survival, making me feel worse and more anxious than ever. How could I tell him I thought we might be parents in less than a year? Would he really be that opposed? What was I supposed to do if he remembered our conversation and woke up tomorrow, furious with me?

Irene scooched up close and laid her head comfortably in my lap. She sighed a content sigh, walking two fingers up my thigh as she whispered, "You *are* joking about the baby, right?"

I ran my fingers through her ponytail, picking at a knot in her thick black hair, "I'm not joking."

She looked up at me, her eyes wide and slightly unfocused as she said, "You really made a baby? Ohhhh noooooo...that...that complicates stuff."

"Stuff," I repeated, staring up at the tunnel hatch.

"I'm not gonna remember this tomorrow, you know that right? Even now your face is all mashed potatoes to me, sexy Raine," Irene slurred, giggling and rubbing her temples. "I can give you some drunk advice if you want it, though. I'm just full of wisdom right now. Overflowing with it."

"Go for it," I said, smiling weakly as she lifted her head up. Irene began to stare intensely at the puddle in front of her where Ai had been lapping up water. She raised a shaky finger, closing her eyes. Her lips parted, the wise words waiting on her tongue.

"All you have to do, Raine Ylevol," she started to say, tucking her chin and suddenly making a sour face. She pursed her lips, and before I could stop her she had vomited a bellyful of brandy and sage advice into my lap. I leapt out of the final spray, scooping Ai into the crook of my elbow and pinching my nose to keep the smell from making my stomach turn inside out as well. Irene shook her head, "I think it's time I hit the sack."

"I think so, too," I squeaked, holding my breath as the puke-drenched dress clung to my legs and middle. "I'm pretty sure the cyborg has chosen to visit another time...I'm gonna go put on something not so vomity."

The spy held a shaky thumbs-up and then let the hand drop to the floor with the rest of her. She was snoring before I even made it up the ladder to the dining room. Everything seemed to be closer than it appeared to me, making climbing a slow and frustrating process and walking even harder. I was so angry with myself. Not only had getting drunk made me dumb as a sack of rocks, I could fall and break my neck because of how unsteady this made me, and only now did I question whether alcohol was okay to consume while you may be pregnant. I'd taken four shots of whiskey and random sips from other concoctions I hadn't cared to identify. I was stupid and reckless and tripping over my own feet with the stench of vomit fresh and gross in my nose.

We'd stacked all sorts of junk in the windows and in front of various doors to keep the cyborg out, and the piles were just as we'd left them. He hadn't come in. He hadn't even tried. I staggered over to the wardrobe in the upper bedroom to change into something not covered in Irene's stomach fluids, and then went to the bathroom to guzzle as much water as I could. I thought I'd heard once that water helped to get you through being drunk. After sitting and drinking for nearly an hour, my head still felt heavy and my eyes were still bleary, but the dizziness had gone. I still didn't trust myself going down all of those stairs and into that dark and gloomy tunnel.

I instead walked morosely to the bookshelf, hoping to find something that could take my mind off of everything. My fingers ran over their dusty spines, feeling leather, cloth, paper bindings. Some of the titles had been rubbed off with age and use, but with my eyes now level with the shelves I could still manage to make out a few familiar ones. First I saw the collection of Spirit Tales every Underbrusher child had been read to get through the cold and hungry season. This volume was bound in red silk and the edges of the pages were painted gold. I flipped through and saw page after page of endless words, no pictures to show. Whoever had owned the book had also filled it with illegible marginalia; nearly every page commented on with personal diagrams and captions. The copy my mother had read to me was much thinner and waterlogged, and completely told in pictures, which made it all the more fun to learn the stories when I was so little. I also recognized a few dictionaries, some famous historical novels I'd read (or had pretended to read) in school, and a field guide for medicinal plants.

Once I'd skipped to the next shelf, however, I noticed that the spines had changed and were all the same. It seemed to be a set of uniform bundles of parchment, sewn together into books with multicoloured string. Each volume stood side by side, leaning against one another in the dust, and the row of strange books stopped before reaching the end of the shelf. I gingerly tugged one from its place, blowing through the film of dust on the cover. The letters danced a little bit in and out of focus since I was still a tad intoxicated, but they came together coherently in the end. *Journal 3*, I read to myself, sticking it back in and taking out the one at the beginning of the row. *Journal 1...okay, now this is interesting,* I thought, glancing around to find a candle for some light to read by. *Hopefully the ghost of whoever wrote this isn't here and going to haunt me for snooping.* I dug around in the drawer of the bedside table for the candle and sparking stones, then found a comfy spot to settle down with Journal 1.

One week before, it began. Before what? I pulled my knees to my chest and kept reading without letting my thoughts interrupt with questions.

One week before, last day of winter.

I no longer believe that our plan will work. He's told me that the passage from his end is nearly cleaned out, but Chodak isn't finished clearing out the caved-in section of ours and every day closer to it is bringing me farther and farther from my wanting to see him. I love him, I do, but is it worth the risk? I'm lying to mother and father and I'm even lying to Indira now, as if we weren't already lacking sisterly love. Chodak only knows because he found some of our letters, but Solomon swears that we won't get caught. His parents are really getting on his case though, I'm afraid. He's been arranged to marry some girl from his mountain level and he told me that she is absolutely sour and he misses me more and more every moment we are apart. I believe him and I love him, but I'm scared and can't help it. It feels like a century has passed since the day he saved me from his mountain's wretched police, and yet I remember it all so clearly as if it were yesterday. But I can't tell if I'm filling in my memory with what I wanted it to be like, and he's just a faraway stranger, a ghost I'm trying to make real again. With that being said I still can't keep myself from thinking of him. His piercing blue eyes, like water bathed in the light of the moon. His skin, looking so pure and white against mine when he held my hand and guided me *into the woods to make our escape. The kiss we shared before the blasted palace guards finally took me away. So short but so tender, replaying in my mind the entire ride back home and even now, months later as I sit watching the ocean tide go in and out. Damn it if I don't take the leap and find out for myself if it's real between us. I will meet him even if I have to grab a shovel myself and dig until my hands bleed.*

She drew the tunnel, and I traced my finger along the inky smudges. The tunnel beneath the tower ran in two directions from Fluxaria to Thgindim, and the Tower was built closer to the Fluxaria end by ten miles or so. Ten miles. Only ten miles left, only *ten miles from here?*

My heart beat against my ribs so hard and fast that it made it hard to breathe; hard to sit still. I no longer felt drunk and unfocused, I felt as if I could take off down the tunnel right now and come up to see Fluxaria in all its splendour. But at the same time, I had to keep reading to know what had happened.

<u>*Two days before, the snow is melting.*</u>

I had been waiting until I could hold myself together to write, but even with my brother being dead for days now my hands won't stop shaking and it's good I'm the only one who has to read this because my writing is beyond illegible right now. The whole mountain is calling it an accident that the crown prince died while digging out a tunnel underground, a tunnel that my sister is sure I had something to do with, and I feel like I killed Chodak. I killed him. I went into one of my fits again when father told me and I just blurted out everything. About the plan, about Solomon, and I have to thank the spirits for making me so distraught my parents were convinced I was spouting nonsense and they only listened to half of it before sending me off to the healers. I don't remember all of it, just bits and pieces while my energy was brought back to normal. Being in a hospital bed didn't keep Indira from bursting in and dumping a waterfall of accusations into my lap. I had enough sense at that point to keep my mouth shut about my full intentions. I admitted that he and I were building a passageway beneath Mythland to reach the Thgindimmer who saved me on the other side, but I didn't let slip that Solomon was also building a tunnel, and was finished and waiting a little more than halfway to Fluxaria for me to meet him. She called me idiotic saying that was the most ridiculous and dangerous and selfish scheme, and she never thought I was that messed up in the head that I caused our healthy twenty year-old brother to have a heart attack because I tried to make him do the impossible. She threw my meal tray at me and in return I chucked my piping hot cup of tea at her face and we started <u>really</u> fighting, it was unbelievable! We had never gotten physical in even our worst arguments, but now we were punching any bit of each other that we could reach, screaming and pulling hair, pinching and digging our nails in as deep as they could go. It didn't go on long enough for either of us to be injured. My mother came in and broke us apart. Indira rattled off everything to her, resulting in me getting locked in my bedroom. I tried so hard to convince mama she had to let me see Solomon again, and she sympathised with the fact that I had strong feelings for him but nevertheless said she couldn't bear to see another one of her children lose their lives. I couldn't do anything after that but let her hug me for a long while. She said she'd have a constant flow of maids at my door to make sure I didn't leave my room unattended. And that my father had ordered for the tunnel to be destroyed tomorrow afternoon. That means I'll have to find a way out and go before any of the filling in of it begins. I sent a letter off to Solomon today, but now I just hate this escape and I'm beginning to hate myself. I should stay and mourn my brother who's been there for me and Solomon since the beginning, but at the same time he died so that Solomon and I could reunite. How could I possibly not go when he died for this? I am so torn and feel that I have almost completely disappeared. I half wish that I will disappear, I just want to see my brother again and stop feeling this terrible guilt. I hate myself. I should just let Solomon marry the sour girl. She's probably much better and not as selfish as I.

One hour before.

I am packed and I am going, no more second-guessing it. I can feel Chodak's spirit with me, encouraging me to go forward and not look back until after we've met and had some time together. Then I'll return. For mother's sake. And maybe I can convince Solomon to come back with me and once my family meets him and sees how amazing he is they might let him stay. Not to mention it doesn't matter so much who I marry because Indira's getting the throne, so it could maybe work. Fluxaria hardly needs the royals, and in truth, the royals hardly need me, the baby of the family who has been "raising hell from the womb" {according to my father}. Maybe it is selfish of me to run away with him after all that's happened with Chodak, but I can't bear this mountain any longer. I feel like I'm suffocating with every breath I take, and empty words I give to all of the people coming to grieve and offer their condolences. All I want right now is to escape into Solomon's arms as I did that last night we were together. I can't bear the hatred festering toward Solomon's home, I can't bear the dull palace life and letters I have to send through to Solomon in secret. The feilong of his is horrible with scents and so only flies on blood moons and I have to rely on faithful Han to travel through what's been built of the tunnel so far and deliver messages, but that takes weeks at a time to get there and back. I should also mention that Han has agreed to break me out of my bedroom when she takes on her shift to keep guard of me. I act so prickly towards her in front of mother so she'd never suspect we'd been conspiring together for months, so my mother will also never suspect Han to be the culprit who let her wild daughter loose. I am done with putting up with my sister's perfect everything and seeing the shame on my parents' faces whenever my name is spoken. I don't want to go to that dark place again. I'm finished with hurting myself and trying to die, with letting my emotions cause me to do whatever they please no matter who it hurts, but I will get hurt and risk everything to get to a life I can live. I need to see if a life with Solomon is a life I don't ony have to bear, but can truly love living. Chodak believed I would be better off with Solomon in a cottage in the valley than in this palace on the mountain. He knew how toxic Fluxaria has gotten for me so I will just have to trust him and trust myself with this.

I shut the journal, placed it back carefully in its slot and grabbed the next one. I tried to wrap my head around it. These journals belonged to a Fluxarian princess, a Fluxarian princess in love with a Thgindimmer? I peeked at the inside cover and rubbed hastily at the coating of grime to read the name. *Property of Shardza Taiyang, age 16.* How long ago was this? Was I the only one who knew this story? And had she given a clue about Ai and how she would fly home on the blood moon? A feilong, she had called her, a means of sending letters. I wouldn't waste another moment not knowing, I pulled back the cover of Journal 2 and heard the spine creak beneath my fingers.

If it weren't for this tiny shard of candlelight, I'm not sure if I could write! But I am on my way to Solomon, pumping the cart Han used to deliver our letters and I just hope that nothing has happened and everything will go as planned. It's freezing underground, my skin feels like it is lined with snowflakes and it smells so terrible down here, like the earth is diseased or rotting. Mythland is sick in its roots, it seems.

One week after, full moon. The centaur is high in the stars.

I'm sorry I haven't written in a while, I had to actually live my life and not just record and ramble on about it. Solomon came to meet me in the tunnel and I can't remember ever being so happy. Suddenly, all my worries are gone. The little cottage in the valley turned out to be a magnificent tower he built himself in this wildly beautiful and exotic jungle of a forest, and he's painted me and sketched for me so many beautiful pictures and we get to sleep in a pool of moonlight every night because it comes singing in through the grand glass window of the top floor and we made love for the first time last night and I have never felt so absolutely alive and myself after all these horrible months without him. He said that we mustn't stay though. Only for a week or weekend this time because not everything is in order. He says he has to fake his death in order to escape that horrible Justice Police, that he'll have to completely vanish before being able to know we're safe here, together. I told him about coming to Fluxaria, but he said he couldn't risk that either, no matter how much he wished he could. He just knows Thgindim would blow his disappearance out of proprtion and call it a crime Fluxaria is committing against her sister mountain. I told him I could stay here and wait for him to return, but he told me unless I'd cut all ties with my family, I shouldn't dare stay. Returning and leaving will be excruciating, and I don't know if I can just slip out again, even with Han's help. My mother will do more than ever to keep me trapped. And I do have some more things I'd want to take along with me from home, just some trinkets and things of Chodak's, but how can I leave this paradise? Ever since coming here, so cut off, in this illusionary dream, I am realizing how real it could be just to stay here and never go back. He's stored enough food to last for months, and by the time it runs out, we will have figured out how to glean food from the land. Plus, hunting is always safe. We have a strong structure to protect us from these awful storms that rattle us every night, and he even brought me a ton of yarn and tools so I am able to craft my own clothes. I know there must be something he isn't telling me because I cannot for the life of me see why it is so pertinent he go back once more; why vanishing this time isn't enough. I want to trust him, but he's changed since we were first together and while my love is stronger, my faith in him is wavering. He says he has nothing to return home to since his parents perished in the factories and his arranged marriage is all that remains of what could be seen as family. The Justice Police do nothing but abuse him and he works under oath to the same Council who locked me in a cage for months. I can't bear it and I can't bear how scared he looks when I catch him on his own somewhere in the tower. Just last night I woke up to an empty pillow beside me, and there he was, entire body trembling, squatting in the hallway and weeping. I was so shocked and frightened, I just lay very still in bed and pretended to be asleep when he joined me again. Maybe I can change his mind. Maybe I can convince him that we'd do just fine here, start a life and move on from the awful past we both had to live through. I owe my life to him, eternally. When those police caught me and took me to Thgindim, I was positive that I was going to die there. But instead Solomon risked his life to save me and broke me out in disguise and led me through Mythland until my guards showed up. He is the reason I am alive and after bonding with him, I now know he is the reason that I continue living. He bonded with me before we even physically bonded, he understands me and cares about me, not who he wants me to be. That is most important of all. He believes that together we can be free from the royal life of Fluxaria and the horrible oppression on Thgindim and paint to our hearts' content out here. We'll have children and pets and learn to ride tiangou and build tree houses up so high we can kiss the stars at night. It's a silly dream, but this is my journal and I will write all of the silliest, most selfish, worst things I want because there is no one else who will listen. Except for Solomon. Having him here, I no longer keep everything locked in ink and parchment. He accepts my scars and mistakes and I can tell him anything. Most things I don't even have to tell him, he just knows or senses how I feel, what I'm thinking. I hope someday I can return to Solomon Shirong Ylevol all of the wise and beautiful things he has offered to me. Until then, I am grateful.

chapter sixteen

"I have a headache, dude..."

"You're not the one who drank five pints."

"Yeah, I had *six*, scarface."

I rubbed my temples, feeling a headache of my own brewing. "Guys, I know your hangovers suck but please stop complaining or else I might just jump through the window," I muttered, hearing both of them sigh and get back to eating the meat we'd scored from yesterday. I hadn't bit into my little rabbit leg yet. Every time I looked at it, my stomach heaved. Leaning back in my chair, I sipped my water, watching my friends stuff their faces.

"Sorry, Bluehead," Destan said, rubbing my shoulder and sticking his grinning face into my grumpy frame of vision. "On the bright side, Mr. Cyborg is nowhere to be found, we have this snazzy food, and the eclipse is tonight, which will be fun to see."

"Ooo, man I wish I was back home right now. Fluxaria goes all out for the first red moon. Cakes, lanterns, fireworks, the whole shebang," Irene said, dreamily leaning her cheek on her hand.

"Wait." I glanced up, "What did you say?"

"'Shebang' isn't in Thgindim terminology?"

I shook my head, "No, no, before that. What about the red moon?"

Destan spat out a bone and looked at me in surprise. "You've never seen a total lunar eclipse, Bluehead? The full moon goes all red and looks huge and mighty for a night. It's quite the spectacle."

I stood up, pushing my plate towards Destan to eat. My thoughts ran back and forth from one end of my mind to the other, and as I tried to catch hold of a single one, I noticed I too was pacing. My voice shook, "I've heard of it, I just hadn't connected the dots until now...wow...an eclipse. On Ai's egg, on her egg, Chan had written 'will find me on the blood moon,' the red moon, during a total eclipse. That has to be when Ai gets called back to Thgindim or something, maybe it's an intuitive thing and she just knows when to fly."

"Okay, hold up, girlfriend," Irene interjected, scooting her chair into my pacing-track and stopping me suddenly. "Who the hell is 'Ai'?"

"You didn't see it yet?" Destan raised an eyebrow, "Raine's got herself a mini-dragon thing. One of her friends back home snuck the egg into her hair before we got kicked into Mythland. It's pretty fucking sweet."

I nodded, "She's been sleeping by the fire, and sometimes I'd put her in my knapsack, so that's probably why you didn't notice her. She's pretty quiet." My eyes found the stairs and I wondered if I should fetch Ai now and bring her down, both to give her something to eat and to show Irene. Then I remembered I'd seen her stalking her own breakfast of bugs and mice, and I leaned back against the table, turning to Irene.

The Fluxarian stared at me long and hard, her mouth opening and closing, the words stuck on her tongue. Then she swallowed, whispering, "So, you're telling me, that on your grey, corrupt, craphole of a mountain, there are feilong just casually living and laying eggs? And there's one just snoozing by the fireplace upstairs? *Right* now?"

I squinted, uncertainly, "Yes? Maybe...what did you call her?"

"Feilong, a.k.a. mini flying dragon thing," Irene rolled her eyes, pushing out from the table and striding over to the stairway. Judging by her speed, I took this as something of urgency and followed after her, hearing Destan hastily chug the rest of his tea and jog behind me. The back of Irene's neck was bright red. Why she was so upset I had no idea. "Jeez, I cannot *believe* you didn't give me a heads up about this...do you have any idea how important this is to saving Fluxaria?"

Destan and I exchanged equally confused looks, coming into the bedroom to see Irene crouched by the fireplace. She sat on the balls of her feet, palms pressed to the ground as she glared ahead into Ai's wide, dark eyes. The little creature had its long, ribbon-like body bunched up in anticipation for whatever the stranger across from her had planned. Her whiskers fanned out and swiped at the floor, nostrils flared and eyes narrowing to slits. I felt a jolt of maternal instinct take over, and I walked right in between the two of them, bending down and scooping Ai safely into my arms.

"Okay, Irene, enough. What is going on?" I demanded, cradling Ai close to my chest. Irene looked appalled at how I held her.

"Contacting Fluxaria, that's what," she scoffed, pointing a short finger at the bundle still tensed and anxious in my arms. "Raine, feilong are *spirit messengers*. Or at least they were before the mountains split. They were humans' only contact with the spirit world, and then when we fucked up and heaven closed up, all of the feilong as well as other beings connected to the spirits were said to be stripped of their divinity. Left on earth to settle in alongside the basic animals. Before the mountains split, the tribes had been given a warning. If the fighting between us could cease by the blood moon, then the spirits would let their messengers remain intact as well as our singular mountain. Of course, we couldn't stop fighting.

"When we heard that not only would we lose half of our territory, but also lose our connections to the spirit world, it became a free for all. Your tribe and my tribe both started grabbing all of the divine messengers we could get our hands on and slaying the ones already claimed. The midnight tribe–your tribe, what became Thgindim– pretty much won all of them. Which ultimately sucked because then your mountain got all industrial and secular, and had allegedly wiped out all of the remaining divine messengers and rubbed it in Fluxaria's face that you'd finally brought an end to the 'tyranny of the spirits' or some Majesty Council bullshit.

"But if this is really a feilong, which I'm pretty damn sure it is, then we have a sure-fire way to send a message to Fluxaria that we survived the Peak Tower heist, that we're on our way in Mythland with life-saving information, and that if they can send troops to come and pick us up, it would be greatly appreciated."

I glanced down at Ai, at her little head, at the tiny golden claws pushing into my skin as she clung to my wrist. How could this small, scaly gift from my best friend be what Irene was describing? Where would Chan find such a creature, and how could she know its significance? I looked from Irene to Destan, my stomach turning as another thought crept into my head. *Chantastic had written that it would find HER on the blood moon, not Fluxaria. If it doesn't reach her, she's going to think I'm dead. She's going to think I'm dead. She'll tell her sister, Carmen, everyone who loves me, whose depending on me.*

"So...what's our course of action?" Destan asked, withdrawing a hand from his pocket to grab my waist. Somehow, the touch didn't bring me the comfort it intended.

"Draft a letter. Make it sound fancy and impress the hell out of them with our survival skills and dedication to strong vocabulary. Then send it off at moonrise," Irene said.

"Wait," I whispered, pulling excuses from the air, "but how do we know Ai can make it all the way to Fluxaria? We might not be even halfway through Mythland yet, and she only hatched about a week ago. And what if she's intercepted? If the cyborg gets her we could be in even more danger."

"These things are *called* by the blood moon, Raine. Even if the feilong popped out of her egg this morning, she'd be ready to fly where destiny takes her. To Fluxaria."

I argued right back, "But what if she goes the opposite way, Irene? What makes you think she'd be called to Fluxaria and not Thgindim: where she's from?"

"Because unlike your mountain, Fluxaria is a spiritual magnet. We've got temples from before the split, untouched and still brewing with all sorts of mystical shit! Even if she's from Thgindim, there's no way that a divine spirit messenger would be pulled in the opposite direction of where the spirits are still worshipped, that's completely backwards."

"But she's not a divine spirit messenger! She's just an animal, a baby animal with animal instincts to return home. That is all that's left," I exclaimed, my cheeks burning up, "You said it yourself, all of the make-believe magic stuff was taken out by the spirits. The spirits, you, for some reason, still depend on."

She shook her head slowly, smirking, "Why are you being such a bitch about this? Don't you want Fluxaria to get us out of here before the cyborg blows us up?"

"Irene, of course she does," Destan said, "so quit it with the name-calling. Let's just think on it for now and stop spouting whatever comes into our heads, okay?" He looked from her to me, a frown creasing his mouth. "We don't have time to fight. Not with each other."

"He's right," I whispered, sliding out from his hold and walking towards the window. Ai chirped excitedly, ready to taste the wind and catch some bugs for breakfast. As I fastened the yarn back around her neck, I added, "There's something more urgent I need to tell you."

Irene gave a short laugh, quietly muttering, "More urgent than preventing a war..."

Destan shot her a warning glance and she returned it with an eyeroll. She stuck out her tongue as he turned his head. "What is it, Raine?" he asked.

I launched Ai into the wind, her body winding in and out of the air currents and then disappearing in the trees. I walked away from the window, over to the pile of journals I'd left scattered on the floor. Destan and Irene followed, kneeling beside me. I opened the first one, passing it to Irene, "I know how to get us to Fluxaria, safely. The tunnel below us? It connects Thgindim to Fluxaria– and I know how to get back to Fluxaria safely," I said.

"You know what now?" Irene asked skeptically, slowly reaching for another can of food.

I pointed up at the ceiling, "I found these books upstairs last night, journals, really. Journals of the girl who lived here, or I guess escaped here to meet with...her lover. Thgindim lover."

"Not exactly the most charming place for a date." Irene said.

Destan shrugged. "I dunno. The giant hole in the roof is great for stargazing."

"Anyway, the tunnel goes from Fluxaria to Thgindim, straight through. The tower was built closer to Fluxaria because this was where the girl was coming from and she met...." All words had dried up in my throat as I stared at my father's name in Princess Shardza's loopy cursive. After reading it last night I'd ended up waltzing in that same sort of hallucinogenic dream that I'd been in the night I'd found Destan's body and gulping down pints of ale until my head was emptied. I'd gotten so drunk that the world had begun to drown with me chained to the bottom, only to throw it all up this morning. Solomon Ylevol, Solomon Ylevol, *Solomon Ylevol?* It couldn't be, it just couldn't.

"Raine?" Destan's voice was soft, yet broke into my tangential thoughts. I blinked slowly a few times, realizing he and Irene were staring. I opened my mouth to speak, getting the words out before my lips decided to seal again.

"Solomon...Solomon Ylevol built the tower. He was the Fluxarian princess's lover. Solomon Ylevol, my father," I said.

Irene was first to gasp, she stood up and jabbed a finger at me in confidence. "Princess Shardza! It's Shardza, right? Not Indira?" I nodded. "There were rumours about her disappearances that nobody could decipher...Raine, you just solved one of the biggest mysteries of my country. Fucking A+ job."

"But..." Destan said, his eyes flickering onto mine, "...your *dad?*"

Even though I pretended it didn't happen, Destan's gaze danced from my eyes to my blue hair in recognition of what we all knew had to be true now. But he went silent again, shoving his hands in his pockets and acting as if he hadn't connected the dots. *"You're not my daughter!"* said my mother, the night she kicked me out. Could it be she wasn't just angry and disowning me? Had she let something she'd been hiding slip? If my father had been intimate with both my mother and an exotic princess, what was the likelihood that his weird blue-haired daughter had come from the black-haired Underbrusher? Pretty damn low. I'd finally shattered the glass bubble I'd built up around my worry that after all of this fighting and work to bring peace, I didn't even belong on the mountain I called home, I'd been lying to everyone including myself my entire life.

"You know, Raine...since the moment I got a good look at you after you saved me, I detected there might be some kinship between us," Irene smirked. "But after getting to know you, to be quite honest I'd just thought you'd dyed it to stand out a little or seem more badass and wouldn't admit to it. I guess...shit, the reason I didn't decide you were definitely Fluxarian is because the only Fluxarians with hair like that are the royals. So, of course you couldn't be related to them, I thought. Now that that's a possibility...things have gotten a little interesting."

"I don't think we have time for interesting," I sighed, rubbing my eyes with my knuckles and trying to clear my head, "What's most important is that now we have a tunnel that runs straight from here to where we need to be. We could leave by tomorrow if we really wanted and had enough supplies." The prospect of having to walk for miles in the dark with all of these new and nasty thoughts and worries made my stomach heave, but I knew it was what we had to do. Especially with Mr. Cyborg knowing where we were camped.

"Sounds like a nice and sturdy plan, Bluehead," Destan nodded, squeezing my shoulders and shooting me an encouraging smile. He bent down to the bookshelf and slid out one of the not fully completed journals, paging through and tearing out some leaves of parchment. As he waved them in the air, he looked from me to Irene, "Sooo...who's going to write this brilliant letter to Fluxaria saying they should pick us up in our fancy underground tunnel?"

There were two letters. One, written by Irene. Succinct and to the point, even providing coordinates she was able to gather from Sebastian's tablet, and a hand drawn map copying Shardza's description of where the tunnel wove underground and led into the Fluxaria catacombs. The second letter, written by me. Hurriedly, in the private space of the bathroom, with shaking hands and a pounding headache. It was almost sunset. Destan had spent the day catching up on wrestle-time with Siri, Irene on her letter and experimenting with building a clockbomb, and me with reading nearly all of the following journals. Even with the letter to Chantastic in my hands, sealed and identical to Irene's– save a tiny thumbprint I'd smeared on the tiny scroll to distinguish them —I was back and forth about which to put in Ai's claws. I realized I was less positive, and more hoping that this feilong would fly from whence she came, and into the hands of the girl I loved and depended on so greatly. I was risking all of our safety by sending it the opposite way, to the opposite mountain we were trying to fend off. Now was not the time for me to be selfish, to value the feelings of my best friend and my own over that of an entire nation depending on us making it out alive, and soon. But deep down, I just couldn't accept that Ai would go to Fluxaria, even with Irene's message. She had not been born there, I doubted that there was any spirit left in her that would call her to some random temple of monks who see the spirit tales as pure fact. Here's what I wrote:

C—

I love you I LOVE YOU I LOVE YOU I LOVE YOU I LOVE YOU I LOVE YOU

I had to say that first, before anything else was put on this sheet of parchment. I'm lucky to have found parchment to write to you, but believe me when I say I've found stranger things scattered all around this twisted valley. Secondly, I'm okay. Sort of. Maybe. I'm with Destan and Irene (the spy) and we're travelling together now. The Majesty Council had split me and Destan up last minute and so it wasn't until a couple of days ago that I wasn't alone or with more unfriendly company. But before I get into things, I'm dying to know how you came across this little creature. Irene thinks it's something called a "feilong," some mystical creature. When she hatched, I actually had this flashback to some drawings I used to do when I was little, so I must've come across them at some point, but other than that I'm not sure what to think. I named her Ai, so that half of you is here with me. I miss you so much I've been dreaming of you every night. So, where did you get Ai? How did you know about her flying home on the blood moon? If this is actually being read by you right now, then that means she's made it to Thgindim, even though Irene had been positive it would end up on Fluxaria. I don't know. Both Irene and Destan are under the impression that this is a letter to the Fluxarian government, asking them for aid to get us out of Mythland. I don't think I've ever lied to them before. I didn't want to. But if I didn't contact you, then you would think I had died or hadn't taken care of the egg or kept it warm and it just terrified me and I couldn't let you believe that. Not to mention, you can pass along the knowledge to Velle and Carmen as well. If only Gwen could understand. She must think I've abandoned her. Was it selfish of me to send this? I feel so guilty but less so than if I'd used Ai to get to Fluxaria. Nothing feels real here, Chan. Even with Destan here and this shelter we've discovered, I still feel like I'm dragging myself through a neverending nightmare. I hate to be so melodramatic. There's just so much pain and fear inside of me that I don't know what to do with, how to get it out. Mythland has filled my head with so many questions I need answers to. I've seen creatures uglier and more fantastic and strange that I never thought could possibly exist outside of spirit tales. I've lost hope more times then I can count and it's so hard to stay strong when I know I'm in it so deep that if I screw up then it could lead to the destruction of an entire nation. Help me think of home. How's Gwen, how's my mother, how's Velle, Carmen, Auntie Jun from the Laundress pavilion, how's your granny, how are YOU? Have things changed greatly since I left or are things pretty much the same? Things were so scary in Underbrush right before I left, but then I remember the scariness was because they still hadn't hunted me and Destan down as the thieves so please tell me it's safe and people aren't being executed every day anymore. Tell me all you can. I don't know how many scrolls of parchment Ai can carry yet so I must sum up things here. Chantastic, I'm scared I might be pregnant. I'm overdue on my cycle and even though I first thought this was because of the lack of nourishment Mythland offers, I can feel my body changing. You see....Destan and I bonded. Only once, the night before we were taken to Peak. I know I haven't shared with you the details of our relationship, so I'm sorry this skipped from "partners in crime" to "engaging in sexual activity" since the last time we spoke about him. But since then I've bonded with another as well, against my will, many, many, horrible times before I was able to escape, and I'm terrified that monster's child could be inside of me and not Destan's. It's only been a couple of weeks since that happened, so it couldn't be his, right? Destan doesn't know yet, neither what happened with the other man, or what I think could be growing inside of me. I'm so scared to tell him and I wish you were here to hold me and lie and say everything will be okay because when I'm with you everything is okay and I need my best friend more than ever. There's one more thing, Chantastic. What happened in Peak Tower will remain between us, and I love you so much. May we see each other soon, all safe and sound.

All my love,

R

It seemed too short, there was so much to say, but for the first letter it would have to suffice. When Irene called me down and said the moon would be rising in less than an hour, I stowed my letter under my waistband and met her and Destan at the tunnel hatch. I took Ai and had her sit on my shoulder, and when we made it outside I knew she already sensed a change in the cosmos. She sniffed the air, her whiskers drifting up to brush my cheek. The sun was not quite set, a moody purple sky melting through the trees. Destan stood guard with two arrows nocked on the bowstring, pacing in a circle around us in case a hungry tiangou or vengeful cyborg decided to make an appearance. Just as we were losing light, Irene came over, passed me her letter, nodding at Ai.

"Think this little thing can hold this?" she asked. I nodded, taking Ai around the middle and sliding it through her clawed feet. She tossed her head defiantly, releasing the letter to land in damp and muddy moss. Irene caught it speedily as only a spy could manage, cursing under her breath and slicking back her hair. "Okay, let's do plan B. You got that leash?"

"Yeah, right here," I said, removing the long yellow string from my pocket and struggling to fasten it around Ai's right foot. I'd realized that with all of the body-morphing she seemed to do, it wouldn't be secure enough to attach the letter around her middle, or even her neck. She could completely flatten out from her neck to her tail, and I was not going to risk the letter slipping out from the tie once her body became an inch thinner. Her arms and legs, however, remained round and tucked to her side as she glided.

Irene glanced away as I worked on securing her scroll, and in the split second she yelled to Destan to see if the coast was clear, I tossed her letter behind me and switched it for my own. I stepped back and covered it with my boot, squinting to see in the fuzzy darkness as I made the final knot and Ai could suppress her energy no longer.

The moment my fingers left her scaly leg, she shot upward, completely vertical and ribbon-like as she flew. The moon floated like a pot of blood in the sky, and Ai soared higher, higher, her instincts taking over as the pull of the moon erased all other impulses than to fly home. Irene and I stood side by side, her hand gripping my arm tightly, nervously as she watched intently at our messenger glide above the shuishan trees and out of sight.

"You think she'll make it? All the way and everything?" Irene whispered, her eyes still glued to the sky above her. Even Destan had been spellbound, his bow lowered; his focus only on the crimson moon ruling the night.

I nodded to the spy, rubbing her hand gently, "I'm sure she's gonna make it. All the way home."

chapter seventeen

"True or false: I am sixteen years-old."

"False...wait...yeah, false."

"Nope. True, I hit the big one-six last month," he said.

I sat up in bed. "You're kidding."

Destan grinned, shaking his head and laughing softly. "Not kidding, Bluehead. Your turn."

"But wait," I demanded, turning to gape at him, touching his wrist, "when was your birthday? What day?"

"July 22."

"And how did you manage to keep track of what day it is, Destan?"

He lifted his arms up, chanting to the hole in the roof, "The *stars*, Bluehead. I'm an expert at stars, remember? Duh."

I traced a finger along the bare plane of his chest, over the valleys his ribs made, murmuring, "Then tell me what day it is, smarty-pants."

"True or false: you wouldn't believe me even if I told you."

"Probably true. I can't really fact-check, can I?"

He looked at me, reaching out and stroking a finger down my cheek. His front teeth came over his lip, a sigh breezing through his nose. He wanted to kiss me. Pretending I hadn't noticed, I averted my eyes and combed gingerly through his curls, accidentally brushing his scar. He playfully snapped at my finger, teeth coming together with a click and making me jump in shock. He pulled me in closely so that our foreheads touched, nose nuzzling mine softly. "True or false...you still wanna marry me?" he whispered, drawing back and meeting my eyes. I didn't know what he saw in them, but it made a worried crease trace into his forehead.

I smoothed it out with my thumb, replying, "True. Of course I do. Why?"

He shrugged, burrowing his head deeper into the pillow. "Just checking. I...I've just been a little worried about you."

"Worried about me?" I repeated. I could feel my heart begin to beat faster. "Why?"

"You just got a lot on your shoulders, I guess," he said. "It's one thing to be in Mythland, it's another thing to be *hunted* in Mythland by a cyborg, kidnapped and tortured by some refugee camp, find your fiancé dead-looking, and then realize your father could be harbouring a dark, dark secret and you're not who you thought you were. Don't tell me that's not a lot, because *holy fuck*, Raine! I don't know how you make it through the night." He nudged me gently, his smile fading as he added, "Not to mention you sacrificed your connection to Chan back home to help Fluxaria. Irene was being pretty harsh but I understand how hard it must have been for you to do that."

Guilt, guilt, guilt. I looked away, too ashamed to meet his eyes. *Don't be proud of me, Destan. I'm a coward, a liar. I care more about one girl than the fate of one thousand on Fluxaria if we don't make it back in time.* I opened my eyes, only able to stare at my own fingers as I brushed them through his hair. "True or false," I whispered, "you think we're actually going to make it and somehow save the world even if Ai doesn't reach Fluxaria?"

Destan pursed his lips, humming as he considered. "Is there...a middle answer? Like a 'hopefully-sorta-maybe'?"

There came a clattering from below us, and both Destan and I started, grabbing on either side of the bed where we had our bows resting; nocked and at the ready. We waited in tense silence, bows raised and drawn, until there was a sneeze and the mumbled cursing of a Fluxarian spy trying to tinker together a bomb, and we relaxed again back into the covers.

"False alarm. *Again.*" I whispered, leaning my head against his shoulder. From here I could see my rucksack, now bursting with warmer clothes, as many of the journals that could fit, and various cleanliness and first aid supplies I'd found lying around. Destan's bag slouched emptily against the wall, waiting to be stuffed last minute before we left the tower for good. I sighed, "I'm not looking forward to traveling in that dark tunnel, but feeling like a cyborg could charge in any moment and shoot you isn't all that great either."

"That's for sure. Good to know all that cussing and rattling is just our ponytailed friend, though, right?" Destan smiled. His fingers walked like a pair of calloused little legs up and down my arm, chills racing under my skin. "I wonder if she can actually make one of those clock bombs. Remember how nasty that explosion had been? Even though she says she's gathered about everything she needs I just don't know how she can pack such a punch inside a makeshift thing like that."

"I think it's about time to stop doubting her, though," I shrugged, looking back on the times when she sat in our meadow, going down a list of countless passwords she'd memorized and hacking through what had supposedly been unhackable. "When she gets serious about something, she has a pretty good success rate." Our conversation stalled as we were interrupted by a soft ticking. Shocked into moving for my bow again, my fear immediately transformed into excitement as Irene gave a *"WOOHOO!"* from below us and I realized there was now a working Majesty Council weapon in our possession. "See!" I grinned, jumping out of bed.

Slipping in my socks as I ran on the cold wooden floor to the stairway, I called down to her in congratulations, "Irene! I hear it ticking, did you really build it?"

Destan came up behind me clapping and hooting, "Yeah! Ten points for the Fluxarian!"

There was a commotion at the foot of the stairs. "What are you two talking about?" she hollered back, poking her head in to look up at us. She had something in her hand, and waved it back and forth for us to see. "I found a secret goodies drawer! My case of the munchies is cured!"

Irene bounced happily out of sight, the crunching of nuts barely heard over the now louder, more insistent ticking. She couldn't hear it down there, it was getting faster, faster, Siri's ears had perked up at the sound and now rose from her lounging by the fire, growling. Panicked, I turned back to the stairwell, screaming down to her, "Irene? Irene do you hear that?"

"What?"

"Found it."

I spun around at the sound of Destan's voice. A clock on the mantle above the fire, not dusty and untouched in the slightest, wacky numbers, smoke coming from the center–

We burst into motion. I snatched my rucksack, Irene's spy bag, hesitating to get Ai but then remembering she was already safe in the clouds. Destan stuck his feet in his boots, his hat on his head, and with his quiver slung over one shoulder and his bow in hand he didn't even reach for the empty knapsack. We dashed down the stairs, Siri thundering behind us, the thump of her paws in between the constant *tick tick tick* of the bomb.

Irene toppled out of her chair, dropping a handful of sweets as we surged into the dining room. Before she could even ask what was going on, I answered, "Get the tablet, get it out of the drawer!"

She nodded, leaping to her feet and sliding over the table to the kitchen counter, yanking out the drawer and tucking the silver and glass contraption under her arm. Her makeshift bomb lay in pieces on the table. As Destan forced open the floor hatch, I scooped my arm across the table surface and shoved as many of the parts into her spy bag, not pausing to even catch my breath. Because as soon as every piece had been saved, our time was up.

My feet hadn't even touched the floor of the tunnel when a deafening crack split our eardrums. It shook the walls, the ground, every bone inside our bodies, and we took off blindly, holding hands to stay together in the madness. Suddenly, a wave of hot air rolled over us, coating the dank air with the stench of sulphur. My ears popped, heat rushing from behind us, and the tunnel was illuminated by the flow of incoming fire. The force was so intense that Destan's knees buckled, Irene ploughing into him and me on top of her. She quickly shoved me off and dashed full speed toward the pillar of light marking where we could resurface.

The dark turned orange, bright and hot and getting hotter, I could feel the fire on my heels as Destan pulled me behind him. Irene kicked straight up, knocking the hatch door completely open, and leapt out, offering her hand down as the flames caught up and washed over us. The pain was fierce and terrible but short, as Destan gave me a boost to the surface and his entire back was struck with fire before he could escape. I felt fire bite down on the backs of my knees and neck even as I flew out into the open air, landing with a smack on the crispy frost-licked grass. Destan crashed down beside me, coughing clouds of grey as fire rushed up and out the hatch like a volcano.

I scooted up to sit, reaching for him on one side of me, and Irene on the other. We gripped each other's wrists for dear life, watching as stone by stone, the tower came crumbling down into the swamps and trees around it. Shardza's wardrobe of sweaters and dresses, gone. The journals that wouldn't fit in my bag, the goodies Irene had just found waiting for her in the kitchen. The warm bed and fireplace and gold mine of ale, all gone in the flames. The fire roared and roared, smoke billowing into storm clouds into the sky. Destan looked from side to side, scrambling to his feet, gasping. "Where...where's Siri?"

"She came down with us, didn't she?" I asked, something cold and dreadful clenching my heart. Destan's face had dissolved into the expression of a sad little boy, his bottom lip trembling as he searched through the haze of smoke. From within the crackling and roaring of the fire, there came a low howl. Destan took off full speed back toward the tower, whipping out his flute and playing shrill note after note until his companion emerged from the smoke. Siri whined and howled, dragging a limp leg behind her as she crawled through the crumbling pile of rubble. The ground above the tunnel caved in beneath each footstep as Destan ran to her, and he leapt away from the sinking ground and into the rocks. He eased her out, holding tight to her neck as she stumbled to the grass. Irene and I rushed over to help, brushing through her fur with our fingers, looking for injuries. From the sagging of her middle and amount of blood, it was clear she had broken the entire right side of her ribs. Her silver fur was sticky and dark with blood, her whimpers becoming more and more like human sobs as she collapsed at our feet. Destan knelt by her, whispering something into her shredded left ear that I couldn't quite make out. I dug in my rucksack and pulled out the first aid supplies I'd raided from the bathroom, joining him and wrapping a bandage around Siri's injured leg. I used up the rest of the roll, coiling it tightly around her ribs to secure them in place and reduce the agony she'd already suffered. As I tied it off, she pulled herself up to her feet, digging her nose affectionately into my shoulder and then Destan's.

Moving well out of the way of the falling walls, we crouched by the edge of the forest and stared ahead, amazed at how quickly our hope had been destroyed. I pulled my knees to my chest, feeling grass cling to the melted, sappy soles of my boots. The top level of the tower tipped over, a burst of white flame blowing out in a ring around the destruction, the sound of impact making my heart stop and eyes fill with tears.

"It's all gone. The tower, the *tunnel*...we...what are we going to do?" I croaked. A tear raced hotly down my cheek, more threatening to spill. I wiped at my eyes with the singed edge of my sweater sleeve, turning to look at Destan. His face was unreadable, his eyes shiny with angry tears he wouldn't let spill.

He continued stroking Siri's side, gruffly replying, "We move on."

Irene had been staring forward, jaw tight and eyes narrowed. But at Destan's voice she crumbled, forehead on her knees and arms hugging herself as she wept. It was the crying of someone stolen from the hope of heaven and sent to hell, a crying I had never seen of anyone in my life. She rocked back and forth, tears falling to the grass, her mouth gaping but no sound coming out. I threw my arms around her, burying my face in her shoulder, feeling Destan encase us in one big huddled embrace as she continued to cry.

"We'll be okay, we're going to make it through," Destan whispered, squeezing us both and then letting go. I broke from Irene's hold and together we stood up, brushing ourselves off. The spy couldn't tear her eyes from the burning remains of the tower, and what used to be an entrance to the tunnel back to her home.

"I'm so fucking done with Mythland," she muttered, her voice cracking as she turned on her heel and strode away from us, "Let's go. I can't...I just can't do this right now." She turned halfway, sticking out her arms, and I tossed her spy bag, which she caught without flinching.

"She's tough, isn't she?" Destan murmured, shaking his head and shrugging his quiver back onto his shoulder as we followed behind her. I nodded, my long hair itchy and hot on my neck as I realized I hadn't tied it up.

I pulled it over my shoulder, whispering, "It had to be that cyborg, that metal guy, whoever that bastard is." Destan nodded, Irene glancing over her shoulder and stopping so we could catch up. "It has to be. We were so foolish to think he'd back off for even just one night after he found out where we were staying..."

"...and he's probably not far from us now, watching, or waiting to go in and look for our bodies," he added.

The emotion that had previously overcome Irene's evaporated. Hard black shadows lay beneath the cruel jewels of her eyes, and she brandished both middle fingers at the tower behind us. Half of her mouth turned up into a smile, and she sneered, "Well, fuck him. He's not finding bodies." She lowered her hands, pushing aside the barbed branches blocking our entrance back into the deep woods and continuing, "Screw the tunnel, it's blown up and probably had caved in other places anyway, so it wouldn't have saved our lives. We have a letter going to Fluxaria that'll save our asses a little sooner anyway. So, for now, let's just get as deep in the woods as we can so that the cyborg can't track us."

We walked on through the trees with prickling pits in our stomach. Every now and then I had to suppress the urge to throw up, sick with whatever the thing inside me was doing and sick with the fact that what I'd decided with Ai could be the end of us. Of all of us. We walked through swamps, too solemn to speak, too deep in thought for new strategies, and too scared to go through without our hands held by one another. It felt like a field trip day I'd gone on when I was seven. A portion of my Underbrush class was going to a Majesty Council monument built in the middle of Canopia's square, and then on to the factories where we could see the state-of-the-art machines in action.

As we walked on the side of the road, we clutched each other's hands for dear life and edged along slowly. My classmates had been terrified of the rickshaws and carts frisking about, and some would even freeze and get a spanking before continuing forward. I'd thought they were such scaredy-cats, and tugged those behind me along, wanting nothing more than to let go of the sweaty hands. But even now in the nearly pitch darkness of the Mythland forest, going forward into more of the unknown, I could hardly stand to hold their hands. I wanted nothing more than to run the opposite way where I couldn't hurt them anymore, and disappear into the darkness.

We walked until the moon was shrouded by storm clouds, wind and rain thrashing the trees. The sky cracked open with a stroke of thunder. Irene tried to keep going, but Siri's injuries were slowing her down, and the nausea was becoming almost too much for me to take. Destan must've sensed the lag, because he whistled, causing us to stop. Raindrops dripped from his hair into his eyes as he spoke, "Hey Irene, in that bag do you have a super-secret-spy tent we could pitch to rest for the night?"

She looked side to side, an eyebrow raised, "You really think we're far enough away that it's safe to just pitch a tent and go to sleep?"

He nodded, "We've been moving in zigzags, haven't heard anything other than our own footsteps, and I'm sure if we camouflage it right we'll just look like another bush." She still looked doubtful, her hand curling in and out of a fist around the strap of her bag. Destan gave the spy a weak smile, "For Siri's sake?"

Rolling her eyes, Irene dropped the spy bag. "All right. I guess we should make sure our furry means of transportation is all rested and healed and stuff. But..." She dug around through her stuff and then shook her head, "No good. I used to have a waterproof tarp but I lost that on my way over the first time. Sorry."

"What can we do instead?" I asked. I didn't dare open my mouth any wider to risk the sour breakfast rising in my throat to come pouring out. I rested a hand on my stomach. *C'mon, baby, if you're really in there could you be a nicer guest and not make your human-house vomit all of the time?*

Destan dug his fingers beneath the rim of his red beanie and scratched his head, muttering, "If I had an axe, I could chop some of this wood around here and build us a little cabin in an hour, tops. But I didn't get to grab the one in the tower, so..."

"It'll be fine. We don't need a fancy cabin," I said, forcing a smile. "We've been spoiled in that tower. We're outlaws, wanderers, right? Certainly we can spend a night beneath the stars."

"Certainly," Irene agreed, bending down and scooping up some fallen branches in her well-muscled arms. "When I came through here to get to Thgindim, I'd build myself a little nest just out of some branches and it was good enough."

"And I can fix up a roof to keep the rain out. No better natural umbrella than layers of leafy branches, am I right?" Destan said.

"Then we're good. Raine, you watch Siri and guard our stuff. I'll gather the supplies over on the left, and Destan you do the right. We come back to build in the middle. Sounds good?" We nodded, and I was grateful to sit down and slouch against Siri's warm side. I took care to lean on the side not suffering broken ribs, mind you.

Quick pricks of icy rain prodded us to move more quickly, and as they dropped off materials, I helped to weave and layer the branches into a nest that could hold us all. But by the time their arms were full and I was waiting for more building materials, it had begun a windy, blinding downpour.

The 'nest' had turned out better than I'd imagined. It was a snug fit for all three of us to squeeze into the woven circle of branches, but after Irene had returned she helped me fit them more tightly together so that we couldn't even feel the mud beneath the thick floor of twigs. The rain barely made it through the roof of leaves and branches Destan had constructed like a dome over us, and being pressed together made the cold not as bad without blankets.

"Nice job, everybody," Destan said, through chattering teeth, nudging Irene, who lay beside me. I was stuck in the middle. "Feels like the tower's mattress already."

"And we look like a bush," I said, noting the foliage.

"A stealthy bush hiding fugitives," Destan added. "You really are Fluxaria's finest, I'll give you that. Some mad spy skills, indeed."

Her brown lips curled into a slight grin, and it looked as though she might say some witty retort back. But instead she scowled, sitting up to look at us both. "If I tell you something sort-of-really-fucking embarrassing, do you promise not to be too mad?"

"We already know you suffer from chronic pottymouth," I smiled, hoping to ease the anxious look on her face. She continued to frown and I blushed. "I promise. What's up?"

She swallowed, twisting her hands in her lap. "I haven't been completely honest with you..." She took in a deep breath, and let it out with a rush of words. "I'm not a certified Fluxarian spy. I'm a spy *in training*, a *rookie* spy, I guess, if you could even call me that. I wasn't the one sent to get war information from Thgindim, I took another spy's job because I wanted to prove I could do it."

Destan and I both gasped in surprise at the truth, but didn't say anything, letting her continue to explain. Irene yanked out her ponytail and ran her fingers through the part of her hair, admitting, "I... I was just so tired of training and I thought I was ready. I took her ID to get through clearance when they sent me off, but if I go back I'll be kicked out of the academy. I'm surprised Fluxaria didn't send in another agent to get the job done." Irene was beginning to shake, and being so close I knew Destan could feel her tremors as well. "I flunked half of my lessons, the others I passed with the average level of skill as anyone else. Nothing extraordinary. I could climb, I could decode and memorize, but when it came to the important stuff like knowledge of Thgindim and proper strategy and protocol, I fell short. My teachers said I was too careless and rash and wouldn't get out of Mythland alive." The side of her mouth twitched and she smirked, "I did though. Got out, I mean. After months, I somehow made it through, and found you, and got the tablet, and I'm on my way back.

"When your home is on the brink of blowing up or getting conquered and enslaved and nothing your government does seems to be working, you start to wonder if you can play the hero and save the day like in comics and stuff. And the minute I was actually in Mythland I knew I was just an arrogant doofus who went through elaborate sneaking and scheming just to end up worse off than I was before. You take one look at the villain face-to-face and you know you aren't the hero. You're just holding onto the hope you'll at least die feeling like one." She fell silent, staring up at the leafy roof above us. Slowly, a smile crept onto her face. She pointed above her, "But, fuck it. Look at this. I...*we* got us somewhere. *I* was arrogant and dumb to think I could do it, but not because I wasn't ready, because I was trying to do it alone. The only reason I'm still here and have accomplished anything is because you yanked me out of the way of a rockalanche my first day on Thgindim. We're going to walk into Fluxaria and stun all my rookie spy friends and the big deal spies because a cruddy spy, a scarface, and his badass-blue-haired-archery-girlfriend saved the day." She plopped back down beside us, rubbing her eyes sleepily as she sighed, "So there it is, the truth. I'm a phony, I'm not 'Fluxaria's finest' or even close to what I told you. I'm sorry if that changes anything between us."

The rain created a rhythmic hush against the leaves, giving the quiet a gentle heartbeat. After a moment of thoughtful silence, Destan leaned over me and placed a hand on each of Irene's shoulders. She raised an eyebrow, and Destan smiled impishly whispering, "You are *clearly* still Fluxaria's finest, Irene. You'd be nuts to think otherwise"

Her hard, onyx eyes seemed to soften. Irene attacked him with a fierce hug, burying her face in his back and then yanking me into it as well. I laughed, planting a kiss on her dirty tan forehead, feeling a nauseous swell in my stomach. She'd told her secret. A huge one. I had to tell mine now, but which one? How could I have let so many fill up my heart like this?

But before I could speak, a hissing whirred around the nest. We froze in fear, but before we could calculate what sort of threat could be lurking outside of the nest, lights began flickering between the branches encasing us in the nest. The lights floated blurrily, illuminating the gaps in the walls; at first I thought they were fireflies, but they were completely luminescent and transparent, different ethereal shades of green and pink and gold. About twelve of them bobbed above our heads, clumping across the leafy roof like bunches of floating flowers the size of a child's fist, and they were making that dull hissing sound.

Cautiously, Irene outstretched her arm, pushing aside some of the roof. An orangey one of the bugs drifted through the parted leaves and landed on the tip of her index finger, swirling out all four of its wings like lily petals, changing colour as it spun like a top. As it turned in circles, pockets in the creature's body opened up to release the timid sound of chiming bells.

How can Mythland have such beauty and ugliness at the same time? I thought, catching my breath as a cloud of four more bobbed into the nest; pink, blue, white, pale green. They swam in a synchronized dance above our heads, ducking in and out, the fanning of petals, the chiming of bells heard over the sound of rain and thunder, our eyes sparkling in the reflection of the gentle light. None of us spoke as they flew around us. Despite how much had happened, I couldn't accept that any place or living thing in this universe could have been created only to destroy, to cause despair and exist in toxicity. Even this wasteland apparently put in place by the spirits had a gentle healing creature like the qilin, and swarms of harmless beacons that swam above our heads and made our eyes heavy with sleep.

One that flickered in between soft blue and grey light landed on my stomach, tickling as it spun. Hesitantly, I brushed it away, careful not to touch it and hurt its barely touchable body. These beings had calmed all of us, and instilled a slight urge of courage within me. Taking a deep breath, I gathered up my words and spoke. "I have a secret too."

I could feel Destan's twitch of shock beside me. I placed a hand on my middle for security and then drew it back almost more scared than I had been before. The glowing blue bug hovered away and slipped through the cracks of the nest. More followed, leaving only the first orangey one to keep spinning above us.

"Go ahead, spill your guts, Raine," Irene chuckled, nuzzling my shoulder.

No turning back now. Words, words, I needed words. I hated and loved words. I hated how the peace could fracture with a single word. No way of phrasing it felt right, did it justice, I felt like infinities had passed in the minute before I spoke. I drummed my gloved fingers on the slightly raised slope of my stomach. Destan was just about done waiting, wriggling anxiously beside me.

"I think I'm pregnant." The weight of the world rose from my chest. "I know I can't be that far along, but—"

Destan sat up too fast and his head conked hard against a big branch. "Wait, what?"

"I KNEW IT!" Irene screamed, "I knew you two had hooked up! All those gooey eyes and closeness, man I knew I was setting it up when I gave you the bedroom alone a couple of nights ago. But c'mon, Raine, it doesn't happen that fast."

"We didn't..." My cheeks flared with heat, remembering how badly it had gone the other night. "It wasn't a couple of nights ago."

Her eyes widened. "It happened back home? Oh, shit, tell me I wasn't sleeping a few feet away in that meadow when you did-the-do?"

"Of course not, it was...in a cave," I said, unable to look at her or the still silent boy beside me.

Irene was enjoying this way too much. She clapped and clapped so loud, the last of the luminescent bugs were scared away from the nest. Destan sat stiffly beside me, legs pulled to his chest and chin on his knees in silence. Irene opened and closed her mouth a number of times, but couldn't seem to find the right words. Finally, she plopped back down beside me, tentatively hovering her hand over my stomach. "So...you really think there's a baby-thing inside there?"

I shivered, rubbing the goosebumps on my arms. "I don't want to, but it just sort of adds up. My body and emotions have been all out of whack, and even though I'm eating hardly anything, I haven't lost any weight. I've actually gained some or look round and I've never...I tried to tell you the night the cyborg broke in, but you were too drunk and after I was just so scared to say any—"

Destan turned and pressed his lips to mine for a fervent kiss. I could feel tears, not mine, rolling across my cheeks and I drew back to look at him in alarm. He had already turned away, head between his knees and fingers knit deep into his hair. His hands shook.

And suddenly he was crying.

Sobbing, breathing in guttural gasps, his face red and covered by his hands. Tears dripped between the gaps in his fingers, and for a split second he opened one bloodshot eye and looked at me. I looked back. "Raine, I didn't think you could...I'm sorry. I'm so sorry, I can't believe I did this to you," he said. He shut both eyes again, growling and yanking at the roots of his hair.

"Destan, no, stop it," I begged, my eyes stinging as I gently touched his cheek. Irene didn't seem to know what to do, and kept her distance. "I'm not mad at you," I said. He shook his head and I bent down, trying to pry his fingers away from his face. When I finally could, he could hardly look at me, the most tortured expression in his eyes. "I'm not mad at you," I repeated, lip trembling. "Why are you?"

He didn't answer, just kept on crying like the world was coming to an end. And he cried and cried until he'd drowned himself into dreaming, and I lie awake through to the morning, haunted.

chapter eighteen

"What? *What?* Dude you have to be joking."

"Smells great, right?"

"*Smells?* Looks, tastes! Holy crap, Destan, since when could a teenage lumberjack cook?"

I opened one eye grumpily. I'd been dreaming for sure, but I couldn't quite remember what I had been dreaming about. The leafy roof of the nest was brilliantly green with light, so it must have been morning. Bewildered, I realized that someone had wrapped me up in something warm and soft, and as I pulled it off and held it up, I realized that it was Destan's sweater. I scrambled to my knees and peeked my head out from the nest. Irene was slouched against a big oak tree, drinking something from the belly of a big leaf. Destan busied himself over a fire, where he'd set a flat stone over the flames, and stirred whatever he was cooking with an arrow of his. His cheeks were red and chapped from cold, his tongue between his teeth as he carefully scraped the gravy-like substance onto another big leaf. Since he'd given his sweater to me, he sat there only in a thin undershirt. I could only watch a moment until he glanced up and broke into an unprecedented grin.

"Bluehead!" he gasped, setting down the arrow and bounding over to me. He caressed my face in his ratty gloved hands and pecked me quickly on the lips. His eyes flickered onto mine, "I didn't think you'd be up so early. You sure you don't want to get some more rest?"

I shook my head, cautiously stepping completely out from the nest and passing him his sweater. "Yeah, I feel rested enough. Are you...okay?"

He chuckled, turning back to the fire and poking the glowing, burning branches. "Sure, why wouldn't I be?" Irene and I exchanged suspicious looks. Had something happened in between the time he went to bed crying and woke up happy as can be? Had a spirit come to him in a dream and reassured everything would be all right or something? Whatever it was, he didn't want to mention it, and neither did Irene or I, for that matter. I was just relieved he wasn't weeping anymore.

Irene set down her empty leaf, rubbing her belly in contentment. "Raine, this guy has been on a cooking rampage for the entire morning. Take a whiff." She pointed a short finger at the bubbling brown stuff over the fire.

I obeyed, bending down to inhale the savoury aroma of whatever was cooking. "Mmm," I murmured appreciatively, "smells good."

"Come and try some," Destan said, in a bit of a stammer, nervously scratching the back of his neck. "I caught some game. Three bunnies, and I tried to do a stew of sorts with their meat and some wild spices I found growing. It's really no big deal."

Irene's eyes widened and she mouthed, *"It's a pretty big deal,"* behind him. I put a hand over my mouth to keep from laughing, and picked up a leaf for Destan to fill. As the rabbit stew warmed my hands, Irene spoke up again. "There's an issue with the bomb. I'm missing one crucial piece."

"What?" Destan asked, sprinkling some spice on top of my stew and passing it back to me with a smile.

"Fuel. I can fashion solar power for the more minor properties of the weapon, but in order for it to have enough juice to blow up, I need to make a natural battery," she explained, frowning at the work in front of her.

"Do you know how, or what you need to make it?" I asked, "Because I'm more than happy to go out and search for whatever you need."

"Mmm, I don't think that's a good idea, Bluehead," Destan interjected, "You need to rest, not stress so much. I can get whatever Irene needs."

"I mean..." Irene looked from him to me, a little amused, "I appreciate the chivalry but we *all* gotta go, probably. I know what we need to find, but it's not gonna be easy. It's this carnivorous swamp plant, something called mao gao cai. Also nicknamed 'sundew.'"

"Sundew?" Destan grinned, "I think I know that plant! Pink petals and little sticky, dewy hairs all over the leaves, right? Grows in sunny swamps?"

"That's the one. How do you know it?"

"My brother used it to cure a cough. And you're telling me it can blow stuff up?" Destan rose a doubtful eyebrow.

Irene nodded, "Yup. The mao gao cai plant has these organic compounds in it that carry electrons and can be used to create a flow-battery. In basic terms: we need it to fuel the bomb and give it the explosive factor." We crowded around the fire, helping ourselves to more and more of the rabbit stew, discussing and re-discussing new plans. When Irene's bottomless stomach was finally satisfied, she took out the clock bomb and got back to work; twisting wires with tweezers she'd stolen from Shardza's vanity, and installing the strange numbers. All the while, Destan kept up the bizarre behaviour he's had all morning; shaking his knee restlessly, shifting beside me so that one moment we were touching and his fingers were laced with mine, the next there was a not so casually huge gap between us. Every time I made a movement, he looked at me with instant focus, and when I spoke he'd grab my arm and rub it in a way he must've thought was reassuring or something but actually just made me feel weird. We'd only been sitting for an hour when I couldn't take it any longer.

"Hey, Beaniehead?" I asked, leaning my cheek on my fist and glaring at him. Destan looked genuinely worried at this, so I rolled my eyes and smiled, "If something's wrong, or you have something to say about last night, just tell me, okay? Why are you acting so weird?"

He frowned defensively, but his flushed cheeks gave him away. "I don't know what you mean, there's nothing wrong."

"C'mon, you're treating her weird. Like really, *really* weird," Irene said.

"Am not," Destan protested, crossing his arms.

"Fine," I sighed, taking off the sweater he'd shed for me, "then prove it. I'm not cold, but *you* are, so put your sweater back on."

"I'm not cold."

I narrowed my eyes. "Put. On. The. Damn. Sweater."

Destan threw his hands up, waving at both Irene and me beside him, "You two are the ones acting weird! I just wanted you to be warm and not get frostbite or something. You and the..." He cut off, stalking over to Siri as she snoozed against a tree, his back now to us and his head in his hands.

Irene filled in the blanks. "Her and the mini-Destan inside of her?" Destan froze, glancing over his shoulder as the spy continued, "She was pregnant yesterday and the day before, just because you know now doesn't mean she's suddenly more breakable or something. Just take a chill pill, really, dude."

Withdrawing his hand out of Siri's fur, Destan snatched the sweater from me and wrestled himself back into it, grumbling, "I'm just trying to help. Sorry if I'm a bit unprepared for this sort of thing."

I dug my boots into the soft ground, looking at Destan with sympathy. "None of us are, Destan. Thanks for...trying. Don't stress it," I said.

"Don't *stress* it?" He echoed, too loudly, waking up a very grouchy and growling Siri. He stormed over to me. Oh no. That hadn't soothed him at all. "Because of me you're in more danger than ever, not to mention a kid who wasn't supposed to exist! There's no safe, straight shot to Fluxaria anymore, and we still don't know if the cyborg has given up on us. And I shouldn't stress it? I don't want any chill pills! I just want to do something that will actually help us, for once!"

"Good lord, Destan," Irene rolled her eyes, "this is not the time to feel sorry for yourself and blow things out of proportion. We're going to be fine."

"No, Irene, he's right," I said, shakily, earning a raised eyebrow from the Fluxarian. "This is a bigger mess. But I don't need you suddenly treating me like I'm made of glass just because we're now dealing with the consequences of our...actions." *Your screwing, you mean,* my head scoffed. I bit my tongue against the thoughts, finishing, "I felt taken care of enough with the way things were, and you know I hate special attention. Please, just trust me, Destan?" I offered my hand out to him.

He didn't look completely reassured, but the anger faded from his expression as he stared at my hand. Silently, he took it, rubbing my fingers thoughtfully as he nodded. He planted a soft kiss on my knuckles, trying to smile at me, but producing more of a grimace. "Let's come up with a Plan B," he said, shooting to another topic so instantly that at first I was alarmed he was still referring to the pregnancy. "The tunnel is a bust, so what now?" As he spoke, the bushes behind us rattled. I glanced at it curiously, but then shoved the observation aside.

"Well, I had a thought," Irene said, trading the tweezers for a butter knife as she tinkered. "We should try and figure out just how far away we are from the mountain. But since this forest is so thick, it'd be best to get above the trees."

I tilted my head to the side, "Above...?"

"We climb," Irene said, coming over and plucking up a thin stick. She knelt by a tree and arranged some leaves. One green, one yellow, one speckled by bug bites. "Look at this. I'd say let's go...three miles from our nest?" She designated a pinecone to be the nest and moved the bug-bitten leaf about a foot away. "I'll climb a tree all the way to the top and get a view of how close we are."

"But what if Fluxaria is somehow closer or even farther away than where we go to look?" Destan asked.

"That's what the rest of my plan is for," she said, eyes flashing excitedly. She set the other two leaves equidistant apart in between the pinecone and the bug-bitten leaf. "Destan goes two miles, Raine you go one so as not to stress the little bundle of joy in your belly. It'll be guesswork, but back at the Fluxarian camp, I learned that if you're running, a mile is about 1,400 steps. We'll have to count carefully–"

I held up one hand to stop her, the other touching the leaves on her diagram. "Okay," I began, "I like it...but how will we make it up the trees? They're huge, not to mention covered in poisonous plants and bugs, most likely."

"Yeah, they're huge, but still not as tall as Peak Tower, and you handled that just fine, right? You were a natural!" she said, knocking my shoulder.

"I didn't go all the way up, though, only halfway..."

"Then it's just what you've been trained to do. C'mon, you and Destan will get to use the climbing spikes, and I've been trained to free-climb so there's nothing to worry about."

A sort of grumble thundered through the trees, and we exchanged nervous glances. Destan cautiously began packing up our supplies, saying, "I think maybe we should move on from here. You know how much Mythland loves kicking us out of wherever we're comfortable."

We nodded and followed suit, shoving the few things we had back into our packs. But only moments after we had climbed onto Siri and she started bounding away from the nest, she began to whine, her body sagging lower and lower to the ground until she nearly collapsed. Destan soothingly patted her side and then stroked his fingers along her muzzle. "You okay, girl? What's wrong?" He asked her, concerned. Siri tossed her head and stood back up, whimpering as she made herself keep walking. She could only manage a staggering trot. Worried, Destan dug his heel into her flank to signal her to stop, and she sank back down on the grass, panting.

"Is she hurt or something?" Irene asked, peering over my shoulder. Destan shook his head, sliding off and checking her body for any unknown injuries.

"She wasn't beaten up too bad from the explosion," he murmured, "but she's got a bum leg, which significantly affects how many people she can carry. Even in her normal state she can't support three for very long." He shook his head sadly, the blond curls dancing out from under the brim of his red hat. "Not to mention we haven't been able to sacrifice enough meat for her."

Irene nodded, stroking Siri's silky ears, "Wolves need meat. Maybe we should let her go on her own to hunt for some rabbits or squirrels or something–"

A grumbling vibrated once again through the forest, the leaves of the shuishan trees shivering and rustling around us. Siri growled in response, barking at the disturbance in the woods. Reluctantly, Destan mounted her again, glancing around with eyes narrowed in suspicion. "We gotta keep moving. Are you two cool if Siri polishes off the rest of the rabbit stew? It might give her some strength to keep on."

"It's better than facing whatever that grumbling is," I said, Irene nodding vigorously in agreement. Siri finished what remained of Destan's concoction in only two licks, pulling herself back to her feet. She struggled ahead, moving slowly but persistently, her clear green gaze focused ahead of her and teeth bared as the sound became louder. Out of the corner of my eye I thought I saw something emerge from the bushes, a pair of red eyes, then maybe five pairs of them. Destan urged Siri on, nervousness quivering on the edge of his voice as we continued to move at the pace of dripping molasses. And then– a terrible howl, a flashback to a den underground packed with sleeping, snoring beasts.

I grabbed Destan's arm in panic, but just as I opened my mouth to warn him, a hulking tiangou burst from a tall clump of bramble bushes and charged. Destan jerked Siri's reins to the left, making her swerve out of the way quickly as the beast continued flying to where we'd just been. Irene held on tight, squeezing the breath out of me. I gripped Destan's shoulder with my fingertips, the other hand desperately trying to steady myself on Siri. The tiangou's slavered fangs snapped down on nothing as it pounced where we had just been standing, a horrible scream ripping from its throat as it swivelled around back at us. His cruel red eyes suddenly went completely black as the pupils spread like a drop of ink in water. Its bristling black lips curled back from its teeth as it snarled, and a pack of four more emerged slowly from every side of us, stalking in the same creeping rhythm of placing one clawed paw at a time in front of them. On the moss, their steps made not the slightest sound. Amid these moldy, soggy plants and trees, we were a group of walking steaks. And they were hungry.

"Shh, tiangou-beasty...just keep walking," Irene squeaked, clinging to me more tightly and letting out a yelp as one barked for us to quiet. Siri barked right back, her soft grey lips peeling away from her teeth, adopting a threatening stance. She lowered her haunches to the ground,

228

making it difficult for us to hang on, and she let a tremor roll through her body, as if she was trying to shake us off.

"Siri, Siri, girl, stay calm, stay calm," Destan whispered hurriedly, unable to hold on. We landed on our feet at her back legs, and she curled her body around us protectively.

My instinct told me that we needed to run. Just run, just flee...until they caught up and snapped our necks. I looked furiously around for a way out, but the circle of beasts around us was getting tighter and tighter, no holes in between to slip through without losing a limb first. "We need them distracted, we can't outrun them," I said, breathless.

"They're probably starving, I don't know what it'll take to get their minds off of four tasty morsels, Bluehead," Destan whispered. His hand then went from my arm to my stomach, and he gulped, adding, "Five, actually." I felt like the ground had disappeared beneath my boots, and I was falling so fast I couldn't catch my breath. *It's not just me going to get eaten. There's a baby. Destan's baby, my baby.* The word made me feel sick, but at the same time a jolt of power seemed to fill the panicked void inside of me. For the first time, it wasn't burden, it was another one of the precious items I was responsible for carrying safely out of Mythland. And this baby felt infinitely more precious than the tablet, than the bomb, even more precious than my own life

For the first time in my life, I felt like a mother.

The realization sent me staggering, and in the split second all of this raced through my thoughts, the first tiangou attacked. It lunged at Siri and took a swipe at her, only grazing her flank before she lunged and chomped hard on its front leg. As the tiangou whined and began to brawl with our wolf, three came once. Destan and I jumped into action with our bows, rapidly shooting two of them in the throat before they could even touch Siri. The tiangou that hadn't been hit by our arrow sank into a deep crouch and launched itself over me and Destan, leaping straight into Irene. She had twin butterfly swords in each fist, holding tight as the beast crashed on top of her and snapped its jaws. Irene and the tiangou yowled together, both struggling in pain, no longer preoccupied in attack, and as the terrible sound of flesh being sliced whipped through the air, the tiangou's struggle ceased. It lay limp, Irene's face crushed into its bloody belly and her screams muffled. Destan knelt and tugged on her legs, helping her to pull her out from beneath it. As her face emerged, I saw her cheeks sprinkled with blood, and the hands that grasped Destan's were nearly black with the tiangou's spilled insides. I had continued aiming and shooting while Destan helped her out, fending off the ones who just wouldn't give up, but they were getting better at jumping out of the way and soon I was out of arrows.

I threw my bow down, stepping forward and screaming as loud as I could, "GO HOME!" My throat felt scraped raw from that single roar, Destan and Irene's faces masks of shock. I sucked in a breath and screamed it again, causing the tiangou in front of me to growl, eyes narrowed as it stalked around me. Sweat beaded on my brow as I stared it down. Back in Underbrush, rabid dogs and foxes would sometimes come out of the woods foaming at the mouth absolutely crazed with hunger and whatever else the Majesty Council might have injected them with when running tests up at Peak. My Dad had taught me forever ago to say that, to just tell them to go home as loud as you could and usually they would go whining back into the bushes. Now I knew tiangou were more than just rabid dogs, but I was at my last nerve, and yelling seemed the only thing I could do now that I didn't have a weapon.

The tiangou came closer, so close that my face was inches away from its snout, and its mouth opened wide for the loudest, booming, most bone-rattling, milk curdling roar I'd ever heard. Bloody breath attacked my face, hot and wet and making my stomach want to empty itself on my boots. Destan reached to pull me back, but I shoved off his hand and came even closer to the beast, shrieking so loudly into its face that I felt a blood vessel pop and sting in my eye.

Irene licked her lips and joined in, "GO HOME! GO HOOOOME!" Then she looked at me and asked out of the corner of her mouth, "That's what you said, right?"

I nodded and bared my teeth, growling and walking forward at it, causing it to slowly retreat. I bared my teeth in between screams, surprised at how abrasive mine and Irene's voices sounded when they clashed together. They were bigger than us and still not scared, but they had become disoriented, or a better word for it might be surprised. I guess it wasn't every day prey roared right back at the predator. Destan's voice chimed in every now and then, but he was focusing on untying Siri's reins. His gaze flickered back and forth from the surrounding tiangou to the skillfully tied ropes around Siri's neck.

"I'm gonna rein 'em in," he whispered, breathless as he finally yanked out the knot.

My eyes bulged. *"How?"* I hissed

"Working on it, Bluehead. Keep them scared!" he said, as Irene shook my arm to keep yelling.

The tiangou formed a tighter circle around us and all howled in unison. They were getting tired of this. Maybe at first it had seemed almost like a challenge, but now they knew it was all just a bluff, there were no secret weapons that threatened them...or, were there? *Scare them, scare them, keep them scared,* the words echoed back and forth in my mind as I reached back at my rucksack, blindly pawing through the contents as a single tiangou prowled forward with its claws popping out. It wouldn't get the chance to use them, I'd found what I'd been searching for.

"Irene, get that branch!" I commanded, backtracking as the tiangou took the first warning swipe. The claw grazed my knee and I bit down hard on my lower lip to fight the pain. Irene somersaulted out of the way and came up with the dead, leafy stick we'd taken for kindling. I struck my flint stones violently, hands shaking and not producing a single spark. One of Irene's hands covered mine and steadied it, the added pressure causing a few flares to leap and catch on the thick tuft of leaves, then the stick itself. Our weapon had been created.

"Go home! Go home!" Irene called at them, waving around the now blazing torch and successfully causing them to shrink back, snarling as the fire became dangerously close to their long black snouts, "You wanna mess with us? No? Then go home!"

Struggling to dash forward in the deep snow, I stole it from her and thrust the torch forward again and again, making two bound back down the path behind us, only three foolishly stubborn beasts remained. Just as they seemed to want to give up and dash away, Destan charged at one and lassoed the ring of rope around its jaws, clamping it tightly into a muzzle. The companion beast tried to attack, but Destan had the captive tiangou rear back in front of him, and toss the other reins he'd strung to Irene and me.

Crouching low to get enough momentum, I launched myself up and caught the ropes in one hand, Irene snatching the other. And then as I was about to copy his action and come straight at the tiangou, I suddenly froze. A panic filled my chest and my hands began to shake, I couldn't breathe or think and Irene snatched her reins and ran for her beast. Her torch swung in her other hand, the flames causing this smaller beast to cower down to its belly, not even fighting as she fixed on the muzzle. The remaining tiangou Destan had left me to wrangle was slinking back farther and farther, almost smiling as I struggled to move.

"Hurry, Bluehead, go!" Destan said, struggling to keep his tiangou from squirming out from under him.

"What's the matter?!" Irene shrieked, looking wildly at me, her calves pressed hard against the greasy black sides of the animal.

My torch was going out and my tiangou spun around to bound away, shocking me into action. I dropped the smoking stick and went after it, running with leaden legs, the spaces between us becoming longer and longer. I slowed to a stop and bent over, my hands on my knees as I breathed exhaustedly. "Shit," I whispered, tears stinging in my eyes out of embarrassment. "Shit, shit, shit, *shit*..."

"Raine, what happened?" Irene asked incredulously, her and her beast trotting up to my side.

I swallowed and trudged back over to Siri, the muzzle loosely in my fist. I looked up and met Destan's eyes. The skin around his scar was red and chapped with cold; the cut itself was nearly smoothly healed. His eyes, those pure silver moons, had taken on that sad glaze of concern I'd seen too many times now. The same eyes that looked at me when I'd freaked out and broken off our bonding in the tower, the eyes that saw the whip marks and asked questions I couldn't answer yet. Just looking at them made mine fill with tears, my lip begin to tremble, and I was forced to look away as I heard him say, softly, "Don't stress it, Raine. Siri can surely support you, we didn't really need another one."

I nodded, "Mmhmm, I know." I slid my hood up to try to warm my ears, and gently eased Siri into a mounting stance. "I'm sorry...I don't know what came over me, I really don't."

"Well, I wouldn't blame you," Irene replied, her dark eyes scanning across the snow-frosted woods. "They're terrifying and unnatural, and experiments from your mountain, actually. Wolf-bear-some-crazy-chemical-hybrids, but too unruly to keep there, I heard, so your Council dumped them out to keep Mythland dangerous. Not to mention they named them after an evil Fluxarian spirit."

We remained quiet for some time after that. We all walked together in a line of two beasts and one weak but loyal wolf. As Irene took the lead, Destan drifted back to my side. "Hey," he murmured, an arm appearing behind my waist. "Is there something else going on? That you wanna talk about?"

I wound my scarf tightly around my neck and over my head, staring at my boots as I walked. *Destan, it wasn't the tiangou that scared me,* I thought, trying to figure out what to say to him. *It was that feeling of helplessness I hadn't felt since Tieran...how can I tell you? It would make it real, right now it's all in my head. I feel messed up and out of control and ashamed and I just need to forget and move on because there isn't time for me to keep hurting and being scared.*

I stopped walking, the hands in my pockets curled into fists. I was still fighting the urge to cry, my hand shaky as I pulled one out of my pockets and touched his cheek. He covered my hand with his own, and I went on tiptoe to kiss him. His lips were warm and firm, but cautious, even as I moved in to kiss him deeper. *I'll tell you everything. Please give me time.* I drew back, not wanting Irene to notice why we were so far behind, and kept walking. Destan held my hand tightly in his own, not saying another word.

Snow was falling and catching on my eyelashes. These white woods felt too fake and innocent for all that had happened inside of them. My anxiety about the tiangou and the cyborg and the Shuishan kept me reeling until I glanced behind me and saw that there were human footprints mixed in with the animal tracks. Human footprints that didn't match mine, Irene's, or Destan's; that meandered along the side of the trees and disappeared into the bushes. I squinted into the brush, picking out a gleam in the leaves. Two blue eyes stared through a glossy black visor of a Justice Police helmet. Then disappeared into the darkness.

chapter nineteen

I slid out from in between Destan and Irene, scooting up to sit and then shakily getting to my feet. They were sound asleep, Irene's snores falling between Destan's. I draped my coat across them and turned away. The crescent moon leaned against a cluster of stars, winking at me in between the leaves. Our campfire had dwindled to hot sticks, and I stoked it only so I could light a torch to see if the eyes were still watching from the bushes. I waved it to and fro, watching as light caught onto something shiny. My stomach flipped in fear, and dropping the torch back in the fire, I slung on my quiver, picked up my bow, and strode with determination into the thicker trees. I heard a panting, and then felt something large and soft rub up against me. Siri looked up into my eyes, the message clear in her own. *"You don't think I'd let you go in there alone, do you?"*

I nodded at her in reply, rubbing her nose affectionately and grabbing a tuft of her fur to hold onto as we dashed into the bushes. The hairs on the back of my neck prickled at a crunching of boots on leaves just ahead of us, and Siri growled in acknowledgement. I nocked in an arrow, shoving aside some branches and ducking in between the trees, following the rapid sound of footsteps and the distant black silhouette of someone moving in haste. Siri kept up diligently, paws making not the slightest sound as they touched down on the bed of rotting leaves. I now knew I was far enough away from Destan and Irene not to wake them, and close enough to the cyborg that he would hear my call in the darkness.

"You've been following us," I said, too softly. Terror pulsed through my veins, and Siri growled warningly as the shadow stopped moving away, and began moving closer.

"Yes," the voice was deep, with a cold and metallic edge. The cyborg's piercing blue eyes shone in the darkness, illuminated by the moonlight shining through the trees. Clenching my fist around my bow, and giving Siri a reassuring pat, I met him in the center of a circle of berry bushes.

"Why haven't you tried to kill us again?" I asked, only a few footsteps between us now.

I detected a smile behind his mask as he replied, "Timing is key."

My eyes narrowed. "Who are you?"

"You mean my Career?"

"No, you," I specified, my knuckles white as they squeezed my bow ever the more tightly. "Who sent you, why are you trying to kill a bunch of teenagers in the woods, who are you?" He didn't answer, just folded both hands and rested them on the butt of his monstrously huge crossbow, and continued staring. I sucked in a breath and spoke more loudly, "Are you a cyborg?"

"A *what?*"

"Half human, half mechanical? Not real?"

"I'm real," he said, plainly.

Nausea swirled in my stomach, and I wondered how he'd react if I puked on his metal boots. Probably not a good idea. I set down my bow and held up my shaking hands. He in turn laid his weapon on the ground and pressed his arms flat to his sides. "What do you want?" I asked, each word carefully enunciated so that it would make it through that iron skull of his.

"To bring justice."

Oh please. I sighed, "Can you be a little more specific?"

"You are a persistent threat to Thgindim," he replied, avoiding the question. Again.

"I'm still a threat? Here? The Council beat me, I'm banished, what more is there to worry about?"

"You have reunited with your two companions, one of which who has in her possession classified Majesty Council material. The chance of this material reaching Fluxaria increased dramatically once she was no longer on her own in her mission. I have been sent to make sure that neither you, nor the tablet, arrive at the enemy's mountain."

"I'm flattered that the Majesty Council believes in us so much..." I muttered, rubbing the back of my neck. How long until Irene and Destan would wake up to take over watch and notice my absence? I couldn't think about that now. Only the killer in front of me.

The cyborg's posture straightened and he took two steps forward, so close I could feel his breath on my forehead. "This is your final warning," he whispered, the smell of smoke filling my nostrils. "If you keep forward, I will be forced to spill blood. It won't just be that boy's face getting cut this time."

I reached back at my quiver and withdrew an arrow, jabbing it at his metal, armoured chest, "And this is *your* final warning. Hurt any of my friends and I'll..." I glanced at the prosthetic hand at his side, a vivid memory suddenly playing through my head. I was in Peak Tower, rushing from Sebastian Lao's office, shooting three arrows at a JP holding Destan by the throat. Tearing the officer's hand from his wrist. "Try anything and I'll shoot off the other hand," I finished, unable to keep myself from smirking.

The cyborg began to emit a mechanical growl. His prosthetic hand balled into a fist at his side and he boomed, in a voice suddenly very human, no longer measured at all, "Miss Ylevol, you don't know what you're meddling in. Councilman Lao thought you would've surely perished by now, but seeing as you are still posing a threat to our national security, your mission must end. Whatever war you think you are interfering in is not the war we are fighting. The Majesty Council is

236

more than a crowd of black robes, they are more powerful than a silly girl and her friends could ever realize. You are on the verge of sparking an all-out bloodbath against your own people—oh, excuse me," his eyes narrowed, and he took a step forward, hissing, "those who are partially your people."

I backed away, numb all over. "How do you know I'm only…how–?"

"I am aware of more than you are prepared to know. Surrender now and I can escort you safely home where a chair has been left open for you, for a memory wipe. Wouldn't you rather be blissfully ignorant again? Tell me that a part of you wants to forget all that's happened in these woods, what's happening between the mountains you appear to care so much about," he came towards me, at least three heads taller, and hesitantly he laid a hand, his real hand, on my shoulder. "Come home and start over, nothing held against you."

Through the glove, I felt the heat of skin, of blood running through it. And his chest heaved with breath, even if the breath whistled out like exhaust from an engine. I had begun trembling, and I backed out of his touch, demanding, "Why would the Council give me this chance after what I've done?"

"We are not the villains, Raine Ylevol. Why spill blood when there is no need?"

"You seemed fine with us dying back at the tower you blew up, and when you tried to break my neck."

"My orders changed," he said simply, letting out a whoosh of breath. "Councilman Lao now deems you worth saving, worth fixing; and I agree, seeing as how valiantly you've fought my attempts on your life thus far. You've proved to be a potentially valuable asset to the Majesty Council, if only your skills were redirected in the proper direction."

"You lost me at 'Majesty Council,'" I said, "and I would rather die than be redirected to serve those monsters ever again!" I spun around and grabbed my bow, pain blaring through me as both of his hands seized my shoulders and shoved me face-first into the rough bark of the nearest tree.

"Dammit, Raine! Why won't you see reason?" he bellowed, his mask pressed coldly to the side of my face as he pinned me to the tree.

His strength was that of a machine, his voice, his anger, completely human. "If you continue, all you know will burn and more than just your companions will suffocate in the ashes. Even if your own life means nothing, what about your mother's, your sister's? What about your father's life?"

I twisted my shoulders out of his grip and kicked back hard with my foot, not strong enough to shove him off, but I wasn't alone in this. Siri charged in between us, teeth bared and dripping as she growled and stalked forward toward the cyborg. As I raised my bow, so did he, without flinching. That strange likeness we shared, that archer's intuition. I nudged Siri with my boot to keep her from proceeding, and yelled, "What of my father?" My bow trembled unsteadily in my shaking fist, and a buildup of frightened tears welled in my eyes, making everything blurry.

"Let the memory wipe occur and Solomon Ylevol will be released—"

My eyes bugged. "Released from where?" I screamed, backing away with Siri at my flank. "Sebastian's given me this bribe before, and my answer is the same. Now tell me what did you do to my dad?" My cheeks were soaked in the tears my eyes could no longer contain. Was he even in the JP? Had the Council known everything about his affair with Shardza and had him locked up somewhere all of these years while my mother and Gwen and I waited for our family to be complete again? The cyborg moved toward me, and Siri snapped at him, growling with ferocity measurable to that of a tiangou. Then I tugged on her neck and we turned and ran. The cyborg chased after us, not even taking his crossbow.

"Miss Ylevol, it is imperative we reach an agreement!" he screamed after me. "Running won't keep your fate from catching up with you!"

"LEAVE ME ALONE!" I howled back, tripping over my own feet and glancing blindly around for a path back to the camp. In that split second of hesitation, he caught up, grabbing my wrist and pulling me in the other direction.

"Our patience is running out, abandon your quest," he said, shaking me back and forth. Why was he still trying to talk to me? I could barely keep from vomiting, as he boomed, "Would killing them all, your mother and sister and those friends of yours, would that bring you home?"

That was the last straw. I dug the string-nock of my bow into the first chink I saw in his armour; piercing between his knee and thigh. He reeled back in shock and pain, and I took off, running so fast that I felt that I'd even left myself behind in those bushes. Siri swooped her head in between my legs, and I landed securely on her back. I clutched on for dear life, every so often taking a glance behind me. He hadn't followed me. Good.

Bringing my family into this? Who did he think he was? Horrible visions of Gwen and Chantastic and Carmen and Velle and even my mother being dragged off to Peak clouded my mind. I could already recall the sensation of snakes winding up the arms of the chair in that torturous room, the suffocating darkness that made your body seem to disappear. Just the thought caused me to cry out, icy panic squeezing my insides and making it hard to breathe. *No, no, don't dwell, just keep going. They are okay. He's bluffing,* I thought, fighting the anxiety attack with all my might. *My father, my father, he keeps appearing everywhere I turn. First in Shardza's journal, and in my Lilah-induced hallucination, and now the cyborg's handing him to me on a silver platter?* Sobs rose in my throat, and I focused on swallowing them down by the time I reached camp.

By some miracle, they were all still asleep, and as Siri skidded to a stop on the cold ground, I slid off and dashed over to them. I knelt and shook them both awake, Destan being first to stir. He looked groggily up into my face, confused. "Bluehead? What's goin' on?"

"The cyborg," I gasped, giving Irene an extra elbow to the stomach to get her up. She squealed, cursing and glaring at me through sleepy eyes.

"Where?" Destan asked, struggling to get to his feet and striding over to the two tiangou we'd secured to a tree. He turned in a circle, peering into the lightening darkness, "Are you sure you saw him?"

"I talked to him," I whispered, bangs falling in front of my face as I bent to sling on my rucksack. Irene followed suit, stuffing her blanket back into her spy bag. It took her a moment to register what I'd just said. When she did, her eyes bugged.

"You *what?!* Has being pregnant made you crazy or something?" she hissed.

"C'mon, we'll talk about it later," Destan said, eyes flashing from me to the spy. He jerked a thumb at our three beasts. Siri remained alert and stuck to my side, her fur standing on end as Irene and Destan went over to the captured tiangou. They first fought against Irene and Destan's riding them, but soon gave in, bowing their heads and accepting leftovers from dinner as payment. I climbed back onto Siri, wrapping my arms around her neck and taking off in the lead.

We ran and ran, the sun rising behind us. Dawn blushed against the trees, the snowy trail made rosy in the light. We had maybe been going for two hours when Irene suddenly yelled out, and I glanced back to see that Destan had skidded to a stop. I turned Siri around, riding over to them. Destan had dismounted his tiangou and stood with his head tipped back, a finger pointing at the highest layer of leaves hovering above us.

"Is that what I think it is?" he whispered, Irene and me joining his side and gazing upward.

"What?" Irene asked, going up on tiptoe and grabbing his tall shoulder for support.

"It's Ai," I breathed, heart racing as a turquoise ribbon wove in and out of the branches. Tied to her claw was what looked like a small red bundle, a scroll. The one I'd sent off had been pale parchment, this blaze of red was a blazing declaration that Ai had made it out of Mythland and into someone else's hands. *But did it reach Chan's hands?* My breath caught in my throat, and I looked from Irene to Destan out of the corner of my eye. *If it did, I can't lie to cover it up any longer. There are already too many secrets between us.*

"Should we call to it or something?" Destan suggested, sticking both hands in his coat pocket. Ai was preoccupied with trying to snatch eggs from a hawk's nest, not even glancing as I cupped my mouth and called.

"Ai! Ai, down here!" I hollered up at her, "It's Raine!"

Irene sighed, stooping to pull a rock from the mud. She tossed it and caught it in her palm, a mischievous smirk playing on the edge of her lips. "I could throw something at it? That'll get its attention."

"We are not throwing anything at her," I scoffed, looking at the spy incredulously and stomping closer to the tree where Ai dipped in and out of the branches. "Ai? Ai, please..."

There was a *zing*, a *thunk-thunk-thunk*, and I was just in time to catch sight of three consecutive pebbles hammering the hawk's nest and making shreds of leaves and twigs shower down, and a very alarmed Ai zoom out of the way and begin to soar lower. I spun around to glare at Irene, but she was still holding her pebble. Destan smiled guiltily, hands in the air.

"I wasn't gonna hit her," he said sheepishly, "just had to try another strategy, sorry Bluehead."

"And look," Irene gasped, "it worked, here she comes!"

The feilong wound around and around the tree, her blue scales glittering in the snatches of sunlight peeking through the leaves. I extended my arm as far as I could, awaiting her return, and staggered forward to the tree. Her cold claws brushed my skin and dug in, her head lunging in to nuzzle my neck. I held her closely, doing a little spin and running back to Irene and Destan, a victorious grin on my face. "She came back," I declared, heart racing, "she made it back from Thgindim!"

Irene's smile quivered. "Fluxaria, you mean," she said, "we'd sent her to Fluxaria."

I didn't say anything, glancing from her to Destan. His own smile faded, and he stepped forward, touching my arm, "We *did* send that S.O.S to Fluxaria, right, Raine?"

I hesitated, slowly detaching the red scroll from Ai's leg and beginning to unroll it. Irene's hand snatched it away, and she flung it open, eyes scanning the handwriting I instantly recognized as Chan's. The flash of happiness I felt seeing it was snuffed out by the fury in the spy's eyes.

"I...I don't understand," she said, looking at me with her face set in a dazed sort of rage. "We wrote a letter to the government...why isn't this a reply? Why didn't Ai go to Fluxaria?"

"Because Ai isn't from Fluxaria," I whispered, fear pulsing through my veins, "and I was positive she would be called to where she is literally from, which is Thgindim. I know you said that feilong originated in Fluxaria but—"

"But what?" she screamed, splashing mud onto my legs as she stomped through a puddle over to me. "You should've trusted me! You shouldn't have just assumed!"

"I was trying to follow instructions," I pleaded, reaching to touch Irene's arm. She wrenched it away, facing away from me and crossing her arms. I stared at the ground, too scared to see Destan's expression. "Chan had given me instructions and it would have been betraying her to not follow them, to not use Ai how she'd directed me..."

"But betraying me would be okay, though? My entire nation is on the line, how could you sacrifice that for the sake of some girl that means absolutely *nothing* to our cause?"

"I didn't mean to betray you, Irene I would never–"

"But you did."

She turned and glared, tear tracks shimmering on her cheeks. We stared and stared at each other, Destan silent and unobtrusively frozen on the sidelines. Irene wouldn't have that. She whipped around and shoved against his shoulder, "Aren't you going to say anything? Aren't you going to take her side, betray me, too?"

Destan narrowed his eyes, pushing her away and backtracking farther from the both of us. "I'm not on anyone's side, I think both of you are acting pretty mental, to be honest," he said. He met my gaze, and in his eyes the message was clear. *Another secret, Bluehead? Why didn't you tell me?* I took a shaky step towards him but he shook his head, stepping back and averting his eyes.

"I can't be around her right now, I might end up doing something I'll later regret. Or not regret," Irene growled, her hands curled into a fist around the red scroll. "Either way, enjoy your fucking letter, Raine. I hope it was worth it." She threw it in the mud, wiping her boots on the beautiful red paper before storming off into the trees with both tiangou trotting behind her. After some hesitation, Destan followed her, shooting me one sad smile before he too decided I was best left alone for now. Siri went after him, and then it was just me, my shame, a letter in the mud, and a feilong on my shoulder.

My feet felt heavy as bricks as I walked to the letter. Ai was chirping, still trying to glean some affection from me and nuzzling my neck. But I was numb, hardly able to breathe as I tried to just focus on Chan's response buried in the mud and not the pain I'd caused both Irene and Destan. I knelt by the puddle, pulling off my glove to pull the soggy, half-opened scroll from the mud. Luckily, none of the parchment had torn beneath Irene's boots, but I had to wipe and wipe to clear off the grime before I could make out a single word. Her ink had smeared, but my eyes decoded every character:

R-

The moment Ai showed up at my window I cried and cried I was so overjoyed to see that all of my cryptic nonsense actually made sense to you. Of course I never doubted your abilities to see through me. You understand me better than I understand myself.

If my handwriting is illegible I'm so sorry, I haven't been sleeping much at all, so I've been bleary in nearly all aspects of my life. Now maybe I'll get a little peace since you are alive after all, thank you, thank you, THANK YOU ☺!!

I'm glad to hear you are with them, but I admit I never knew you were split up so if I'd known you were alone this whole time I might have never left my bed and just gone crazy. Already I've been getting scolded and shoved around at work because my head and heart are with you and not with the flowers I should be cutting or arranging. Multiple times I've been threatened with a Career transfer to a less Chantastic-y position if I don't catch up, like Rice-picker or Test Subject. Oh yeah, about that last new one.. This year, the majority of new Underbrush adults have been designated Test Subject for their lifelong Careers. The thing is, that while the benefits and pay are better than most jobs, the estimated life expectancy for these Underbrushers is only another 15 years at the MOST. They'll be all dried up and filled with needles and not even know their own name by the time they reach 30, if they even live that long.

I'd like to say things have gone back to normal here but even with you and Destan and the spy gone, Thgindim is all shaken up. If they didn't trust Underbrush before, now we're all pretty much criminals in the eyes of both the JPs and the Majesty Council. There haven't been any more executions, but what's worse is people are just beginning to disappear. Literally, Raine. Poof. Gone. And no one is saying anything. Whoever makes a scene just disappears next, and so now everyone's just quiet about it and suffering in silence as their wives and children and friends are snatched and taken wherever. I'm worried sick about Velle having to commute to Peak to work every morning because you know she isn't the most aggressive and couldn't fight off whoever is kidnapping people. She's so committed to her work, though, it's annoying. And the level of brainwashing she's getting from being up in that Tower full of airheads is frighteningly high.

I suppose I should tell you this, too. Velle doesn't know about this communicating of ours. Carmen does. It's scary but I just don't trust her anymore, my own twin. She sees me all a mess worrying about you and even though at first, you remember, <u>she</u> was the hysterical one saying goodbye, now she's turned up her nose and tells me things like "she should've known better than to defy our government who's just looking out for us," or "I miss the Raine she was before she turned into a traitor against our mountain." We hardly talk anymore because we just end up arguing and making Granny upset. Carmen's trying to fill your position and be the peace-maker between me and Velle, but we share the same stubbornness in our matching DNA, so it's pretty useless.

I know you want to hear about your family, but sadly there is just nothing much to tell. The day after you left, I stopped by with flowers for your mother and Gwen and she took one look at me and slammed the door in my face. I tried again the next day and she told me I was no longer welcome in your house. I asked why and she accused me of knowing about everything, about the spy, about Destan...I think your mother misses you. And feels sad and just as worried as I am, no matter how mad she might have seemed, you're still her daughter and she loves you. She and Gwen have been sealed up inside hardly leaving at all except to open the door for taxes or handing off her soups to the delivery girl. If it makes you feel any better, I'm sure both of them are safe from whoever is stealing people.

Going back to what I know about Destan...is it bad that I sort of maybe saw maybe all of this kind of coming? Maybe? I don't know, the intensity with which you spoke of him last year when we left Skye's birthday cotillion just really shook me, and I just had this feeling things would go down a rocky path. I went home that night and on top of all of the other shocking things you said, I just laid there replaying in my head your expression and the look in your eyes when you defended him against what I was telling you about it all being his fault. So...you really love him, don't you? Could you tell me more about him, how things developed the way they did and so fast? I'm sorry I'm so skeptical. I really wish I could say I support it and that I want you to be happy with him and

I'm glad you're in love, but I just feel so stupid and angry at myself. Because even though you said the kiss would remain between us, now I know I overstepped my bounds. I had no idea you two had bonded and committed to each other like that, and now that there might be a child involved, I feel even more stupid about trying to show you my feelings when you already had them for someone else. Please forgive me, Raine, you're my best friend and we can just pretend it never happened, okay? I'm going to stop with this here.

In regards to the pregnancy stuff, I'm no expert but I can assure you that it would be much too soon to feel symptoms if it was from the other man. So if you are, in fact, pregnant, it has to be Destan's. I'm not sure if that makes you feel any better…you're scared, I know. Raine I hate that all this is happening to you. The thought of that monster hurting you like that makes me scream inside and want to charge into Mythland brandishing a sword to chop his head off. It is so cruel and unfair and please stop apologizing because it is nowhere near your fault that this happened to you. Once you feel ready to tell Destan, I'm sure that if he really, really, loves you then he will understand and not hold any sort of bizarre grudge.

You apologized so much for how you're feeling, how you think you're complaining, but Raine you have fought through so much more in just a month than most people have their entire life. You are more than allowed to feel these negative emotions. I don't know how you possibly couldn't, not after all of what has happened. If you don't think you can let it out to Destan or Irene, send it all to me and I will whisk the bad away and try to leave you with some peace. Please, I beg you, be angry and be sad and feel all you need to feel, but just don't let it become you blaming yourself or feeling guilty.

You made a good point in writing that little Ai can't carry all that much, so I'll finish it off by answering your question about how I knew about her. In short...I didn't, really. I had been on my way to work when in those chips that had been quiet since Career Day, just went off and blared the news that the Peak Tower Thieves had been caught and you were one of them. I felt like the whole world was ending hearing your name spoken alongside "banishment." I ran to your house and banged on your door and I saw Gwen peeping through the window, waving, thinking it was all a game, and then your mom taking her away and the sound of multiple locks being secured. I ran next door to Carmen's and she wasn't at home. I could hardly breathe; I was a frenetic mess in the middle of the street and somehow made it back home where Granny was still cooking her breakfast.

She let me cry for awhile, laying with my head in her lap, rubbing my back while she smoked. And then when her cigarette had burnt all the way down, she just shoved me off of her to get up and instructed me to pack up a sack of food and fill our water gourds, as if we would be going out. And you know Granny, she's been inside for at least twenty years, never stepping off the porch. But suddenly she had on an old coat that smelled like mouse droppings and mildew, and she went charging out the door motioning me to follow. Then, as we were walking down the main Underbrush road, she pointed vigorously for me to pull up every yellow dandelion crossing our path. I did as I was told, wondering if finally Granny had gotten a bit odd in her old age. Whenever I looked at her in question, she'd take on this stony and impatient expression and urge me forward to pick more or walk faster.

We walked very north up through Underbrush, and just as the Starshade gate came into view, she veered off to the side and dove through the bushes! It was insane! I'd never seen her move any more than shuffle around in her slippers or take an hour to cook some rice at the stove! I followed, so confused and even more distraught at this point and tried to keep up as she hobbled over roots and through the low-hanging pine branches.

As we walked, the tree trunks started turning red. A rusty red, like the colour of that scarf you always wear. And then I started to realize, they weren't so much trees anymore as columns. Some were carved or covered in chipping paint, all sorts of different colours. Hanging from the trees were little houses, like bird houses, but smaller, of a different shape. It's indescribable. I think we were in the remnants of an old temple...have you ever seen any of them during your travels in the forests? Granny stopped in the middle of a circle of these columns. These were ones that started out normally but then rose up into the sculpted forms of women, goddesses, maybe.

Granny took the sack and reached in for all of the bunches of dandelions, and started tossing them all around us— at the columns, at the little houses, out into the trees. I just stood there and watched, completely confused about what she could be trying to do. But then there was this sound. A chirping. Sort of like crickets, sort of like birds. And from inside one of those little houses came these strange creatures that flew without wings, gliding through the air as if swimming. I thought they were some kind of lizard or snake with their scales, but the more

I watched them the more I felt as if I'd entered a spirit tale. Maybe forty of them filled the air, all different colours. Some red, some purple, blue, green, gold, even silver and black. They gobbled up all of the dandelions Granny tossed, and as they all circled and caught the weeds in their mouths, my Granny suddenly gave me an urgent look, nodding her head at one of the columns.

On top of it was one of the little houses that had fallen out of a tree. The arched roof had been split open and I could see what looked like a nest situated inside. There was a tangled bed of grass and pine needles, and a stack of small eggs in the belly of the nest. I climbed up the column as far as I could so that I could reach an egg, and the moment my fingers touched one, the creatures whirled around and came at me like a swarm of angry wasps. Caught off balance, I fell back and luckily the egg I'd snatched hadn't broken. Granny helped me up as the creatures flew down and pecked and pulled at my hair, clawing at the hand that held the egg as we ran back toward the edge of the woods. They stopped chasing us the minute the sounds of the street were audible. I had never wished more in my life that my old Granny could talk.

At home I sort of lashed out at her asking why we'd gone there, what those were, why did I take an egg and

251

how was this supposed to make me feel better or help the fact that my best friend would be sent to hell on earth in a night. She just smiled sagely the entire rant, driving me CRAZY. By the time I'd vented all of my frustration, she had shuffled back to the kitchen to put a kettle on the stove for tea. She'd placed a beaten up copy of spirit tales on the windowsill, by the egg bathing in the sun.

I took both the egg and the book up to the loft, and flipped through to see if anything connected. Somewhere in the middle of the book near the discussion of humans and how they can reach out to the spirits, I came across the spirit messenger passage. There were those little flying things, even the little houses and sketches of men with their long black braids and old fashioned robes hammering them together. I read about how they need heat to develop and to hatch, how they are called home on the blood moon and can learn to follow scents as they age. You and your spy were right, they are called feilong. Fluxaria must be more spiritual, then, despite what we've learned about it?

I read the tale and knew that if I could only get the egg to you, you could work out its purpose once it hatched and we could stay in touch. I knew it was a reach, but I saw no other option other than to get banished myself and go in there with you. That was actually a serious thought that had crossed my mind. I had known about your plans and the spy, I figured I could get banished too and that seemed like a more comforting option than being miles and miles away while you had to fight to survive.

I hate having to stop but I have to send this off as soon as I can. I've been giving Ai plenty of milk and bugs and dandelions to keep her growing and happy, as well as various drawings and borrowed clothing you've given me over the years so that she can learn your scent. I'm bathing this letter in plenty of perfume from the flower shop so that Ai can return to me as well. I love you so much, so much more than words can say.

I love you and have more faith in you than ever. Send news soon. We shall surely meet again...after you've saved the world, of course.

xOxOxO

Chantastic

chapter twenty

I stretched out on the pad of moss, staring up at the stars. I'd read her letter three, four, six times and still every time I did I found myself as excited and blown away as the first time. One certain moment repeated and replayed through my thoughts, somehow in the low lull of her voice,

So...you really love him, don't you? I really wish I could say that I want you to be happy with him and I'm glad you're in love, but I just feel so stupid and angry at myself. Because even though you said the kiss would remain between us, now I know I overstepped my bounds. I feel even more stupid about trying to show you my feelings when you already had them for someone else. Please forgive me, Raine, you're my best friend and we can just pretend it never happened, okay?

I pressed the heels of my hands into my eyes, listening to the sounds of the forest. The air stirring the leaves, Ai's soft snores, and the creaking of the branches above me. *Your feelings? Chantastic, what feelings? Was that kiss supposed to mean more than just "goodbye?"* I shook my head, no, of course not. We were best friends, not to mention, both girls. That just wasn't a natural thing to happen. We loved each other that was certain, I loved her so much that I'd do anything for her, and her for me. But was I *in* love with her? I couldn't be, the way I felt for her was completely different if not the polar opposite of how I felt about Destan. But the more I thought about it, the less convinced I was. Chantastic, Chan Ai Song, my best friend, had feelings for me. Romantic feelings. And if I did, I was too scared, too busy with everything else going on, to find out. Especially, because the one and only Destan Abrasha came stumbling through the trees into my clearing, putting a stopper in any more Chantastic thoughts I could possibly have.

"Is my time-out over yet?" I asked, sitting up and smiling at him. He managed a small smile, but it soon faded, and he looked conflicted again.

"I understand, you know. What you did," he began, kicking at a cluster of fungus and coming closer. His words made a swell of relief rise inside me, but his cold grey eyes sent it shrinking back into nothing. "But it wasn't cool. And I just don't get why you'd keep it secret until now. You've been hiding so much and I just don't get it, Raine."

Swallowing the lump in my throat, I rose from the ground and came cautiously toward him. "Destan," I whispered, "I just don't want to hurt you, put any more stress on you."

He rolled his eyes. "Come *on*, Bluehead, I'm a grownass man—I can take whatever it is, whether it's the pregnancy or some sneaky thing you did or why you freak out at random things you never used to or why you won't bond with me. What happened when you were taken by the travellers? What did they do to you?" he demanded, a vein pulsing at his temple. He must've seen the fear that flooded me at his words, because he jogged over and rested both hands on my shoulders. With one finger, he tipped my chin up to look at him. I couldn't and focused on his coat collar as he spoke. "I can't help make it better if I don't know what's wrong. And I can't stand that you're keeping all of this hurt inside of you. *That's* what's stressing me out, Raine. Not knowing is hurting me."

My lip began to tremble, and his calloused fingertip traced from my chin to my mouth, feeling the tremors. His arm slid behind my back and pulled my body to his, holding me close. He gently stroked my hair, pushing the bangs out of my eyes as I quivered in his arms. I dug my fingers into the thick coil of his scarf, squeezing my eyes shut and burying my face in his chest. Even pressed close to him, I felt like the force of the earth was pulling me away to somewhere dark with nothing to hold on to.

"I love you. Nothing could change that. I'll forgive you for anything, for everything, if you just tell me what's wrong and what happened," Destan begged, squeezing me more tightly and then releasing me from his embrace. He moved away and sat onto a boulder, patting the space beside him for me to join. I hesitated, staring at his broken expression and knowing it would take more strength not to say anything.

"After I was captured, the leader of the travellers poisoned me," I began, moving dizzily to sit with him, and staring up into the endless blue of the sky. "But it wasn't a poison that makes you sick or is supposed to kill you. It...it was the blood of this creature, and it completely immobilized my mouth and throat and it made it so I couldn't speak. There were a lot of girls he had done this to...to keep under his control."

Destan's warm palm fell over mine. "Under his control to do what?"

Tears balanced on the thin cliff of my eyelids, daring to create waterfalls on my cheeks. I tipped up my chin to keep them at bay, and removed my hand from under Destan's. "He would make us dance for him and his men. Every night. He'd hardly feed us, keep us trapped in a tent during the day, and then dress us up in these costumes and makeup and make us dance on a stage."

Destan didn't say anything. His hands rested on his knees, curling in and out of fists the longer I let the silence last. As the first tear fell, every word came rushing from my mouth, "Then he would take a girl or a few to bed with him. Every night. And once I arrived he'd always pick me, because I was new, because he thought I was exotic, I don't know, but he'd pick me and he would just force me to..."

I dissolved, my head falling forward into my hands as Destan knelt before me. I could hardly breathe between sobs. "Destan, I didn't have a choice, I couldn't fight him because he was too strong! And I know I should've told you and even though I doubted it, I know I should've sent Ai to Fluxaria, but I felt so alone and messed up and I had to tell *someone* but I couldn't tell you because I was too ashamed..."

"And that's why you wrote to Chan? To tell her about this?" he asked, his voice breaking and forehead touching mine.

I nodded. "I couldn't sleep, I can't sleep without dreaming it all over again and I just needed to hear from someone that it wasn't my fault and that's what she said to me." I didn't want to know what expression was on his face, and I just kept talking and talking, my entire body shaking more violently every moment. "I want to be close to you again. I want to bond with you so badly, but when we tried, it just brought back everything that he made me do, that he did to me, and I didn't want to bring it up because there's so much more to worry about! Like the war and getting to Fluxaria and I couldn't just give us another problem to deal with..."

"Raine Ylevol, listen to me, okay?" Destan whispered, stroking a hand over my hair. "The only way we can help stop this war and get to Fluxaria is if we're all in one piece. And if you're being torn every which way with a pregnancy and secrets and trauma like this, then there's no way you'll make it. And without you, we won't make it either." He drew back and cupped my face in his hands, forcing me to finally look into his eyes. His eyes were bloodshot and streaming. "I had no idea this could've happened to you...Raine, it *kills* me that this happened to you, that I wasn't there—"

"It's not your fault," I said quickly, shaking my head, "there's nothing you could've done."

"Then let me help you now, okay? We could...I don't know, tell Irene? She can be harsh sometimes, but she knows it isn't like you to do what you did with Ai and the letter. If she knew why, she'd understand," he said.

"How can you be sure?" I whispered, "I'm scared she's never going to trust me again."

"Then maybe...you could somehow make it up to her." Destan turned and dug around in his pocket, withdrawing a sheet of notebook paper I recognized from Irene's pocket journal. "I think this is her to-do list, and on it there's a drawing of that plant she needs for the bomb. Mao cao...mao gao cai or something? Find this for her and she'll know you would never betray her or the mission."

I nodded, examining the crude sketch that must've been balled up in her spy bag for who knew how long. I could navigate my way through a swamp and find this, no problem. I wiped my streaming nose with the back of my sleeve, sighing, "I'll try it. But I don't want to be away from you two, not with the cyborg clearly planning on more sabotage. I talked to him, remember? He said he'd do more than just slice your face up."

Destan scowled. "Were those his exact words?"

"Pretty much."

"Well, it's not like you're banished from the fearsome-threesome. Like you said, it was more of a time-out. To let things cool down some," he shrugged.

I tucked some hair behind my ear, staring off into where he'd come through the bushes. "Then maybe I should take the long way back. Go through the swamp instead of the brush and grab the plant on the way."

"Well, be careful, all right? I only want to be two minutes ahead of you in case anything happens," Destan said, looking at me seriously. I touched his cheek, bringing my lips to his and kissing him softly.

"I love you," I whispered, "I love you and I promise, no more secrets."

"Good," he chuckled. "I love you too. And you have to tell me what you need to get through this. If it's space, if it's telling Irene or not telling Irene, whatever you need, okay?"

"Okay."

"And as long as I'm here, no one is ever going to hurt you like that again. Say the word and I'll go off into the woods with a big stick and hunt down that bastard. I don't want you to be scared or feel forced to act like everything's okay when it isn't, but it is going to be okay, eventually...whatever the fuck that means." He scratched at his head under his beanie, staring at the ground. "I don't know if this helps at all, but when Griffin died I felt all messed up, too. I never thought I'd get over it. And I'm not 'over it,' you can't be when things this huge happen. But after a while it just doesn't hurt the way it used to, and things can feel normal-ish again and new good things start happening. Like you, for instance." He looked back up at me, eyes crinkling at the corners with a slight smile. "You sure you wanna go get this thing alone?"

I sighed, rising from the boulder. "I don't know if Irene would count it as me redeeming myself if I had my lumberjack boyfriend chop through the swamps so I could pull up some flowers." I went over to a peacefully snoozing Ai and stowed her carefully in my knapsack, glancing back at Destan and trying to smile. "I think I can manage. Thank you, though. For everything."

He did a clumsy bow, "Just doin' my job. Don't get too filthy." Destan gave me a last peck on the cheek, and as he started into the trees, I followed the stream of mud into the swamps.

"Ah, there you are..." I murmured, making my way carefully from stone to stone. The swamp smelled like a hundred skunks had sprayed their stink into it. Water-hoppers lightly danced across the surface, their spindly legs hardly disturbing the noxious flow of bog water. Looking timidly around, I noticed that the trees surrounding me all grew at a diagonal tilt; half-submerged, their trunks covered in mucus and fungus as some sort of infection spread from the water to their roots. Islands of moss were scattered spontaneously about, on one of which a squirrel stood stranded with no other option but to wade in the acidic mud if he wanted to make it back to safety. It was on the tiny island slightly beyond the squirrel that I saw my target: the mao gao cai plant. With leaves weaponized with sticky drops of carnivorous dew, and spoked pink petals erupting from the center blossom, it beckoned me to come and pull it up by the roots and bring it to Irene to do with it whatever she wanted. I didn't know how many samples she needed to make the bomb blow-up-able, but peering through the green clouds of swamp vapour, I could identify at least five different clumps of mao gao cai scattered throughout. *I better get as much as I can find,* I thought, leaping carefully over a sunken log and landing on the first grassy island. *I wish she'd specified quantity on that list of hers.*

I combed through the grass with my fingers, looking for flashes of pink, but found nothing but spiderwebs and weeds. I moved onto the next island, this time accidentally brushing the water with the heel of my boot and hearing the faint sizzle of melted rubber. Biting my lip, I shook out my foot and unsheathed my dagger. Crouching by the mao gao cai, I sawed gently at the stem, not daring to touch and get stuck to one of the leaves. The dew on them was only supposed to be able to capture and dissolve bugs, but I didn't want to find out what damage it could still do to human skin. I wrapped it up safely in a leaf and stowed it in my pocket, jumping from island to island, repeating the same method for an hour until I was positive I'd gotten all of it. My pockets were busting with potentially explosive plants, and my stomach seemed to rumble emptily for something to eat. But then I felt something else, and I stopped in shock, nearly tripping and plopping into a puddle.

It felt like a tiny finger running down my stomach, making it flutter, and then there was a flicking sensation. A tiny flick to the inside of my belly. *Holy crap,* I thought, trying to get out of the swamp even though now my heart raced and raced and a second flick caused me to trip and melt my other shoe heel. *HOLY CRAP! There IS an actual living thing in there! I have to make it back and tell Destan!*

I leapt over the last island in haste, pushing away the dangling vines in my way and feeling thorns tear into the thick fabric of my coat as I ran. Luckily, Destan and Irene were only two minutes away, and when I spotted a hole hacked into the tangle of brambles, I dove through and found myself once again face to face with my Beaniehead. He screamed as I burst into the clearing, falling back onto his butt with me crashing down on top of him.

"Bluehead! Where did you come from?!" he squealed, looking up at me incredulously and tickling me to get me off.

I rolled onto the grass beside him, laughing, "What do you mean where was I? I went and got the mao gao cai! All of it, actually!"

"The what?" Destan tilted his head to the side in confusion, one eye winking as I noticed Irene watching a few feet away. "Ohh...you mean the super important plant that will finish the weapon and save Fluxaria? Wow, Bluehead you're a hero!"

Irene rolled her eyes, "Very subtle, Destan. I wonder where she got the idea."

I went to my knees and then to my feet, walking nervously over to the spy, heart hammering in my chest. "The mao gao cai. I...I got it for you," I said, reaching into my pockets and holding out the leaf-wrapped plants. Irene's eyebrows shot up her forehead in surprise, and she took a few suspicious steps forward. She pried away one leaf with her pinky, peering at the pink petals sticking out near the top.

"Hmm. That's a lot of stuff all right," she muttered, looking back up at me. She crossed her arms against her chest, her bicep muscles flexing as she did and making me feel even more like a toothpick. "But why are you showing me this, traitor?"

I flushed, setting the plants down on a stump beside me and nervously meeting her eyes. "Because...because I wanted to show you I still care about the mission. A lot. I'm sorry I went behind your back, it was wrong of me. If we don't reach Fluxaria it's on me for not listening to you. And I knew you needed mao cao gai to fuel the weapon so I just wanted to help."

"Even if all of that's true..." she shrugged, absently kicking over a mushroom, "...I don't see how this shit's gonna help any of what you just said."

My throat went dry. "W-what do you mean?"

"I mean, that's not mao gao cai," she said, snatching up the plants from the stump and turning on her heel.

Destan ran up from behind me, his cheeks bright red. "*Yes*, it is," he protested, "that's what you drew on your to-do list, at least."

"Is it so shocking that maybe I just wanted some of these pretty swamp flowers to adorn this butt-ugly campsite?" she scoffed, her back still turned to us as she yanked out the not-mao-gao-cai and tossed them into a bowl where she'd ground up various other herbs. "Your Bluehead is going to have to do much better than this if she wants to be within less than twenty feet of me. I'd tell her to go hunt some mini-beasties, but she's pretty horrible at that so..."

Heat flooded my cheeks. "Irene, I'm sorry–"

"No, Raine," Destan said, slowly shaking his head, "don't apologize to her, she's acting mental. Either she's mental or she's fucking with you."

Irene was now fiddling with the tablet, her shoulders shaking with silent laughter. I didn't know what to make of her. A fuzzy, crackling sound filled the air...radio static? It was hard to tell because now she was giggling.

"Irene, what in the world are you doing?" I asked, exasperated and striding over to her. She held up a finger, the other hand yanking a slender antenna from the top of the tablet and adjusting the angle.

"Just hold on," insisted the spy, shooting me a quick glance before returning to work. A braided wire I was sure she'd scavenged from the tower wound from the bottom of the tablet into a pink and green ball of the ground up herbs and not-mao-gao-cai. And before I could connect the dots, a ghostly image of various numbers hovered above the glass and Irene prodded them systematically, tongue sticking out in concentration. The static continued, but then through the static, I could hear what sounded like laughter, a man speaking, and Destan and I crowded around the tablet in awe.

"*Chhhh*....I have to say...*chhhh*....of the up and coming Entertainers in Emergent....*chhh*... playing for the Majesty Council at the annual cotillion...*chhhmmm*," the radio voice crackled, interrupted every few moments by the fuzz caused by our extreme distance from Thgindim, much less one of the highest levels of the mountain.

"Irene," I said, "did you use those swamp flowers to power a *radio?*"

She couldn't hide her pleased grin. "Are you insinuating that you have a problem with that?"

"But you said she got the wrong plants!" Destan exclaimed, "Is this mao gao cai?"

"Yeah, I lied. Just wanted to torture her a bit longer to get even."

"Remind me never to cross you ever again," I muttered, shaking my head and observing the holographic radio dial. "Could I look for something on here? A certain channel?" I'd tuned in to music sometimes when working on homework or sketching alone in my room, but except for one channel, it all came from Emergent and featured fluffy lyrics and upbeat melodies that often made me want to smash the radio to bits. The one channel I could actually stand broadcasted solely from Canopia, so I crouched beside Destan and Irene in a swamp miles and miles away from home to find it.

"I hope it'll come in," I murmured, twisting the strange dial delicately to another channel. "I think it was...eighty-nine something? Eighty-nine point...seven."

The sound cut from static to another voice, nostalgia coating my heart in something warm and yearning as it announced, "Now without further ado...*chhhh*...Yuqing Ma partnered...Alec Tso...*chhhh-mmmm*...on...the...*chhhhhh*....brandnew...*chhhhhhmmm*....Mountain Air in E-flat. Enjoy, folks."

The music began and there it was. No sugar-coated melodies or wealthy Entertainers showing off their years of private tutors and beautiful instruments that cost more than an Underbrusher's home. This station was run by factory workers performing in a basement, not afraid of sad songs or playing instruments made from scrap or deemed out of style by the Department of Entertainment. There was nothing overtly political, so not even the toughest of censors could manage to shut it down after decades of broadcasts.

A piano began to play; the blunt sound of the instrument sizzling through the tablet speaker and wandering through the trees, making the branches shiver at the unfamiliar presence of music. I found myself shivering too, and Destan took my hand, put one in Irene's, calming the tremors right away.

"I think this calls for a celebration," Destan said, grinning broadly, "would you ladies care to dance?"

"Spies don't dance," Irene said.

"Don't or can't?" he probed, successfully pulling me to my feet, but unable to make the Fluxarian budge.

She smiled, eyes narrowed. "Won't. Not unless there's some moonshine in your knapsack to numb the pain of the whole experience."

"What kind of weirdo puts on music they don't intend to boogie to?" Destan asked in exasperation. "C'mon, please? Let's handle serious stuff tomorrow. You know you wanna get down with cool kids like us."

Irene looked up at me, something I hadn't noticed before in her eyes. Pain. Before there had been only anger, never ending anger and ferocity at what I had done. But now I saw that all of that had been just another defense. I hadn't made her angry, I'd done worse. I'd killed maybe the last shred of hope inside of her that things would work out.

She glanced away, leaping to her feet and brushing off the knees of her pants. "Fine. But only one song, you hear me? I just wanted to test if the radio component of the tablet could work if I gave it some extra juice– OHHH NO, DESTAN, PUT ME DOWN!"

The moment she agreed, Destan snatched her by the waist and spun her around, legs kicking in the air, screams resounding throughout the forest and scaring away the pairs of eyes watching in the bushes. I couldn't help but laugh even as he tossed her up once and then caught her, earning a smack to the back of the head. His beanie went flying and Irene seized the opportunity to free herself, her cheeks flushed.

"My fancy new hat!" he gasped, dashing to pick it up from the grass. He unstuck a solitary leaf from the knitting and then smiled up at me. "No harm done. Fancy beanie is intact."

I grinned back at him, surprised when I noticed Irene at my side. Her hands were balled into fists, lips pursed as she seemed to be contemplating if she wanted to dance with a traitor like me after all. Destan didn't allow her to overthink it, and took both of our hands, nodding at us to do the same. Hesitantly, Irene moved to hold mine, a grumpy crease in between her brows. Even the crackly music seemed to be building with tension as her fingers came closer and closer to mine, finally gripping my wrist in a painfully tight hold and yanking me to the side as Destan led us in a gallop.

His laughter overpowered the trill of piano and drum, his clumsy stomping and attempt at singing along causing Irene to join in next, her face truly happy for the first time since we were drunk and cramped in that tunnel. As we continued galloping in a circle to the music, I met her eyes, offering a timid smile. Her hand relaxed on my wrist but didn't let go.

Can we start over? I asked her silently, unable to catch my breath as Destan ducked under our arms and we unwound, dancing around and around again until the song changed and a dozen drums began to play.

The spy shrugged, *"Whatever."* With a smirk, she did a quick twirl and her ponytail whipped me hard in the face. Destan cracked up, not noticing how Irene narrowed her eyes warningly at me. *"But cross me again and you're toast."*

The music suddenly cut off, leaving the air full of static. The three of us skidded to a stop, tripping into each other as a chilling voice buzzed through the speakers.

"Do you read me.....*chhhh*...recalculating coordinates...*chhhmmm.*"

"The station's all messed up," Destan said, starting over to the tablet and reaching out to move the dial. But no matter which way he turned it, all that came in was static. Static, and that voice.

"Do...fugitive spy, do you read?" the voice chanted, Irene's jaw dropping, all colour leaving her face. "This is...*chhh*...of national security... *chhhmmm*....we are locating the use of this Majesty Council device....stay where you are to avoid further—"

Destan shot at it in a quick movement, sweeping up his bow, sticking a wad of mud to the arrow tip, and hitting the tablet straight on the power button. The woods were now an eerie, terrible quiet. Irene's hand fell limply out of mine, and she took a few trudging steps toward the tablet.

"I guess it's safe to say..." she began, tracing a finger over the silver edge of the device, "...party's over. Let's get back to war."

chapter twenty-one

I guided Siri through the swamp, counting her steps to myself. *222, 223, 224, 225.* It was going to take forever to get to 1,400. The plan was in action now. After the scary Majesty Council broadcast, we reviewed what we'd gone over before. We needed to know how far we were from Fluxaria, and so Irene would take herself two miles ahead of me, Destan one mile ahead of me, and I'd stay put at the one-mile mark— about 1,400 paces. Then we'd climb a tree at each of our stopping points, and look out to see just about how much farther we'd have to go to reach Fluxaria.

Leaping over a small stream, Siri zigzagged us through the oncoming crowd of bamboo. I kept us running straight behind Destan and Irene; checking to make sure we lined up with the bobbing dot of red that was his hat, and the swinging tail of the tiangou he rode. I was keeping up, but I didn't have to go as far as them, so at some point they would disappear and I'd have to stop and begin to climb.

I fixed the strap of my quiver more securely across my body and checked my bag for Irene's climbing spikes. She'd given me the full set, both her and Destan claiming they could free climb well enough. I didn't even try to argue that I didn't need them all. It was surprising enough that Destan let me contribute at all now that he knew there was a mini human inside me.

378, 379, 380, 381, 382, 383. They were getting so small and far ahead of me that I had to force Siri's slender grey legs to pump us ahead even faster by smacking her sides, careful not to brush her bandages. She was still healing from the tunnel collapse, which was why I'd taken her and not Destan. *460, 461, 462...jeez!* The baby kicked, reminding me to remind Destan that this freaky phenomenon was now occurring. Then I was reminded I'd let seconds go by without paying attention to my wolf's footfalls. *Crap. Let's just add five and go from there.*

As we ran, Mythland blurred by in a snowy green haze. Everything looked the same in the way that everything was completely different from one another– as it always was in Mythland. I was bored with Mythland's spontaneity and even more bored with its surprises. At first, the valley was terrifying. But now I wasn't expecting anything to go as planned, and ever since I started thinking this way, I hadn't fallen into any more dens of tiangou or been completely thrown by a storm. Fearing the eyes in the dark made them come out, fearing the storms made them beat me, it was the fear that screwed things up, I knew this now. Running ahead now, counting steps, finally at 1000 paces, I knew I was just another breathing piece of the complete puzzle of the forest. It was the fear and separation that had made the woods so daunting and impossible. It just didn't scare me anymore.

The sound of mechanical breathing scared me.

I glanced over my shoulder, seeing a glint of black metal disappearing behind a low-hanging bow. *1261, 1262, 1263,* I tried to stay focused, holding tighter to Siri and urging her along. I recentered us to where Destan was ahead of me, now hardly a pinprick. *1295, 1296, 1297, come on Siri, come on, we can't let him catch up.*

A whirring noise sounded from the left side of me, a spray of leaves shooting into my path. Slicing through the brush looked like spinning blades, connected to some metal contraption on which the cyborg was straddled. He revved the engine, closing in on Siri's left flank, his voice booming as if through a megaphone, "Abandon this quest, Miss Ylevol. It doesn't have to end this way."

I swerved farther right and he followed, the rapidly spinning propellers grazing Siri's side and causing her to shriek in pain as it shaved into her skin. I sat back and drew my bow, squeezing my thigh muscles to try and sit upright. "Back off or I'll shoot!" I screamed at him. "Not everyone has a fancy Justice Police bike. Touch my wolf again and I'll fill your engine with arrows!"

"I suggest you preserve your ammunition for our journey back to the mountain," he said, coming in close again. I fired the second he moved, my arrow glancing off the shiny exterior of whatever he was riding. I shot again, this time securing two arrows on my bowstring and using all my strength to fire straight at his beady blue eyes. They pounded the bulletproof glass of his visor, giving me just enough time to veer Siri off into the bushes where his bike would have trouble navigating.

Shit! I thought, fury flowing hotly through me as we ducked under a fallen tree and I yanked on Siri's reins to stop. *Not only have I lost track of what number of steps we were on, I'm now way off course from Destan and Irene.*

I slid off of Siri, not wasting a moment to slide on the hand and foot spikes and make it over to the nearest tree. Before beginning my ascent, I turned back to Siri, resting a hand on her muzzle. "Siri, I don't want that cyborg to hurt you," I whispered, looking solemnly into her green eyes. I pointed at the bamboo grove sprouting a few paces away. "Go in there and hide until I come down, okay? Don't let him see you. Please, go." I guided her in the direction of the grove and she understood, whining a little in protest, but then obeying and disappearing inside the thick vat of stalks.

The lethal end of the hand spike sank easily into the bark. So hastily apologizing to the tree and whatever spirit might reside in it, I dug in my feet and hoisted myself up as I'd done nearly a year ago at Peak. I couldn't dig the spike too deeply into the tree or else taking it out would be a task in itself, so I had to be quick and only get a proper hold and support before moving quickly again.

I fell into a rhythm— right foot, left hand, left foot, right hand— I went on and on submerged in absolute focus, only taken out by my aching, exhausted muscles. I had been climbing a straight ten minutes before the branches became thick enough to trade for the spikes. Wheezing and out of breath, I swung myself up to sit on one, every limb quaking as I unhooked the diamond spikes form my hands and feet. Before stowing them in my rucksack, I turned them over in my hands, looking for some hint of wear. Nothing. They were as pristine and sharp as the first time I'd used them, save the smear of dirt where my hands had been pressing. I stuffed them away, careful not to disturb the napping feilong curled up at the bottom. I rested a few fingers on Ai's back, stroking gently as I took a minute to breathe and recharge.

Back on Thgindim, you had to be a good climber. The mountain was prickly with pine trees and prone to avalanches in which the only escape was usually scooting up a tree and holding on for dear life as an ocean of rock rushed around you. I was a good climber, it was in my blood. Even my mother, gaunt and weak and hunched, could make it onto our little house's tin roof in seconds if we needed to find higher ground during an avalanche or even just to hide out from the JPs collecting taxes. I remember the first time she brought me and Gwen up there. We were hiding so the JPs could pillage our house of any valuables that added up to the taxes we owed. Gwen was having the most trouble getting herself up the gutter, so Mom single-handedly tossed her up and Gwen floated onto the roof gentle as a parachute. We waited up there for about a half an hour, finding shapes in clouds to pass the time and kept our minds off of the destruction below us.

It's time to keep going, I thought, looking up. The leafy branches above me swirled dizzily, and I grasped the branch below me harder to stay balanced. *Okay, not doing that again. Just focus on what's in front of you, Raine...*

I kept on; reaching up for the next bough. The blisters on my palm split against the rough bark, and I gritted my teeth against the sting, trying with all my might to pull myself up. My arm seemed to turn into jelly, and I luckily caught myself on the branch below me before I plummeted to my demise. I fell into another rhythm of reaching, pulling, holding my breath and exhaling as I made it up. There wasn't any room for the thoughts or painful worrying about the people I loved back home or even the cyborg looking for me down below. My mind was empty, only following the instructions my body gave, climbing,

climbing, my eyes wide and unblinking. No glancing down, no glancing up, just my hands and feet, and I stayed in this trance until finally the branches began to thin.

It was getting brighter very quickly, and actually...warm? I slowly drifted from my concentrated place, feeling the warmth of the shuishan boughs in wonder, climbing as fast as I could in desperation to reach the sun. My heart raced and raced inside of me. The snow was long gone now, and the wood was smoother to the touch. As I finally broke through the leaves, I was swallowed in such light that I blindly toppled back and had to resurface.

From this height, Mythland was a sea of emerald green speckled by white. The sky was blue, a blue I'd forgotten, the blue I'd loved so much that back home I'd run inside and dig through my messy desk until I found my paints and mix forget-me-not with bluebird to achieve that ethereal blue and save the moment. Ahead—the clouds were stacks of cream-coloured pillows resting beneath the sun's drowsy head. Behind—charcoal clouds dragged shadows over the valley, jagged bolts of lightning and the blur of rain continuing all the way to Thgindim's big gates.

Thgindim. It was so very beautiful, I found myself crying this time out of longing rather than fear. The magnificent gates seemed to make everything around the mountain shimmer and waver. Thgindim was a perfect triangle of precious jade, appearing so huge it seemed we were still right at the beginning of the valley despite the miles we'd travelled. And even from here I could see each individual tile of Peak Tower sparkle proudly, the pointed top poking a hole in the clouds and continuing up endlessly. *I guess the Majesty Council wasn't being boastful when they told us Thgindim looked powerful even from across the valley. I had no idea how big the Tower could actually be...it's nearly impossible.* I also saw, for the first time, what lay beyond Thgindim, beyond Mythland. But the longer I stared, the more I felt a strange queasiness in my stomach that I knew had nothing to do with being pregnant.

There was nothing beyond Thgindim. I made to look toward Fluxaria, but then I decided to concentrate on the nothing, trying to see how that was possible. It was like looking through a bizarre lens, one that bent the focus all around me no matter which way I turned my head. There was nothing to the east, nothing to the west, I'd turn my head and Thgindim would *still be there.* As if I'd never turned when I knew for sure by the placement of my feet or twist of my neck that I'd indeed moved and Thgindim had somehow moved with me, not allowing me to see past it. No matter how I tried to focus on what lie behind the mountain, Thgindim stayed sharp and everything beyond was a greyish blur that just looking at it made me disoriented and my eyes burn and blink until I glanced away.

As weird as that is, Raine, I know *you're just putting off what you actually need to see,* the voice in my head hissed, causing me to slowly rotate back around and face my destination. I prayed anxiously that from here, Fluxaria wouldn't still look so tiny. *Just don't be any smaller than…I don't know, my pinky nail. Head-sized is fine. Or my hand, or even a fist wouldn't be so bad, just please don't let it be impossibly far, for our sake. For Irene's. It's time for her to go home,* I thought, my eyes closed in anticipation. The leaves were smooth as silk beneath my fingers, the sunlight a bath of purest warmth on my neck. I could taste the life in the air, I could smell that all of the decay of Mythland was below me and now I had risen above and was within the borders of a calmer place ahead. My eyes opened. Before I even took notice of Fluxaria, I zeroed in on a red dot not so far ahead of me. The dot moved and a small arm stuck out and waved.

"Destan!" I called, screaming my throat raw in the hopes my voice could reach him. "Destan, it's so beautiful!"

I thought I could hear him answer, I swore he made a funny face, but from here it was inscrutable. I craned my neck farther and soon located Irene's black ponytail tiny but distinct just beyond Destan. She stood higher than both of us, perched like a bird on the tiniest, tallest branch. Her shape transformed from a bird to a star as she stretched out her arms toward her home, swinging the treetop back and forth happily.

Fluxaria was a mosaic of vibrant violet, rose petal pink, sapphire and midnight blue. It was dotted with colour all around; and from here we were so close that I could see sprawling temples and what looked like gardens and waterfalls. Behind the mountain, the land ended and a vast blue-green basin stretched endlessly into the sky. *Ocean. It's real, after all. Just like in the spirit tales,* I thought, feeling so giddy and relieved and yet so terribly confused; glancing back and forth from my mountain to the one awaiting me, unable to make sense of what I was seeing.

From Thgindim, Fluxaria had been a black spot. Why hadn't we seen the colours? The beautiful sky and greener trees, where were the storm clouds that swirled infinitely around our twin mountain? I'd painted Fluxaria so many times in my landscapes. In history class we were shown photographs a spy over a hundred years ago had taken of the presumably desolate and dangerous place. Had they been fake, edited, something? But what about what I'd seen from the meadow? I'd stared off at it with my own eyes, never seeing anything but the black stain on the horizon, no ocean, just foggy darkness beyond. *Maybe you've gone crazy, Raine,* I thought, considering the possibility, *maybe you never survived the Shuishan after all and now you're in heaven. If so, it's not too bad, is it? Paradise is straight ahead, whether you're alive or not.* I held out my hand toward it and burst into exhilarated laughter: Fluxaria was almost the size of my palm; we couldn't be more than four miles away. We could get there in a day's time if we continued at a good rate and didn't run into any more obstacles.

Just then, I saw Destan raise his bow, and an arrow came flying my way. There was something pinned to the end. I tried to act fast and catch it, but it soared straight through my fingers. Destan put his hands on his hips as if scolding, "*Really, Bluehead? Really gonna make me shoot another one?*"

I threw my hands up in frustration, still overcome with laughter, and waited for him to take a second shot. He held up a finger, seeming to be fastening something new on the end. This time I clapped my hands right around the smooth metal arrow, and tugged off a wide green leaf. He'd carved words into it. I looked up at him in shock, then back down at the hardly legible printing he'd done. He hadn't told me he'd been practicing his reading or writing, but now that I thought about it I'd noticed him perusing the comic book Irene had brought along with her, his lips silently forming the sounds of the letters.

iREEN SAYS WEER SO
CLOSS. PARTEE TOUITE.
LUV YUU.

I grinned and touched the small smiley face he'd carved at the bottom of the leaf. I took my arrow tip, plucked free a big leaf, and scratched in a reply with the arrow tip, purposely misspelling so he could read the beginning message:

LUV YUU TOO! GIVE TO IREEN.

After thinking for another moment, I scrawled a message just for her on the back:

So much for being a rookie spy ☺ All of them will know you're a pro! Let's do some flute-playing and dancing and eating everything left when we get back down! YOU DID IT! WE DID IT! WE'LL BE THERE TOMORROW!!

Sticking it securely through the arrow, I shot it back to Destan and waited. He caught it, read the first part, and gave a thumbs-up. Then he waved to Irene, who turned to face us. She jumped up seeing me and I could tell she was trying to scream something but I just sadly waved and pointed at Destan and the arrow. Irene stood perfectly still in anticipation for the message, and Destan straightened his anchor, the arrow nocked in. The arrow flew gracefully through the blue of the sky like a shooting star, and Irene did a skillful flip (scaring me half to death) before catching it in her hand.

I stretched my arms up like she had done, tears streaming down my cheeks and laughter unable to stop spilling from my mouth. I placed one on my stomach and could almost feel the baby cheering up. The nausea had passed and the sky cradled us with the clouds and wind, Destan was blowing me kisses and waving his beanie in the air, Irene's black dot of a head turned away from me as she gazed at her home, and then so caught up in the wonder of the moment, my ears didn't register the sharp blast of the shot and Irene's head vanished from view, and Destan's thundering scream sliced through the distance and sent me plunging back to reality.

∞ *R . R . S* ∞

chapter twenty-two

All colour seemed to drain from the world the moment she fell.

I climbed down so fast that I'd slip, plummet a few feet, cut myself on some sharp branch, have snow fly into my face, and it seemed to take so long to come down and then suddenly I was running. I wasn't breathing. I wasn't smelling, seeing, hearing. I'd lost all sense of what was around me as I ran. I could barely tell if Siri was running beside me or if she'd left her hiding spot. I couldn't run straight. I hit into tree after tree, and it was only after one sent me to the ground did I come to realize what I was doing, what had happened, and what could possibly keep me from exploding into a bunch of little blue pieces.

I scrambled back to my feet and screamed, "IRENE! IRENE, I'M COMING, IRENE!" Once I'd opened my mouth I couldn't stop screaming her name. My legs burned from running through the snow, had there been snow before? I couldn't remember, nothing looked familiar and it was getting so dark so quickly that I felt myself sinking into that state of hysteria where I was half awake, half asleep, in some nightmare, and in my head repeated the vision of Irene's head appearing, disappearing, her being perched up there like a happy raven, and then falling down after a gunshot. A gunshot. Yue's head blown open. A gunshot, the force of the world tearing through me, lying in a pool of blood and a thousand Lilahs bearing down on me. Irene with her head blown open, Irene in a pool of blood–

And then I collided into him, my face bouncing off his chest and his teeth leaving an indent in my forehead and both of us breathing so hard and loud that it sent the forest creatures into retreat to their nests and tree holes or burrows, wherever they go, I don't know, but then Destan grasped my face in his shaking hands and I realized he had been yelling something.

"Raine! Raine, calm down, stop screaming, calm down!"

I tried, I tried so hard, but it just got worse, I felt like I was vomiting every word, "She fell, Destan we have to catch her–"

"Raine, I know, but we have to calm down," his voice broke, and for a terrifying moment I thought he was going to cry, but then he kissed my forehead quickly and lifted me up and we both began riding Siri so fast that I could feel my skin sticking back against my skull. Even Siri seemed to know that this was a state of emergency, she was no longer weak and starving. She flew as fast as she'd done back on Thgindim that time we'd saved Irene from the avalanche, and as she soared in between trees and over streams and swamps, I tried to keep talking to Destan.

"The trees are so thick, you don't think maybe she could be caught in the branches?"

"It's possible. But Raine..."

He didn't continue and I didn't finish for him. That might not have been a gunshot. And even if it was, maybe Irene fell on her own accord, maybe she lost her balance after all of that stupid flipping and goofing around she was doing so high up.

Siri lithely leapt over a patch of something bubbling and burning, skidding to a stop in front of a cluster of thorns. Destan peeked around for Irene, and I craned my neck to see around him, but she wasn't here, so why'd Siri stop? But then the wolf quivered, her fur rippling as her body summoned up the most forlorn howl we'd ever heard. The howl went straight to my bones, and soon I was screaming Irene's name again, wanting desperately to hear Irene scream back, "*WHAT RAINE? WHY THE FUCKING FUCK ARE YOU FUCKING SCREAMING?*" And then she'd come clawing her way out of the thorns, saying that some idiot had shot the branch she was standing on and she fell, but she landed in a lake or a swamp and that's why she's all wet. She's fine, but pissed and now really wants to party to get this crap off of her mind–

With a nauseous surge forward, Siri was off again, edging her way around the thorns and then stalking around whining all the while, her nose pointing straight up and sniffing. My nails dug deep into Destan's shoulders, and as I tried to relax my hands, he reached back and held it there, giving it a soothing squeeze, telling me to stop calling for her, I didn't even realize I was still calling for her.

Maybe she isn't answering because she's knocked out, unconscious. Yeah, that's reasonable, more logical. If she'd fallen from so high up, there's no way she'd be well and cracking sarcastic jokes or even wanting to party. She'd need some nursing back to health. Destan and I are good at that...we built up her strength and protected her before back home. We might not have my mother's bandages and first aid stuff, but surely we could make her well enough to struggle through to Fluxaria and then let the professionals handle it, right?

"Get off here," he whispered, taking me out of my mind.

I gulped, releasing my hold on his shoulders. He was shaking all over and clumsily dismounted Siri, staggering through the snow up to his knees. I didn't see her, he seemed to have seen her, but all I could see was a small clearing completely covered in white, icicles razor sharp and dripping from the boughs of the trees like jagged crystals. There was something black by a tree. Destan crossed to the center of the clearing, leaving a carved out tunnel of snow. I forced myself to follow, my throat too swollen with fear to speak another word. And then he stopped moving. He

crouched by the tree and picked up what I realized to be her spy bag, then dropped it, with a gasp. Slowly, he brought a finger to his forehead. His head tipped back, a cloud of breath whooshing from his mouth as he stared straight up. A red spot suddenly dropped onto his forehead. Then a drop on his nose. And as he fell to his knees, I made it to his side, and dared to look up.

Irene was maybe thirty, forty feet up the tree, sprawled across a few branches. Spread like a star. A star with a fountain of red flowing down its neck, making crimson rain. What looked like a collar was fastened around her throat, a light blinking rapidly. When it began to beep, Destan shot up from the ground, his hand locking around my wrist.

"We have to get out of here," he rasped, looking around wildly. He stumbled backwards, trying to drag me with him but I wouldn't budge, unable to keep my eyes off of her. Of her ponytail, still swinging back and forth in the breeze.

"Raine!" he boomed, storming back to me. Tears poured down his cheeks, his eyes shadowed and bloodshot. "C'mon, there's no time, that thing on her neck could go off any second–"

"We can't just leave her," I said, my entire body racked with tremors. The ground shifted below me, the beeping becoming a blaring, hot drops of her blood splashing on my forehead. "We have to save her...Destan we can still get her..." My words died in my throat as he slung me over his shoulder and bolted back to Siri, a crack of thunder interrupting what had just been such a sunny afternoon.

"Go! Siri, go!" Destan kicked her hard, launching her past Irene, past the beeping, into the darkening wood where snow had continued to fall.

I was in a battle of trying to hold on and trying to find a way to get the wolf beneath me to slow down and turn around. I pounded Destan's back with my fists, crying, "We have to go back! Destan, turn around she needs us!"

"No, Raine, she doesn't!" he yelled back at me, hardly sparing a glance over his shoulder as we swerved out of the way of a falling branch. "There's nothing we can do."

"How can you *say* that?" I demanded. I'd never been angrier in my life, and I never dreamed it would be at Destan. And never about this.

279

"We could've climbed, we could've gotten her down, taken that collar off and thrown it in a swamp. We need to turn around!"

He cursed loudly. "And, what, the gunshot was imaginary? All that blood?"

I screamed in anguish, desperately trying to pry his hands from the reins. "Turn back, Destan I'm begging you just turn back we'll be too late—"

"WE'RE ALREADY TOO LATE! SHE'S DEAD, RAINE!"

A blast sounded from behind us, a hot wind suddenly sweeping through the trees. Destan yanked hard on Siri's reins and we jerked to a messy stop, neither one of us able to stay on and tipping over into the snow. I raised my face from the biting cold of the snow, watching in horror at the distant blaze behind us. Trees shivered in the smoke, the fire so powerful even from here that my eyes felt aflame. As aflame as the girl still spread across the branches, waiting for us to save her.

All of the commotion had woken Ai, I could hear her incessant chirping from my knapsack. I kept it zipped tight, not daring to let her see. I used all of the energy I had left to get to my knees, feeling Destan's hands land atop my shoulders, his tremors running from his body into mine. I took his face in my hands, pulling him closer, both of us struggling to breathe. I touched his cheek, trying to wipe his tears, but he turned his head, his voice now hardly a whisper.

"She's dead. He got her...he finally got her," he gasped, his nails digging into my skin as he tried to contain all that was building inside of him. There was still a smudge of dark blood on his forehead, quickly replaced by snowflakes. I hadn't even noticed how cold it had gotten, how quickly night had fallen, as if standing atop the trees in a sea of blue had been nothing but a dream. There was a sharp intake of breath, and Destan drew back from me, his eyes focused somewhere beyond me in the darkness. "It's him," he whispered, cheeks ghostly pale as I whipped around just in time to see a glint of armour disappearing in the bushes. Destan was on his feet and bolting towards him just as the engine of a faraway bike began to rumble.

In a fury, he nocked in two arrows at once, shooting rapidly into the pitch blackness ahead of him. I chased him, desperately trying to catch hold of his arm and keep him from going any farther. Destan kicked through a cluster of thorns, a few first tearing across his

280

exposed neck. "FACE ME, YOU BASTARD!" he roared into the dark, looking wildly around. I'd seen the cyborg's motorbike. There was no way he'd still be anywhere near us. Destan didn't care, and kept clawing through more bramble, reaching back at his now empty quiver again and again as if more arrows would appear. "DON'T RUN AWAY FROM ME, YOU MURDERER! YOU COWARD! COME BACK!"

"Destan, stop, please stop," I pleaded, blocking his path. Tiny cuts peppered his face from where the thorns had gotten him, and his eyes shone with an unsettling gleam I'd never seen before. He tried getting around me and I shoved him back, yelling, "The only way you're going in there is if you use your full strength and *force* me to back down, and if you do that I'll never forgive you."

At that, he seemed to deflate. The tension in his body melted to limpness, his eyes filling with tears. "He can't get away with this," he said, the tears spattering down his cheeks as he shook his head. "He killed her, Raine. She's, she's just...gone."

I tried to keep the fire going, but the wind wouldn't let me. Sparks flew so far around us you'd have thought we were sitting in the sky. Shuddering, I pushed my bangs out of my eyes, scooting over to give Destan room on the log. He'd been trying to set up camp, make a cosy nest like usual. But when all of your materials were either wet or buried under snow, there wasn't much else to do but sit and wait. And wait. Our tears had run out hours ago.

"The next time I see him," I broke the silence, hardly able to manage a whisper, "I'm...I'm going to kill him." And by this wimpy fire, listening to the sombre cries of Siri behind us, mourning the death of one of the most fearless people to exist, I meant it. There was no more hesitation, no more moral compass inside me spinning this way and that about what to do. I didn't just want to escape him, there was no escaping him. He'd warned me and I'd just run and continued doing what he said would get someone killed. I'd thought he'd been trying to put my friends' lives back on Thgindim in danger, and that I could stop him before he could make his long journey home. But now he hadn't only hurt someone I loved. He'd killed her. And I would never forgive him or let him live because of that.

"You've never killed anyone before," Destan said quietly, eyes glued to the fire.

I turned to look at him. "How do you know that?"

"It changes you."

I searched his face and eyes for some sort of answer, but he just continued gazing into the fire. Tears rolled down his cheeks so silently and rapidly that it seemed he'd keep crying forever. "Raine, let me kill him," he said, wiping his nose on his sleeve and tugging his hat over his ears.

"No," I whispered, shaking my head. "No...I can't just let him....let you." I moved to kneel in front of him, gently touching his cheek. "You've never killed anyone either. And...I want to. For Irene."

His ratty gloves felt comforting as he moved my hand to his lips, planting a soft kiss on my fingers. But as he met my gaze, his face seemed to take on a skeletal darkness, shadows making him look centuries old. And then he spoke. "I've killed three men so far, Raine." The fire crackled, coughing up a cloud of sparks and then continuing to smoulder. I slowly dropped my hands, every inch of my body going cold as Destan, my Destan, confessed in a strangled whisper, "The first was a guy at Peak, during the heist? It wasn't even intended to be a fatal shot, but he kept bleeding and...and I heard another officer pronounce him dead before we even made it to the lift..." Destan couldn't meet my eyes, he scowled and put his head in his hands. "The other two were two men I ran into my first week out here. They were sick, or cannibals, or starving, and they were going after each other, but then they saw me and I killed them. I couldn't get the bow I'd made in time, I just cut them down right there with my bare hands and whatever I could find. I already have that on my conscience. I want you to stay pure and innocent as you are now, so just let me do it, please, Raine, I beg you..."

His head rose from his hands, the firelight illuminating the scar stretching across his face. I'd unconsciously begun to finger the wooden infinity charm he'd given me, my brain slowly registering what he'd just confessed. My toes curled and uncurled inside my boots. The ground felt like it was caving in, and joining us around the fire were those weird, floating light bugs that had visited us some nights ago. Destan and I looked round at the whole swarm of them, all shades of silvery white, their petal-like wings fanning out as they landed on each of our shoulders.

"Destan," I began, my heart racing, "I'm not that...'pure' anymore. Not innocent. Remember? What I told you about the camp?"

"Raine, there's no way you can pin that on yourself," he sighed, his hand moving behind my waist and pulling me closer. "The only stain from any of that is on the bastard who hurt you, not you. Not at all."

I stared at his lap. "That's not how it feels."

"I can't imagine how it feels," he muttered, jaw clenching. "And I hate that you have to feel it and hate that I can't undo it or make it go away. And I don't want you to go through any more of it so that's why I want to handle the cyborg. The guilt you get from killing someone...it'll eat you up like nothing else, even if the person deserved it, if it was only to protect yourself or someone else, you feel like the scum of the earth."

"I don't want you feeling that either, though," I said. "You've already been through that before, I don't want you going through that again."

"But I'm prepared for it, I'm willing to feel it, Raine." He moved me to sit on his lap, my legs wrapped around his waist, my arms around his neck. Hesitantly, he leaned in, and brought his lips to mine. I kissed him back, deeply, twisting my fingers through his hair and sliding my other hand up his back, feeling the pulsing warmth of his skin under his coat and sweater. I wanted him so close that he couldn't be ripped away. Irene had been two miles too far. I tried to keep kissing him, but soon a panic rose in my chest, and before I knew it his lips felt dry and cracked, his hands ice cold and cruel as they held me tighter.

He immediately drew back looking at me with caution as he must have sensed me going back to that horrible place in my head. Biting his lip, he looked nervously up into my eyes, and whispered, "I love you. Maybe it's me being selfish or too controlling or something, but I can't let you feel that pain. You're strong and I know you could handle it, but I just don't want you to, so please let me. I love you too much and you're carrying enough inside of you already."

Tenderly, he stroked one hand over the curve of my middle, where I felt a flutter in my womb. "Destan..." I gasped, sliding his hand lower and laying mine beside it, looking expectantly up into his eyes. There was the flutter again, this time a kick for sure and Destan could feel it, his eyes growing wide.

"There's really a baby in there, isn't there?" he said, his mouth quivering into a smile. Tears sprang to his eyes and he threw his arms around me, standing up and spinning around laughing. "There's a baby! A mini-Bluehead!"

As he set me down, I found myself smiling, too; gazing up at him. Wanting to kiss him. Then wanting to tell Irene to come here so she could feel it kick, too. My smile vanished, replaced by a punch to the stomach as the reminder she was gone came at me full speed. He seemed to sense it too, and we sat back down by the fire, lost. Siri appeared behind us, laying down so we could lean back against her fur, staring up at the clouds of those bugs dancing so delicately through the branches. I think we stayed awake for another few hours. Not talking, not moving except to hold each other's hand. We stayed awake until the last petal of snow drifted to the embers of the fire, until the trees turned silver with frost, until the hazy clouds of those bugs became thinner and thinner, and we had no more tears to cry.

chapter twenty-three

The tablet buzzed in my hands, the robotic voice chanting back, "Access granted. Proceed, Councilman Lao." Panicking about the volume, I pressed my thumb over the small speaker-hole at the bottom of the metal rectangle and glanced nervously at Destan, who stirred but remained fast asleep. Irene had carved the password lightly on the back cover of the tablet, and it took me awhile to decipher her writing due to the dirt smeared all over our stuff, but eventually I was able to get in by pushing the buttons that floated above the screen. Her nearly finished clock-bomb sat beside me, ticking innocently and setting me on edge. She'd jammed in the rest of the mao gao cai and I'd been testing it today to see if it ticked. Not wanting to blow anything up, I took out the battery again, stowing it in her bag.

Turning back to the tablet, I stared at the screen and all of the choices of files and folders and programs and all sorts of nonsense I couldn't dream of understanding. I selected one randomly. A thin image rose up and out of the glass, wavering like a mirage in front of my eyes. Rapidly, the square image was dotted with numbers and punctuation, sun and moon symbols; at the bottom reading:

WIDESPREAD ANNIHILATION.

Face heating up in anger, I jabbed the power button and the tablet whined to a stop. The image disintegrated in the air like smoke, and as I stuck the stolen items into my own knapsack, I felt a hand on my back.

"Did you get any sleep?" he asked, combing his fingers through the tangles of my blue hair. I hadn't even tied it up yet, and it pooled messily down my back ending below my hips.

"Some sleep. I don't feel especially tired," I replied, scooting around on my knees to look at him. Destan's eyes were still completely bloodshot from crying, and the circles etched under them were storm-cloud grey. I stood and gave him a peck on the cheek. "You?"

"Not a wink. See anything interesting on that?" He motioned at the tablet poking out from my bag and my anxiety about understanding any of it came back full-speed, giving me a headache.

"No. I think it's better we save it for the Fluxarian government to figure out," I sighed, brushing off my leggings and getting to work. We sank into the familiar rhythm of cleaning up the sight and preparing some breakfast, but kept stopping and starting again as we now had to take care of what used to be Irene's responsibilities. I dug up some mushrooms and roots until my fingers bled from trying to work through the frozen earth, and Destan grew frustrated trying to construct a fire when all the wood was soaked in snow and too damp for anything to catch.

As I washed the fungus and roots, the quiet morning was interrupted by a sudden, booming bark. I looked at Siri, but she was busy cleaning Ai with her tongue, her big paw holding the ticklish feilong still. Then glancing behind me, I realized one of the two tiangou we'd wrangled had returned, still muzzled, coming out from behind a large rock. It had some sort of animal carcass locked in its jaws, and its ears were folded down flat against its head. Its ruby red eyes watched me intently, a muffled whine coming from the beast.

"Oh...Mr. Tiangou?" I asked, lamely, internally smacking myself for sounding so stupid. I cautiously approached it, noticing Siri had quit bathing her new little friend and all of her attention on the approaching beast. "You've brought something for us?"

It just kept staring at me, blood dripping in thick black globs from the animal in its jaws. Looking more closely, I realized it wasn't some small creature, but a small piece of a much bigger animal. My stomach turned and I stopped in my tracks, not wanting to find out which body part it happened to be. The tiangou whimpered again, and Siri began to prowl a protective circle around me, rumbling out a warning sound to the animal she'd seen try to eat us just a day or so ago. A little wary of the creature myself, I called for Destan behind me. "Hey, Destan? Destan, come here– your tiangou came back."

"Came back? For real?" he shouted in reply.

"Yeah..." I averted my gaze from the bulging red jewels of the tiangou's eyes so as not to intimidate it, and slowly, the beast lay down. I heard a slashing of some branches, and Destan came jogging over to the river where I'd been washing the mushrooms. His cheeks were wind-chapped, his beanie falling off of his crazy mane of blond curls. He readjusted it and wiped his nose, stepping across the mossy rocks to stand beside me and Siri on the other side of the river, eyeing the tiangou in wonder.

"Holy shit," he muttered. "How did it manage to take that big a bite out of something with that muzzle on?" he asked me, raising an eyebrow.

I hadn't thought of that. Maybe that's why it hadn't dropped the prey yet? I shrugged and lowered myself to the ground to get my hand on my bow, "I have no idea...maybe it just used its claws or something?"

The tiangou came closer, limping and dragging its back foot behind it on the ground. It was in that creamy coating of snow that I noticed that the beast itself was also leaving a trail of blood; and the trail seemed to be getting darker and more widespread as it neared us.

"Easy, beasty," Destan warned, raising up his hands and blinking quickly at it. The tiangou struggled against the frayed binds of the muzzle and clicked its jaw up and down, unable to loosen it. Destan strode forward and carefully began to undo it, keeping his fingers as far from the fangs as he could. The tiangou snapped at his hands at first, but then stilled when it realized Destan was working to get it off; digging its teeth deeper into the soft flesh of the animal and whining. Once the muzzle fell off, the tiangou released the meat it had been holding and then crumpled to the ground, lying on its back and writhing around, shrieking.

Horrified, I ran up to Destan. "What happened? What did you do?"

He gaped at me. "Nothing! It just started....it's definitely hurt, Bluehead, look at all that blood."

"What was it carrying?" I asked, unable to bear watching it writhe in such intense agony, and approaching whatever it had dropped instead. "Maybe...you don't think it brought this back for us to eat, do you?"

"Depends on what it is," he scoffed, moving behind the tiangou and attempting to calm it, laying his hands on its belly and withdrawing quickly as it howled in pain. Siri returned the growl, not sure what to make of it, glued to Destan's side.

Not daring to smell whatever the tiangou had brought, I held my breath, taking an arrow from my quiver and using it to flip the lump of meat over so I could see more clearly what it was. I instantly regretted it. Two eye-sockets, one partially empty with a sliver of oozing red eyeball and a gaping pupil; a half of a jaw still fanged and dangerous, the makeshift muzzle seemingly singed and barely intact, the skin around the mouth melted or burned off; a shredded ear and long cord of skin with some clumps of fur still attached. I fell back in shock, crawling away with a yell, trying to get as far from the mauled tiangou head as I could.

"What? What is it, Raine?" Destan asked, rushing to my side.

I couldn't contain my nausea any longer and turned away from him so I could vomit what little of the mushrooms I'd ingested during breakfast. He held my hair out of the way, leaning in close as I managed to cough a response, "It's...it's the other tiangou's head, or part of its head. Don't look at it, it's awful." I forced myself to stand and I ran to the river to wash out my mouth with some handfuls of the muddy water. Then I splashed some on my face to snap out of the state I was in and added, "You don't think it killed and ate one of its own kind, do you? Brought it for us to show or something?"

Destan shook his head vigorously, "No, I wouldn't think so, but I don't know..." The still-living tiangou vibrated on the ground like it had been hit with a lightning rod, and then it sprang up and limped over to the head, whining and nudging it with its nose. Siri barked to try and get the rabid beast away from us, but the tiangou just lay down in a pool of blood panting by the head. And then it looked as though something profound had dawned on Destan, his eyes rounding out to huge silver moons, landing right on me in horror. "Or..." he began, running backwards and glancing over his shoulder to make sure not to hit a tree, "...maybe it was running *away* from something. Maybe something attacked them both but this one made it out alive. Maybe it was *warning* us." And before I knew what he was doing, he nocked in one of the arrows he'd just made this morning, and shot the tiangou in between the eyes, ending its misery.

I ditched the stupid mushrooms by the stream, chasing after Destan as we returned to the clearing where we'd slept. Siri loped behind me and then sank low to the ground so that we could climb on with our rucksacks, Irene's safely squished between Destan and me. *Something more dangerous than tiangou?* I thought. *How could that be? Irene had said they were king of these woods. Wait, where's Irene? We have to—*

No. The reminder sent a jolt of pain through my entire body and I shut my eyes, trying to breathe and not start crying again or calling for her. I held tight to Destan's shoulders. All around us, it seemed the Mythland creatures were on the run. Squirrels, foxes, rabbits came out of hibernation and tried to dash through the snow alongside us, their squawking and yowling filling the woods with noise. Even the trees seemed to be groaning, behind and ahead of us was screaming, such loud screaming that my skin prickled with paranoia and Destan could hardly stay focused on avoiding the trees ahead of us. Siri travelled as quickly as her bony legs could carry us, and had been the only animal in sight not crying out in panic until suddenly she released a pained yowl and tripped a little in her great strides. Now whatever was wrong was affecting her, Destan couldn't continue, yanking on the reins and looking behind him. He gasped. "Gas! Raine, some kind of poison gas coming up from the ground!"

As I whipped my head around to see, he urged Siri forward again, her silver legs picking up speed on the packed-down snow. The jolt forced me to face forward again, but it was then that I heard it. A sickening sizzle hissing all around us, the smaller animals falling behind and thrashing in pain as green clouds rose through the snow and engulfed them. The gas was rising up faster than we were running, melting the snow, smoking out in hazy green plumes. It was as if the forest was purifying itself, detoxing itself of the contamination lurking in the swamps and under the frozen soil. But now that it was clouding around us, Siri could hardly stand the pain. The fur on her legs was melting off with the skin beneath it, turning them raw and red. It wouldn't be long until she was in the same state as that tiangou: destroyed by the acidic mist, and us with her.

Destan rode her so that she would jump every few seconds, giving her paws some height away from the burning ground. But the gas continued to rise and even though it was thinner the farther it was from the ground, it still singed her flesh and even I began feeling that my boots on her flank were growing hot. Without warning, I stole the reins from Destan's grip and drove Siri in another direction where I could hear a rush of water. The mist now came up to my stomach and all three of us cried out in pain as the stinging air drove in between the tough wool fibres of our coats and the thick layer of Siri's fur. Using her last bit of strength on her ravaged legs, Siri leapt and propelled us straight into the river.

My first thought entering the thundering white water was the cold. I was shocked to near numbness the moment I plunged in and felt myself tossed forward with the rushing current. My second thought, however, was for the tablet and the bomb. I sprang back to awareness and struggled to take off my knapsack and raise it out of the water, hoping desperately that the weapon Irene had worked so hard on wouldn't go off and that the tablet's hardware wasn't completely ruined by the water. Next came my head, jutting out from the frothing surface and coughing up lungfuls of water. My bangs were plastered flat over my eyes, and I shook my head this way and that to shake them out of my vision. "Destan?" I called, kicking my feet to stay afloat as the current continued to carry me forward. My knapsack was still held above my head, water dripping from it into my eyes. "Destan, where are you?"

There was a splashing, and a voice emerged behind me, "Here! Raine, here!"

I paddled to turn around, but felt the unbreakable path of the current swing me back around and hit me into the shore. I caught a glimpse of his red hat, but that was all as a wave pulled me under. I clawed my way to the surface again, grabbing a rock and holding tight as water flowed over me. Now the current was working for us, carrying Destan my way so quickly that he banged into me and held onto my shoulders to keep from drifting ahead. "Are you all right?" I asked, hardly able to see him clearly.

"Pretty much, where's Siri?" he said, eyes darting frantically around us at the empty river.

I shuddered from the cold, "I...I don't know. Maybe she's still under or swam ahead or–"

"Siri!" he called suddenly, cutting me off and then releasing my shoulders so that he could be carried forward in hopes that he'd run into her silver body or see her snout poking out. He grabbed hold of a rock with the pruney tips of his fingers and waited for me to return to him, stammering, "It's...it's no use. She's nowhere near."

I clutched onto the same rock and battled against the current's push. Looking along the shore I saw that the gas still hovered in low-lying clouds of green fog. But whether it was that the booming of the river had drowned out all other sound or that continuous flow of gas from the ground had stopped, I could not tell. All I knew was that the hissing had ceased and the poison was in a state of rest. Without warning, my hands gave out and Destan caught me in his arms, letting us rushed back into the current while in a tight embrace.

We floated like that in tense silence for a long while. My entire body felt numb and nonexistent from the constant battering of icy water. I was in his arms and yet felt as though I was simply floating within them, not feeling the security of his muscles or comfort of his hand that I watched move up and down my back. Seconds flew like hours and minutes like days in which the sun never disappeared behind the trees. I was fading into a frozen state of rest when Destan caught onto a large slab of mossy rock and hoisted us onto it. We lay sprawled on the slippery surface, taking deep breaths to thaw out our lungs. My knapsack lay beside me and I yearned my unmoving fingers to untie it and check for the tablet, but I just continued laying there. Watching the clouds spiral around the sky so quickly that it must have been me that was existing in slow-motion.

"Bluehead?" Destan whispered.

I shivered back into myself, "B-Beanieh-head?"

He laughed throatily, sitting up and resting his head on his knees. Destan stared out intensely, scanning the river we'd finally gotten out of, back and forth at either shore where the gas seemed to be nothing but thin green ghosts now, sluggishly swirling but no longer so threatening. "I hate this place," he murmured. "Thgindim might be pretty screwed up with the Council and all, but at least the woods weren't equally screwed, you know? The spirits were damn smart putting this between the mountains. It's always coming up with new ways to kill you." He threw a stone roughly into the river, and then another, exhaling loudly through his nose.

"This is not the time and place for a child," I whispered, running a finger over my middle. "At least we'll be out of here by the time the baby comes. Fluxaria will be better, right? It has to be..." Destan pitched the last stone back into the rapids and then stood up, slipping on the moss but catching himself. Suddenly, he threw a punch at the rock beneath us, cursing as he pulled his fist back towards him. I sat up in alarm, "*Why* did you do that?"

"Because..." He covered his eyes with the ratty palms of his gloves and then threw them down, his eyes seeming to shoot flames into the water, "because of me, because...I'm just so sorry—"

"For what?" I felt absolutely frozen, and watched, completely terrified, as he knelt before me and took my hands. His trembled. His eyes were tortured.

"That I did this to you, that I can't undo it and keep you safe because it's already done," he said, his gaze wandering to my middle, and voice sounding shaky with fear. "I shouldn't have just rushed into bonding without thinking of the outcome, or at least that there might be a chance that we would live and have this insane responsibility for something so fragile and vulnerable—"

"It was my choice, too. I ignored the risks. Destan, stop this!" I cried, regaining my ability to sit up and speak more clearly. "We both kinda screwed up, but it's over and there's nothing we can do now! Please, I hate fighting like this—"

"Nothing we can do?" he repeated, in disbelief. "Yes, there is! We can kill it! We are in a position where if you so much as fall off Siri onto your stomach, or eat the wrong thing, or are exposed to something like, I don't know, *toxic forest gas*, that the living thing I put inside you will die! Not to mention this place has made you so weak, you were already so small, Raine, and what if it's too much for you? What if giving birth...breaks you? Kills you?"

I couldn't look at him, my vision swimming as I felt his hand caress my cheek. As one tear skidded out, I spoke, trying to keep my voice measured. "I don't know, Destan. I just don't know, what do you want me to say? That I'm going to leave you for putting me in this position, that I don't forgive you?" I looked up into his eyes, shaking my head. "Because I don't want to do that. I just want us to get out of here and figure it out later."

"There might not be a later. I've been sucking it up so far and just going along thinking it would all be okay," he said, his eyes beginning to shimmer. "But Irene still died. That guy still did those messed up things to you. Siri's probably drowned and I just keep getting this feeling it's my fault somehow."

My stomach faced another sickening lurch at Irene's name, I shut my eyes and tried to swallow the pain with some deep breaths, but it wouldn't work. I struggled to keep myself from crying as I said, "Destan, it's my fault that Irene..." I couldn't say it; no I wouldn't. I didn't want it to be true, I would make it not be true. No, I wouldn't. I couldn't. I furiously wiped my eyes, "...my fault that she died. When I last saw the cyborg, he threatened me that he'd do something if we didn't go back with him. I got scared and ran away instead of just shooting him and making sure he wouldn't." It was no use, I was gasping with sobs, my stomach sucking in and out as panic caused my lungs to work overtime, my voice breaking, "It's my fault she's dead, not yours."

He fell apart, finally. Collapsed into my arms and I in his. Unlike in the water I could feel him all over me, his fingers knotted in my undone bun, the warmth of his breath on my neck within the seemingly eternal cold around us. "I forgive you, Raine. I forgive you and I love you so much," he sobbed, his voice so broken that just hearing him try to speak made me cry even harder. "Do you wanna know what her last words were? I heard them...just right before that collar shot onto her neck and pulled her down." I nodded and dug my teeth over my lip to keep it from quivering. Destan's grimace somehow managed to transform into a smile as he laughed, quite accurately mimicking her lively way of speaking, "*Oh shit!*"

I melted into horrible laughter, so easily inserting that into the memory as she must have realized she was about to get shot. Maybe she'd seen the glint of his armour, heard the buzzing of his motorbike from way down below. Maybe he'd climbed up the tree to get a clearer shot and she'd seen him there, poised like a metal vulture with a rifle beneath its wing. I took a deep breath, burying my face in his shoulder as I whispered, "Destan, we're so close. So close. Let's finish this for her."

"Screw the war," Destan agreed, squeezing me, "this is for Irene."

We kissed and I was flooded with the taste of him, with the love and the pain and the promises all dancing together on the tip of his tongue. There were no flashbacks to a tent in a tree, just him here, now, on a rock in the middle of a river in the middle of the worst forest on earth. And then, his lips began to form words against mine. "About...the baby, and all that. You're right. We can't undo anything and maybe we don't have to. Maybe this combination of a bluehead hero and her screwy boyfriend will do some good, or Fluxaria will have some miraculous doctors to make sure it all goes okay, I don't know." He must've been able to feel my smile, because he returned it, kissing me once more before continuing, "All I know is that's it's there, inside you. And we're too close to getting to where we need to be to give up or regret it now."

"Exactly," I said, kissing him again, wanting to dissolve into the moment and not have to leave and continue down this river or along the gas-clouded ground. "I love you. We can figure out this mess together."

His forehead touched against mine gently, and we both sighed as reality continued to dawn on us. We'd have to move on soon or else our wet clothes would freeze onto us. And even though I was shaken by all of the words said, when I rose to my feet and cautiously tested the grass, I felt as though something heavy had been lifted from my chest. I hadn't truly known how Destan felt about the pregnancy news, because he had just cried the first night and then tried his hardest to avoid the topic altogether.

The gas was so thin now that it only hovered warmly around my ankles. The woods smelled like some sort of citrus and algae combination. The perfume of the gas melted into the air, only so subtle now that as I lugged my knapsack and shivered, my head spun slightly and skin prickled rather than burned.

Destan and I reluctantly split up; he looking for dry wood to build a fire and shelter, and I for something to cure the ache in our stomachs. Mythland was getting dark so quickly that every time I shut my eyes for a few moments of rest, I opened them and found the trees to be a darker shade of brown, the leaves turning from fresh spring green to rich jade. But as evening began to fall, I became ever more paranoid. The last time I had been alone, it had been with the cyborg. If he found me again, this time he would just shoot me, slit my throat, kill me to end the threat I posed to his Majesty Council's diabolical plans.

And I don't think I could stand any more of his threats either. As I tried to hack away at some bark with my dagger, each strike of the dulled blade seemed to shoot a new horrible thought into my skull. My mother coming home to find Gwen gone, or worse, taken up to Peak and trapped in a padded room in a straitjacket and her eyes blindfolded. After weeks of this isolation, they just kill her. Chantastic and Velle and Carmen being stopped on their way home from work, asked if they had conversed with me about my motives, if they in any way aided with the thefts. And then they'd say no, they were just my friends, but then the Majesty Council would find some evidence of Chantastic's contact with me, and she'd be tortured until I came home or gave up and let the cyborg asshole put a bullet in my brain.

A cracking of twigs.

My forehead had been resting tiredly against a tree, but at this I was frightened into alertness, my fumbling fingers trying to nock an arrow on my bowstring. Each breath was like a knife in my lungs as from behind the nearest tree, a figure came prowling out, holding his lightning rod. So this was how the cyborg wanted to do it? In the dim forest light, he inched closer so quietly that I couldn't hear the gears of his legs tick, I couldn't hear the mechanical whirring of his existence.

Or maybe I heard it, but in this state I was pinned by terror to the tree, unable to overcome the fact that he was raising that rod, that me and baby would be gone, and if I was gone then Destan might be gone, too, and Fluxaria and everything we'd fought so hard for.

"Please," was all I could say, I couldn't help it. He lowered the rod, taking off his helmet and seeming to lean forward with his eyes like two dark blue beacons in the nearly black woods. And without warning my brain began rapidly spinning through a panicked alluvion of memories that didn't add up to who I knew to be in front of me: *Can't breathe, can't scream, aching wrists, his teeth biting down, his voice like a dagger saying 'mine, mine, mine...'*

"Irene?"

chapter twenty-four

He said it again, "Irene?" and then I couldn't see the world in front of me; I was weeks away; my back aching as it ground into the wooden floor, his hand on my cheek forcing me face-down as the sharp tear of fabric sizzled through my ears and I was invaded, skin cold and tight, forced warm and willing, never willing, I had never been willing and he loved it that way.

I staggered forward and watched his form brighten and become more real, face paler, eyes worse, body bundled up in leather and furs, scarf concealing all but his eyes, scarf tugged down so I could see the chapped lips whitened by the thousands of tastes he'd had of the qilin's blood. It was not a lightning rod he was holding, it was a sword. Not a helmet he removed, but a hat. His hands gloveless, clean fingernails, *nails scratching, digging, clawing, leaving a red line down my leg as it dragged down, down—*

"No," I said, all I could say.

Tieran inhaled sharply, backtracking until he ran into a tree, and he rasped, "You...y-you're alive? I shot you..."

"Zhaorong shot you," I echoed, hands fisted and curled, bow dropped, thumb quivering over the hilt of my dagger. He saw and took a step forward, his own hands tightening on his sword and hovering over the set of knives strapped to his belt. There was an aching ringing in my ears, I wasn't thinking, I wasn't breathing. I came forward with my dagger shaking in my grasp and tears stacking like small hot gems behind my eyelids.

"We don't have to do this," he hissed, eyes narrowed. It shocked me that my least favourite person in the universe, someone I loathed even greater than the oily and creepy Sebastian Lao, would suggest just parting without even a single act of vengeance against each other. "Irene, let's just run back to wherever we came from–."

"Stop calling me that!" I screeched, pointing the tip at his chest and beginning to walk faster, coming towards him at a near sprint.

Tieran snarled and raised his weapons as well, "What the hell's happened to you?" As his eyes combed over me, I caught them sticking to where, in my wet clothing, my pregnant bump was now clearly defined. He gazed into my face in bewilderment, a smirk curling the edge of his mouth as he whispered, "That's new. Am I a daddy?"

I snapped, charging at him through the snow, tearing the hem of my coat on a branch, feeling the tiny pieces of ice raining down slice against my cheek. My feet were numb and throbbing inside my worn out boots, lifting in and out of the snow without any exhaustion. Catching my wrists, Tieran squeezed until I dropped the dagger. It made a deep cave in the snow where it fell and as I tried to wrestle free from his grasp, he thrust his head forward and knocked his forehead against mine, making me wonder if Lilah had taught this dirty move to him or if it had been the other way around. The sudden painful headache sent black fuzz across my vision, and I stumbled back into a tree, trying to fight off the pain and see where he was running.

"Fight me, you coward!" I howled into the swirling world, running as fast I could with my boots sinking into the deep, cold white. He wasn't faster than me, I saw his red head bob like a spot of blood in between the coming trees and sometimes he'd glance back and change direction and disappear into another thicket. I took a shortcut in between a frozen bog, and as he came running onto the iced-over water I slid to the floor of the ice and swung out my foot to trip him. He landed facedown and slid a few feet, making the surface of the bog splinter in places. I jumped onto his back, stealing one of his knives that had clattered out from his belt and I held it to his throat, arching up his neck like the cyborg had done in the tower. But as soon as I felt the fire roar in my head, pushing me to do it, just do it and get rid of the foul creature that hurt me and so many, I had one moment of hesitation and that was all it took for the bog to cave in and send us plunging into the cold.

The shock of the water overcame me, and Tieran instantly took this chance to escape my hold. He kicked his legs and began swimming back up to the surface, but I grabbed the loose shoelace spiralling from the eyelet of his boot and tugged, sending him down again for a moment. But I wasn't strong enough to drag him down and so I surfaced with him, coughing and feeling my limbs jellify with frostbite and cold.

He yanked me out roughly by the hood of my coat and slammed me onto the grass, peering over me with those terrifying eyes and lips so pale and still cracked at the edges where he used to paint on the poison. And suddenly I was suffocating in that tent of his, neck bruised and made raw by his kisses, mind flaming as he forced his way into me again and again while I couldn't even scream. Tieran's eyes softened from the hard sapphire to shiny and trembling.

"Do you want me to kill you?" he whispered, his hands gripping tightly on my shoulders and his legs spread as he crouched over me. "Do you? Because that's what it fucking seems like, Irene."

No, no, why had I chosen that to be my fake name? I didn't want his mouth saying her name, I couldn't let her name pass through those lips that did so many bad things. "My name...is Raine. Not Irene. Raine," I gasped. Tieran dug my shoulder blades deeper into the hard ground and I cried out, trying not to remember, trying so hard to just move and run. I didn't want to fight him anymore. Running away would end him enough for me. As long as he would just leave me be.

"Well then, *Raine*, what more do you want from me?" he roared, and I felt something hot splash onto my face. He was crying. "You've taken everything from me!" He slammed me down again, and the breath was knocked straight from my lungs. As I tried to breathe, he shook me violently, more tears dribbling off his gaunt cheeks onto my skin, "Well?"

"Nothing. I don't want anything from you," I gasped, my eyes fluttering closed.

His fingers squeezed more tightly and then relaxed as he hissed, "You sick bitch." He stood up, tremors rolling through his body like he'd been electrocuted. And he picked up his knives and I felt his foot land on my ribcage, holding me down and I waited for him to do it, to get the blue-haired bitch off his trail, to just get his revenge already, but he chucked them into the frozen lake and kicked some snow onto my face. He picked up my dagger and stalked away. I blew some of the cold spray out of my eyes and sat up, the tips of my hair frozen to a point, my entire body feeling numbed and weak. I couldn't stand without my knees giving out. But I blinked quickly and could see that Tieran hadn't left. He was kneeling in the thicket of the trees a little distance away from the frozen bog, that splotch of red hair and black coat surrounded by white. And I could hear him making some sort of ugly sound, like a choking or weeping, and then there was a moment where I saw one arm extend, and then the next, gripping my dagger and suddenly realizing what he was doing, I staggered forward, falling into the snow that felt no colder than my. I crawled in a panic, rasping, "Tieran...Tieran what are you doing–"

He plunged it deep into his chest, I didn't see a spray of blood and he only grunted when my dagger soared through his torso but I scrambled toward him in such shocking desperation that the forest seemed to be spinning beneath my body.

"Raine!"

The voice shot from the woods like a birdcall. I stopped crawling and panted, looking around for Destan to appear. Tieran was lying a few yards away, twitching, fingers digging into the ground and eyes begging at the moon as he must have realized he would not be dying so quickly. I made it to his side, numbly watching how his body rippled with tremors, silent as he was finally the one in pain, the one on his back helpless and hurting.

Destan came dashing from the woods, bundles of lumber under his arm, "Raine, oh thank the gods you're all right. I heard screaming and," he stopped, eyes finding Tieran, eyebrows coming together on his forehead. And then he saw me, silent and still as this strange man suffered and bled a flood of crimson into the snow. "Who's...Raine, what's going on?"

Tieran's eyes were closed, chest heaving up and down and up and down, and beside him I struggled to remain in this reality and not the one where I was the one gasping in pain. Destan's touch anchored me back to this moment, and he hurriedly put snow on Tieran's wound to clot and cleanse it, his mouth bubbling over with commands, "Find some leaves, look for some dandelions maybe or those lace flower roots. We need to stop the bleeding soon or else he's gonna have nothing left to go through his veins. We have to work quickly," he met my eyes and his expression went beyond confusion. "Raine, why aren't you doing anything?"

I was breathing at such a rate that I couldn't slow down and speak, looking helplessly into Destan's eyes as Tieran drew a horrible breath and weakly motioned for Destan to come closer. Tieran's eyes could hardly stay open as he spoke, "Just...just leave me." He coughed up a spray of blood that seemed to bounce off of the snow. His wobbly gaze landed on me for a flickering moment and there was no air to breathe. At the point of such panic and remembrance, I nearly forgot that Destan was shaking my shoulders and shouting my name.

"Raine? Raine, what's wrong, who is he?" Suddenly his two silver moon eyes were an inch from mine, so frightened and urgently blinking. My lungs gave up their dangerously fast pulsing, and I stared Destan straight in the face, the words rolling from my tongue before I had even thought how to order them properly.

"He is the man who raped me and tried to kill me."

All colour drained from Destan's cheeks. He slowly turned to face the man beneath him.

"I have...a house. Built it...not far." His eyes stared emptily beyond us, struggling to stay open. It wouldn't be long, and Destan knew it so he forced himself to look away from me and address Tieran as he lay dying.

"How far?" he demanded.

Tieran's head lolled over and he choked out more blood, "Th-that way. Three minutes to walk."

And then Destan drove his fist as hard as he could straight at Tieran's face, knocking him out cold and causing blood to spurt from his nose. Destan drew back his arm for another and then he hesitated, the fury racing so hotly in his veins that he was unrecognizable. I'd never seen him so completely murderous looking, so terrifying. I hated it, and I let my strength finally give way, taking his attention from killing my rapist and directing it back to how desperately we both needed shelter and fire soon or else we'd be in the same near-dead state as Tieran.

Destan supported me as we fought our way through the knee deep snow and steady downpour of ice that had begun. He had one arm around my shoulders to keep me standing, and the other was behind him; dragging Tieran by a handful of his cherry locks. Ahead was a cabin of sorts. A badly made one now that I could compare it to Destan's handiwork during our times together, but it still looked sturdy, and large enough so that all of us could fit, even stand inside without bumping our heads on the ceiling.

Dropping Tieran (more like throwing him back down into the snow), Destan struggled to unjam the door that had iced over. It was a big slab of bark, riddled with holes made by hungry bugs, and once Destan forced it open, our faces were greeted with a heavenly rush of warmth. We entered and glanced about the tiny little house Tieran had made. There was a messily constructed table with some cups and plates I recognized from the Shuishan camp, a dug out hole with a pot on top for a cooking fire, and then a separate area reserved for the fire heating the cabin. A big square of stained satin had been hung up from the ceiling, separating the house into two rooms.

As Destan dragged Tieran inside, I cautiously pulled back the edge of the fabric and peeked into the next room. It was chillier somehow, like the warmth couldn't seep through even a thin sheen of material, and there were two separate piles of blankets and pillows; one vacant, one taken. As the person rolled over, I couldn't help but curse loudly.

"Oh, joy. It's blue-hair." Lilah narrowed her eyes and coughed, her face wrinkling in pain as she did so. "Must be my lucky day."

I stared back coldly, "What's the matter with you, then? Did the demon possessing your body decide to take a vacation?"

"Haha, very funny," she laughed hoarsely and rubbed her eyes with the heel of her hand. "Dying, actually. It seems that I have some sort of forest infection. Tieran went out looking for some painkilling mushrooms I knew about, but I'm guessing you chopped his head off at first sight?"

My stomach heaved and I touched it instantly, feeling the baby seem to say, *Let's get out of here. Too many memories. Too many jerks.* But as I tried to give my child a voice, it just came out as Irene's in my mind and a terrible jolt of missing her chilled me to the bone.

Destan pulled back the curtain. "Come out here, I've made a bed."

After ransacking Lilah's stash of brews, Destan and I knelt by the fire, slurping from the cans and thick glass jars. Tieran was back with Lilah now, getting patched up by her tiny, evil hands. Their whispered conversation hissed through the curtain unintelligibly, and I didn't want to make sense of it. I was busy making sure Destan's fury didn't boil over. He sucked in a rattling breath, eyes flicking to and from the curtain. "Do I have permission to kill him?" he spoke from the corner of his mouth, hands balled into lethal fists. As I was about to open my mouth to respond, I heard a cough from behind the curtain.

"Wait, Irene–Raine," it was Tieran, "I have something that could help you two."

"Don't want it." Destan's fists got even tighter, the vein at his temple visibly pulsing. I touched his hand, stroking it gently until it relaxed against his side, giving him a reassuring nod as I stood up and went to the other side of the curtain.

I eyed the two of them, Tieran draped lamely across his little witch's lap, asking, "What is it?"

"You're trying to get to Fluxaria, correct?" he said, turning his body so Lilah could spread more ointment on the knife-wound.

I narrowed my eyes, "How do you...?"

"You've come from one end of this hellhole to the other where we all know that big sparkly mountain is," Tieran drawled, rolling his eyes. "But there's no way you're gonna be able to make it in if you don't have official identification that you are, indeed, Fluxarian. Even the hair won't cut it."

"And that's where we happen to be able to...help," Lilah grimaced at the last word, as if the thought of doing anything positive for me it left a bad taste in her mouth.

"We have some Fluxarian IDs. Most of my dolls were from there, remember?" his eyes glinted like sapphires and anger boiled up my throat like vomit as the image of Yue's murder flickered through my memories. "You and your gorilla of a boyfriend are welcome to them. Under one condition."

"See, I knew it." Destan came stalking in, getting down to Tieran's level so that he could yank his collar, "You're not getting shit from us, you sick bastard!"

Tieran choked out some hoarse laughter and looked up at me in amusement, "What do you see in this guy, may I ask?"

Lilah smacked Tieran's shoulder, saying sharply, "Hey, quit it. If he rips off your head, who's going to take care of me?"

"Smart girl." Destan smiled sourly and dropped Tieran with a *thunk*, making him wince and groan.

"We don't necessarily want anything from you. There's just a favour that I think you could afford to do for us. Seeing as we've taken you in and everything instead of killing you like we've been dreaming of ever since you got us banished from our own kingdom," Tieran said.

"Oh, so we should be grateful that you didn't kill us?" I tilted my head to the side incredulously and scoffed, "Yeah, that's really just so nice of you. Of course we should now do anything you ask. And it's not like you two *deserved* to be banished or anything."

They didn't enjoy my sarcasm. Lilah and Tieran exchanged glances and Tieran sighed, saying through gritted teeth, "All I ask is that you take Lilah with you to Fluxaria. I can't properly take care of her here, she needs real doctors."

For a moment or two, I actually felt myself soften a bit. He didn't want anything for himself or even anything that would affect me or Destan too greatly. I hated how human he seemed when it came to Lilah, how they treated each other like brother and sister and saved their empathy only for each other. Destan ran his fingers through his hair, under his hat as he thought it over, and then he exhaled loudly, looking at me, "It's your call, Bluehead. You're the one who was tortured by these two so I'll understand if you just want to leave them."

I nodded, hearing how raggedly Lilah's breathed was, her eyes so sunken and bloodshot, her face so thin and cheekbones so sharply jutting out that she looked skeletal. And truly dying, suffering. She didn't deserve to be saved, neither of them did. They were far from being good people, much less people at all, but at the same time I pitied them. Not compassion. Pity. I looked at them in disgust and fear that people could really sink this low and be this unhappy and broken inside. And with pity came that stupid spark of hope that always seemed to catch light in me that there's always hope for anyone. There's always a way to be saved and move on from the past. That, and we needed the Fluxarian IDs.

I pursed my lips and looked down, saying quietly, "We'll take Lilah with us." They both sighed and exchanged immensely relieved glances. Lilah sank down into her bed and shut her eyes, her breathing slowing to a sleepy rhythm.

Awkwardly standing before Tieran and a softly snoring Lilah, Destan and I hesitated over our next move. The day had been exhausting, and in light of Irene being gone and Siri still missing, I felt that if either of us tried to stay up and communicate to a jerk like Tieran, we'd just keel over and never get back up. So without another word, we went to the other side of the silk divider, and curled up by the fire. It was warm and I took off my coat and sweater, next my leggings, leaving me in my undershirt and underwear and snuggling close to Destan, wanting desperately to feel the soft comfort of his skin on mine again in any way possible. He followed suit and slipped off his so that I could press my cheek to his bare chest and make sure that he of all people still had a heartbeat. Tenderly, one hand stroked up and down my bare arms, and the other combed through my hair, smoothing it down against my back. His heartbeat was slow and steady. It was now my favourite sound.

∞ R.R.S ∞

chapter twenty-five

I dipped my wet brush back on the chalky square of paint, and then smoothed a canary yellow across the top of the page. The smooth gliding my hand did was soothing, it made me sleepy, and I felt a chin lean on my shoulder, some black hair falling in a glittering curtain around my face. I smiled, "It's not done yet."

"What's taking you so long?" Chantastic mused, her cool fingertips running over my forehead and then covering my eyes, "Wait for it...okay, open."

I gently pushed her hands away, and when I regained sight, I saw that the canvas in front of me was finished, it was even dry and had mine and Chan's signatures in the bottom right corner. "Wow...good job," I whispered.

We were in the meadow, poppies sticking out from the emerald-green grass like red and violet feathers, twirling as a breeze rolled through. The pines were free of snow, they dripped with coppery pinecones and had meadowlarks' nests woven in the grass beneath them. It was sunset and I had painted it perfectly. Both the canvas and the sky burst with pastel pinks and bruised blues and purples. In the distance Fluxaria was white and brilliant. But...something' wasn't right. My forehead crinkled, I leaned forward on my knees and traced over the Fluxaria I'd painted.

R . R . S

Then I glanced from the painting to the horizon where it actually lay. "Chan, does this look right to you?"

She tilted her head quizzically to the side, "I...think so?" And then she laughed really loudly, it was unsettling and strange and made me suddenly very afraid. "Raine, that is just what it looks like. Why are you acting so silly?"

"What it looks like," I repeated, staring off blankly at the horizon. It was wrong, Fluxaria was that black spot again. Had it always been this way? What about when I'd looked at it from the trees? It had been so beautiful. Something flickered in my vision, sparkling again and again off and on, appearing in different places. Spellbound, I stretched out my fingers and felt a gossamer sort of veil before me, shimmering like dragonfly wings but feeling like a thin sheet of lace.

"I'd be more concerned with how this place looks, if I were you. That mountain is fine. Let's just go back to town, Lilah and Gwen are waiting," she said, rising to her feet and brushing off her skirt. She offered a hand, but I was preoccupied with my own. I no longer felt the veil in between my fingertips and reached forward again, I still saw the glittering but couldn't seem to grasp it. I turned back to her, desperately, "Chantastic? Chantastic, it's gone; did you see it?"

She rolled her eyes, she looked tired of me asking so many questions, acting so panicky when we apparently had things to do. She held up a pair of scissors and sighed, her eyes cold, "I got it done for you, Raine. Weren't you paying attention?" In a quick movement, she threw the scissors to the ground and waltzed away, a tunnel appearing through the trees and gobbling her up in its dark depths.

A wet plop of snow hit me on the nose. Grouchy, I opened one eye and glared at the leaky roof Tieran had attempted. At least I knew that Destan and I probably wouldn't be staying here another night. I sat up and shivered, feeling around the dirt floor for my sweater and leggings. Last night I had been fine with my arms and legs exposed, but now that Destan was gone and the fire was barely smoking, I was covered in goosebumps and absolutely freezing. The dream was still running violently through my mind, vivid and horrible. And before the impulse could vanish, I quickly dug through my bag for Irene's notepad and began to write a reply to Chantastic's letter.

C—

I felt the same type of joy as you when I saw Ai returning with a letter featuring your handwritten words. I have to admit though, my friends didn't know she'd gone to Thgindim and not Fluxaria, so there was some fighting over that. It's all worked out now, though. Sort of. Maybe. I'm sorry, it's just that so much has happened and not a lot of it good.

The assassin going after us killed Irene only a night ago and it's just made everything a bleak mess. I can't bear to start talking about her in the past tense because she's just one of those people who seem indestructible, you know what I mean? Like they're just too alive to ever not be. I wish you could've met her. She ~~is a~~ WAS a little intimidating at first, but after you hang out with her, you start acting more confident yourself. She just made everything brighter and now there's a gaping hole between me and Destan that Irene used to fill. I have to stop writing about her now. It's still too fresh and this wasn't supposed to be a dreary letter telling you how bad it is out here.

One good thing is that after your letter I was able to tell Destan all that had happened when I was captured and he also knows I'm pregnant. There are officially no more secrets eating me up inside, and he's been honest about some of his own things, too. So, that was also pretty comforting; to know I wasn't the only one struggling with what had gone down when we were separated.

Thank you for giving us your blessing, by the way. I really do love him, Chan, and trust him with my life. I never thought I'd ever find anyone who could love me even close to as much as you do, but now that he's here I feel like my heart has grown so much and I'm so lucky to have a family like you two. Irene was a part of that family, too. That's why it's been so hard. Things will be hard until we make it to Fluxaria, deliver what we stole, and can sit back and let the government finally handle this mess.

You'd be happy to know that we are now a mere two miles from the Fluxarian border....it's insane! We will be there TODAY if there's no more snags in our plans (which there always seems to be because Mythland is freaking evil, but I can still hope).

I have to admit, just hearing about what home is like now is making me sick to my stomach. I don't like the sound of those snatchers. You have to promise me to just keep an eye out and stay out of the way, okay? There's only room for <u>one</u> rebel in this relationship, and look at the trouble that got me in, so you just focus on staying under the radar, okay? Because at this point, if you get caught and blasted into Mythland, it would be weeks, maybe months until I could go back and find you and that just won't do.

I can't believe your Granny knew about the feilong! That was one wild story. If you ever figure out exactly how she knew about them, you must tell me. I'm sorry to hear about Velle. I understand you're mad at her, but please try to just focus on staying together, please? For my sake? It doesn't make me especially happy that she thinks I'm a totally brainwashed criminal now, but she works at Peak under the influence of some really scary people so I don't blame her for turning her back. I'm sure she'll come around once this war is finally over, and Thgindim sees the truth about the Council and Fluxaria. I hope so, at least. There's not much else to do but keep going and keep hoping because otherwise I'd just go crazy.

The fire is dying down in here, making it really hard to write, and I don't want the scroll to be too heavy for Ai to carry along to you, so I'll end it with this: I love you. I'll make it home to you. And when I do, I'm going to hold your hand and probably never let it go ever again. Stay safe, write whenever you can.

xoxo Raine

I rolled up the letter, kneeling and rummaging through my knapsack to find her letter to me so Ai could get her scent again. But as I dug through, I felt a chill settle through the cabin and I took the liberty of getting out my sparking stones first to re-light the fire. Kneeling by the kindling, I tried to strike them cleanly. They just wouldn't go, not a spark, maybe they'd dulled or something? I didn't know, but frustrated,

I threw them down and looked grumpily at the fire pit through my bangs, wrapping my arms around myself and shivering. Just then, there was a clicking sound, a whoosh, and something warm was suddenly near my ear. Slowly turning, I saw Tieran holding some sort of lighter, a blue flame flapping like a flag on the end of the copper nozzle. I hadn't even heard him come into my side of the room, and I remained frigidly still and silent as he bent forward and held it to the sticks, waiting for the flames to catch.

"Technology is an amazing thing," he smirked, sinking to the floor beside me and lying back on the pile of blankets. He was shirtless, his hand resting over the bloody bandage of his self-inflicted dagger wound. Breathing deeply through my nose, I kept staring at the fire, trying to become completely hypnotized by the steady flickering so that I wouldn't have to acknowledge who was beside me. It wasn't working. His voice came creeping into my ears again, "Thanks for agreeing to take Lilah back with you. I...appreciate it."

"Don't," I whispered, my eyes burning holes in his. My coldness seemed to only amuse him.

"Make me," he said, his gaze lingering on my lips. Heat flooded my cheeks. And before he could say another stupid thing, I hit him hard across the face, his head snapping back with the sharp clap of my palm reaching his cheek. Tieran then shook his head, the long cherry hair flying around as he rubbed his jaw and laughed, "Good job. I officially no longer appreciate you taking Lilah back with you."

"Good." I made to stand, but then his hand latched around my wrist, his skin icy cold. I used all my force to wrench it out, and I succeeded, but then as I made to walk briskly away, both of his hands grabbed my shoulders and I could feel his cold breath grazing my neck, he'd stood up so quickly.

"Wait," he said, urgently, and I reached for my dagger that was no longer in my hilt. *Dammit! He took it during our fight earlier!* "Could we just talk for a second...Raine? Human to human?"

"Too bad you aren't one," I said. "And if you want to talk, I'd appreciate it if you let me go and let me choose to speak to you of my free will, rather than being forced to do another fucking thing for you. This superiority complex you've got is just making me want to put that dagger back in you."

"Ooh, I forgot how feisty you get. What does your boyfriend call you? 'Rainestorm?'"

My hand flew back and took a knife from his hidden belt I regrettably knew about, pressing the lethal edge of the blade flat against his windpipe. He didn't fight, just stood perfectly still, eyes closed. I examined his face, unable to make sense of it. "You really have a death wish, Tieran," I said, backing him up against the wall of the cabin, enjoying how suddenly nervous I was making him. "First you try to dagger yourself after our fight. And now you're provoking the girl who you know can hardly stand letting you breathe another second. And so I'm not even sure if I'll kill you because you seem to want it so much."

A bulge appeared in his throat as he swallowed, and I realized that he was mustering all of his strength to stay on his feet. His teeth were grit together and he bullets of sweat trailed down his neck as his fingers seemed to coil and twist over his bandage. He was in pain, so why was he wasting his energy? Did he really want to die?

"Who would want to live?" he rasped, a slight smile rising on the edge of his mouth. "In this place? With this hell of an injury? I'll either be going the slow way or could get a girl like you to just get it over with."

"Why'd you try to kill yourself before, then? When you still thought you were Lilah's only hope?"

"People do crazy stuff, sometimes. You would know," he said, chuckling darkly to himself, and finally crumpling to the ground. I dropped the knife and reluctantly helped him lie back down on my makeshift bed by the fire, as he continued to try and speak. "I wasn't thinking when I did it. Just feeling. I've lost nearly everything that defined me. Why exist if you don't exist?"

"That makes no sense at all," I whispered, seeing him scowl and cringe as his wound seemed to flare again. He began breathing in ragged gasps, so weak-looking that for the first time since I'd seen him, I wasn't afraid. Maybe he was right about no longer existing. I couldn't see any trace of the Tieran who had swaggered around the Shuishan camp, relishing the atrocious things he did to people. He had no more power over me, over anyone, and he knew it. He hardly had power over himself, anymore. He was a ghost.

Sinking back down to my knees, hesitantly positioning myself a safe two feet from him, I said, "I'll make sure Lilah's okay." His eyes opened and looked at me in wonder, so I quickly looked away, trying to keep my voice steady. "Not for your sake, and not so that you feel like saving her will forgive all the horrible things you've done. But because she's still young and has so many chances to do better than she has while being around you."

Tieran exhaled loudly, nodding, "I get it, I get it. It's too late for me, but she still has a chance for a happily ever after." The smile he gave me was one I'd never before seen. It wasn't mocking or arrogant, it was simply...a smile. The hard blues of his eyes softened, and his words left his lips in something even frailer than a whisper. "Do...do you think I would have had a chance if you'd taken me down years ago? That I could have had a happily ever after?"

An ache weighed in my chest, my eyes stinging and throat feeling as if a bee had made a nest right where I needed room to breathe and swallow. I couldn't bear to look at him, and instead gazed upward, watching snowflakes leak through the chinks in the wood and sprinkle onto the dying man beside me. I bit my lip, struggling to answer him, "I...I don't know. No offense, but it isn't like I want you to."

"Understandable," he whispered. "I'm...I'm sorry, Irene."

"Raine."

"I'm sorry, Raine."

My throat clenched. "For what?"

"I'm just...I'm just sorry," he gasped, piercing me with his eyes. As soon as I averted my gaze, I returned my stare as he made a choking sound and seemed to recoil, clutching his chest. I watched numbly as he fought against the unconsciousness claiming him. And then Tieran couldn't fight it anymore. He'd wasted all his energy in the raw hours of the morning to apologize to me and then passed out. By the time he'd wake up, if he'd wake up, Destan and I and his little Lilah would be gone.

"Goodbye, Tieran," I whispered, taking a last glance at his bone white face, his blood red hair, his chapped mouth. And then I rose to my feet, sticking them into my boots and tying up my hair. I pulled my thick wool coat back on, tied around my scarf, and then I woke Lilah, guiding her outside to where Destan waited in a sober sort of silence. I kept Chan's letter under my arm, going towards Ai. She looked sad lying in the shade of a bramble bush, clearly missing Siri. They'd seemed to have bonded within the last week. Ai no longer wanted to nap in my rucksack, but in between Siri's paws. Siri had even taught Ai how to manage what sounded like a bark. The wolf's sudden disappearance had even put Ai in a state.

"Ready to see Chantastic again, Ai?" I asked her, crouching by her as she gnawed on a twig. Hearing Chan's name, Ai leapt up to standing on her four little legs, the long whiskers whipping excitedly at the ground. She chirped, nuzzling my hand, and I smiled, securing the scroll to her foot and letting her roll around for a minute or two on Chantastic's letter to me. Once she had her scent, Ai was off again and Destan appeared by my side.

"Ready to go?" he asked, rubbing my shoulder. Lilah wheezed beside him, clutching onto his arm with her cold and skeletal fingers. I nodded, slinging my bow across my body and quiver over my shoulder. I took a last glance at the little cabin, at the orange light of the fire shining from in between the strips of wood, and then I took Destan's hand, listening as he played his flute for Siri to come.

We walked and walked for hours, Destan playing song after song in hopes that our wolf would hear and return. And after what felt like ages, we heard an answering howl, and Siri came bounding toward us, tackling Destan to the ground and licking his face and up his nose and under his beanie. Lilah screeched and hid behind me, "It's killing him! Why aren't you doing anything?!"

Destan was making a guttural sound that to some ears sounded like cries of pain, but to me I knew it was his unstoppable laughter, he was able to twist his head to look at me in amazement, tears of joy dribbling from his eyes. I began laughing too, nudging Lilah and shaking my head, "Oh, calm down, Lilah. It's just Siri."

When Destan finally rolled out from under Siri, his face was dripping with slobber and his beanie was hardly hanging onto his head while his curls sprung about. He fastened his hands around her nose and pressed his forehead to the prickly grey fur, closing his eyes and nuzzling her gently, "It's so good to see you. I'm so glad you came back. I'm so happy to see you, girl." Siri whined and pawed his knee so that he'd back away, and he obeyed her, stepping back and leaning forward to scratch behind her ear. He glanced at me and Lilah, grinning broadly, "Looks like we won't be walking to Fluxaria. How's that make you feel?"

"So much better," I said.

"Thank *gods*, I thought this was a plot to have me walk myself to death before reaching the dumb mountain," Lilah said, glaring at me and staggering over to Siri. Then she paused, her face frightened as Siri growled at her. Destan smacked the wolf's nose to stop, but Siri only lowered the growl to a grumble, clearly remembering Lilah's existence at the camp where we both had been held captive.

Destan bopped her on the head once more, looking at Lilah apologetically, "Sorry 'bout that. Siri's not usually this way with people she's just met."

"Oh, they've met. Siri also spent some time with the Shuishan," I said, giving Destan a pointed look. He raised an eyebrow.

"Never mind, then," he said, "she hates you. Watch out."

Lilah forced herself to move an inch, and then before rethinking myself I picked her up and sat her down on Siri's back, me following behind. Lilah wriggled about, crying to get off, but I cemented my arms around her middle and held her still, groaning, "Come on, Lilah. Don't freak out or the animal will freak out, okay?" She nodded feebly and then awkwardly put her arms around the wolf's neck. Luckily, Lilah was so tiny that carrying all three of us was no problem for Siri. So with Destan hopping on, we took off with a jolt into the forest.

"Feeling okay, blue-hair?" Lilah asked me, over the buffet of air hitting our faces. "I heard that girls who are preggers usually don't feel too good after a lot of motion."

I clenched my teeth. "I feel fine. I appreciate your concern." Of course I was lying, the baby was tumble-saulting all over my insides every time Siri took a leap, making vomit burn up my throat and have to be swallowed back down.

"Well, if you have to barf, wait 'til we're slower or else it'll hit me in the face, okay?" Lilah said, and the delightful image of chunky and smelly puke splattered all over her made me dig my heels into Siri's side so she lurched forward even faster, narrowly missing a tree.

"Everything all right?" Destan shouted from behind, slowing Siri back to a steady run. I gave a thumbs up and he guided us onto a path of smooth grey rocks, the trees splitting around us and hanging over like a green tunnel. For some reason, Lilah just wouldn't shut up.

"Is it Tieran's? I didn't think he ever got a girl pregnant—"

"Lilah!" I exclaimed, exasperated, "Would you please stop talking to me?" I was at my last nerve with this brat. If I had only realized how much I hated her before saying yes to bringing her along, then Destan and I could have been riding in tranquil silence. But now Lilah was chirping about everything I didn't want to talk about and I couldn't contain it anymore. "You know, if you're really so sick and dying and in need of Fluxarian care, then how come you're just as much of a bitch as always? Why'd you even leave your 'big brother Tieran' if you're fine?"

Lilah scooted ever so slightly closer to Destan and farther from me. We rode in silence for a perfect thirty seconds. And then she had to speak again, "It was your decision to take me." We said no more, it was getting strangely warm as we rode forward, the trees growing farther apart from one another. The grass was long and kissed with golden sun because the sun actually was able to pierce through the leaf cover. I slipped off my coat and stuck it in between me and Lilah, rolling up my sleeves and even debating whether or not to take off my gloves. But as I was about to ask Destan if he thought we were going the right way, we heard a rapid movement scuttling ahead, coming through the bushes.

Tugging on the reins, he veered Siri to the left, gasping, "Something's coming. Keep your voices down." We all nodded, dismounting and crouching behind a bushy fern. It sprang out as soon as we'd ducked down to the dusty dirt and had to peek through the fronds.

It was a boy, his hair a dark blue, darker than mine, his clothes a burnt orange with patches on the knees and elbows. He was running very clumsily, his mouth agape and chubby childish cheeks flushed with pink. He jumped onto the nearest tree stump with a grunt and cupped his hands around his mouth, hollering, "Maaaaaamaaaaaa! Baaaaaabaaaaa! I found a good camping spoooooooooottt!"

More movement, the sound of branches being pushed away, a girl with short hair the colour of grapes, in a big red t-shirt and shorts walking out with long strides. Her parents followed behind, both in the same casual attire, wrinkled tan faces, black hair that glinted blue as they passed into a pool of sunlight. My eyes widened in awe of them.

"Poh! Poh, you can't just run off like that," his mother chided, coming forward and touching his cheek, trying to help him down off the stump.

He shook his head fervently and gently freed his hand from his mother's. "But *Mama*, I just wanted to find the perfect spot to pitch our tent." He pouted and his father came from behind to grab him under the armpits and lower him back to the ground.

"Oh, honey we need to stay *inside* the fence. We're too far away from the other campers," she said. I couldn't believe my eyes, the mother draped her arm across her son's small shoulder, rubbing little circles on his back soothingly. If I'd been a little boy who went past the fence on Thgindim, I'd be shot on sight by the JPs, and if they didn't shoot me, it would be my mother who'd get it done!

"I just wanted to help..." Poh sighed, his father ruffling his downy blue hair.

"We know. It's all right. And you know...I found a great spot just through here..." said his father, pushing through some of the prickly bushes and disappearing over on the other side. Before the boy could follow, his sister tapped his shoulder and he turned around, making a grumpy face at her.

"You know, if we'd pitched the tent out here, the tiangou and wolves and cannibals would bite off your head and bounce it around like a rubber ball," she teased, making a scary face.

"Nuh uh!" Poh wrinkled his nose indignantly, "Cannibals don't *play* with heads, they eat heads!"

They continued arguing as they crossed over through the line of bushes as their parents had done, and once they were out of earshot, we slowly rose to our feet. I swayed, the realization that I'd just seen a living, breathing Fluxarian family made my head swim. Lilah leaned against Siri, looking green and faint, but otherwise unintrigued by what we'd just seen. Destan's hand found mine and held it tightly, looking at me intensely, grey eyes like to shiny stones.

"Do you have a plan? An idea for what comes next?" he whispered.

I sucked on my bottom lip, brain working fast, my gaze still pinned to his in silent communication. Then I reached up with my free hand and began tucking his stray curls under his hat, poking all blonde back under the rim so that it almost looked like he was wearing a dark red mushroom cap. He frowned, poking the pillowy hat and raising an eyebrow.

"Should I understand?" he asked, slowly. And then he got it, blinking quickly and an identical grin spreading across his face. "Oh shit. You think we can pull it off?"

I nodded. Behind me, I could hear every breath Lilah took. She wasn't even standing, but panted as if exhausted. "What...what are you two idiots talking about?" Concerned, I helped her stand and put my palm on her forehead. Burning hot. Whatever sickness was inside her was working faster, working more cruelly, making her so weak that her legs shook in effort to support her tiny body.

"We're going to have to do some acting, are you up to it?" I asked her.

"Do I have a choice?" she wheezed, tossing her long, white blonde-hair. Limp strands clung to her clammy forehead. But before I could answer, Destan scooped her up, slung her over his shoulder and we began walking toward the line of bushes.

chapter twenty-six

"Hi there! Wow, it's so...green out here today, don't you think?" I stammered, my whole face feeling hot. Smiled hugely, I put both hands on my hips confidently declaring, "I bet you're wondering why I'm talking to you. Well, wouldn't you know that my brother and little sister have lost our parents! And golly, they said they'd be by the entrance to Fluxaria, our home and where we live. But it's our first time out and we are sure as heck lost. Do you think you could show us where to...uh...go? We need to make it home for lunch."

Both of their faces were two red balloons ready to pop. Even sickly Lilah had regained the energy to smirk and suppress her cruel giggling. I rose an eyebrow, "So? How's that?"

Destan pursed his lips and looked at me sympathetically, "Er...well, Bluehead..."

"How about this then," I cut in, dropping my hands from my hips and beginning to pace, my palms over my stomach as I began to moan.

"Oh, oh! Pregnancy! Such pregnancy, the baby is coming someone let me and my not-pregnant friends on the mountain before I burst!"

They both cracked up at this one, and for a moment I could hear Irene, see her pointing at me, *"That one will work for sure. That's my vote!"* My smile quivered and I blinked quickly to whisk the incoming tears away and get focused again.

"Very funny, but too hard to pull off," Destan said, giving me an apologetic smile. "Sorry, Bluehead."

"Why can't we just present our real case?" I demanded, grumpily crossing my arms. "Do you really think we have a better chance of getting into Fluxaria if we lie, in comparison to saying we're coming with important evidence from the enemy mountain to be given to the government and save everyone?" I groaned, covering my eyes and plopping down in defeat on the grass. "We'd be taken right where we need to be, I think," I mumbled.

Destan came over and began playing with my bangs, pinching them in between his fingers and tossing them this way and that, "Oh Bluehead, I agree that would be best, but we can't just go in there and expect them to believe us. Not all of us have hair like yours, remember?"

"I thought you said you were from Thgindim?" Lilah chimed in, managing to sit up against Siri.

I slid my hands away from my eyes. "It's complicated."

"And that's why we can't drop the entire novel of our existence and our spiral into pro-Fluxarianism and banishment stuff right at the gate. It's too risky. Plus, we got these sweet fake IDs in case we need proof, right?"

Lilah squealed suddenly. "Oh *no...*"

I shot up from the ground. "What 'oh no'? We *do* have the fake IDs, right Lilah?" She looked too guilty. "Lilah?!"

"Okay, okay, don't get mad," she whimpered, twisting her hands in her lap. "We do have fake IDs. It's just...Tieran and I only got two. And both had been altered so that mine and Tieran's faces are on them." She withdrew them from her small bag and passed them over to Destan.

"Well maybe we could explain that my red hair was actually a hat?" he suggested, tugging thoughtfully on his beanie.

Ignoring his comments, I stared at Lilah in utter amazement. "Why didn't you tell us this *beforehand?*"

"Because you wouldn't have taken me with you!" she said, eyes watering as she entered a violent coughing fit. I wanted to stay mad at her, but she just looked too pathetic, too weak. I fell back to the ground, shielding the sun from my eyes.

"They're never going to let us in," I whispered. "What are we going to do now?"

I could sense Destan leaning over me, and then I felt his lips on mine. He kissed me lightly, his mouth in a sweet sort of half-smile as he said, "For now, let's run through it again?"

"Yeah, give it one more go. And he's right about the pregnant one; while you might be able to pass as having a bun-in-the-oven, you definitely do not look ready to deliver, honey," Irene said, poking my bellybutton.

I nodded, "That's a good point..."

"What is?" Destan asked.

My stomach heaved and I scooted into a sitting position, shutting my eyes and breathing through my nose. *I need her here, she was always here to make plans with us. How are we supposed to know what to do on her mountain when none of us know it in the least? Just having her here would have solved all of this,* I thought fervently, looking back up at Destan with a smile plastered on, "Nothing. So...run it again?"

I was last to go over the fence, Destan waiting on the other side to catch me as he'd done with Lilah. The fence was constructed of sturdy metal and left no gaps for Mythland beasts to wander through, and yet it was far from threatening and not even a third as high as the one completely circling Thgindim. I supposed Fluxaria just didn't expect anyone to want to escape.

Once we were up and over, it was only a few paces until another cloud of children came screaming by us, all with such strange hair, deep blues and purples that made me do a double take as they rushed toward a ball one of them had kicked. The only hair like that I'd ever seen had been mine in a mirror. I backed out of the way as some younger children came by pulling ribbons and kites behind them. It was disorienting that Mythland was less than a few feet away and already Fluxarians were everywhere.

There were Fluxarian kids dangling from the trees by their knees and Fluxarian couples holding hands and lying in the shade on a blanket. There was a series of colourful canvas tents dotting throughout the trees, and Fluxarians were coming in and out, lugging firewood and tin plates, setting up a fire or already sitting around one to warm their hands or stick marshmallows near the orange and glowing wood. And amid all of this noise and bustle of families and couples around us, we realized we were holding our breath. As if that would keep us invisible in the presence of people who were technically our enemies. But no more. We would face them, we would do this.

"Let's go," I whispered, signalling Destan with a small nod so that he kissed me one more fleeting time and then slunk away into the dark of the trees, leaving me and Lilah to the campers. He would be watching us from the edge of the campground with an arrow nocked in and ready if any sort of trouble arose. Lilah was now wearing Destan's beanie, her long blonde hair tucked up into it just in case it was a giveaway that a twelve year-old didn't have the hair colour of other kids her age. She was breathing really shallowly now, so pale that I could see the blue veins writhing under her skin like parasites. Reluctantly, I put an arm around her, letting her weight fall against me. "Hold on. I still hate you, but hold on."

"Sure, why not?" she wheezed, coughing into her hand and drawing it back with red splattered across her knuckles. I stopped, staring at the blood. I'd seen it so many times in Underbrush. People coming to my mother for healing potions and paying everything they had only to keel over in the next few weeks. I looked away and began towing us into the commotion of campers, having to limp to keep her standing beside me.

"Excuse me? Darling, is your friend okay?"

I stopped in my tracks, looking around to find who was speaking. A man with long black hair braided down his back stood behind us, one hand on his daughter's shoulder, the other drifting towards Lilah. His eyes were big, black, and kind. But worried.

"Well..." I stammered, thinking fast for an explanation. "Not really. She was bit by some sort of snake and has been getting worse really fast."

"A snake?" he shook his head sombrely, his daughter clinging to his leg shyly, her eyes like two orbs as they stared and stared at me. "You're not saying one got into your tent?"

I shook my head earnestly, "No, sir. Back by the fence once must have slithered through."

"Well, she's gotta have that looked at, you have no idea what sort of sickness Mythland snakes carry," he said, coming in front of us and beckoning for us to follow. "Where are your parents?"

"They're...back on the mountain."

"And her parents?"

"We're sisters," I said. Lilah snorted, her eyebrows shooting up her white little forehead. I know, it was a stretch, but from what the man could tell, Lilah could have blue hair under that hat and our eyes weren't too different; hers a light grey, mine a light blue. If anything, she resembled me more than my own sister Gwen. *Not that Gwen might even be related to me after all at this poin*t, I thought, the reminder another punch to my gut.

"So your parents let you down here on your own? How'd you manage that?" he asked, exasperated. He put both hands on his hips, the gold earrings swinging from his lobes as he tilted his head to the side. We were in front of his tent, his little violet-haired daughter scurrying through the flaps and zipping it up tightly to keep us out. My heart was going real fast now, my breathing and stomach fluttering and the baby starting to wriggle nervously inside me. I averted my eyes to the trees, wishing I could see through the thick green and see even just the glint of Destan's arrow, a clump of blonde curls peeking through the leaves, anything so that I knew he was watching over us.

"We were supposed to come back yesterday ago, but my sister Lilah got over the fence right when we were supposed to be getting back, so they left without knowing we weren't with them," I said in a hurry, palms sweaty inside my gloves.

He tapped his chin with his finger and then nodded, crouching to undo the zipper on his tent. "I see. What are your parents' names, maybe I know them?"

"RED ALERT RED ALERT GET OUT NOW!" Irene's warning was loud enough in my ears to be real, and I flinched, trying to come up with something.

"I...I d-don't think so. They work so much and hardly get out—"

"Where do they work?"

I laughed, thinking I might go hysterical, my entire body quivering at this point, "Well...they work...um, they work...at the spy training camp."

His face split into a glowing smile, "Impressive! I've never met a trainer who had children, the job being so demanding and all."

"Yeah, me neither," I said, smiling so hugely my face ached. Lilah slumped even more against me, this time completely unconscious. I panicked and touched her wrist quickly to make sure there was still a pulse. Feeble. So feeble and weak.

The man said pardon me and scooped her up into his arms, calling out to the other campers, "Excuse me? Excuse me, everyone? Do any of you know where the closest communication booth is?"

A woman cradling twins hollered back in reply, "Just by the shrine, outside of the cafe."

"Near the statue or the fountain?"

"Fountain."

He nodded and touched his tent with his foot, "Karma? Karma, darling, Baba will be right back, okay? I have to get this sick girl some help, go to Miss Wu's tent." There was a rustling and some sort of mumbled reply from inside, and then he took off with Lilah tucked close to his chest, his black braid swinging behind him like a glossy string of liquorice as I jogged behind him. I was completely dumbfounded. A stranger helping two girls with a very fishy backstory when he had more important things to do? It was unheard of! On Thgindim people knew better than to look after someone other than themselves or their family. But here he was: leading me through the thinning crowd of people to where, suddenly looking up, I could see some sort of cable-like structures extending from the base of the mountain all the way to the top.

The tents stopped here, but to my surprise this was not the end of Fluxaria's assimilation into the Mythland woods. Where the campground ended, a new sort of place began. There were poles draped with ivy and golden string lights, not yet lit, lining the path cobbled by greyish purple amethyst. Statues of spirits I recognized and did not recognize stood in circles of trees with little pools of water around them, coins tossed in and glittering. And at the end of the path was the greatest statue of all; a gold-plated sun perched atop a stone pedestal as violet water flowed out from each sunbeam and twirled down into the fountain base at the bottom. Carved into the sun were the words: *Fluxaria, retsis of eht noom, dlihc of thgil dna nus.* The ancient Thgindim tongue, I could tell by recognizing words I'd had to memorize for the bonding ceremony. Behind the statue, a great golden fence curled around the beginning of the mountain and disappeared into either side of the woods. I knew there had to be a fence.

Yet the man was motioning for us to cut past the statue and go down a path to where the decorations dwindled to only some occasional lanterns swinging from low-hanging tree branches. That's when the fence reappeared, along with the entrance to Fluxaria, not a door or gate, but a sort of contraption of cables and boxy metal cars that drifted up and down the mountain. I craned my neck and saw that there were landing bases every few miles for people to get off. There weren't police stationed at the base, but there were some women in official-looking violet uniforms toting mini crossbows and wearing small triangular hats. They were ushering Fluxarians in and out of the carts, taking tickets and clicking little handheld scissors of sorts that left a sun-shaped hole in the paper. Captivated and suddenly scheming to find a way to get us on one, the man called me over to a phone station beside the loading dock. Lilah was now slightly more awake, struggling in his arms uncomfortably, obviously trying to cuss him out for picking her up in the first place. He didn't seem to notice.

"Here, come and plug in your village number. Or– you could always try the training camp's number if you think they could be there. I'll alert some officials to bring her to a hospital," he said, carrying Lilah over to the ladies in the violet uniforms.

I felt my face flame with rosy heat. I shakily entered the glass box, staring at the device and deciding it wasn't too different from a phone. I pressed the handheld speaker to my ear and stepped close to the microphone that jut out above the keypad. Then using the amount of numbers Destan and I'd dialled to connect to Peak Tower, I jabbed some in randomly. After a few rings, there was a sort of chiming sound and a woman's voice chanted back to me, "I'm sorry, but the number you have inputted cannot connect to any communication receptors on the mountain. Would you like to try again, or perhaps state your name?"

I hesitated, on the verge of hanging up until the man came back, a victorious expression on his face and Lilah being taken away on a stretcher. I turned back to the phone, "Oh, hey Mom! Sorry about all the mix up, can you pick us up in a bit? Lilah is pretty sick."

"Excuse me?" the voice replied, this time less systematic and with a curious rising at the end of the sentence.

My face managed to get even hotter, it wasn't a computer voice! I'd thought it was a recording, but now there was a guy staring at me hoping that I reached my imaginary Fluxarian parents and a lady on the phone who was very confused and waiting for me to make some sense. I scratched my head and laughed a little, "Yeah, it was a snake again. You know how Lilah can be. She's being taken to the hospital now. I swear this won't happen again." The lady started asking more questions but I continued acting as if it was my Mom on the other end yelling at me for not keeping a better eye on Gwen. After some more conversation, I hung up the phone and turned around to the man.

"She said my Dad will pick me up from the..." I paused, staring up at the floating cars on wires, "from the highest docking station of those cars."

"Good, good. And I talked to the officers and your sister's already getting treatment as we speak," he smiled. Then he stuck out a hand, "I'm Ární, I don't think we'd been properly introduced."

"Raine," I said, bowing slightly out of courtesy and glancing anxiously at the trees behind me. I needed to somehow let Destan know what was going on, not to mention get a ticket on those cable cars. "Ární ? Would you be able to get me and one of my friends waiting back at camp a ticket for those cars? Once I'm with my parents, I can pay you back."

"Seems fair. Go get your friend and I'll stand in line at the booth," he said, waving and jogging in the other direction.

There was a not so subtle cough from the woods behind me, and so, inconspicuously I drifted toward the edge of the woods, keeping my eye on the guy as he moved up in line and took out some coins from his pocket And then, an arm curled around my waist coming from the dark, and I smiled, murmuring, "We're so close. Lilah's getting help and that man is buying us tickets onto the mountain."

"Good," he said, but his voice was all wrong, robotic. I slowly tried to turn around but then the arm tightened, a hand going for my throat. "You've left me with no choice, Miss Ylevol," the cyborg whispered, his gears clicking and clicking in my ears as I heard the clean sound of the safety being unhooked from the gun. He raised the round, cold metal nozzle to my temple, pressing it in hard. But as I could sense his finger hovering over the trigger, he said something more, "Councilman Sebastian Lao instructed me to ask for your last words. He said to tell you, congratulations."

I couldn't breathe or think. Lao, Lao, Lao, Tieran, Lilah, Thgindim's favourite laundress, Yue has a hole in her head, your friends are in danger, flying glowing flowers, Irene is falling, there's a baby I'm a baby I have a baby, Scarface beanie head blue head blue hair, Solomon and Shardza, Chantastic kissing me through the bars, I'm Raine, who's Raine? Everything was spinning out of control and the longer I waited, the sooner it would go still and stop, everything would stop all at once.

"Did you already get Destan?" I whispered, staring ahead as Ární left the booth holding two tickets and looked around for me, not even glancing at the trees.

The cyborg grunted. "Are those your last words?"

I closed my eyes. "No," I slipped my hand behind me in my knapsack, and he caught my wrist. The other hand patted it down, probably looking for some sort of weapon or knife. Then he relaxed his hold and I sighed, "I have something for Sebastian." Slowly, I pulled out Irene's clock and pushed the battery in with a satisfying click. I looked at my murky reflection in the smudged glass, the numbers and lines flurrying across my vision in a blur. I smiled, "Tell him...I've had a blast."

The cyborg was confused, he steadied his hand and as I felt the slight flex of his fingers to shoot, I threw down the clock hard behind me. My ears popped at the force, and I felt the cyborg drop the gun as a cloud of flame engulfed us both.

Many, many thanks go out tooo…

KADIAN I just had to list you first because without you I would not be typing on this file and this novel would still be on a laptop in Iceland where the wifi comes and goes as it pleases and I am eternally grateful for your help and hope we can meet again one day and perhaps share in an adventure together!

Natalie for putting up with my nonstop writing during the Snowbama 2016 and for reading it when it was a bunch of loose papers. You da bomb and I love you.

ALSO my mother for putting up with my nonstop writing during Snowbama 2016 in which I spent most of my time writing and not shovelling out the cars or doing the laundry which has been long overdue. I promise that before I commit to book three I will empty my hamper!

Greenspring Montessori School and the entire staff who would come in the lounge to relax and end up having to listen me type furiously the entire time. If you ever need me to get off the computer so you can spend your break on the interweb or get personal things done, just kick me right off.

Anna and Bjarni for letting me use your amazing laptop to finish up formatting as well as your Wi-Fi! And really the fact that you took me into your home so openly and made me feel so welcome, boosting my confidence in my drawings, buying me that cat pillow, voyaging to waterfalls and a glacier lagoon because you knew I wanted to see it, takk fyrir, þakka þer fyrir.

Ronen, for, once again, a stunning cover. The struggle is real but you always come through and I'm so so grateful to have you as a friend and contributor to my series.

MIAAAAA BECAUSE YOUR ART MAKES ME BELIEVE IN PEOPLE HAVING SUPERPOWERS LIKE HOW CAN YOU BE SO NICE AND PRETTY AND ALSO SO TALENTED AND JUST I LOVE YOU YOU MADE IT COME TO LIFE OKAY? OKAY.

Yiqing Zhao for bringing Raine to life in my book trailers! You were such a sweet and talented person to work with and I wish you best of luck in New York City to pursue your acting! We will surely keep in touch and you'll always have a job back in Baltimore as long as I'm cranking out the books in this series.

Sargasm for looking at this when it was a scrappy first draft in 2013 and pushing me in the proper direction when I still had no idea where the heck this sequel was going.

Umma, for showing me how to make these pages sparkle.

Nick for helping me with the cover and not being grumpy when I got too sick to clean your house and repay your service. Also for the A+++ book trailers!!!

Free font websites. ***Free font websites.*** Notably, dafont.com and the artists who created the fonts used for much of the characters' handwriting: Darcy Baldwin, Kimberly Geswein, and countless others who had their fonts free for personal and commercial use. Bless your souls.

Tammy Pierce for picking up a copy of *Piercing Midnight* at Chessiecon and even insisting that I sign it. The fact that one of the most legendary girl-power fantasy goddess writers of everything has my book in her possession still baffles me and makes me light-headed. I'll be seeing you this summer and if I find you also READ *Piercing Midnight* and want to TALK to me about it, please be prepared to catch me as I faint in disbelief.

Taffy, for showing me I can still produce novels even when my darling cat insists on lounging across the keyboard.

Irene and Chan for letting me take creative license with yoUR sOuLS eHehEhhEeH

Dad, for keeping Mythland mythterious.

And all of you who check my book out at the library and talk about it to your friends and write reviews on Goodreads and Amazon, you give me the confidence in my writing like nothing else and to have an audience is something strange but wonderful to get used to. I appreciate everything and I'm eternally grateful.

about the author

Since the publication of *Piercing Midnight*, R.R.S. has been living the hardcore writer life: cleaning up broken glass, getting rump-rot in front of the staff lounge computer, not getting haircuts, crying over sinus infections, and sleeping on Iceland moss to feel more one with the earth. R.R.S. is always up for sushi, so if you're ever in town, give the writer a heads up and we can make it a party.

R.R.S.'s email:
faery.ring.press@gmail.com

R.R.S. is now on Goodreads! Check out the writer's blog and feel free to ask questions and leave reviews for the series!

about the cover artist

Ronen Yakubov is an emerging artist currently based in Baltimore, Maryland. He won a Scholastic Art and Writing Award Gold Medal this past year for drawing, and while he can obviously do some pretty sick watercolour and ink book covers, he specializes in graphic design and portraits. You can view his portfolio from his Instagram and commission work through email. He's a bit of a local legend, so feel free to check out his Facebook fanpage, titled "The Ronen Yakubov Experience." He also really likes sushi so you're welcome to invite him to the sushi party as well.

Ronen's Instagram:
ronen96

His email:
ronen16@gmail.com

Want more of the Infinity Chronicles?

Check out the blog for videos, quizzes, and exclusive bonus content from the author!

the-infinity-chronicles.com

www.ingramcontent.com/pod-product-compliance
Lightning Source LLC
Chambersburg PA
CBHW021530250626
47154CB00006BA/2052